MW00674508

"Judicium is a brilliant idea, an all-star mini-series waiting to happen. I'm truly jealous I didn't think of it first!"

-George Anthony, author of *Starring Brian Linehan*

"Only two powers are greater than words. One is the the deft combination of words to tell a riveting story. The second is the power we all recognize as supreme. Gerald miraculously melds these two powers into a page-turning journey that will rock your moral foundation, revive your soul, and resonate for ages."

-Pat Cugliari, professor of Advertising at Humber College Toronto and director of Creative Services for Astral Radio Canada

JUDICIUM

JUDICIUM

An Investigation into the Missing Body of Christ

GERALD HESS

TATE PUBLISHING
AND ENTERPRISES, LLC

Judicium
Copyright © 2012 by Gerald Hess. All rights reserved.

No part of this publication may be reproduced, stored in a retrieval system or transmitted in any way by any means, electronic, mechanical, photocopy, recording or otherwise without the prior permission of the author except as provided by USA copyright law.

This novel is a work of fiction. Names, descriptions, entities, and incidents included in the story are products of the author's imagination. Any resemblance to actual persons, events, and entities is entirely coincidental.

The opinions expressed by the author are not necessarily those of Tate Publishing, LLC.

Published by Tate Publishing & Enterprises, LLC
127 E. Trade Center Terrace | Mustang, Oklahoma 73064 USA
1.888.361.9473 | www.tatepublishing.com

Tate Publishing is committed to excellence in the publishing industry. The company reflects the philosophy established by the founders, based on Psalm 68:11,
"The Lord gave the word and great was the company of those who published it."

Book design copyright © 2012 by Tate Publishing, LLC. All rights reserved.
Cover design by Rtor Maghuyop
Interior design by Mary Jean Archival

Published in the United States of America

ISBN: 978-1-62024-804-1
Fiction / Mystery & Detective / Historical
Fiction / Christian / Historical
12.10.22

ACKNOWLEDGMENTS

Writing a novel is a very solitary experience; however, that doesn't mean that the final product doesn't owe much to the contributions of others. Number one on that list of silent contributors is my wife, Angela. For the past four years, as I researched and wrote *Judicium,* she has been the one solid thing in my life, the rock to which I have been lucky enough to tether my boat. She is the love of my life and the one indispensable person in my life. Without her there would be no *Judicium.* Thank you, Angela. God blessed me when He brought you into my life.

To my friend Paul Kahnert: thank you for your unwavering support, your commitment to the idea of *Judicium*—and oh yes, for the title and prologue.

To Gary Wall: thanks for showing me how to turn on my computer and for saving me and the manuscript when the computer was about to crash.

To my best buddies Johnathan Beach, Derek Dorey, John Mars, and John Kurlowicz: thanks for the encouragement, the education, and for putting up with me.

To David Cairns and Derick Brent: thanks for the books that were invaluable resources. Without them, *Judicium* would have been only half a book.

To Dave Wannan: thanks for the promotional input and your great ideas for the cover.

To Scott Wallace: thanks for the enthusiasm.

Sometimes things happen for a reason. Knowing Pat Cugliari is one of those things. Through thick and thin, he has believed in me and *Judicium.* His intelligence, support, and sense of humor have never let me down. I owe him more than I know, or at least dinner at the MacDonald's of his choice.

And lastly a heartfelt thank you to the woman who gave me life: Thank you, Mom, for everything.

PROLOGUE

Judicium is a Latin word meaning a "legal investigation" or "judicial inquiry" into an incident.

One such incident happened around the year 33 AD in the ancient city of Jerusalem when the body of a carpenter's son from Nazareth disappeared three days after He was executed by crucifixion.

Because Roman law declared the bodies of those crucified to be Roman property, there was an investigation—a *judicium*—into this apparent theft and the strange circumstances surrounding it.

And So It Begins

Golgotha Jerusalem, Dawn, AD 33
Forty Days until Bethany

The cold, predawn fog was thicker than usual, cloaking everything in an eerie, ghostly miasma. Standing in front of the stone that guarded the entrance to the tomb, Aaron pulled his cloak tight around his neck and cursed his luck. He was supposed to have had the week off. Some time by the sea with his wife and young family had already been planned, but he was stuck in Jerusalem with three raw recruits guarding some dead prophet's tomb. They'd been there the entire weekend on a midnight-to-midday shift that was scheduled to last for at least another week.

Aaron was an ambitious man, his dark brown eyes always wide open to the next opportunity. A squat but muscled torso supported a face that looked as if it had been chiselled by desert sand. Well-defined cheekbones flanked a long sloping nose that led to a small, thin-lipped mouth and a proudly jutting chin. His shaved head protruded from a thick neck like the point of a javelin. Not exactly slow, he knew no one was going to mistake him for a scholar. From a family of poor, landless peasants who worked land owned by Annas, a former high priest of the Sanhedrin, Aaron had grown up expecting little from life except hard work and death. But diligence and a genuine love of the martial life had served him well. At twenty-five, he was the youngest captain in the temple guards. He believed great things were in his future. He just didn't know what they would be.

Resting his back against the great stone, Aaron considered the man on the other side. He had heard of the miracles. He had also heard of the prophecy. For the past three nights, a single question had lingered in the back of his mind: Would the Nazarene walk out of his own grave? His ear against the stone, he listened for the sound of fingernails desperately trying to claw their way out.

The three recruits—Jacob, Ezra, and Azekah—were gathered around a campfire ten yards from where Aaron was standing. They had built their fire under the protective branches of a large olive tree, its small, cream-coloured flowers just beginning to open. They were gambling away their week's wages. Ezra was losing. He wasn't too happy about it.

Jacob reached for his wine cup.

"What do you think that is?" he asked his two comrades, pointing at the shaking cup.

"Earthquake!" shouted Aron, doing his best to keep the fear out of his voice.

The roiling earth sent dice, money, wine, and gamblers rolling, scattering, spilling, and stumbling in every direction. Lightning struck the earth inches from where Aaron was standing. The brilliant flash blinded all four of them. The ear-splitting roar of the thunder deafened them. A sudden rush of air swept them off their feet, not so gently depositing them on their backsides.

Azekah was the first to run.

Jacob was next. Ezra followed as soon as his legs would let him.

Aaron had taken the worst of it.

His head throbbing, he forced himself to sit up. He couldn't believe his eyes. The great stone had been rolled out of the way. At first he thought it might have been moved by the earthquake, but the other tombs nearby looked undisturbed. The dark, cave-like tomb was open to the morning light. Aaron swallowed his fear and looked inside. The altar was empty; the shroud and the cloth that had covered the Nazarene's face were on the ground beside it, carefully folded.

Aaron had only one thought: *How do we explain this?*

Looking at the great stone, a second thought came to him. There were men in Jerusalem who would pay handsomely to be the first to know that the tomb of the Nazarene was empty. "And they might as well pay me," he said, smiling.

FEAR BATTLES FAITH

FORTY DAYS UNTIL BETHANY

A woman dressed in a simple cloak running through the empty streets of the not quite awake city stumbled and fell, scraping her knees and the palms of her hands on the rough cobblestones. Heedless of her injuries, she was back on her feet in a heart beat, her breath coming in deep, haggard gasps as she resumed her run through the labyrinthine streets of the ancient city.

At the door of a poor house in the lowest section of the city, she pounded desperately, her lack of breath forcing her to her knees. The door opened and two men, seeing the woman prostrate on their door step, helped her to her feet. "Mary, what are you *doing?*" asked the taller of the two men.

"Let her catch her breath, John," scolded the taller man's friend.

"I'm all right, Peter," Mary said, collecting herself with some effort.

"What has happened to you?" John asked nervously.

"I've been to the tomb of our Lord. They have taken Him away!"

"Taken Him where?" asked Peter.

"Out of the tomb, I don't know where!"

John was in the lead as the two men, their lungs burning from a lack of breath and their flanks clammy with sweat, finally reached the open tomb. They could barely believe their eyes. He was gone! Going to the altar, Peter picked up the shroud that had been wrapped around the body of Jesus. "Why did they remove His shroud?" he asked.

"So He could walk, Peter."

John's simple statement brought Peter up short. *Why did I just assume His body had been stolen?* he asked himself. "You think He's alive, John?"

"Yes, Peter, I do."

"But what if His body was stolen?"

"Thieves would not unwrap His body."

"What if it was Caiaphas?"

"It wasn't Caiaphas, Peter! Our Saviour has returned to us."

"That is what we believe, John, but what if we're wrong? What if the high priest took His body?"

"Why would the high priest of the Sanhedrin steal our Master's body?"

Peter paused to pull his thoughts together. "Think about it," he began. "Caiaphas knows that we are a threat to him. By stealing the body, he hopes to make us criminals in the eyes of Rome."

"How does Caiaphas turn us into criminals if he is the one responsible?"

"We'll be Rome's primary suspects. We have the most to gain."

"And the shroud, Peter?"

"Thieves would never bother to unwrap our Master's body. Only someone who wanted to make it look as if our Master walked out of his own tomb would have wasted time removing it."

"Meaning us?"

"Caiaphas will tell Pilate that the shroud proves that we took the body."

"Do you not believe that Jesus is the true Messiah?"

"Of course I believe," replied Peter, forcing himself not think about the night of His arrest and the three denials. "But what we believe doesn't matter. What matters is what Pilate believes and what Caiaphas can convince him to believe."

"What do you want to do?"

"The others have all made their way back to Galilee, and that is where we should go—now!"

"But what of His miracle?"

"What of it?"

"Should we not return to Jerusalem and tell everyone the truth?"

"If we return to Jerusalem, we will be arrested and crucified. How can we tell people the truth hanging from a cross? Galilee is our home. We'll be safe there. Jesus first came to us there. Most of those who believe in Him are there. From Galilee, we can spread the truth about what has happened here."

"Perhaps you are right, Peter. We have good reason to fear both Pilate and Caiaphas. And Jesus will find us in Galilee just as surely as He would in Jerusalem."

"Then you'll come with me?"

"It will be good to go home."

"Yes it will."

"What about Joseph of Arimathea?"

"What about him, John?"

"Shouldn't we tell him what has happened to his tomb?"

"We can see him before we leave."

"Should we take His shroud with us?"

"No, John. Jesus left it here. I'm sure He had a reason."

The two disciples made their way back to Jerusalem. In the branches of the nearby olive tree, a frail old man sat hidden behind the lush spring growth. Pulling back the hood of his cloak, he scratched the top of his wrinkled and disfigured head. After the disciples were gone, he came down out of his tree. Limping badly, he ambled over to the tomb. At the altar he picked up the shroud. Gently he fingered the blood-stained cloth. He looked to the east and smiled at the rising sun. "And so it begins," he said.

Rumour of a
Miracle Spreads

Forty Days until Bethany

For the life of him, Jonah couldn't figure out what Joseph of Arimathea was up to. Although not a member of the Sanhedrin's highest ranked Chamber of Priests or the second ranked Chamber of Scribes, he was still a wealthy member in good standing of the Chamber of Elders. He was not the sort of man you would expect to find seeking out the darker quarters of Jerusalem so early in the morning. Watching Joseph enter the one-room drinking shop, Jonah could only scratch his head and follow.

A large man, Jonah was nearing forty and was as hard and constant as the great desert that had borne him and as deadly as the Arab tribesmen who had sold him into slavery after murdering his family and stealing their meagre flock. He had earned his freedom by deftly slitting the throat of a pickpocket about to make off with his master's purse. Free, but without two bronze coins to rub together, he had enlisted in the Roman army, where he spent eight years killing Rome's enemies. After Rome, he went into business for himself. From his Arab captors, he had learned to be cunning. From Rome, he had learned the value of planning and discipline. And from life, he had learned to always get his money up front. His tunic was well-made and clean, and the travelling cloak wrapped around his shoulders was warm and comforting.

Joseph of Arimathea snaked his way to a table in a secluded corner of the shop. Keeping a few bodies between them, Jonah turned his thoughts back to trying to understand why Joseph

Caiaphas, High Priest of the Sanhedrin, had ordered him to never let Joseph of Arimathea out of his sight.

"See who he meets with, Jonah," the high priest had told him. "See if you can find out why he gave his tomb to the Nazarene."

Why Caiaphas was interested in what Joseph of Arimathea had done with his own tomb, Jonah had no idea.

The owner of the now-empty tomb sat down at a table that was already occupied by two men, whom Jonah recognized as Peter and John, disciples of the crucified Nazarene. He chose a bench against a wall that placed him behind his subject but close enough to hear every word spoken. Then he sat back to watch and listen.

"All right, Peter, I'm here," said Joseph, petulantly wiping the sleep from his eyes. "Now would you please tell me what's so important that you had to drag me out of bed at so early an hour?"

Peter gave the room a quick once over as he waited for their waitress to finish bringing them their drinks. Jonah was fortunate to turn his head away in the nick of time.

"Mary Magdalene came to see us this morning," Peter said.

At the mention of Mary's name, Jonah's back stiffened. He knew the woman—intimately—and although their paths had not crossed for some time, he still carried a fondness for her in his heart. A fondness that he feared might actually be something more profound. He leaned forward and listened intently.

"She told us that the tomb is open," interjected John.

"But the tomb is sealed with an enormous stone!" exclaimed Joseph.

"It has been rolled away," whispered Peter conspiratorially.

"But that's impossible!" asserted Joseph with a contemptuous snort. "Perhaps the earthquake moved the stone?"

"I thought about that, Joseph," replied Peter, "but it was a very minor quake, and it is a very big stone."

"What about the guards?" continued Joseph. "Caiaphas has the tomb guarded day and night. He knows what is supposed to happen on the dawn of the third day."

"Mary says the guards ran away." John shrugged.

"There's more," said Peter, elbows on the table. "John and I went to look for ourselves. We discovered that the tomb isn't just open—His body is missing."

"You mean..."

"He is risen!" burst out John, causing Peter to turn an angry eye his way.

"Will you keep your voice down," demanded Peter. "You don't know who could be listening."

"A missing body doesn't prove anything; it might have been stolen," said Joseph, getting them back on topic.

"That is certainly what Pilate will think," said Peter.

"Pilate will blame us," added John.

"You didn't, did you?" inquired Joseph hesitantly.

"Of course not," asserted Peter defiantly.

"Then who do you think would do such a thing?"

"Peter thinks Caiaphas."

"The high priest? But he's the one who ordered the tomb guarded."

"Caiaphas took the body so that he can blame us and order our arrest," said Peter sharply.

"It's an interesting theory, Peter."

"Aren't you both overlooking one thing?" asked John.

"And what might that be?" asked Joseph.

"That our Master walked out of His own tomb?"

Joseph sat back in his chair. Emptying his cup, he signalled their waitress for a refill. "What if the prophecy has been fulfilled?" he asked.

"I believe it has," replied John.

"Either way, we will know for sure soon enough," said Peter. "In the meantime, we must take the necessary precautions."

"I agree," said Joseph, straightening up. "The two of you should join the others in Galilee."

"We have no money, Joseph."

"Don't worry about that, Peter," said Joseph, reaching into his cloak and taking out a small purse. "Here, take my purse. There isn't much, but it should see you to Galileee. Just go, please."

"Thank you, Joseph." Peter smiled, rose, and took the offered purse.

"We shall forever be in your debt," said John, also getting up.

"Just go and be safe. And one final thought, gentlemen. I was studying the sky last night, and I noticed that Jupiter, the star of Kings, was brighter than usual."

Jonah stood up. He knew he was supposed to stay with Joseph, but something told him he'd better go and see for himself.

When he was in sight of the tomb, Jonah picked up his pace. There was a haunting stillness in the air. Up ahead, he could just make out the vague image of a skull looming out over the valley. Golgotha—Place of the Skull.

He didn't go directly into the tomb. He took his time, first examining the area around the guards' fire. He made note of the spilled wine and the discarded dice, but he could see no sign of a struggle. No blood, no broken weapons, no dead bodies. He thought perhaps the earthquake might have opened the tomb, but if that was the case, why only this one? Why not any of the others?

In the middle of the empty tomb stood a crude stone pedestal on which a body could be placed. Only, there was no body. He picked up the linen shroud and the rope bindings that had once held it in place. He wondered why the thieves had gone to so much trouble. He crouched down and saw that the pedestal was cracked from top to bottom. He stuck his index finger in the crack. It came away covered in soot.

Once again in the light, Jonah lifted a face shaped by a thousand desert storms and scared by a hundred battles up to the rising sun. He marked its position in the sky. *I suppose I best see Caiaphas before breakfast,* he decided. One last look into the inexplicable emptiness of the tomb, and then he headed back to the waking city.

THE SCHEMING GETS UNDERWAY

FORTY DAYS UNTIL BETHANY

The guards at the entrance to the Tower Antonia, the great fortress that controlled Jerusalem, would not let a Jew, even a captain in the temple guards, through the gate. Aaron had to cool his heels inside the guardhouse. It was a square, one-room, single-storey stone structure with wooden benches to sit on and narrow slits designed more for shooting arrows than taking in the view. It made Aaron feel as if he were waiting inside a prison cell.

He was waiting for Pilate's second in command, the tribune Lucius Verus Clemens. Aaron had first been approached by the tribune during a joint military exercise carried out against Parthian bandits by temple guards and legionaries. The attack had been a complete success. During their triumphant return to Jerusalem, the tribune had mentioned to Aaron that, as head of security, he was in a postion to pay, and pay well, for any information that helped Rome nip political unrest in the bud.

Most people found it difficult not to stare at the young tribune. Aaron was not most people. He believed in the Spartan virtues—discipline, loyalty, frugality, bravery. The tribune was…well, none of those things. He'd just turned thirty and possessed a captivating beauty more voluptuous than virile. High cheek bones set off dark, alluring eyes under long, seductive lashes. A soft, round chin was topped by a full, sensuous mouth. His perfectly coifed hair had not a single strand out of place. Of modest stature, he was turning to fat despite his youth. He disgusted Aaron, but his money was good.

The tribune's two bodyguards were at his side. They were a pair of violent-looking former legionaries who Lucius had personally selected before leaving Rome three years ago. They had both proven to be loyal to the tribune's money. Seeing that Aaron was alone, Lucius ordered the guards to wait for him outside.

"Hail Caesar!" shouted Aaron, raising his hand in salute as Lucius sauntered into the room.

"You can dispense with the false show of loyalty, Captain. It isn't going to earn you a single extra sesterce," droned Lucius in response.

A little embarrassed, Aaron lowered his right arm as if he wasn't sure what else to do with it.

"So, Aaron," began Lucius, wandering over to a polished brass mirror that hung opposite to where Aaron was standing. He was dressed in full armour and a red traveling cloak. He carried his helmet under his right arm; his sword was buckled on his left. In his left hand, he held a pear so ripe as to be on the very edge of rot, just the way he liked his fruit. "This better be important," he said, pointedly keeping the back of his head turned towards Aaron as he contemplated his reflection and flicked away a speck of dirt from the front of his cloak. "I've got a centura of anxious legionaries waiting for my order to move out."

The moment of truth was at hand, and Aaron swallowed hard. This had to be handled right. He wasn't here to serve Rome but to get paid. Like any good salesman, he knew the hardest part of any transaction was determining who wanted it more. The tribune wanted to hear what he had to say. He wanted the tribune's money. *The trick*, he told himself, *will be to not tell the tribune too much. Get him interested, but leave him wanting more.*

"Well, come on, Captain. Speak up," snapped Lucius, sucking in his stomach as he checked out his profile.

"This is not the usual sort of information," Aaron commenced. "It's not barrack gossip or drunken barroom rumours."

"Oh really," said Lucius, before biting into his pear, juice squirting out the sides of his mouth and running down his chin. "What kind of rumour is it then?"

"I saw this with my own eyes."

"And what you saw," asked Lucius, flexing his biceps, checking out their shape and size in the mirror, "was it animal, vegetable, or mineral?"

"It's something I'll want extra for."

Lucius moved to the centre of the room. He stopped a couple of feet in front of Aaron. He wiped pear juice off his chin with the back of his hand. His eyes never left Aaron's. "This really is a very fine piece of fruit," he said, offering Aaron the half-eaten pome. "Care for a bite?"

The tribune's behaviour didn't surprise Aaron. Lucius was not known for his adherence to military protocol. First, no salute, and now this disgusting bit of fruit thrust into his face. "No, thank you," he said, forcing a smile. "I'd rather we settled on a price."

With a shrug, Lucius returned the offending fruit to his mouth. "Why don't you just tell me what you saw, Captain," he said while chewing, "and I'll tell you how much it's worth?"

The impertinence was another thing that did not surprise Aaron. The tribune was used to having the upper hand. *Not this time*, Aaron reminded himself. He thought about all the bills he had to pay. The home he had inherited from his father-in-law was spacious and far enough above the lower city to avoid its nastier smells, but the taxes and upkeep were killing him. He was also sending his son to the home of a Greek scholar. He was determined to give his boy the advantages he had been denied. Thinking about money, or rather his lack of it, steeled Aaron's will. "I already know how much it's worth," he said flatly.

"How many sesterces are we talking about?" asked Lucius.

Aaron swallowed hard and stared fixedly at the tribune. "I don't want sesterces," he said. "I want gold."

"Gold?" Lucius smiled. "My, my, aren't we feeling ambitious?"

"It's worth it. But only if you hear it while there's time to act."

"'Time to act.' Sounds serious," said the tribune mockingly, "How much gold?"

"Ten coins."

"I'll tell you what, Captain. I'll give you five gold coins now and the rest after I've heard what you have to say."

"Ten now," demanded Aaron, holding out his hand palm up.

For a long heartbeat, Lucius stared into the captain's eyes. Aaron had told him just enough. With a reluctant shrug of his shoulders, he dropped ten coins into Aaron's outstretched palm. It was a pittance to him. To Aaron, it was a small fortune. "Excuse the pear juice," he said.

Aaron looked down at the coins. Pear juice made them glisten in the growing sunlight. With a curt nod of his head, he slipped the coins into a purse securely tied to his belt. "It happened just before dawn this morning," he began, wiping the sticky fruit juice off his hand and onto his cloak. He opened his mouth to continue then paused. He had been about to tell the tribune the truth, but at the last second thought better of it. *No point telling him I ran away*, he supposed.

"For the last time, Captain, get on with it. I haven't got all day."

Aaron smiled weakly. "We were attacked," he said in a matter-of-fact tone.

"Attacked? By whom?"

Aaron looked away. It was an unconscious action. He was lying, and liars look away. "I don't know, Tribune. They wore masks."

"Did they say what they were after?"

"They were after the body."

"They told you this?"

"They knocked me unconscious, but they took the body."

"What about the stone?"

"They rolled it out of the way."

"What of the earthquake?"

"I thought about that, but the other tombs are still sealed."

"Who else knows about this?" Lucius asked, conspiratorially moving closer to Aaron, his voice barely above a whisper.

"Just me, my men, and now you," answered Aaron, sidling away. He didn't trust the tribune being that close.

"Can your men be counted on to keep their mouths shut?"

"I ordered them not to say a word. They're scared. They'll do as they're told."

"Good." Lucius nodded, walking back to the mirror. He took a last bite of his pear then tossed it uncaringly on the floor. "The longer we can keep this our little secret," he said, smiling and checking his teeth, "the better."

"My shift ends at the end of the sixth hour. I will have to say something when the second shift arrives to relieve us and in my report."

"Don't worry about that. I'll contact Caiaphas. Your second shift will be replaced by legionaries from the Antonia."

"And my report?"

"Say whatever you want, but take your report directly to the high priest." Lucius turned from the mirror and looked sternly at Aaron. "Do not, under any circumstances, Captain, allow anyone but Caiaphas to see it. Are we clear on that?"

"Whatever you think is best, Tribune."

"So the Nazarene's body is missing," Lucius wondered aloud, lifting his chin examining his neck for wrinkles, "and on the dawn of the third day. You did well to bring this to me, Captain."

"Glad to be of service, sir," smiled Aaron, his hand fingering the gold coins through the leather skin of his purse.

After the captain left, Lucius did not return to his centura. Still captivated by his reflection in the mirror, he pulled at the tiny wrinkles around his eyes and considered what he had been told. The tribune had advised Pilate to execute the Nazarene. Now, with the theft of the body, it looked as if the execution might lead to more trouble than it had prevented. *The question I have to ask myself,* pondered Lucius, *is how do I make money off of this?*

The Lying Continues

Forty Days until Bethany

Aaron found Jacob, Ezra, and Azekah waiting for him inside the wine bar, where he had told them to wait for him. All three of them were anxious to hear what Aaron had to say. They had taken over a large table at the back of the place, away from prying eyes and ears. They ordered some wine, but when their waitress asked about breakfast, they were all too upset to eat except for Aaron, who splurged on a plate of fresh bread, honey, some olives, cheese, half a dozen boiled eggs, and, for a special treat, sweet raisins.

"Where have you been, Captain?" asked Jacob, putting words to the anxiousness they all felt.

"Where I go is none of your concern, Jacob," asserted Aaron sternly. There was no way he was going to tell them about his little side trip to see the tribune.

"But you were gone so long, Captain," whined Ezra, nervously twisting the ring on his right index finger.

"You all need to calm down," said Aaron with as much of a smile as he could muster, "because there is nothing to worry about."

"Nothing to worry about?" exclaimed Jacob. "With all due respect, Captain, we left our post, and the tomb we were supposed to be guarding is empty."

Aaron looked at the three worried faces boring in on him and wished they weren't so young. He was confident they could all get through this in one piece. Their Roman replacements wouldn't arrive for hours yet. They had plenty of time to get back to the crime scene and make the alterations necessary to back up the story he had decided on. The one thing they had to avoid was panic, and panic was what he was looking at. "Men, men, men, what's important here is that we all stick to the same story."

"And what story is that, Captain?" asked Azekah.

"The simplest one possible: we were attacked. We were knocked unconscious. When we awoke, the body was gone."

"They'll never believe us, Captain," argued Ezra. "Never!"

"We were attacked!" erupted Aaron, banging his fist on the table. "Right?"

An ominous silence settled over the table. A bead of sweat fell from the tip of Ezra's nose. They all watched it hit the table. "Right?" repeated Aaron quietly.

The pause lasted longer than Aaron would have liked. Jacob was the first to break it. "You really think they'll believe us, Captain?"

"Would I have recommended it if I didn't?"

"No, I guess not, Captain," conceded Jacob.

"Look, men, we have to tell them something, right?" Aaron looked around the table. Slowly, each one of his men nodded his head in agreement. "This is the best story I could come up with. If one of you has a better one, let's hear it."

Azekah looked to Jacob, who looked to Ezra, who looked back to Azekah. "I didn't think so," said Aaron, smiling thinly. "Good! I'm glad that's all settled. Now where's our food?"

As if on cue, their waitress appeared with their order. She set out a serving plate with the cheese and bread. Around it, she placed bowls filled with honey, olives, eggs, and, last but not least, the sweet raisins. "You sure you won't have a little something?" offered Aaron, tearing off a piece of bread and dripping a goodly amount of honey over it. "The bread is fresh, and so is the honey."

They were hungry. The smell of the bread hot out of the oven that morning was too tempting. The three of them dug in.

Aron watched them eat and smiled. They were starting to relax. He decided they were ready for his last bit of bad news. "There is one other thing, men," he said affably.

"What's that, Captain?" asked Ezra.

"If we're going to say we were attacked, we're going to have to go back to the tomb and make it look as if we really were attacked."

"How do we do that, Captain?' asked Jacob.

"We have to go back and break a few branches, scuff up the dirt. Make it look like we put up a fight."

"Is that all, Captain?" asked Ezra.

"We're also going to have to look the part."

"I don't like the sound of that, Captain," said Ezra, shaking his head.

"You're going to like how it feels even less."

THE DOUBTS AND
WORRIES GROW

FORTY DAYS UNTIL BETHANY

Caiaphas's home was situated on the summit of the southern hill far above the clatter and stink of the lower city and accessible by a long, stone staircase. At the top of the stairs, Jonah came to a locked gate. Behind the gate stood two temple guards. Behind the guards stood a sprawling stone house constructed in the Hellenistic style. Spacious rooms with translucent talc windows looked onto a central courtyard surrounded by stone columns and entered into through a portico. Seeing Jonah approach, the guards hustled to open the gate.

Jonah avoided the portico and made his way to a narrow tunnel near the front of the house. The tunnel led to a formidable brass door. Several loud bangs caused an eye hole to slide open; a moment later, the door. Jonah didn't bother to acknowledge the guard. He hurriedly made his way down a dark, damp hallway until he came to another brass door guarded by a second heavily armed man. The guard, recognizing Jonah, immediately put his shoulder to the heavy metal door.

On the other side of the door, seated at a large, rectangular, stone table, Joseph Caiaphas, High Priest of the Sanhedrin, was busy making sure the accounts for the sacred treasury of the temple, the Corban, were current and in order. The temple collected money from tithes and temple dues as well as the compulsory half-shekel tribute paid not only by the residents of Jerusalem but also by every adult Jew the world over. These monies were in addition to the votive offerings and the gifts of gold.

The money was important. The temple had many expenses—sacrificial animals, salaries for priests and temple guards, daily maintenance and repairs, seemingly endless repairs. But the truth, and it was a truth Joseph and the rest of the Sanhedrin didn't like to talk about, was that the temple had acquired quite a healthy surplus from an annual income of over eight hundred gold talents. A surplus that sometimes found its way into projects that might not have met with the approval of those forced to pay the taxes.

Like Pilate's grand aqueduct, thought Caiaphas. The aqueduct was a perfectly worthy project, but it was not one in any way associated with the maintenance and upkeep of the temple. But Jerusalem needed the water. And the people needed to see the benefits of Roman rule, not just the consequences. Pilate's handling of the Standards Affair and his slaughter of the Galileans just one year ago had left Judea angry and resentful. The aqueduct, and the water it would bring to the city, would be tangible proof that not everything Roman came at the end of a sword.

Not if the people find out that the Corban is helping to pay for it, Joseph reminded himself. He looked up and noticed that his hour glass had run out. He turned it over and rose from his chair. He stretched his back in a vain attempt to ease the dull ache that started in his hips and worked its way up his spine.

The high priest of the Sanhedrin was of a noble appearance; his face was long and lined by the worries only a man who sees himself responsible for the future of his people can comprehend. He had intelligent eyes—bright, piercing, perceptive, and the color of coal. His beard was long, streaked with grey, and richly perfumed. His apparel was costly and fit well. Born in Beth Meqsheth, a small village near Jerusalem, into a wealthy, aristocratic family of high priestly lineage—his grandfather, Elionaeus, had been appointed High Priest by King Agrippa—Joseph had, by marrying the daughter of Annas the former High Priest, merged two of the most powerful families in all of Judea.

As High Priest, he held the highest office he could ever hope to achieve, and yet he was not at peace.

He worried for his people. They were approaching a crossroads, and he feared they would make the wrong turn. It had taken all of his negotiating skills to keep the Standards Affair from exploding into an all-out war against Rome. His diplomatic skills and Pilate's willingness to back down were all that had kept his people from courting disaster. And all because the second cohort assigned to keep law and order in Jerusalem had had the temerity to put Caesar's profile on the front of their battle standards.

Such rigidity to the demands of the modern world would, Caiaphas feared, one day lead Rome to wipe his people from the face of the earth as they had once done to Carthage. At least Carthage had good reasons for going to war. *What reasons do we have?* he asked himself. *Under Roman rule we have prospered beyond anything our forefathers could ever have imagined. There are as many Jews in Caesar's empire as Greeks, and we're just as influential. But if we continue to shut ourselves off from the rest of the world, if we continue to rise up every time Romans behave like Romans, we will soon find ourselves nailed to crosses.*

His back feeling somewhat better, Caiaphas sat down and was about to get back to his financial accounts when Jonah was escorted into the room. A solemn look came over his face. Turning to the guard, he said, "You can return to your post."

"Yes, Excellency," replied the guard, backing his way out of the room.

"What brings you here at such an early hour, Jonah?" asked the high priest, almost afraid to hear the answer.

"There's something you need to know," stated Jonah ominously. "It's about the Nazarene."

At the mention of the crucified prophet, Caiaphas was all ears. "Have you discovered why Joseph gave up his tomb?" he asked anxiously.

"Mind if I have a little wine?" Jonah asked, sitting down on a chair across from Caiaphas.

"Not at all, Jonah."

Jonah poured himself a goblet, downing half of it in one motion.

"Feel better?"

"A little." Jonah smiled. The windowless chamber was doninated by a large stone table. Behind Caiaphas stood a small brazier, the walls were frescoed with colourful mosaics that, in conformity with Jewish law, avoided figural art, decorating instead with geometric and floral motifs.

"So, what is it that you needed a drink before you could tell me?"

Jonah leaned forward conspiratorially. "I've been following Joseph of Arimathea, and, this morning, a messenger came to his house. Moments later, he left and went into the lower city."

"Why would Joseph go into the lower city alone before first light?"

"That's what I wondered. I followed the priest to a cheap wine bar, the kind of place that caters to the caravan trade, mostly Greeks and Egyptians. He met and talked with two of the Nazarene's disciples. Peter and John, they called themselves."

Caiaphas felt his pulse quicken. Although Joseph of Arimathea had spoken out against putting the Nazarene on trial, he had done so on legal and humanistic grounds. His appeals on behalf of the accused blasphemer were, on their own, not enough to prove that Arimathea had become a member of the Nazarene's flock. But to be meeting with two of the Nazarene's disciples secretly, before the first hour, was proof of something more than mere compassion. "Did you hear what they talked about?" he asked.

"Peter and John told Joseph that the tomb was empty."

Caiaphas sat back abruptly. "Empty?" he asked incredulously. "How is that possible?"

"I don't know. I only know that it's true. I went there myself to make sure."

"What about my guards?"

"When I got there, they were gone."

"And the great stone?"

"Rolled out of the way."

"Rolled out of the way? How is that possible? Could the earthquake not be responsible?"

"I considered that, Joseph, but the other tombs were all still sealed tight."

"And the tomb, you're sure it is empty?"

"Except for the shroud."

Caiaphas leaned forward, shock turning to curiosity. "They left behind the shroud?"

"They did. The way I see it, Joseph, the thieves mean to confuse us, make us think that the body got up and walked away on its own, which..."

"It couldn't do if it was still wrapped up in a shroud," overrode Caiaphas. He gulped his wine and turned to watch the flames dance inside the brazier. He had gone to great lengths to put the Nazarene in his grave. He had thought it would put an end to the false prophet's growing popularity. Now he wasn't so sure

"So what's next, Joseph? Do you want me to continue to follow Joseph of Arimathea?"

Caiaphas took a sip of wine before answering. *I told that spineless jellyfish, Pilate, to give me Roman guards, but he's so worried about that madman Tiberius Caesar that he can't make a decision. His irresolution has put all of Judea at risk. Well, that's all in the past. What I need to do now is find the body and put an end to this as soon as possible.*

"I think," began the high priest, turning his eyes back to the large man sitting across from him, "that you must continue to keep an eye on Joseph of Arimathea. Find out if he is connected to the followers of the Nazarene."

"So you think the Nazarene's followers are behind the theft?"

"That's what I want to find out."

"They have the most to gain, Joseph. But the two disciples sounded as confused as we are."

"Confused in what way, Jonah?"

Jonah closed his eyes, doing his best to recall exactly what had been said. "I remember the one called John said he was convinced that the Nazarene had walked out of His own tomb. The other one, Peter, he said he thought the body had been stolen."

"He said the body had been stolen? Are you sure, Jonah?" asked a startled Caiaphas.

"Oh, I'm sure, Joseph. Peter definitely seemed to think the body had been stolen."

"Peter didn't happen to mention who he thought had stolen it, did he?"

Jonah smiled broadly. "Peter seemed to think you stole it."

"Me? Why would I steal the body?"

"So you can blame the theft on them and use the crime as an excuse to stamp out their new religion."

Caiaphas smiled to himself. *Not a bad idea*, he thought, *too bad it never occurred to me.* "Where are they now Jonah?"

"They've run off to Galilee. They're scared, Joseph."

"Scared of what?"

"You and Pilate mostly—and their own people."

"Can you keep an eye on them in Galilee?"

"I'd have to hire more men."

"Then go ahead and do it. I don't know what these disciples are up to, but I don't believe them when they proclaim their innocence."

"Then why did they deny it to Joseph of Arimathea?"

"They don't trust him."

"But wasn't he in on it? That's what you suspect, right?"

"The disciples could have gotten Joseph of Arimathea to donate his tomb without telling him they were going to steal the body."

"What about your guards? How did they overpower them?"

"There were only four guards. There are twelve, I mean, eleven disciples."

"Fishermen and peasants—two dozen wouldn't have been able to defeat your guards."

"Well, they did. Perhaps they bribed them."

"With what, Joseph? These men don't have any money."

Caiaphas looked contemplatively at his friend, his left hand tugging at his beard. "You raise interesting questions, Jonah, as usual. But what we need now are equally interesting answers."

"You want them watched?"

"I do. And don't forget the women who were close to the Nazarene, like Mary Magdalene."

For the second time that morning, Mary's name had come up. Jonah's eyes narrowed. His head tilted to one side. "Surely," he said, "you don't think Mary stole the body?"

Jonah's reaction surprised Caiaphas. "Do you know Mary Magdalene?" he asked.

"What makes you think I know her?" asked Jonah defensively.

"You seem to be very sure of her innocence if you don't."

"I knew her once, that's all. It was a long time ago. But I can tell you this—Mary might lift your purse, but she's no more capable of stealing our missing body than you are of flying."

The high priest considered the connection. *Why is Jonah so quick to conclude her innocence? And why is he trying to convince me that the disciples are innocent? He couldn't be one of the Nazarene's followers, could he? No,* Caiaphas assured himself, *not possible, not Jonah.* "Not by herself, obviously, Jonah," he said, "but the followers of the Nazarene are our best suspects. We need to watch all of them."

"Keeping an eye on that many people won't be cheap."

Caiaphas unlocked a drawer, reached in, and pulled out a purse. "Here," he said, tossing the purse to Jonah. "This should be enough to get you started."

Jonah did a quick count then stuffed the purse into a deep pocket sown into the inside of his cloak.

"It's more than enough, Joseph."

"You can keep what you don't spend," said Caiaphas, taking hold of Jonah's arm. "Don't let me down on this, Jonah. It's too important."

"Have I ever let you down before, Joseph?"

"No. You're the most reliable man I know."

"Well, the most reliable man you know is in need of some breakfast and a few hours sleep."

"Tell my cook to prepare you something and feel free to rest in one of my guest bedrooms," said Caiaphas, as he rang a bell for the door to be opened.

"That's very good of you, Joseph. I just might take you up on that." The heavy door creaked open, and Jonah left.

After the big man had left, Caiaphas wondered if Jonah understood the true implications of what had just happened. He stared at the flames dancing inside the brazier and asked himself, "Did I make a terrible mistake?"

A Scoundrel's Last Chance

Thirty-Nine Days until Bethany

The sun had set by the time Lucius ordered his men to set up camp half a day's ride from the newly constructed city of Tiberias. They were supposed to be chasing down Parthian raiders, but the tribune had to see someone, and that someone was important enough for him to risk a ride across the desert at night with only his two bodyguards for an escort.

He was risking his life to see Herod Antipas, the most politically ambitious of Herod the Great's three sons. Born in 21 Bc, his life's one great ambition was still unfulfilled. After his father's death in 4 Bc, Augustus Caesar had divided Herod's kingdom amongst the three sons. He gave Antipas Galilee and Perea. Judea he gave to Archelaus, and, to the third son, Philip, Augustus awarded the area east and northeast of the Sea of Galilee.

Antipas had spent his life trying to correct what he saw as Caesar's mistake and reunite his father's kingdom. Naturally, he saw himself as king. His first opportunity to realize his dream came when Archelaus proved unsuitable as a ruler in Judea. Rome was forced to replace him with a Roman prefect. Ever since, Antipas had been scheming to convince Rome to rid herself of her prefects and put him on the throne in Judea. Over the years, he had acquired a number of influential friends—men close to Tiberius Caesar. But his health was beginning to fade; the energy and drive of his youth was gone, and the tetrarch's dream was still unfulfilled

Morning found the tribune outside the gates of Tiberias. Riding through the south gate into Antipas's newly constructed city, Lucius was struck by how empty the place was. "Serves

Antipas right for building over a cemetery," he muttered to himself. "When the engineers told him they'd found human remains, he should have cancelled the entire project and built his new capital city somewhere else." Lucius shrugged. "I suppose tyranny requires one to never admit to a mistake."

The city itself was magnificently constructed with excellent views of the Sea of Galilee. Built from scratch on the sea's western shore, where the hills receded enough to allow easy access to the water, the city, like Jerusalem, straddled the major trade route that ran north to Syria and south to Egypt. The warm springs of Ammathus, much favoured by the tetrarch, were an easy half day's ride to the south. Among the city's many amenities were a large synagogue, a sports stadium, and a beautiful, golden-roofed palace. "Such a sublime city," marvelled Lucius. "It's a shame the Jews are too superstitious to enjoy it."

At the royal palace, the tribune was ushered into the throne room, which was well known for its impressive, Romanesque style. The floor was travertine marble. The windowless walls featured colourfully painted scenes from Greek mythology. Promiscuous gods chased demure but beautiful maidens. The tetrarch was dressed for the hunt in a tunic of the finest wool, having just returned from a hunting expedition.

"Lucius!" Antipas smiled as the tribune entered the room. He was a small man with cruel, wide-set eyes that looked out onto the world over a long, aquiline nose. A carefully trimmed beard masked a weak chin that was held up by a scrawny neck, narrow shoulders, and a soft, slight frame. "Have you come for your money?" he asked.

"Amongst other things, Excellency. Might I have a moment? Something important has come up."

Antipas sighed. "Very well," he said. He snapped his fingers, and a slave ran over with a goblet of wine. "I suppose we might as well be comfortable," he said, smiling laconically then ponderously plopping himself down on a well cushioned reclining couch.

"I couldn't agree more, Excellency," replied Lucius, helping himself to some wine and reclining on a couch facing the tetrarch.

He looked at his retinue of slaves, dancing girls, and hangers on, and said, "I believe, Tribune, we should do this in private." He clapped his bejewlled hands loudly, and everyone scurried away. Once they were alone, Antipas leaned forward, his eyes hard and calculating. "So, Tribune, you've arranged for the zealots to obtain their weapons?" he asked, running an ivory comb through his well-oiled beard. The oil glistened in the candle light.

"I have, Excellency. You've arranged for the money?"

"How can you betray Rome this way?" asked Antipas suspiciously.

Educated by the finest minds Rome had to offer, Lucius had long ago learned to see through what he believed were the false pieties of patriots. History, he believed, taught the wise man that right was always decided by the strong. "Excellency," he said, "as a Roman, I understand that questions of right and wrong are simply a matter of who wins, don't you agree?"

Antipas picked up his wine goblet. "Not completely, Tribune," he said thoughtfully, "but if your fidelity is so conditional, how can I trust you?"

"Since you're going to win, Excellency, my loyalty is absolute."

"Good answer, Tribune," acknowledged Antipas, tossing a large purse into the tribune's lap.

Lucius looked down at the purse and smiled. "Two thousand?" he asked.

"That's right. I presume you'll be taking your usual ten percent?"

"Of course, Excellency," answered Lucius, hoping his smile didn't give away the fact that he planned to take twenty.

"So, Tribune, you implied that my money was not the only reason for your visit."

"I've devised a new plan, Excellency," he said, casually picking up a ripe fig sitting atop a large plate of fruit that had been strategically placed on a table between the two couches, "a way for you to reunite your father's empire sooner than we had expected."

"Isn't that why we're arming the zealots?" asked the tetrarch.

"It is, Excellency, but this will speed up your success," replied the tribune, biting into his fig.

The tribune had been coming to Antipas with ideas for getting rid of Pilate almost from the moment he had arrived in Judea. First, the Janus-faced young Roman had assured him that he could remove Pilate simply by getting the prefect to order the second cohort into Jerusalem. The idea was that, because of their blasphemous battle standards, Judea would rise up in protest over such a blatant disregard for Jewish religious law, thus opening the door for the tetrarch's return to Judea. The tribune had taken a large retainer for that manoeuvre, and it had almost worked. Unfortunately, just as Roman soldiers moved into position to attack the unarmed Jewish citizens who had gathered underneath Pilate's throne room in Caesarea, Caiaphas convinced the prefect to back down. The second cohort was replaced by a cohort whose battle standards didn't offend Jewish law.

After that failure, the tribune had approached the tetrarch with a second, even more expensive scheme—arm the zealots. The tribune had argued that once the anti-Roman religious fanatics had weapons, they would create enough trouble to unseat the prefect. So far, like all his other ideas, this one had also failed to produce any meaningful results. Antipas sighed deeply and put down his comb. "So what is this new plan of yours, Tribune?"

Lucius finished his fig, emptied his wine goblet, and then stood up to make his presentation. "As I'm sure you will soon know, Excellency," he said, starting to pace, "there's been a theft at the tomb of the prophet."

The tetrarch's eyes widened, "The Nazarene's tomb?" he asked.

"That's right, Excellency, and on the morning of the third day," continued Lucius, raising a finger to emphasize the significance of the third day.

Antipas gulped down more wine. "Morning of the third day," he repeated wistfully. "Just as he said…but how does any of this get me Jerusalem?"

"Excellency, I'm going to present Pilate with a basic fact of Roman law," answered Lucius, a self-satisfied grin on his face. "Roman law states that the bodies of those crucified are Roman property, and any theft of said property requires a legal investigation. Under Roman law, it is called a Judicium."

The tetrarch looked sceptically at the young Roman, who was again surveying the fruit plate for another fig. "I know what a Judicium is, Tribune. What I don't know is how it gets me Judea."

"It's simple, Excellency." Lucius smiled condescendingly. He couldn't help himself.

His Excellency didn't miss the condescension. "Explain it to me anyway," he said, his voice flat.

"My plan, Excellency, is brilliant in its simplicity. I intend to lay a trail of clues that will lead the investigation straight to Joseph Caiaphas. And what do you think happens to Judea when Pilate arrests the high priest?"

"The High Council of the Sanhedrin will call for mass demonstrations."

"Business will grind to a halt, Excellency. All those fat caravans will stop coming. Taxes will stop flowing. And Tiberius Caesar would soon be demanding that you, Excellency, take charge."

The tetrarch's eyes widened lustfully. "Yes, your plan just might work, Tribune. But Pilate would never agree to do something so reckless."

"I'm not going to leave him any other option. The Judicium will find Caiaphas guilty."

"You're sure?"

"The clues I intend to lay in front of the investigator will leave the man no choice, and once the investigator goes to Pilate with his indictment, the prefect will have to act."

"He'll be committing political suicide."

"There won't be anything political about it, Excellency."

"And what is all this going to cost me?"

"Well, Excellency," said Lucius thoughtfully, finally selecting a second fig. He looked Antipas in the eye as he bit into it. "What I have to do will be very dangerous."

"Just give me a price, Tribune."

"As you wish, Excellency." Lucius smiled, pacing again as he finished his second fig. "I think five hundred thousand would be a fair price."

"Sesterces?" asked a shocked Antipas.

"For Judea, Excellency."

The size of the number left the tetrarch momentarily speechless. After regaining control of himself, he realized that, considering what the tribune was offering, it was a price he had to pay. "Fine," he said, "Half a million it is."

"A wise decision, Excellency, one you won't regret."

"I better not, Tribune," warned the tetrarch turning a baleful eye on Lucius.

Lucius, ignoring Antipas's less than subtle warning, sniffed the air. "Is that Frontinian chicken I smell, Excellency?"

"Good nose, Tribune."

"Oh, I do love the aniseed in Frontinian chicken."

"You want to stay for lunch, Tribune?"

"Well, Excellency," said Lucius, all thought of his men waiting for him in the desert gone from his mind, "I am hungry, and it's a long ride back to my men."

"Then you'll stay."

"We can talk more about how I'm going to hand you Judea on a silver"—Lucius picked up the purse and gave it a shake, tinkling the coins pleasantly—"platter."

After the tribune had left, Antipas ordered everyone out of his throne room. Alone with his thoughts, he admitted to himself that what he had just discovered worried him deeply. One of his tax collectors claimed that Jesus had returned his son to him from the grave. Joanna, the wife of his chief steward, Chuza, believed fervently that the Nazarene was the Son of God. And now the tomb was empty—just as the Nazarene had predicted.

Going to a window that overlooked the sea, he remembered the words of John the Baptist. *I should never have killed him, not just to please a woman. Could the crazy old man have been right? Has John's prophecy come true? Did I behead a true prophet of God?*

The thought of having defied God so blatantly caused Antipas to shudder. He felt cold and walked away from the window. "What did I do?" he called out to the empty throne room.

I Believed Him

Thirty-Nine Days until Bethany

Still in her bedclothes, her robe wrapped tightly around her, Reisa Caiaphas looked over at her husband's bed and, finding it empty, sighed. He'd been having trouble sleeping, and she wanted to make sure that he was all right. The high priest's wife was approaching her forty-fifth birthday, and her figure, once considered voluptuous, had grown plump. Her raven-coloured hair had long ago turned white. She had soft, understanding, brown eyes set somewhat incongruously in a strongly lined face whose features were a little too sharp for a woman—the chin a little too prominent, the jaw line a little too obvious.

Her husband's fitful nights had started with the arrest of Jesus of Nazareth. She had begged him not to do it, but Joseph was certain of the righteousness of his decision. And yet now he could not sleep. "Serves him right," she scolded, immediately begging God for forgiveness. Shaking her head resignedly, she wished, and not for the first time, that there was some way, some magic potion, some brilliant words of the prophets, some wise insight into the nature of man and woman, that might convince her to truly love her husband. Of course, the problem was not with her. It was with her heart. And while hearts may be easy to break, they are impossible to argue with.

She had only married Caiaphas because that was what her father, Annas, had wanted. That had been fifteen years ago, the year Joseph Caiaphas was appointed High Priest by the Roman Prefect Gratus. At the time, she had been happily resigned to her spinsterhood. She'd had plenty of suitors, but they had all seemed more interested in her father's money than in her. So with her mother gone and her thirtieth birthday right around the corner, she had found contentment, if not real happiness, in looking after her father. Then one sunny spring afternoon, her father had come home with the surprising news.

She knew her father had been behind the difficulties that had forced Gratus to quickly hire, and then fire, the three high priests appointed after her father's dismissal. What she hadn't been aware of was the deal her father had made with Gratus. Earlier that same spring day, Gratus had agreed to appoint Caiaphas high priest in return for a promise of a little peace from Annas. Her marriage was just a way for her father to get back into the game as Caiaphas's father-in-law.

Not that she didn't try to love her husband; she did. Unfortunately, she had had to settle for merely admiring. Joseph Caiaphas was a man with a difficult job. A job that placed a wall of ceremony and circumstance between the high priest and the people he served. It was a job that made the most basic and intimate human relationships into Chinese puzzle boxes.

He was expected to wield power in defence of his people when, in reality, he had none. He was expected to balance two great forces—Rome and Judea—neither of which he controlled. He was the most pathetic of creatures, a diplomat without leverage. The people, who could annoy Rome enough to win small concessions when they wanted to such as during the Standards Affair, had a will of their own. To them, the high priest was like the banks of a river; he could channel their emotions, but he could never control them. And Rome? Rome listened when he talked and then did whatever it wanted. With defeat lingering around every corner, her husband had grown cold and aloof. He was a man to be respected but not loved.

After her eyes adjusted to the darkness, she sat down on her husband's empty bed. *Did some part of him*, she asked herself, *understand the enormity of the mistake he had made? Was that what was keeping him from his bed? But how could he, when to acknowledge his mistake would be to accept Jesus of Nazareth as the true Messia?*

And to accept that would be to accept the end of the Sanhedrin, of the entire Jewish religion. She did not think he was capable of that. What man would be?

She stood up and called gently into the night, "Joseph? Joseph? Where are you?"

"Out here," came her husband's voice from the balcony just off the bedroom.

She stepped onto the balcony and into the cold night air. She hugged the collar of her robe tight around her neck. "What are you doing out here at this hour, Joseph?" she asked.

"I couldn't sleep. Thought I'd look at the stars," he said.

"So now you've looked. Come to bed, please."

"Don't you think the night sky is God's greatest creation?" asked Caiaphas, ignoring his wife's pleading and staring up into eternity.

"I have no idea, Joseph. I only know its cold out here."

"Do you think the stars can tell us our destiny?" he asked, turning to face her for the first time.

"Our destiny, Joseph, is between us and our God."

"Isn't it a great city?" he asked, turning her to look out over the quietly sleeping city. Their balcony commanded an excellent view from the top of the southern slope, and although most of Jerusalem now rested in darkness, the Roman torches at each guard tower offered a sense of its size and importance.

"It's our home," she answered quietly. "And right now, it's too late to be standing around in our bedclothes staring at it."

"And we are a great people," he went on.

"A great people who need their sleep," she said impatiently.

"Do you think our people are happy?" he asked as he ran his hand lovingly along the side of her face.

Reisa gently kissed her husband's hand. "I don't know, Joseph. Ask me again in the morning," she begged.

"Answer now," he insisted, putting his arms around her.

"Yes, yes." She sighed. "I believe we are happy. Now let's go to bed."

"And do you know why we are happy?" he asked.

"I only know why I'm sleepy."

"We're happy because we have learned to live with Rome."

"Do you want us to become Roman?" she asked.

The effrontery of her question angered him. "Of course not," he replied defiantly as if he had just been insulted. "We must always remain who we are. But Rome will never willingly let us go, and we will never force them. Rome is our future. The Nazarene put that future at risk."

"Jesus was no threat to Judea or to Rome. He said His kingdom was not of this world, Joseph."

"And you believed Him?"

"Yes, Joseph, I believed Him," she answered calmly.

Joseph shook his head. "That's because you don't understand how the world works."

"Really?" she said indignantly.

"Yes, really," insisted Joseph. "Even if the Prophet was innocent, others would have used Him for their own purposes."

"So what the man actually said doesn't matter? Only what others might have thought about it?"

"Sometimes, my dear, circumstances lead the man and not the other way around," replied Joseph, the words more appropriate for him.

Reisa wanted to leave, but she had one final question. "And what if Jesus was not a man?"

"Perhaps it is time you went back to bed," he said without glancing at her.

Something Not of This World

Thirty-Eight Days until Bethany

The next morning, last night's argument still very much with him, Caiaphas, alone in his counting room, looked up after reading the wax tablet that a servant had just brought him. As usual, Jonah's message was terse and to the point: "The disciple's are hiding in the home of a fisherman on the Sea of Galilee. They are afraid. I will pass on more information as soon as I can." That was all it said.

Caiaphas rubbed the bridge of his nose. "If the disciples did steal the body," he asked himself, "why have they left Jerusalem? Jerusalem is where they have the most to gain. They can't build a church hiding in a fisherman's hut. So what are they up to? Do they fear arrest? If so, why steal the body in the first place?" The high priest's ruminations were interrupted by a knock at the door. "Yes?" he asked impatiently.

"Excellency!" said the guard, "I have the captain for you."

Ah yes, the captain, thought Caiaphas. "Show him in immediately!"

"So, Captain, please have a seat," said Caiaphas, addressing Aaron after the guard had left. "That's quite an eye you've got there. I hope it doesn't hurt too much."

"It's nothing, Excellency. Happened when we were attacked," said Aaron as he sat down in the chair across from Caiaphas. "If this is about the tomb, Excellency, I've finished my written report."

"Excellent, Captain, I trust you brought it with you?"

"Of course, Excellency," replied Aaron, reaching across the desk to hand Caiaphas the parchment.

Caiaphas accepted the document and started reading. After a few minutes, he looked up at Aaron and smiled. He knew the captain and liked him. "So, Aaron, I trust everything is well with you?"

"It is, Excellency."

"Your wife and children doing well?"

"They are, Excellency. Thank you for asking."

"Not at all, Captain. Would you care for some wine?"

"Respectfully, Excellency, I'd like to finish as soon as possible. My wife is waiting."

"Yes, of course, Aaron, I won't keep you long," said Caiaphas, returning to the report. "Now, you say here that you were attacked."

"That's right, Excellency, just before sunrise."

"But you are unable to identify your attackers?"

"They came at us out of the darkness from behind."

"You had no advance warning?"

"None, Excellency."

"You didn't hear them approaching?"

"As I say in my report, Excellency, we were playing dice, so..."

"Playing dice? While still on duty?"

"I'm ashamed to admit it, Excellency, but it helps to keep us awake."

"Well that's hardly a capital offense. Any thoughts as to why your attackers didn't kill you?"

"No idea, Excellency. I just thank God they didn't."

"And you've no idea how they moved the stone?"

"I was unconscious, Excellency."

"Or why they unwrapped the body?"

"No idea, Excellency. I wasn't even aware that they had."

"So I see from your report. Well, I think that will be all for now, Captain. You can find your own way out."

"Thank you, Excellency," said Aaron hurriedly.

Caiaphas waited until after the captain had left before rereading Aaron's report. It all looked to be in order, yet it was precisely the neatness of the crime that bothered the high priest. *Even if I accept that the guards were taken by surprise, shouldn't they have put up more of a fight? The captain sported a nice black eye, but shouldn't his wounds have been of a more serious nature?* "I'll have to order Jonah to keep a close eye on him," he told himself, "and see if the captain makes contact with the men who paid him to betray his oath."

Walking down the steep staircase that led to the high priest's home, Aaron regretted having to admit that his men had been gambling. But it did lend credence to the rest of their story. *After all*—he smiled to himself—*who lies himself into trouble?*

At the bottom of the stairs, he didn't turn towards his own home but headed instead even lower, into the poorest parts of the city. He had a meeting to go to. The lies he told his superiors were one thing, but he knew the truth. Something not of this world had happened at that tomb, and Aaron was determined to find out what.

Pilate Is Moved
into Position

Thirty-Six Days until Bethany

B ack in Jerusalem, Lucius went straight to the palace. He wanted to move Pilate into position as soon as possible. He had a good record when it came to getting the prefect to do what he wanted. The wife was a problem, but Pilate responded to a combination of soft-soap and bullying. *I'll have to be careful this time, though. Pontius will be upset with me for having advised him to crucify the Nazarene in the first place.*

He arrived at the palace too late to catch Pilate before he left for the aqueduct. The conduit had its beginnings near the village of Bethlehem seven miles southwest of Jerusalem. There, Pilate's engineers had shown him five natural springs that they assured him could supply enough water to feed the city. To get from Bethlehem to the walls of Jerusalem, the aqueduct first had to tunnel its way under the village which stood between the springs and the city. Then, as nothing more than a stone-lined ditch, it had worked its way around the hilly terrain between Bethlehem and Jerusalem. At the outskirts of Jerusalem, Pilate's engineers had faced one final obstacle: the Hinnom valley. For that, they had designed a traditional Roman arched aqueduct which was now in the final stages of construction.

Originally, Pontius had not been very enthusiastic about such a large and expensive undertaking. Even after Lucius had pointed out the favours naming the aqueduct after Tiberius could win him in Rome, he had remained sceptical. Tiberius was notoriously frugal, and the treasury was always short of money.

Lucius had been unable to change the prefect's mind until he received support from Caiaphas, who convinced his fellow priests to make available money donated to the temple. Pilate had immediately agreed. It was a no-lose proposition. Caesar would get his name attached to a great piece of history. Jerusalem would get its aqueduct. Pilate would get the credit. Procula's warning that using money donated for religious purposes to build an aqueduct might lead to trouble later on had fallen on deaf ears. Pilate had signed the bill authorizing the construction three years ago.

It had proven to be a nightmare ever since. At first, the engineers weren't sure if the slope was steep enough to carry the water. Next, there was a shortage of skilled labour. Then, with the monster almost completed, the tiles had been delayed. The tiles had caused Pilate to become obsessively involved in every detail of the project. He was on site every morning with the rising sun and stayed until the afternoon sun drove him back to the palace.

Lucius hated being anywhere near the construction site. All that dust and noise and stink revolted him. He and his bodyguards were making their way over to Pilate's tent when Elijah, a Jewish contractor, caught up to him with another of his pointless inquiries. "What is it now, Elijah?" barked Lucius as the small, middle aged man, came along side of him.

"Well, Tribune," began Elijah, holding up a scroll, "it's this bill you sent me."

"Not again."

"It says you paid me for two thousand nails, but you only paid me for one thousand."

"And how many did you deliver?"

"One thousand, Tribune."

"Then you've been paid in full, correct?"

"Yes, Tribune, but the bill says—"

Lucius grabbed the scroll and tossed it to the ground, where it was quickly covered in mud. "The bill says nothing," he said contemptuously.

"But, Tribune, that does not answer my question."

"Have you been paid, Elijah?"

"Yes, but for one thousand, not two thousand."

Lucius came to a sudden halt. Looking Elijah sternly in the eye, he grabbed the man by the collar and half lifted him off the ground. "Just deliver what I tell you to," he said coldly.

"As you wish, Tribune."

"Good," said Lucius imperiously. He let go of Elijah's collar, and walked away.

Elijah watched the tribune enter the prefect's tent, and then he went and picked the scroll out of the mud. "Thinks he's going to leave me holding the bag, does he?" he muttered under his breath. Unrolling the scroll, he held it up to the sunlight. He flicked away the mud. "I wasn't raised a fool, and if the tribune thinks he can play me for one, he's in for a big surprise."

Pilate's tent was spacious but crowded. A large table took up most of the room. A coterie of clerks, palace slaves, and nervous engineers took up the rest. The prefect was not happy. An inchoate air of free-floating anxiety permeated every molecule of oxygen inside the tent.

Pilate was chewing on a thumb nail. He was standing in front of the table, looking down at a confusing collection of architectural drawings. The engineers, Roman to his right, Jewish to his left, were huddled around him, trying to explain what it all meant.

As Lucius pushed his way through the confusion, the vexing problem of the day had to do with the cisterns in which the massive flow of water was to be stored. The Roman engineers had measured the cisterns and declared them inadequate. The Jewish engineers were claiming the opposite. Pilate had no idea who was right, but he knew what he wanted: He wanted things to proceed as scheduled. He took his thumb from his mouth and ordered the Roman engineers out of his tent. He turned an angry eye on the senior Jewish engineer. "You had better be right about this, Ira," he said, his voice a subtle combination of anger and anxiety.

"Do not worry, sir." Ira smiled. "The cisterns are more than adequate."

"Let's hope so, or we'll both lose our heads."

"There is no danger of that, sir."

"Good," barked Pilate. "Now get back to work—all of you!" With an imperious wave of his hand, he sent the Jewish half of his engineering team running after their Roman counterparts. Seeing Lucius at his side, Pontius turned an unhappy face on his second in command. "Tribune, why aren't you out there chasing Parthians?" he asked.

Lucius discreetly waited until the tent was empty of all its Jewish visitors. "Sir, I heard about this empty tomb business, and thought I should return immediately."

"What tomb?" asked Pilate, scratching the side of his head.

"The Nazarene's, sir."

"Oh yes, I remember now," said Pilate with a snap of his fingers. "It's that damn High Priest again. I swear, the Jews and their religion will be the death of me."

"Don't worry, sir, I'll take care of everything."

"You'd better. You were the one who said crucifying this Jesus fellow was the right thing to do."

"Sir, Caesar ordered you not to offend the Jewish religion. So when Caiaphas told you the man had committed capital offences against that religion, what choice did you have?"

"My wife said I should have let Him go free," barked Pilate, biting off a chunk of nail from his right index finger.

"Sir, with all due respect, that would have been impossible."

"If I had released the Nazarene, there wouldn't be any empty tomb, would there?"

"There's nothing to worry about, sir."

"There better not be, Tribune, or you are going to find yourself on the northern frontier trying to keep German barbarians from running off with your head."

"Sir, sir, sir," repeated Lucius like a school teacher chastising a student. "Haven't we been down this road before? And don't we both know that my father would never let that happen to his first-born son?" Lucius punctuated his question with the sort of condescending grin teachers reserve for the very dullest of children.

Pilate reached for his wine cup and took a long drink. He wanted very badly to wipe the grin off his tribune's face, but the truth was he had to put up with him. Lucius's father—the very influential Senator Gaius Verus Clemens—held an enormous amount of power back in Rome, especially now.

The elder Clemens had helped to organize the downfall of Caesar's rival Sejanus. He had removed the Praetorian guards who were loyal to Sejanus from the senate, replacing them with guards from the night watch. When the arrest warrant from Tiberius was executed, Sejanus was defenceless, making Gaius Verus Clemens the most powerful senator in Rome.

Pilate suspected that the only reason he had not been recalled to Rome to face charges of treason because of his friendship with the late Sejanus, was due to the fact that he had done Senator Clemens a personal favour by accepting his wayward son as his senior tribune.

For his entire adult life, he had worried about the standing of his family name. The Pontiff's, although of noble heritage, were Samnites, cousins of the Latin Romans who had made their home along the Apennine Mountains from where they once almost conquered Rome. When Rome finally absorbed them into the empire, their noble families were granted equestrian, but not senatorial status. And even though members of his family had amassed great wealth in business and honour in battle, some even regaining their noble or senatorial rank, Pontius still felt the shame—his blood was not Roman. With a sigh of acknowledgement to his betters, or at least to those who held the better hand, Pilate swallowed his anger. "So how exactly are you going to take care of this problem?" he asked.

"By finding the body, of course, sir."

"Try doing it quickly. According to that damn priest, Caiaphas, rumours are already starting to circulate about the body not being stolen but resurrected."

"Well, we both know that's ridiculous, sir."

"What you and I know, Tribune, is immaterial. Caiaphas knows his people, and he thinks that the longer these rumours persist, the greater the danger of a rebellion. Those sparks may be tiny, but great fires start with tiny sparks. Do you know who said that, Tribune?" challenged Pilate.

Lucius rolled his eyes. "That would be my father," he said.

"You'll be lucky if you turn out to be half the man your father is."

"So you keep telling me, sir."

"By the time your father was your age, he was already…"

"A leader in the senate—I know my father's resume, sir. He's a great man, making a great fortune betraying his friends on behalf of a"—Lucius paused for effect—"great madman."

"I'd be careful who I called a madman if I were you, Tribune."

Lucius nodded knowingly. "I think, sir, given your Sejanus problem, the last subject you'd want to bring to Caesar's attention would be treason, wouldn't you agree?"

"What Sejanus problem?"

"Wasn't it the late Consul Sejanus who recommended you for your current position, sir?"

"I earned my current position."

"With a little help from the former captain of the Praetorian guards, sir."

"He was my commanding officer, that's all."

"I believe you, sir, but who knows what Caesar believes."

A drop of sweat appeared on Pilate's upper lip. "What about your Sejanus problem? Weren't you one of those young officers buzzing around Sejanus like honey bees after a flower?"

"I have my father to guard my back. Who do you have, sir?"

"I have my unblemished record," replied Pilate, sounding more confident than he felt.

"Too bad your blood isn't as unblemished as your record," said Lucius mockingly.

Pilate raised his hand as if to strike but merely scratched the side of his head. "Maybe this empty tomb isn't the problem we think it is? Maybe we're worried about nothing," said Pilate, trying to move past anymore discussion of treason.

"Sir, as you yourself were just pointing out, the high priest believes anti-Roman agitators are ready to use this empty tomb as proof that we crucified the wrong man. They will say that if the Nazarene has returned from the dead, He must be their long hoped for Messiah."

"Which makes me the man who executed him," grumbled Pilate, reaching for more wine.

"Not a good position to be in, sir, not with Caesar already looking over your shoulder."

"You don't have to remind me, Tribune," said Pilate, refilling his goblet.

"And we have to assume our friend in Galilee already knows all about the missing body and can't wait to tell Caesar how you crucified the wrong man."

"Why would Herod Antipas bother Tiberius about a missing body?" asked Pilate, a hopeless tone to his voice.

"Why did Antipas change the name of the Sea of Galilee to the Lake of Tiberius? Why did he name his new capital city Tiberia?

"Antipas, sir," continued Lucius, "would like nothing better than to worry Tiberius about potential trouble while at the same time whispering in his ear that he could do a better job."

Pilate suddenly had a mental picture of Antipas whispering into the ear of Caesar. The thumb back in his mouth, he could hear Herod's son reminding Tiberius of how Pilate had been recommended by the traitor Sejanus. "What do you want me to do?" he asked.

"Well, sir," Lucius said as obsequiously as possible, "we could move in a legion or two."

"What?" bellowed Pontius, spilling wine and causing a flock of slaves to rush to his side to clean it up. "A legion?" he repeated, in a shocked half whisper. "I don't have a legion."

"Or two, and declare martial law until we find the missing body."

"Declare martial law? Are you insane, Tribune?"

"Well, sir," Lucius said, refilling his goblet. "There might be another option."

"Then let's hear it," said Pilate.

"You could bring in a special investigator to conduct a Judicium—someone to take the blame if things go wrong."

"A sacrificial lamb?"

Lucius nodded his head. "Always a useful thing to have available," he said.

"Who do you have in mind?" asked Pilate.

Lucius grinned. "I have just the man."

"He'd have to be a man of unchallenged integrity."

"Forget integrity, sir. We need a man we can control."

"How?"

"In my experience, there are only two ways to control a man—fear or greed."

"Which one will we use, Tribune?"

"I think fear is the way to go with the man I have in mind."

"Does this fellow have a name?"

"Philippus Publius Marcus."

"The man who brought that Falco character to justice?"

"The very same."

Pilate considered the name. "What does Tiberius think of him?" he asked.

"He's free of any direct connection to Sejanus, if that's your concern. Although like practically everyone else in Rome, he did do business with the man."

"He's not under indictment?"

"No, but who amongst us, sir, doesn't sweat a little every time a mail packet arrives from Rome?"

"Who indeed?" Pilate winced, remembering how drunk he'd gotten before being able to read his last mail packet. The packet had contained a letter from Caesar. Pontius had been certain it was his death warrant, ordering him back to Rome to stand trial for treason. So many of his friends had already been strangled. How could he not be next? Dawn was about to break, and he had finally broken the seal. To his great relief, the letter had contained no order demanding his immediate return to Rome. Instead, Tiberius wanted to make sure that Pilate took the appropriate care not to disturb any Jewish institutions, and that only Jews legally convicted of crimes be punished. The shock of it had been so great the prefect had passed out right after reading it.

Lucius caught the wince and smiled. "I don't think we need to worry too much about Philippus, sir," he said. "He caught the emperor's personal cook stealing ducks from the imperial table, and ever since, Tiberius has had only the highest regard for Philippus Publius Marcus."

"Doesn't sound like somebody we can control," worried Pilate.

"Well, the man does have one glaring weakness."

"What's that?"

"His wife."

"What about her?"

"She's a practitioner of the Bacchanal."

"But that's illegal."

"Hardly the sort of thing you would want made public."

"Especially if you work for Tiberius Caesar, but how did you find out about the wife's indiscretions?"

"I've seen her in action."

"You don't say. Another of your many conquests, Tribune?"

"Let's just say I have personal knowledge of the woman's... activities," Lucius said.

Pilate considered what he'd just been told. A man whose wife was knowingly engaged in something the senate considered a crime against Rome was obviously a man very susceptible to blackmail. "But can we afford to wait for him to get here from Rome?" he asked.

"He's not in Rome. He's in Antioch."

"What about his wife?"

"Exactly the question we will ask him if the need arises."

"Sounds like our man."

"Then I shall see to it right away."

"And if this all evolves as planned," continued Pilate, "you just might escape that German posting I've been promising you."

"I'm so relieved, sir."

If Not Jupiter, Then What?

Thirty-Six Days until Bethany

She was worried about her husband's health. "He's working too much," Procula told herself as her palanquin made its way to the valley of Hinnom just outside the city gates. She had a fine lunch for her husband. Fresh bread, which she had purchased that morning, pickled tuna garnished with eggs and rue leaves, and an assortment of fruits olives and cheese. She knew he tended to forget about lunch, and she wanted to surprise him. *He's losing too much weight, she worried, and he's drinking too much. It's all the worrying about this aqueduct, about the Jews revolting, about Tiberius coming after him because he knew Sejanus. There soon won't be anything left of his nails. He'll have chewed them away to nothing.*

Still an attractive woman, blessed with a fine figure that had aged well and a warm, inviting face that had smoothly transitioned from pretty to handsome, Procula Pilate was a woman of privilege. Her maiden name was Proculeius, a proud and wealthy Equestrian family. Her grandfather Gaius Proculeius had been a close friend of Augustus Caesar, having personally saved the emperor's life in a naval battle and later capturing the Egyptian Queen Cleopatra for him.

An exception to the rule, she had come to expect only the best from life. But the execution of Sejanus and the threat it posed to the life of her husband was teaching her a new lesson. Life could be unfair, unjust, and unkind.

With this realization came a vast emptiness. She had turned to the gods of her father and found in them no relief. She had even commissioned a new statue of Jupiter to be built near the temple of Roma and Augustus near the forum. At the consecrating of the ground during the statue's installation, the high priest of the temple of Jupiter had led the ceremony and afterwards had assured Procula that, in return for her generous gift, Jupiter, the greatest of all Roman gods, would reward her handsomely. The statue had been completed two years ago and still, in the small hours of the night, when her fear was most depleting, she found herself alone and uncomforted. Whatever rewards Jupiter had sent her way, they had escaped her notice entirely.

She had given up on ever rediscovering the faith she had known as a young woman, resigned to a life of spiritual confusion, but that had changed when she first met Reisa, Caiaphas's wife. It was during a dinner held to celebrate the peaceful conclusion of the Standards Affair. After dinner, the two of them had wandered out onto a balcony to enjoy a little fresh air. Reisa, saw the troubled look that afflicted her Roman hostess, and inquired as to the cause. Procula had responded that what she was about to say had to remain in the strictest confidence. Reisa had assured Procula that what was said between them would forever remain their secret.

"I've lost faith in the gods of my ancestors," Procula then suddenly blurted out.

Shocked, Reisa had placed her arm around Procula's waist and moved the two of them farther out onto the balcony, away from the curious.

"My dear, good lady, that is not something one should say in such a public place."

"I'm well aware of the risks, Reisa, but my loss of faith has left such a void in my life I fear I may never be truly at peace again. I must do something to resolve my doubt."

"I don't know what to say, my lady."

"I know we Romans rarely bother ourselves with anything other than money, politics, warfare, sex, and, to a less enthusiastic degree, the arts. When it comes to our gods, we've reduced religion to a fashion statement. We believe what those around us believe."

"Why come to me?" Reisa had asked. "I have no great understanding of such things."

"But you are the wife of the religious leader of your people. Surely you must have something to say on the question of faith," Procula had insisted. She took Reisa's hands in her own. "I wish I had been born a Jew. Your people have such an all-encompassing faith. I would give anything to be as close to God as your people seem to be."

Reisa had responded to Procula's confession with a confession of her own. "My lady, you have no idea how misleading appearances can be, for I too have started to question my faith."

"But you're the wife of the high priest!"

"I still have doubts."

"Then what are we to do? Is this emptiness I feel something I must live with forever?"

For a moment, Reisa had said nothing; then she had glanced nervously over her shoulder, checking to make sure they were still alone. "Have you ever heard of a prophet called Jesus of Nazareth?"

"I have not."

"He's a young man of great wisdom—a prophet of God."

"Your Jewish God?"

"The one, true God, my lady."

"Does Jesus speak of this God?" she asked.

"He speaks *for* Him."

"And you think Jesus might help me with my doubt?"

"I think, my lady, that you should go and hear Him speak for yourself."

She never went to hear the Nazarene speak, but Reisa's words had stayed with Procula. She had even dreamed of Jesus the night before her husband so foolishly condemned Him. And she had witnessed His bravery in the face of His terrible punishment. It had inspired her even more. But was He the Son of God as He claimed? On that question, Procula was still unsure.

She entered her husband's tent followed by a retinue of slaves carrying food and wine, she found Pontius chewing on what was left of his nails and staring at architectural drawings. "Pontius," she said softly, not wishing to surprise him, "don't you think it's time you took a break?"

"What?" mumbled the prefect, not looking up from his drawings.

"I had a very nice lunch prepared for us, so you can stop eating your thumb nail."

"Lunch?" asked Pilate. "Is it that late already?"

"Yes, dear. I brought your favourite—pickled tuna and fresh bread still warm from the oven."

For the first time, Pontius sensed the lovely, appetising smell of the bread. He went to the tray of tuna, lifted the lid and helped himself to a taste. "Perhaps you're right, my dear. I should eat something."

"I have news, dear," he said, as they made their way to where the slaves had set up a table and two chairs under the shade of a tarpaulin. "I'm bringing in an investigator to conduct a Judicium."

"A Judicium into what?" she asked as the two of them sat down and the wine was poured.

"It's seems somebody has stolen the body of that Jesus fellow," replied Pontius.

Her mind struggled to comprehend the implications of what she had just been told. She knew of the prophecy—that He would rise on the third day. But Pontius had said *stolen*? "How do you know it was theft?" she asked.

"How do I know? The tomb is empty. What else could it be but theft?"

She knew better than to mention the prophecy. "Yes, of course, dear, what else?"

"As if I don't have enough problems with all that's happening in Rome," he grumbled.

"I told you to set Jesus free."

"Yes, yes, yes, I remember. But it was impossible."

"He was an innocent man, Pontius."

"I couldn't say no to Caiaphas. Not with that mob behind him."

"What about the guards at the tomb?"

"What about them?" Pontius asked with a discursive shrug.

"They were there," she continued impatiently. "How could they allow the body to go missing?"

"How should I know? That's something for the Judicium to investigate. But Lucius thinks—"

"Lucius lies for the same reason the rest of us breathe," she said caustically.

"You think I don't know that?" asked Pilate rhetorically. "But he's right. The longer that body goes missing, the greater the likelihood of trouble."

"So who are you asking to find your missing body?"

"Philippus Publius Marcus."

"Not the investigator who brought Falco to justice?" she asked.

"The very same, you've heard of him?"

She had. Her uncle had been the legate of the Second Legion while Philippus was stationed in Gaul. Her uncle had spoken highly of the man who had outwitted the notorious Falco. "And this was the tribune's idea?" she asked.

"Lucius knows the man. He is a friend of his father, the senator."

Procula felt her anger growing. Bringing in a man like Philippus—a man with a keen eye for the telling detail or the missing fact, a man who tended to play the angles, his own interests always upper most in his thoughts—was a risk at any time. But with Caesar looking for any excuse to recall her husband, it bordered on the suicidal. "None of this would be necessary" she complained, "if you had just listened to me about Jesus of Nazareth in the first place."

"I already told you that I had no choice!" he shouted back at her.

"Shouting does not make your words any truer," she snapped.

"Then let me speak them softly," he replied. "Tiberius Caesar has ordered me to respect the holy law of the Jews, and, according to Caiaphas, the Nazarene had violated that law. Had I set Him free, I would also have been in violation of those same laws. And that would have put me in violation of a direct order from Caesar. Can you imagine what that would have meant? Tiberius already has his eye on me because of my friendship with Sejanus. The instant he heard that I had disregarded a direct order, and don't think that son of Herod in Galilee would not have been on the first boat to Rome, Tiberius would have ordered me home to face trial and probable execution. My hands were tied."

"You mean washed, don't you?" she said, unable to keep the sarcasm from her lips.

Pontius looked at his wife with tired, bloodshot eyes. He sighed volubly and hung his head between slumping shoulders. Slowly, like a condemned man waiting to hear his sentence, he looked up. "Very clever, my dear," he said sarcastically. "Yes, washed. But never forget, I don't have your blood—Roman blood. And they're waiting. Always waiting—I can feel them waiting. Waiting for me to fail. So I can't bend the rules. I can never give them an excuse. I have to always remember my place. Never forget that I am not Roman."

"I had no idea you were so proficient at feeling sorry for yourself, Pontius."

"All right then, I'll stop feeling sorry. And for argument's sake, let's suppose you are right. I crucified an innocent man. How does that remedy my current problem?"

"What problem is that?" A look of mock concern spread across her face.

"My problem that anti-Roman elements are using this missing body to rally the people of Judea against me. And on the day that happens, we both might as well pour ourselves a warm bath and slit our wrists."

Procula stood. "Mark my words, Pontius," she said, her voice like a lash. "You will live to wish you'd never heard of the name Philippus Publius Marcus."

To Be or Not to Be

Thirty-One Days until Bethany

Philippus Publius Marcus, an investigator under contract to Tiberius Caesar, was waiting for his wife in the apartment assigned to him in the officer's quarters of the Roman fortress in the city of Antioch. The apartment featured soft, animal-skin rugs over well-polished marble floors. The walls were decorated with stunningly painted murals featuring pastel colours and smiling wood nymphs enjoying life. A balcony looked out onto a tiled courtyard where a fountain provided the restful sound of rushing water. Philippus was stretched out on a lounging chair turned so it faced the open shutters that led onto the easterly facing balcony. He wanted to watch the sunrise. He'd already had too much to drink.

He had spent the night at the top of Mount Silpius arresting followers of Lord Bacchus. Caesar had ordered him out of Rome to scour the eastern provinces for religious miscreants. That was a good thing. Rome was not a happy place. Aelius Sejanus, heir apparent to the throne and captain of the Praetorian guards, had been accused of treason and, on Tiberius's orders, strangled along with his family, his friends, and friends of his friends. Philippus wasn't a friend, but he had worked for the man, and that was enough to place anyone under suspicion—and to be suspected was to be dead. Getting out of Rome saved his life; he just wasn't sure if his life was worth saving.

He'd just turned forty, and he was a formidable man. He was tall for a Roman and well put together with long, blue-black hair and dark emotionless eyes. Sword, shield, and armour stowed away, he had bathed and put on a comfortable lounging toga.

Belted at the waist, it was made of the finest quality wool. Light, leather, walking sandals protected his feet.

Wine goblet in hand, looking around the empty apartment, he knew why his wife was not there, and his melancholy deepened. He was unhappy, but it was more than that. He had lost his will to live. He felt himself to be on the very edge of existence, that critical moment when the burdens of life exceed the fear of death. His work as an investigator had become morally repugnant to him. Once it had been his cornerstone. Now it was drowning him in a sea of compromises.

He took no pleasure in arresting people for minding their own business. He could see no difference between slaughtering a calf for Jupiter and getting drunk for Bacchus. It was all just a bunch of superstition and make-believe as far as he was concerned.

The Senate had justified their suppression of the Bacchanal by rallying around something Rome had lost long ago—her public morality. Just the thought of those decadent, old hypocrites furrowing their brows over the state of the state's morals caused a disgusted smirk to form across Philippus's face. "Nobody," he told himself, "still believes in the old religion except the priests who find it profitable."

"So why do I do it?" he asked himself. "Why do I hunt down and arrest people who I believe are innocent? I need the money. Is that my only reason? If it is I have a quicker, more honourable way to deal with my creditors."

He reached for his pugio, which was on the side table next to his chair. He held it up to the sunlight and ran his thumb along the edge to test its sharpness. The pugio was a very common knife issued to every Roman soldier. Julius Caesar's assassins had used pugiones. He pressed a little too hard, and the blade sliced throught the skin, drawing blood. Philippus smiled crookedly.

He placed the knife against his wrist. Slowly but deliberately, he sliced into the flesh. The skin split open. The blood began to flow, but he had not yet hit his radial artery. A light, springtime, sea breeze that had worked its way up the Orontes valley all the way from the Mediterranean gently ruffled his hair. He paused in his wet work, the knife microns from the point of no return. Basking in the warm, moist air, he closed his eyes, tasting the salt. He was about to finish what he had started when he heard his wife at the door. Embarrassed by the thought of being discovered, he hurriedly used a handkerchief to bind the flesh wound then pulled down the sleeve of his tunic to hide it. "Out all night, Helena?" he asked, sliding the knife into a tunic pocket.

She stood right in front of him, hands on hips, legs well apart, shoulders back, chest heaving, eyes grinding into him. Behind her, through the open shutters, the morning sun was finally making its appearance. "Have they paid you your blood money?"

Philippus looked up at her, backlit by the sun, and smiled drunkenly. He couldn't deny what her beauty did to him or how much he still loved her. With a deep breath, he took in her expensive, utterly divine perfume. He looked up into her fiery dark eyes and knew he would always want her.

"Well, have they?" she asked again.

"Why all the interest? Is there something you want to spend it on?" he asked, his eyes making a second, more-detailed survey of his angry wife. She had on her best silk tunic dyed a deep, purple-red, the colour of the emperor. He remembered that the dye, a gift from her father, had to be imported all the way from Tyre Lebanon and cost a fortune.

"It's all about the money for you, isn't it?" she asked rhetorically.

"I don't see you turning it down," he answered. He reached into a tunic pocket and took out a handful of jewellery he'd extorted from one of the richer Dionysians. He tossed the gems at her feet. "If that's not enough, just tell me. I'll go out and arrest some more innocent people. However many it takes to keep you happy."

Helena looked down at the rings, bracelets, and necklaces. The gemstones sparkled brilliantly in the morning sunlight. She took one purposeful stride and struck him across the face then stormed onto the balcony.

Half the wine in his goblet was on the floor. He looked at the red puddle, and shrugged resignedly. "I should have seen it coming," he mused, rubbing life back into his cheek. He knew her love of money was a sore point—an addiction she couldn't shake. She'd put up with the two men in her life—her father and her husband—for the love of their money, not them.

Her back turned to him she tried to enjoy the sunrise. She was angry with herself. She was an ordained priestess of Lord Bacchus, but she still couldn't decide what was more important—Bacchus or the lifestyle she'd become so attached to. She knew taking up her own congregation would cause her father to disown her and Philippus to divorce her. She would survive, but the expensive seaside holidays in Vesuvio would have to go.

For the first time in her life, she regretted the fortuitous accident of her birth. She was the spoiled progeny of a new class within Roman society—Romans who did not carry in their veins equestrian or senatorial blood. Romans who, despite their common blood, had managed to take advantage of the Empire's growing wealth to build fortunes. Her father, Artemis Caelius Macro, had taught himself to read and count well enough to become a centurion. After twelve years on the killing fields of Germany, Artemis was promoted to chief centurion, with fifty-eight other centurions under his direct command.

The opportunity for loot had been immense. Artemis had made the most of it. By the date of his retirement, he had acquired enough gold from his share of the pillage and the captured enemy soldiers sold as slaves to purchase a very profitable olive grove. After a particularly bad harvest, Artemis took the biggest and most successful gamble of his life. He mortgaged his olive grove and gambled the money on a shipment of Greek olives. Had the olives not arrived, he would have been wiped out. But they did make it, and Artemis pocketed an enormous profit, which he used to buy up the olive groves of his neighbours at reduced prices.

Artemis's success took his family to a new home in the fashionable Fifth District. Helena had been happy there, rubbing elbows with the richest and most powerful people in Rome. Of course, not having the right blood meant that true acceptance by the upper classes was always beyond her reach. But she had been content to merely swim in their ocean. Then she found out she was to be married to a man twice her age.

When she had asked her father why, why this cheap investigator? He had told her that Philippus had access to Caesar's inner circle. "Caesar buys a lot of olives," he had told her the night she found out about her forthcoming nuptials. "And this 'cheap investigator,' as you call him, can help us sell them to him." Philippus never sold any olives, but he did borrow a lot of her father's money making both of them dependant on Artemis's goodwill.

Helena soon discovered that although she and her older husband had little in common, they did share one very addictive interest. They would go days, never speaking, never spending any time together. He would be practicing his swordsmanship or enjoying a morning swim. She would be combing her hair or trying on a new pair of sandals. She would happen to look up. He would glance her way. Their eyes would meet. And they would know. She would go to him silently, the moment between them remaining unspoken until it was over.

The first year of their marriage, that passion had sustained them; it had been enough. Then she discovered Bacchus. Through her high society friends, she had been introduced to a coven of worshipers who met every full moon to drink of the wine and eat of the flesh. Her first night under the influence of the almost electric charge created by so many people seeking rapture in unison, she had experienced, for a moment so fleeting it was timeless, god.

She had tried to get Philippus to understand, but as far as he was concerned, the Bacchanal was just an excuse for a bunch of doughy aristocrats to drink, inhale drugs, and fornicate with people they weren't married to. He had ordered her never to attend another. He had even threatened to tell her father. She had called his bluff. He had backed down.

It was the moment they realized his reputation was more important to him than her fidelity, and Bacchus was more important to her than his love. They never looked at each other in the same way after that. She had what she wanted, but she couldn't keep from asking, "Why is he letting me do this? Why is he not jealous?"

The year they had spent roaming the eastern provinces, Helena having to standby and watch as Philippus rounded up innocent members of her own faith from Alexandria to Antioch, had served only to break her heart. But it didn't extinguish the potency of what he did for her, of what she did for him, of what they did for each other. There was no getting around it. Their need was as real as their contempt. "The people you arrested last night," she said, without turning from the morning sun, "hurt no one."

"Only themselves," answered Philippus, emptying his wine goblet.

"Thanks to you."

"If not me, then someone else."

"There's always someone else, isn't there?"

"Speaking of someone else, where have you been all night?"

"You know exactly where I've been," she said sternly, turning to stare directly into his drunken eyes.

"At least you weren't with the others," he said.

"I wanted to be with them," she said, her voice trailing off. "I did, but…" she didn't finish her sentence. She just lowered her head ashamed of herself.

"But what?" he asked disingenuously.

Slowly but determinedly, she raised her head. "But I attended a smaller, more private ceremony here in the city."

"And why was that, dear?" he asked, smiling and enjoying her obvious discomfort.

"Because," she started before pausing. "Because you told me the ceremony on Mount Silpius wasn't safe."

"And you didn't tell anyone else, did you?"

"No."

"Really? Why?"

"Because you warned me not to," she answered, turning back to the sun wiping away a tear.

"You could at least thank me for keeping you out of prison."

"You did it to protect yourself. You're supposed to be arresting the followers of Lord Bacchus, not marrying them."

"What about divorcing them?"

"You owe my father too much money."

"You could divorce me."

"And who would keep me out of prison?"

"Looks like we're stuck and I'm going to bed," he said, getting up and stumbling to his room.

"I don't like being stuck," she complained to herself.

She was sure she was alone. She walked over to where the jewels lay strewn across the floor. She stared at them, trying to make up her mind. "They are beautiful," she whispered. The gold and silver, the rubies and sapphires smiled at her. She knew that if she just walked away, it would be the start of a new life for her. With an affirmative nod of her head, she turned sharply and walked out onto the balcony, proudly leaving temptation behind her.

It was a glorious sunrise, the sky clear and cloud free. She barely noticed it. All she could think about, all she could see in her mind's eye were those jewels glittering behind her. She walked back inside and scooped them up. A bracelet made of gold threaded like rope caught her eye. She tried it on. It fit perfectly. She held it up in the sunlight. She didn't think about the consequences.

God Is Not an Off and On Switch

Thirty-One Days until Bethany

The moon was high in the night sky when Philippus awoke. He yawned as he came out from the bedroom and was surprised to find Helena lounging on a reclining couch waiting for him. He wasn't surprised to see that she had kept the jewels after all. "Shouldn't you be out dancing naked in the moonlight?" he asked.

"Must you always be so crude?" she asked, getting up from the couch. She had two wine goblets in hand and was coming towards him with pouty lips, dressed in a simple but revealing linen tunic.

She offered him a goblet of wine. Looking into his wife's bottomless brown eyes, he asked, "Does this mean you're not leaving?"

Helena didn't know what to say. She had a new plan. She was not going to walk away from her marriage. Philippus had to drink of the wine. He had to eat of the flesh. She would show him the way. Get him to experience all of what Lord Bacchus could do for him.

It would reunite them, and it would give Philippus the one thing she knew he needed. It would give him something to believe in. She had watched him closely, especially this past year when their travels had forced them to spend so much time together, and she knew he was empty inside. It was an emptiness he seemed unable to fill. Bacchus would fill it for him—with her help.

"Of course I'm not leaving," she said at last. "But I need to ask you to take a chance."

"On what?" he shrugged.

"The one, true god," she said earnestly.

"I thought that was Mammon?" he asked, casually sipping his wine.

"Always the cynic," she said, slapping playfully at his hand. She noticed the bandage on his wrist but said nothing.

"The only Greeks who know what they're talking about."

"You've lost your reason why, Philippus," she said, as if passing a death sentence.

"Reason why?"

"Yes, your reason why. Isn't that why you cut your wrist?"

Phillipus looked at his wrist as if he were surprised he had one. "This?" he asked, holding up his arm. "An accident, it's nothing— just a scratch."

"You tried to take your own life."

"I was drunk and feeling sorry for myself. It won't happen again."

"Feeling sorry for yourself? You need something greater than yourself, Philippus. Something beyond these bags of flesh we inhabit, something to give your life meaning, purpose."

"Maybe I should just snap my fingers?"

"You could try Bacchus," she said imploringly. "You have only to accept him as your lord and master."

"Caesar doesn't allow for any other lords or masters," he said jokingly.

She didn't laugh. "If you drink the wine, I know you will become a believer."

"We've had this conversation before," he said. "Why do you persist?"

"Because I believe!" she said, urging him with her eyes, "and I love you."

"Well I'm sorry, I don't believe," he replied, pointedly leaving out the question of love.

"You believe in Caesar," she declared, noticing but deciding to ignore the one word he hadn't spoken.

"I believe in his money."

"Then you don't believe in anything."

"How many legions does Bacchus command?" he asked.

"What?"

"How many?"

"None."

"Exactly."

"Legions? That's what you worship?"

"And money—don't forget money."

She forgot her secret plan. She looked at her husband as if for the first time. "There's an emptiness in you, Philippus," she said with a touch of sadness in her voice, "and I don't know how I've tolerated it for so long."

Chapter Fourteen:
A Change of Heart

Thirty-Nine Days until Bethany

Philippus found the legate hard at work in his palace office going over the final figures on the taxes he was remitting back to Rome. The legate sat behind a simple oak desk; its large flat rectangular top covered in scrolls. There were no chairs except the one occupied by the legate. He didn't want to encourage guests to hang around. The walls were draped with maps detailing the postion of the empire's legions along its eastern frontier. The legate was so engrossed in his numbers he didn't even look up as Philippus walked in and saluted. "Hail Caesar," he shouted.

"Hail Caesar," replied the legate, his head still buried in his ledgers.

"You wanted to see me, sir?" asked Philippus.

"I've received an urgent letter from Senator Gaius Verus Clemens."

"A good man, sir."

The legate looked up from his scrolls. "He speaks highly of you as well. The senator has been to Jerusalem to visit his son, the Tribune Lucius Verus Clemens."

"Are you sure, sir?"

"I have the letter," said the legate, quickly looking to find a writing tablet. He handed it to Philippus.

"The only reason I ask, sir," said Philippus accepting the letter, "is that I know the senator. I did some work for him back in Rome, and the last thing he'd ever do is visit his son."

"Apparently you don't know the senator as well as you thought," replied the legate dismissively, "because that letter is signed by the senator himself."

"But, sir," insisted Philippus, "what does the senator's letter have to do with me?"

"The body of a crucified Jewish prophet is missing. This missing body is causing quite a stir. In his letter, Gaius says he wants to hold a Judicium."

"A Judicium into what, sir?"

"Into the body—it's Roman property. We can't just let it walk away, now can we?"

"Sir, am I to understand that you want me to conduct this Judicium?"

"You've done it before, haven't you?"

"Yes, sir, but I'm scheduled to go home."

"And now you're scheduled to go to Jerusalem."

"But why me, sir?" asked Philippus plaintively.

The legate looked up with a sigh of exasperation. "Because the senator, in his letter, says you're the best investigator in Rome, and I happen to agree with him."

"But, sir, I—"

"You are the man who brought Falco to justice, right?"

"I was lucky, sir."

"I don't care what you call it. The fact is that when Falco's arena collapsed, ten thousand innocent Roman citizens were crushed to death. But for you, Falco would have walked away a free man."

"I counted some nails, sir."

"You were the only one who saw that Falco had built his new chariot oval without the legally required number of nails. After the thing collapsed, everyone knew Falco was responsible. No one could prove it. Not until you came up with the brilliantly simple idea of counting all the nails."

"But, sir, I've been on the road for a year now and—"

"You're still under contract to the Emperor, are you not?"

"Yes, sir, but—"

"Then I suggest you start packing," said the legate with a finality that left no doubt that this conversation was over. "You have until sunrise tomorrow."

"Do you want Gaius's letter back, sir?"

"No, you keep it."

His worst fears confirmed, Philippus pocketed Gaius' letter, saluted, and turned to leave.

"Oh, Philippus?"

"Yes, sir?"

"What happened to your wrist?" asked the legate, pointing at Philippus's wrist.

"Nothing, sir, just a scratch."

"Scratch from what?"

"A change of heart, sir."

SINS OF THE FATHER

THIRTY-NINE DAYS UNTIL BETHANY

Jonah didn't reach the city until after nightfall, frustrating his plans for the night. He'd just returned to Jerusalem after successfully ambushing a crew of bandits before they could rob his client, a wealthy Jewish vintner. Jonah had been paid well, but as a bonus, he had taken possession of the dead Parthian commander's horse. He had hoped to make it back to Jerusalem before night fall, sell the horse, then celebrate at his favourite brothel. His late arrival had complicated things.

The horse trader had shuttered up his house and stables for the night. Jonah had no place to stable a horse. He couldn't wait until tomorrow to sell it. He went to the horse trader's front door and started banging. His hand was sore by the time the trader gave in and opened up. He wasn't very happy until he saw the horse and heard the price.

His purse full, Jonah made his way to the lower city where his favourite bar and whorehouse could be found. "I like Jerusalem," he said to himself. "At least, I like it tonight."

Over the years, he'd managed to save enough money so that one day, when the time was right, he would be able to buy a farm and a few cattle. It was a long-term goal. Not one he took seriously. Just something he told himself late at night when he needed to convince himself that he actually had a long term.

He never thought he'd have the money to buy a farm. But business had been good, and today he had to face the truth. The idea of earning his living from the soil, alluring as it had been in the abstract, lost its lustre when taken out of the realm of daydreams and placed before one as a real alternative.

Jonah could only smile at his own indecision. He knew that he was happy with his life exactly the way it was. Only one thing could make him change. So far, she had not given him any reason to change anything.

He picked them up the second the two men fell into step behind him. But he didn't know about their two friends hiding in an alley a few feet ahead on his right. He had just finished putting away his purse when he heard the quickening footsteps coming up from behind him. He trusted his instincts and training and spun around dropping onto his haunches. The blades of his attackers whirred over his head. He drew his sword and sliced left and right. He caught the man on the left, his blade sinking several inches into his side. The one on the right, taking advantage of his extra split second, jumped out of the way.

Frightened, the man on the right called out to his friends, alerting Jonah that he had to fight on two fronts. He heard the two men come out of the alley, swung wildly at the bandit in front of him then rolled to his left coming to his feet several yards away from his three attackers. Backed up against the wall of the nearest building, he gripped his sword with both hands, flicking his eyes constantly between the three men, alert for any sudden movement.

Jonah sized up his opponents as they formed a semicircle and slowly closed in on him. They were not amateurs; they'd done this before, but they lacked training. He could tell by the way they held their swords, by the way they moved using both feet at once instead of carefully edging along one foot at a time, and, most importantly, by watching their eyes. Theirs were glued to his, and the first rule of close order combat was that eyes lie.

Jonah feinted to his left then swung viciously to his right, catching the man on his right moving the wrong way. He didn't bother wasting energy on a death blow, which can take a lot of strength, but sliced into an accessible limb, leaving the man to bleed to death. He swung his blade in the direction of the other two men, expecting them to take advantage of their fallen comrade's mistake. He was wrong. The sight of their two friends bleeding on the cobblestones had taken the fight out of them. They were in full flight.

The first man was already dead. The second tried to struggle to his feet, but was too weak from the loss of blood. He could do no more than sit up. For a few seconds, he looked hopefully at Jonah. "Help me," he moaned. Then he fell flat on his face, dead.

Jonah smiled, relieved to still be alive, to still have his full purse, and to have the rest of the night ahead of him. Looking at the two bodies, their blood spilling out onto the stone street, Jonah remembered the night when, as a child of ten, he lost his mother, his father, and then his freedom.

Just before sunrise, the dogs started barking. Jonah's mother scooped him up in her arms and hid him in the root cellar. From inside the blackness of his hiding place, he heard everything.

His father bolted the door. The attackers broke it down. Jonah heard three male voices. His father—a farmer, not a warrior—against three armed men didn't stand a chance. Jonah heard him begging, offering the men food and wine. The men demanded money. Jonah's father brought them every shekel they possessed. The men were not satisfied. They threatened Jonah's mother. Jonah listened as his father pleaded with them to leave her alone. The men laughed at his father, calling him a coward and a weakling. Jonah remembered feeling ashamed of himself for being too small to help and of his father for being too weak.

They beat his father mercilessly. Jonah could hear the blows as they kicked him nearly to death. Then they turned to his mother. He listened to the sound of his mother's screams. The guttural, animalistic moaning of the three men reverberated inside his head as he shivered with fear inside his underground cubbyhole. He heard it over his father's sobbing. It went on and on. He thought it would never stop.

And then, everything was quiet—very quiet.

Jonah listened intently to the silence. Straining his ears for any sound or vibration, sweat poured down his face. Time passed slowly. Eventually, he fell asleep. He woke up a few hours later and made his way out of the cellar.

His father was still alive but barely. His mother, stretched out over the kitchen table, her clothes torn from her body, was dead. Blood dripped from where her throat had been slit. From the floor, his father wept softly. Seeing his son, he cried out for help.

He didn't help his father. He refused him even the water he begged for so pityously. A pool of urine seeped across the dirt floor. His father had relieved himself. The sight of him helpless, beaten, and lying in his own filth filled Jonah with contempt. A boy of only ten years, he just stood there and watched his father die.

After burying his mother and father in a common grave, he swore an oath. He promised himself that he would never be like his father. He would never be weak. He pledged to make himself strong, to never die the way his father had.

The next morning, walking away from the only home he had ever known, he didn't see the bandits until it was too late. The next thing he remembered was the slave auction block in Damascus.

Jonah pounded his chest in victory and then spit on the heads of the two dead muggers. They had tried to take his life, just like the bandits who had murdered his parents. He felt no pity. Not for his attackers and not for his father. He felt only hate—so much hate. Yelling triumphantly, he viciously kicked each man in the head over and over again. Blood sprayed out in all directions, covering his boots and the hem of his tunic.

Finally, his anger played out, the faces of the two bandits no longer recognizable, his breath coming in short, hungry gasps he fell to his knees and started crying. The tears made their way down his cheeks. *How can I be crying?* he asked himself. *These two are not worth a single tear.* With a howl of anger and frustration at his own weakness, Jonah drove his fist into face of the nearest corpse. Whether he thought he was punching a dead bandit or the ghost of his father, not even Jonah knew for sure.

Later that night, the owner of the brothel, after she got past the sight of all the blood, couldn't wait to sell Jonah her most expensive girls and her best wine. Jonah was in no mood to argue. Tonight, nothing was too good for him or too expensive.

Jonah woke up the next morning feeling as if he were going to die. On either side of him was a naked woman. They were both snoring loudly. Neither of them moved a muscle as he carefully extracted himself from the bed.

Out in the hallway, he checked his purse. It was almost empty, but he could only smile and shake his head at his own impetuous spending—until he realized how much that hurt.

He tiptoed his way toward the front door. He judiciously stepped around the bodies passed out across the main salon. He reached the front door and had to jump out of the way when it suddenly swung open and two men carrying buckets and brooms walked in. The two men went to work cleaning up. It wasn't their cleaning that caused him to linger a few moments longer than necessary; it was their conversation.

"That's what I heard," remarked the first man, taking a damp rag to the top of the bar.

"The Nazarene has been seen twice then?" asked the second man, sweeping up broken glass.

"That's right. One of the apostles, Thomas, I think, claims he actually touched His wounds."

Their words picked up Jonah's heartrate. Could any of this be true? Jonah had no answers. Back on the street, he promised himself that he would not rest until he did.

Send Me a Sea Monster

Twenty-Eight Days until Bethany

Helena hated travelling. It was either too hot or too cold and always uncomfortable. Their short journey from Antioch to Jerusalem was proving to be no exception. Despite being buffered by an inordinate number of cushions, pillows, and carpets, she felt every bump. Every turn of the carriage wheels caused her spine to feel as if it were about to break.

Watching Philippus, his head stuck out the open carriage window, Helena caught herself thinking about Lucius Verus Clemens. She knew him—intimately—or had many years ago back in Rome. They had met at a Bacchanal. She had been a new initiate, he a young officer more interested in finding a good time than god. And as the morning sun cracked above the eastern horizon, it was her he was next to, not Lord Bacchus.

That first night had triggered a short but tempestuous affair. Their passion had burned brightly but briefly. He had tired of her beauty as soon as it became familiar to him. Just as quickly, she had come to understand that her charming young officer was capable of loving only himself.

After several frothy and exciting months, by mutual consent, they had parted. She hadn't thought of him in years, not until Philippus informed her that Lucius was Pilate's second in command. That meant they would be seeing quite a lot of him. She had no expectation of rekindling their romance, but the young tribune was ravishing.

She gave her head a shake and tried to banish Lucius from her thoughts. The last thing she wanted was for her feelings towards Lucius to get in the way of her plan. Her first try back in Antioch had been a complete failure. She blamed herself for that. *I lost control of my emotions,* she scolded silently. *I can't do that if I have any hope of salvaging my marriage. Calling Philippus empty and walking away was no way to win him over. And fantasizing about beautiful, young tribunes isn't going to help me either. What I need is some way to bring us together. What we still feel for each other physically will help, but it's not enough. I need some external event to force us back together. Perhaps when we sail home, he can rescue me from a sea monster,* she joked to herself.

Philippus waved to Petronius, the centurion he had selected to command his armed escort, took a deep breath of fresh air, tasted the desert in it, and cursed his bad luck. He should have been on his way to Naples. But instead of luxuriating in an expensive compartment aboard the next galley headed for Italy, he was eating dust and smelling horse manure. "All because the body of some Jewish fanatic has gone missing," he muttered under his breath. He glanced down at the scar on his wrist and wondered if he had really meant to kill himself. Sighing, he looked back inside the carriage.

Despite how he felt, he smiled. Helena was lounging seductively in a short cotton tunic that showed off her excellent legs. Stretched out across silk cushions she oozed a cat-like femininity. There was about her a playfulness that could suddenly turn sadistic and an all-encompassing sensuality that masked an arrogant independence. She was a creature capable of bringing her unfortunate lovers rapture or despair but always at her discretion. Philippus had experienced both.

"Is that all you're going to do—look?" she purred, patting a cushion next to her.

"It's safer," he said with an uncertain grin.

"If you're still worried about Antioch, you can stop. I'm not mad at you anymore."

"You mean I'm no longer empty? Or you've figured out a way to put up with it?"

"Let's just say I've forgiven you," she said, pouting.

"You have?" he asked.

"You were only doing your job. How could I not forgive you?"

"It's nice to be forgiven," he said.

"It's nice to be forgiving," she smiled. "Now come on over here and let me really forgive you," she demanded with a smile, tapping again the cushion next to her.

"First, come have a look," he said, pointing out the still-open window.

"At what?" she asked petulantly.

"Jerusalem! Our new home away from home."

"If you've seen one provincial town, you've seen them all."

"You can see the city walls and the Towers of Hippicus, Phasael, and Mariamne."

"The towers of what?"

"They're guard towers. They're enormous. You really should come have a look."

"Must I?"

"One quick look won't kill you."

"I might die of boredom."

"Very funny. Now are you coming or not?"

"If you insist," she said with a sigh. Throwing him a look that conveyed as much apathy as possible, she pulled herself upright, and joined him at the window.

"There," he said, "did that kill you?"

No one was more surprised than Philippus when a throwing axe buried itself into the side of Petronius's horse. The animal reared violently, throwing Petronius to the ground, and then ran off, the blade of the axe protruding from its flank.

Petronius struggled back to his feet. He didn't know the size of the attacking force so he ordered the Arab driving the carriage to run. His head on a swivel, he hastily formed his five legionaries into a tight fighting line across the road, stopping anyone from pursuing the carriage as it rounded a bend in the road and raced away, hopefully to safety.

The Arab driver brought the carriage to a halt just before running into the roadblock of felled trees. Not interested in dying to protect whoever he was supposed to be taking to Jerusalem, he locked the carriage wheels, jumped down, and ran for his life.

Philippus locked the carriage window. He strapped on his sword and grabbed his shield. "You stay here," he said, doing his best to keep the sound of panic from his voice.

"You're not leaving?"

"I can't defend us from in here."

"But I'm unarmed."

"Take my knife," he said, handing her the pugio that had almost slit his wrist before opening the carriage door. He gave his wife a brave smile then jumped outside.

As the bandits rushed towards them, Petronius ordered his men to fight a holding action. Then he turned and ran off to make sure the carriage had made good its escape. He spotted the carriage and Philippus struggling to calm the panicked horses, and then he returned to his men.

Petronius and his legionaries slowly retreated back to the carriage while keeping the bandits from flanking them. They formed up into a three-sided square, the back wall of the carriage forming the fourth side. Two men on the right, two more on the left, and Petronius and the fifth legionary standing parallel with the back of the carriage.

The horses quieted, Philippus sensed someone coming at him from behind. Sliding to his right, he didn't quite manage to get out of the way, and his attacker's blade sliced deeply into his left bicep. He spun on his right leg and thrust his sword under his attacker's exposed right side, puncturing a lung. He was about to end the man's suffering when Helena screamed. He looked just in time to see one of the bandits kicking in the locked carriage door. He got to the carriage door as the bandit tumbled out, the pugio protruding from his heart. He pulled the knife from the dead man's chest and stuck it into his belt then clambered up into the carriage. He found Helena cowering in her corner. He took her in his arms. She turned her face into his chest and began to sob. "Are you all right?" he asked.

Looking at him with tearful eyes, she asked, "Did I kill him?"

"You did," he said, pulling out the knife. He wiped the blood on his sleeve then handed it to her.

Helena's eyes opened wide with fear. Staring into those eyes Philippus could just make out the reflection of a man climbing into the carriage. He turned bent low and then barrelled into him sending the two men flying out the door.

Philippus's head hit the ground with a thud. The wind left his body. His attacker's hands closed around his throat. He tried desperately to fight back. He went for his attacker's face, but his hands were easily batted away. Spots danced before his eyes. His lungs ached for a breath of air. The roar of the battle dimmed. The light in his eyes flickered then went out.

From the carriage door, Helena could see her husband's lifeless body, a man on top of him. She felt the pugio in her hand. Philippus had shown her how to throw it many times. She gripped the blade just as her husband had instructed her. She let fly in one fluid motion, keeping her wrist still, throwing from the shoulder.

Philippus was sure he was dead. Then, all of a sudden, there was air. His throat went into spasms as life rushed back into his lungs. He coughed uncontrollably. His eyes cleared. Still sitting astride him, his attacker hacked as if he'd just swallowed a chicken bone then keeled over.

Suddenly, the sounds of the battle cascaded down on him. Struggling back to his feet, heart thumping uneasily, he pulled out the blade that had saved his life and returned it to Helena. "You saved my life," he whispered hoarsely.

"I guess I don't want to lose you," she said.

"Don't worry. You won't," he said, kissing the top of her head, holding her tighter.

The bandits had seen enough. The Roman square had reduced their numbers from twelve to eight, and, with Philippus now joining the fight, defeat was just a matter of time. At a word from their commander, they started running.

The legionaries wanted to give chase, but Philippus called them back. "Tend to the horses," he shouted. "And clear this road."

"You're wounded," remarked Petronius.

"I've been wounded before. It's nothing."

"You'd best let the medic take care of it for you."

"Don't worry about me, Centurion. Just get us ready to move out as soon as possible."

Philippus washed out the wound. It was deeper than he had suspected. He cleaned it with vinegar, wincing at the pain. He knew it was serious, but he'd done everything he could. He wrapped it with a piece of his torn tunic and returned to Helena. He found her curled up like a child. He poured her a cup of wine. Then he filled one for himself. "The wine should help calm our nerves," he said.

She saw his wound for the first time and exclaimed, "What's happened to your arm?"

"It's nothing. The blade didn't hit the bone."

"It looks deep," she said, unwinding the makeshift bandage.

"What are you doing?" he asked, pulling back his arm.

"I'm getting rid of this dirty piece of rag and replacing it with a proper bandage. Come over here and stick your arm out the window," she commanded.

"This is really not necessary."

"Please, Philippus, let me do this for you," she insisted.

"Fine," he said with a shrug, sliding over and sticking his arm out the window.

"Hold it straight," she said, picking up the wine jug and pouring the contents over the gaping wound. Philippus grimaced through clenched teeth. She went to her luggage case and pulled out a cotton tunic. She cut off a piece of cotton and wrapped it around the wound. "Now," she said confidently, "that should hold you until we reach Jerusalem."

"You did a fine job," smiled Philippus, looking over her handy work.

"You don't have to sound so surprised."

"I'm not."

"Yes, you are, and I don't blame you. I haven't been the most attentive wife in Rome."

"You saved my life," he said.

"I never realized how much I'd miss you until I saw you on the ground. For one awful moment, I thought, 'I'm going to lose him!'"

"I'm here now," he said awkwardly, "thanks to you."

"I've never been so frightened."

"In battle, everyone is afraid. What's important is how you respond to it."

"Do tears count?" she asked, dabbing away at a wet cheek with her blanket.

"Well, there's nothing in the training manual, but you've earned a few tears."

"I need to pray. Will you join me?"

For a moment he considered it, but he knew himself too well. "I think," he began haltingly, "we both know that my praying is nothing more than me closing my eyes."

"I feel so sorry for you, Philippus, I really do."

"Why sorry?" he asked sceptically.

"Because you've denied yourself so much," she said, the tears returning.

"Why are you crying?" he asked, pulling her close to him.

"You've cut yourself off from the greatest comfort we have in this life."

"It's only a comfort if you believe," he said, trying to force a smile.

"If you *let* yourself believe," she replied solemnly.

"It amounts to the same thing."

A silence grew between them. He let it grow. Outside, he could hear the horses whinnying as his men made preparations for them to be on their way. "I really should go see how things are moving along outside," he said.

"Yes, you do that," she whispered, doing her best to hide her disappointment.

Petronius was ready to resume their journey. They had suffered one casualty, and two other men had been wounded. "What do you want to do with the body of our dead?" asked Petronius.

"We take him back to Jerusalem for a proper service."

"Yes, sir, but I should warn you that bodies out here tend to become ripe very quickly."

"Then I suggest you make sure it's well wrapped."

"What about the bodies of our attackers?" asked Petronius, looking down at the lifeless bodies of the men who had attacked them.

"Dump them by the side of the road. We don't have time to deal with them," Philippus ordered.

"Good idea," said Petronius. "Their comrades will bury them."

"I've never known bandits to worry about fallen comrades."

"These men were not bandits," said Petronius. "Bandits don't shout 'Death to God's enemies.' Bandits don't attack well-armed men."

"They did outnumber us, Centurion."

"But why take the risk? It's not like we're carrying the payroll for the Augustan Cohort."

"Maybe they thought we were."

"I don't think so."

"Then what do you think?"

"I think the attack was religious."

"Religious?"

"They died for their God, not their greed," said Petronius, poking one of the bodies with his sword. "For men like these, death is a promotion."

"If that's true, centurion, they're more dangerous than they look."

Back inside the carriage, Philippus shuttered the windows and locked the badly damaged door. Helena was praying. The smell of incense filled the cabin. She was on her knees before a two-foot marble phallus. Watching her, he could see that her fear was gone. Her faith had washed away all concern for the here and now, replacing it with a sublime resignation to what her god had willed her to face. Philippus couldn't help but be impressed.

The wheels of their carriage began to turn, and she looked up from her prayers and smiled at him. "You look very happy," he said.

"You could be as happy."

"I'm just not ready," he replied a little uneasily.

"My poor darling," she moaned, going to him. Taking his hand in hers, she kissed the scar where his pugio had almost done its worst. "Your time will come," she said.

A bump in the road caused them to fall over, their faces inches apart. She could hear him breathing, feel his heart pounding against her own. She kissed him lightly on the lips.

It was like old times. Like their honeymoon in Egypt. Lost in the urgency of the moment was any thought of who believed and who didn't. All that mattered was their need for each other and the hope that, however briefly, that need might be fulfilled.

Philippus was snoring peacefully. Helena rose and opened a carriage window. The sun had set and in the growing darkness she could make out the glow of Jerusalem far off in the distance.

A smile crept over her face. Lord Bacchus had answered her prayers. He had sent their attackers so that, in the heat of battle, they could both realize how much they still needed each other. He had sent her a sea monster.

She closed the window then lay down beside him. She lifted his arm and wrapped it over her shoulder, snuggling closer. Feeling safe and secure, she quietly went to sleep.

THE DISCIPLES RETURN

TWENTY-SEVEN DAYS UNTIL BETHANY

Jonah was seated at a table in a small drinking shop finishing a breakfast of fresh bread, slices of cold sausage, and a large pot of borage tea. He had spent the night after having had too much to drink. The owner of the shop, anxious to keep such a good customer happy, had volunteered her own bed. Jonah had resisted. He remembered getting up to go home. He remembered taking a step towards the door. He vaguely remembered the floor rushing up to greet him. The next thing he remembered was waking up in the owner's bed, one of her servants offering him a headache powder and freshly steeped tea. Both had been a godsend.

He was pouring himself a second—or was it a third?—cup of tea when Barnabas, trying to look everywhere at once, slinked into the shop and sat down at Jonah's table. Barnabas was a small, wiry man with a pointy nose, lifeless skin, beady eyes that never stopped blinking, a thin, bloodless mouth, and a voice that made him sound as if he were perpetually feeling sorry for himself. Jonah looked up from his tea and asked, "So what have you found out?"

Barnabas's eyes took in what was left of Jonah's breakfast. "Aren't you going to offer me something to eat?" he asked, his Adam's apple rising and falling as he swallowed hungrily.

"Help yourself." Jonah shrugged, pushing his plate towards Barnabas.

"Thanks. I haven't eaten since Galilee," replied Barnabas, hurrying the food to his mouth.

"I thought I told you to keep an eye on the disciples?"

"I am. That's why I'm back here in Jerusalem."

"The disciples are in Jerusalem?"

"That's right," mumbled Barnabas between bites of bread and sausage. "I followed those two guys, Peter and John, to this house near the shore of the Sea of Galilee. A fisherman's place, I think. Anyway, they were hiding there, hardly coming out of the place at all. It was like they were afraid of being recognized. They kept all the doors and windows locked. I know because I tried to sneak a look inside, and everything was locked down tight."

"Sounds like they were scared of something."

"That's what I think, Jonah. They were scared. Of what, I couldn't say."

"Then what are they doing back in Jerusalem?"

Barnabas's eyes completed another nervous inventory of the room. A grey tongue licked a white mouth. "Something happened, Jonah," he whispered.

"Something happened? What happened?"

"I don't know. Every morning, the fisherman who owned the place went out early before the sun. He'd do some fishing and come back just after sunset. The disciples stayed in the house. Then, oh, I'd say about a week ago, I was watching the place— must have been an hour or two before sunrise. Suddenly, all the lamps inside the house were lit up."

"Did you try to get a look inside?"

"Of course I did, Jonah, but everything was still locked tighter than a virgin's legs. So I went back to my hiding place and waited. The next morning, everybody went fishing and they brought back a huge catch. That night, another disciple showed up—Thomas, I heard somebody call him. They all went back inside, so I grabbed a little sleep. I woke up—I don't know what time—and everything, like usual, is dark and quiet. I was just helping myself to some wine and the last of my bread when once again the lamps come on. Next morning, I followed them back to Jerusalem."

"And that's it?"

"Every detail, Jonah."

"Did anyone unexpected visit them?"

"If someone did, I didn't see 'em."

"What about deliveries? Could they have received any weapons?"

"That guy, Thomas, he might have smuggled in a knife or two but—"

"But nothing to start an uprising?"

"Not even close."

"Where are they now?"

"They're all holed-up in that priest's place."

"What priest?"

"You know, Jonah. You had me watching him until you told me to go to Galilee."

"Joseph of Arimathea?"

"That's the name."

"Any ideas as to what happened in that fisherman's house?"

"None, Jonah, but I can tell you this much. Whatever happened, it certainly changed their behaviour. I mean, those disciples, they were afraid of their own shadows, and then, just like that, they're all walking around like they don't have a care in the world. I've never seen anything like it."

"Good work, Barnabas," said Jonah, getting up and throwing a few shekels on the table. "That's for breakfast, plus a bonus for you."

"Thanks, Jonah. What do you want me to do next?"

"Stay with the disciples. I want to know who they see and where they go."

"You got it, and thanks again."

"Don't worry about it, Barnabas, just keep your eyes and ears open and your mouth shut."

"You know me—the model of discretion."

The food settling his stomach, the headache powder his head, Jonah made his way to Caiaphas's home. It was a long walk. It gave him plenty of time to think. The disciples were back in

Jerusalem. Why? "Whatever had happened in the home of that fisherman, it's given them back their courage," he told himself.

Caiaphas offered Jonah a chair right after the guard had retreated to the other side of the door. They were seated once again inside the high priest's fortified and well guarded counting room. The brazier was working overtime, and Jonah could already feel the sweat forming across the top of his upper lip. Caiaphas was sitting across from Jonah on the other side of his large desk. He had his chair turned so that he was facing the red hot brazier.

"Sorry to show up unannounced, Joseph, but I've got news on the disciples," said Jonah hoping to get this over with before his blood began to cook.

"Have they come out of hiding?" asked Caiaphas shifting around in his chair to face Jonah.

"They've come back to Jerusalem."

"They're feeling braver," smiled Caiaphas keeping his voice flat.

"The man I had watching them said something happened a few days ago."

"Something?" inquired Caiaphas, eyebrows raised.

"That's what he said. He wasn't able to see anything because the house was shut up tight."

"What do you think it was, Jonah? Why have they returned?"

"They didn't get any visitors. Nobody delivered any weapons. No new recruits showed up."

Caiaphas pulled at his beard. "Your man is sure that no one came to visit?"

"Just another disciple by the name of Thomas."

"He's a good man?"

"I don't know if I'd call Barnabas a good man, but he knows how to keep an eye on someone."

"You're still watching the disciples?"

"Until you tell me not to."

"Where are they right now?"

"They're staying at the home of Joseph of Arimathea."

Caiaphas's eyes widened. There was no point in denying it any longer. He had a renegade priest on his hands. "I have another man for you to watch, Jonah," he said seriously.

"Who?"

"One of my captains—the one in command when the body was stolen. I suspect he was paid to look the other way."

"You think he might lead us to the men who paid him?"

"I think he might. Find out if he's made any large purchases. If we catch him with money he shouldn't have, who knows what we might be able to squeeze out of him?"

"I'll do my best," replied Jonah, getting up.

After Jonah had left, Caiaphas tried to catch up on his book keeping. He'd been neglecting the more mundane parts of his job since the disappearance of the Nazarene's body, but he couldn't stop thinking about the change in the behaviour of the disciples. The aspect of Jonah's report that bothered him the most was that they didn't appear to be organizing an army. An army would be so much simpler to deal with than the other possibility.

THE TRAP IS SET

TWENTY-SIX DAYS UNTIL BETHANY

Pilate met his new investigator in one of the palace gardens. He glanced over at his second in command and took note of how he was dressed. Like the prefect, Lucius had eschewed his formal, military uniform for civilian garb. But it wasn't the tribune's freshly laundered, white cotton tunic that aroused Pilate's ire. It was the bordering strip of purple that ran the length of the garment. Pilate's tunic had one as well, only his was an *augusticlava* while Lucius's purple fringe was called a *laticlava*. The difference being that the augisticlava was quite narrow, indicating that the wearer was a member of the second rank equestrian order. The tribune's wider laticlava indicated membership in the first rank senatorial order. It was a slight that Pilate did not take lightly. It caught Philippus's eye as well.

Helena was wearing a light cotton tunic. Philippus had put on a clean tunic along with a traveling cloak to conceal his wounded arm. They were seated under a copse of palm trees enjoying the cool quiet. The garden was the first bit of green they had seen since entering Jerusalem, a rabbinical ordinance having permitted no green thing to be grown within the walls of the city. The garden contained a fine collection of rare palms, wild apricot bushes, and walnut trees, all creatively scattered around patches of green and cobblestone walkways.

"Greetings, Philippus Publius Marcus," exclaimed Pilate.

"And to you sir," replied Philippus, rising from his chair. "Allow me to present my wife, Helena," he said.

"A pleasure, madam." Pontius smiled. "I hope you will enjoy your stay in Jerusalem."

"I'm sure I will," replied Helena rising to her feet, "and I have every faith that my husband will find your missing body for you, Prefect."

"Your husband is one of Rome's most successful investigators," agreed Pilate. Looking to his wife, Pilate took Procula by the hand. "And this is my wife, Procula."

"It is an honour to meet you," said Philippus with a slight bow. Procula was demurely dressed in a simple woollen tunic. And, unlike Helena, she wore no jewellery. Her sandals were clean but unadorned and clearly made of cheap cow hide as opposed to her husband's much more expensive footwear.

"The honour is mine. I followed your efforts on the Falco case with great interest," Procula said, brushing away a leaf that had fallen on the sleeve of her pale blue tunic.

"I counted some nails."

"That no one else thought were important," interjected Lucius, smiling hugely.

"I believe you both know Lucius Verus Clemens," said Pilate.

"Of course, how are you Lucius?" asked Philippus, shaking the tribune's hand and giving it an extra hard squeeze.

"Very well, Philippus," answered Lucius, keeping his smile in place, despite the pain in his right hand. "The weather excepted, and you?"

"As stubborn as ever," said Helena, piping in before Philippus could open his mouth, "but I love him anyway."

"Helena, how did Philippus ever convince you to leave Rome?"

"He didn't. Caesar did."

"Well, we are all blessed by your presence, whatever the reason," smiled Lucius, staring deeply into Helena's seductive, brown eyes.

Philippus watched the young tribune in action and had to smile. He knew Lucius had been a player inside the social circle of artists, philosophers, Greek astrologers, and politicians on the make who hovered around the royal palace like vultures waiting for something to die. "I see you still have a way with the ladies, Lucius," remarked Philippus, keeping the sarcasm from his voice.

"Old habits die hard," beamed Lucius.

"I'll have to remember you said that," Philippus murmured, staring intently at Lucius.

"Perhaps if you forget, I can remind you," offered Lucius, staring back, doing his best to appear unafraid, but Philippus saw his right cheek twitch. It brought a thin smile to his lips.

"I trust your journey was uneventful?" interjected Procula.

"It was, praise the gods," replied Philippus, turning to keep his wounded left arm out of sight.

"If you consider being attacked by bandits uneventful," added Helena.

"You were attacked?" bellowed Pilate.

"Were there any casualties?" asked Procula, a note of concern in her voice.

"The bandits suffered four dead. We escaped unscathed except for one unlucky legionary," Philippus assured everyone coolly.

"And what about your arm?" insisted Helena.

"My arm is healing nicely."

"You must see our surgeon," insisted Procula. "He's really very good."

"Greek of course," added Lucius.

"I don't need to bother him with this," countered Philippus, throwing back his cloak to reveal his bandaged arm.

"Well, if you're sure you're all right," said Procula, somewhat hesitantly.

"Quite all right," stated Philippus too confidently.

"Then, may we offer some refreshments?" asked Lucius.

"That would be wonderful," exclaimed Helena. "I haven't had a good meal since we left Antioch."

"I've had a table prepared in expectation of your arrival," said Lucius, waving everyone in the direction of serving tables and chairs being carried in by slaves. Ever the gourmand, the tribune had ordered a feast of fresh breads, fruits, honeyed almonds, dried meats, and exotic viands such as Phrygian grouse, roasted peacock, oysters, freshly roasted pigeons, and Mediterranean mullet. Slaves stood by with jugs of Chlybonium wine from Damascus and other vintages such as Setinian and Falernian—two of Rome's best wines.

"A fine city you have here, Prefect," said Philippus, taking his chair and helping himself to some bread and a few oysters.

"And the wine is good," added Helena, her nose lingering over the wine's fine bouquet, her eyes hungrily taking in the delicacies spread out before her.

"And a busy city as well," replied Pilate. "The Jews are a prosperous people."

"I've seen the tax revenues," agreed Philippus. "Which is why the legate considered the letter he received from Lucius's father, Senator Gaius Versus Clemens, to be so serious." It was subtle. But Philippus's trained eye could not miss it. It was just a slight pulling back of his head, but its meaning was unmistakable. Pilate knew nothing about a letter from the senator.

"Well, we all know how important those tax revenues are, don't we?" asked Pilate rhetorically.

"That's why," interjected Lucius, in between mouthfuls of almonds, "we can't allow a handful of religious extremists to use this stolen body to threaten Rome with rebellion."

"It is our greatest fear," Pilate confirmed, reaching for more wine.

"And most exaggerated," Procula retorted, delicately nibbling a pigeon leg.

"I wouldn't be so sure," said Philippus. "We received a taste of it as we entered the city. A crowd of people fell upon us shouting, 'He is risen,' and 'the Kingdom of God is here.'"

Procula smiled at Philippus. "A few rumour mongers are hardly a threat to Rome," she said.

"And the men who attacked us?" asked Philippus, watching Procula's face closely.

"They're merely bandits and no more dangerous than a common horse thief," said Procula, a little too confidently for Philippus's liking.

"I'm not so sure they were bandits."

"You have reason to believe they were something else, Philippus?" asked Pilate.

"Bandits don't attack armed escorts, and my centurion claims he heard them shouting 'Death to the enemies of God.' Not the sort of thing bandits usually shout as they go into battle."

"I dare say it isn't." Pilate growled. "The problem with these people is that they love to criticize. Their public debate is just one long argument."

Lucius cleared his throat loudly. "Yes, well, the problem here, as the prefect has already pointed out, is the people and their religion. The men who attacked you, Philippus, were not bandits of the usual sort but religious extremists—zealots, they call themselves. The reason they're so dangerous is because the people of Judea are so dangerous. We had to recall the second cohort from Jerusalem just because their battle standards were decorated with the face of our emperor."

"Idolatry, they called it," commented Pilate.

"The whole province was ready to erupt," Lucius continued, in between mouthfuls of mullet. "Then Pilate, at the last possible moment, ordered the standards removed from Jerusalem."

It was just a slight shake of the head, but Philippus didn't miss it. *I don't believe it*, he said to himself. *The tribune regrets that Pilate managed to avoid disaster. Now why would Lucius want to see rebellion in the very province he's supposed to be governing?*

"Over Tiberius's profile?" asked Helena, loading her plate up with dried meats and olives, having finished off the oysters.

"They see it as blasphemous," explained Procula, "our tendency to make gods of our emperors. I'm not so sure they're wrong."

Procula's impolitic remark brought the conversation to a sudden halt. Tiberius had yet to have anyone arrested for not calling him a god, but everyone felt the chill.

"Of course," piped in Pilate, staring fixedly at his wife, "whether Caesar is a god is a matter for the priests to decide, but I can say without hesitation that Caesar is a great leader of Rome."

"I think we all agree on that," added Helena.

"Yes, I suppose we can all agree," said Procula, looking demurely at her food.

Philippus watched Procula as she avoided looking directly at anyone. *She's lying. She doesn't agree*, he told himself. *And Pontius is not very happy about her speaking her mind.*

"A toast," suggested Helena, her cup raised. "To Caesar!"

"Caesar!" shouted everyone, raising their cups and drinking deeply. Philippus watched the eyes flittering from left to right. They were all doing their best not to look at each other. *It's not just the Lady Procula who's lying.* Philippus smiled. *We're all lying.*

The toast out of the way, Lucius brought the conversation back to the ostensible reason for bringing Philippus to Judea in the first place. "My intelligence reports," he said, "indicate a cult is forming around the belief that the Nazarene is alive. Unless we can find the body, this cult will continue to grow."

"I will need everything we know about Jesus of Nazareth," said Philippus, looking up from his food. "Census records, tax payments, trial transcripts, and all the records pertaining to the crucifixion."

"Lucius can see to it that you receive everything you need," replied Pilate.

Philippus wiped his mouth with a napkin and, rising from his chair, said, "I will commence my investigation just as soon as I wash the desert from my skin."

"I have agents all over the city," Lucius said, getting to his feet. "I've offered a reward to the agent whose information leads to the return of the body or an arrest."

"Please keep me informed," remarked Philippus.

"I'll be feeding you everything I can," smiled Lucius duplicitously. Philippus returned the tribune's smile. He knew what game was being played. *The tribune wants to lead me by the nose*, he thought. *I wonder what he wants me to find?*

"Let me show you to your rooms," offered Lucius.

"Until later then," said Philippus. "Prefect, Madam."

"I look forward to it," replied Procula.

"As do I," added Pilate.

As Lucius led Philippus and Helena to their quarters, Pilate motioned for his goblet to be refilled.

"Don't you think you've had enough?" asked Procula.

"Not after your performance."

"My performance?"

"'I'm not sure they're wrong?' Don't you think that was a little unnecessary? Are you trying to get us both thrown down the Stairs of Mourning and into the Tiber?"

"I can't help what I think, Pontius."

"Think what you like, but please, as a favour to me, keep those thoughts to yourself."

"I'll do my best," she said.

Pilate smiled weakly. "What more can a husband ask? Is that our tribune I hear approaching?"

"Then I'm definitely leaving," Procula said, hoping to leave before the tribune's return. Luck was not with her.

"Leaving so soon?" asked Lucius, intercepting her at the portico that led into the garden.

"I've developed a sudden headache," replied Procula, manoeuvring her way around Lucius.

"Oh, that's too bad," said Lucius obsequiously. "I do hope you recover soon."

"I'm sure a change in company will do me a world of good," Procula said curtly, hurriedly making her way out of the garden.

Pilate turned a cold eye on his second in command. He found the tribune's tendency towards self-indulgence difficult to tolerate. *The man lacks any moral core*, Pilate grumbled to himself. *But what bothers me the most about him is his insolence. That cavalier tone of his, the way he lifts his chin so he's always looking down his nose at you. One of these days, I'm going to break that nose.* "So, Lucius," asked Pilate, "what was Philippus saying about a letter to the legate from your father?"

"There was no letter from my father, except the one I forged, sir," replied Lucius, casually sauntering over to a bowl of almonds, helping himself to a handful.

"What?" asked Pilate.

"You know, sir, I must compliment you on these almonds. They really are excellent."

"Forget about the bloody almonds, Tribune!"

"Bithynian, aren't they, sir?" asked Lucius with a smile that completely ignored, or worse, mocked Pilate's obvious discomfort.

"Did you or did you not—" Pilate sputtered.

"Sir, I really think it's in your best interest not to know what I did or didn't do. But you might find it necessary to confirm that my father was indeed here for a visit. Otherwise, how could he have possibly known about our missing body?"

"But why did you take such a risk?"

"We needed to get the legate in Antioch to act, and with all due respect, sir, my father's name carries a little more weight than either yours or mine."

"One day, Tribune, you'll—"

"Go too far, sir?" asked Lucius, popping the last almond into his mouth and heading over to the bowl for another handful. "I'm looking forward to it."

"Even your father won't be able to save you," scolded Pilate.

"Then I will finally have liberated myself from him, now won't I?"

"Yes I suppose you will."

"And in the meantime, sir, I think what's important is not how Philippus came to be here, but that he is here and that we will be able to control him."

"But only if he doesn't do as he's told, right, Tribune?"

"Agreed, sir, but I wouldn't phrase it quite that way."

"How would you phrase it?"

"Well, sir, I would say only if it's to our benefit."

"Don't you mean to Rome's benefit?"

"Whatever you say, sir," said Lucius, his tongue sliding out to wet his lips. Pilate took no notice.

It was the first Roman bath Helena had enjoyed since leaving Antioch. Luxuriating in the marble-tiled bath, the heat caressed every muscle and untied every knot. Her mind floated gently from one thought to the next. The day's worries slowly slipped away.

She heard him before she saw him. Looking up, she watched his shadow pass over her as he walked between the bath and the candles she had instructed the slaves to place strategically around the room. Naked, he slipped silently into the water. "Ahhh," he moaned, "I'd forgotten how hot you like it."

"The water is not the only thing that's hot," she purred with a grin of concupiscent desire.

"Really?" he asked quizzically.

"I was thinking about the bandits who attacked us," she said.

"I'm sorry about what happened."

"I'm not," she said, stretching out her right leg and seductively rubbing her foot along his thigh. "I mean, I'm not sorry about what happened after."

"I'm not sorry about that either."

"It made me realize how much I still want you." Pushing away from her end of the bath, she slid over to her husband, her body floating above his, their lips inches apart. "It reminded me what our love is capable of, where it can take us."

"And where's that?" he asked, forcing a smile.

"Closer to god," she whispered into his ear.

Ahh, he said to himself. *This isn't about me, or us, or even her. This is about Bacchus.* "I think we'd be better off trying to get closer to each other."

"But the one leads to the other," she replied, a lubricious look in her eyes. "Bacchus wants us to express our love. It brings us closer to him and each other."

"I wish I could do what you're asking."

"Don't you want what we once had?"

"Of course I do, but we both know it's not that simple."

"You just need a little faith," she said genuinely.

"Faith is the one thing I don't have," he said, sliding out from under her. He wrapped a towel around his waist and walked away.

Lying back on his bed, hands clasped behind his head, Lucius felt truly serene. *Half a million sesterces,* he thought euphorically. *Combined with what I've already salted away, it comes to over one and a half million. And I'm not finished squeezing Antipas—not even close. I'll be able to purchase enough property to set myself up for life with plenty leftover. The rents should pay me two hundred thousand a year. I'll never have to ask my father for anything ever again. I'll be rid of him. I'll tell him he can take my precious inheritance and give it to the gods for all I care.*

Lucius let his eyes drift over the room. "It's not bad," he told himself. "Herod knew how to spend his money, but all this gold trim and Indian silk pillows, it's too eastern. When I get home, I'll want something more Roman, lots of polished marble and fountains. I don't ever want to be far from the sound of running water, not after all this time in Judea.

Alone, the tribune's thoughts turned back to his favourite subject—himself. Getting up to stand in front of one of his many well-polished brass mirrors, he sucked in his stomach to hide his growing waist line and congratulated himself on his handling of the empty tomb. At first, the missing body had looked like a disaster waiting to happen. Only after assessing the situation had it occurred to him that the body was actually the answer to his prayers—if he prayed, that is. He hadn't, as yet, worked out all the details. How he was going to make the high priest take the blame for stealing the Nazarene's body, he hadn't exactly figured out, but he had supreme confidence in his own intelligence and in the idea that fate would offer him the opportunity he needed. He only had to be ready to seize that opportunity when the gods dropped in his lap. And if the gods didn't come to his rescue, if somehow he failed, well, he'd have the tetrarch's money, and he hadn't offered anybody a money back guarantee. "Yes," he told himself, "hidden behind every problem is an opportunity. You just have to look hard enough for it."

As he sipped his wine, he was struck by a delicious irony. He had never been keen on the army—all that marching around, living in tents, eating cold food, and getting arrows shot at you, was decidedly not for him. He'd resisted for as long as he could, but when his father made it clear that if he wanted to inherit something other than his last name, he'd have to serve the standard ten year hitch, he'd enlisted. And yet, it was the army that had given him what he had always wanted more than anything. It had made him rich. It was going to make him free of his father.

He'd done remarkably well for himself in uniform. He'd learned right from the start that a good posting with a general who was on the rise was more important than anything else. And by *on the rise*, Lucius wasn't referring to said general's combat skills but his political ones. Handling the treacherous shoals and reefs of imperial politics was vastly more important than knowing how to lead a legion into battle. That's why he had worked so hard to get close to Sejanus. He had just succeeded in getting himself posted to Sejanus's staff when, out of nowhere, his father had told him that he was going to Judea. Even the promotion from staff tribune to Pilate's senior tribune had failed to make him happy. Pilate would not even command a legion, just five cohorts, and Judea was better known for breaking rather than making careers. He had dismissed out of hand his father's warning that Sejanus was about to fall. When he heard of Sejanus's arrest, he had had to acknowledge begrudgingly that his father had been right, again.

As it turned out, his time in Judea had proven to be less boring and more profitable than he'd ever imagined. Despite the hidebound nature of so many of the Jewish people, all their idiotic rules about diet and drinking and sex and their positively closed mindedness about art, music, and theatre, Lucius had discovered just enough Greek influence to provide a modicum of entertainment. On the financial side, Jerusalem was a trading town, and Lucius liked to trade, especially considering all the insider information that found its way across his desk. Like the way he and his Jewish front men had bought up all the farms that stood in the path of the new aqueduct before the final plans were made public. *I made a killing on that one.* He remembered fondly deciding how much Rome should pay for land he secretly owned.

WHY THE ONE-WAY
FOOTPRINTS?

TWENTY-FIVE DAYS UNTIL BETHANY

Philippus had planned to make his way immediately to the site of the Nazarene's tomb, where he was supposed to meet up with Lucius. *If he's managed to get himself out of bed on time.* Philippus smiled to himself, enjoying the idea of rousting the tribune from his beauty sleep. He was delayed when a guard at the main palace gate stopped him. "Excuse me, sir," said the guard, "but there's a man at the guard house who says he must speak with you."

"Does this man have a name?" asked Philippus.

"Elijah, sir. He says he's a contractor working on the Aqueduct."

"Did he say what it was about?"

"He didn't want to say. He said he had to talk to you privately."

Philippus looked up at the sun; it was just above the eastern horizon, and he estimated that the first hour had already begun. "Listen, soldier, tell this Elijah that I can't see him today. I'm running late as it is. Tell him to try another time."

"Yes, sir," replied the guard heading back to his post.

Philippus watched him go, wondering who this Elijah person might be. *What in the name of the gods does he want to talk about? And why will he only talk to me?*

Much to Philippus's surprise, Lucius was waiting for him when he arrived at the tomb. *This missing body must be more important than I thought*, he said to himself, picking up his pace. The two men exchanged polite good mornings, and then Lucius followed

Philippus up to the tomb. On the way, they passed slaves mixing bowls of clay. "What are they doing with the mud?" asked Lucius, pausing to watch the slaves at their work.

"Making moulds of all the footprints they can find," replied Philippus.

"Whatever for?" asked the tribune sceptically.

"In his written report, the captain of the guard claims he was attacked by a dozen men."

"So you order up a half dozen slaves to play with mud?"

"I ordered up the slaves because when I looked over the crime scene, I found lots of footprints but discerned only four different sizes. The moulds will determine if I'm right."

"And if you are?"

"Then the captain is lying."

Lucius entered the tomb and was surprised by the lattice work structure that Philippus had ordered constructed. Wood planks resting on stones crossed the length and breadth of the tomb. "And what is all this for?" he asked.

"I don't want my crime scene disturbed, Tribune."

"What are you trying to protect?"

"Whatever is here. Solving a crime is mostly a matter of observation."

The two men inched their way along the main plank that ran straight down the middle of the tomb. At the altar, Philippus squatted down and examined the crack running down the front of it. "How do you think this got here, Tribune?"

"Lightning?"

"Inside a cave?"

"Stranger things have happened."

"You're right about that," Philippus said, standing up. From the top of the altar, he picked up some rope knotted into circles as if meant to hold a gigantic sausage together. "What about this?" he asked, holding up the rope.

"Rope?"

"It was used to secure the shroud around the body."

"So?"

"So if you're going to steal a body, why remove the shroud? And if you're going to remove the shroud, why not cut these ropes first?"

"Could it be the body was so decayed they didn't have to cut the ropes?"

"Not after three days," said Philippus, folding up the shroud and carrying it under his arm.

"What are you going to do with that?" asked Lucius pointing at the shroud.

Philippus looked at the shroud. "I don't know, Tribune, but something tells me it's important."

Back in the early morning sunshine, Philippus walked over to the massive stone and ran his hand along the edge. "How many men do you think it took to roll this thing out of the way?"

"Three, perhaps four?"

"Probably five or six."

"Didn't the guards claim they were attacked by at least that many?"

"Yes, the guards," mused Philippus, kneeling down for a closer look at the soil around the stone. "I'll be speaking to them later, but look down here."

"What is it now?" asked Lucius petulantly, not bothering to actually bend down for a closer look.

"This soil."

"What about it?"

"Well, look for yourself, Tribune. There are no footprints."

"Again with the footprints?"

"I found footprints all over the outer area, and inside the tomb, but here by the stone—nothing."

"I'm sorry, it must be the early hour, but once again I fail to see what you're getting at."

"How do you suppose," began Philippus, getting to his feet "our thieves moved this stone without leaving any footprints?"

"The grounds keeper must have cleaned up."

"He didn't. He says he hasn't been near the tomb. Caiaphas ordered everyone to stay away."

"Then the thieves wiped away their footprints," answered Lucius, failing to hide his frustration.

"Why just these footprints? Why not all of them?" asked Philippus, waving his hand in the direction of the slaves who were now busy filling footprints with liquid clay.

"Perhaps they ran out of time?"

"Because they wasted so much time removing the shroud without cutting the rope?"

"Apparently." Lucius shrugged.

"Feel the edge of this stone," asked Philippus, running his hand along the left side of the stone.

Lucius ran an index finger along the edge of the stone. "What am I supposed to be feeling?"

"You feel how chipped it is?"

"Yes?"

"That's because, when it was rolled into place, they used heavy wooden poles, gouging the rock. Now feel the right edge." Dutifully following orders, Lucius walked around to the right side of the stone and ran his hand along its edge. "What do you feel now, Tribune?"

"Smooth," replied Lucius, "the right edge feels smooth."

"Exactly."

"You find this significant?"

"If you chip the stone rolling it into place, why wouldn't you chip it rolling it out?"

"Come now, Philippus, the answer to that question is too obvious. The poles were only used on one side. The men who rolled it out of the way applied their poles to the same side as the men who rolled it into place."

"Then the stone would be resting on the left side of the tomb, not the right."

"I understand that there was a small earthquake the morning the body went missing. Perhaps the quake moved the stone?"

"I thought of that, Tribune, so I went and looked at some of the other graves in the area, and they were all still sealed."

Lucius considered what Philippus had just said. "I must admit," he said, "plenty of questions."

"I saved the best one for last."

"I can't wait," replied Lucius snidely.

Philippus led Lucius back into the tomb. He walked along the main plank and stopped at the front of the altar. "Look at these footprints," began Philippus, pointing at two imprints about six inches from the front of the altar, toes pointing straight out. "They head straight out."

"Out?" inquired Lucius bending lower for a better look.

"Out, and there are no corresponding footprints leading in."

"But that's impossible."

"I've measured every footprint inside the tomb. There are none this size, pointing in, and the gentleman who made these prints was the only man who wasn't wearing anything on his feet."

"You mean he was barefoot?"

"That's right, Tribune—like a man about to be buried."

"Are you saying that the man inside this tomb walked out?"

"I'm just observing the facts."

"How do you know the man didn't wipe the other footprints away?"

"We're back to that, are we?"

"It's the simplest explanation."

"Why cover your tracks going in, but not out?"

"He was in a hurry."

"But this man wasn't working alone. We've already determined that one man could never roll that stone out of the way. And I've catalogued, just inside the tomb, four sets of footprints, three men, one woman, plus our mystery man who only walked out. Are you suggesting that out of all these prints, the only ones wiped away were one set of prints leading in? And why barefoot?"

Lucius considered the question. A smile came to his lips. Since the beginning of Philippus's tour of the crime scene, the tribune had been trying to think of a way to twist the evidence so that it led in the direction he wanted to take it: toward the High Priest Caiaphas. He'd just thought of a way. "I have it," he said, his smile widening.

"Have what?"

"The answer to all of your questions. The motivation of our thieves is religious not political. Although I'll grant you that here in Judea, religion is political. In any case, our thieves are hoping that by stealing the Nazarene's body they can convince the people of Judea to believe that the Nazarene walked out under his own power, making Him the Messiah. Then they can blame Rome for crucifying the true king of the Jews. That's why there are no barefoot footprints leading in and why the shroud was removed. It's also why the thieves have kept a low profile. If they make a public pronouncement, they risk causing everyone to ask why the prophet hasn't revealed himself. Mystery, innuendo, and rumour are their trump cards. Let the people wonder and slowly grow angry. That's what they want."

"Any thoughts, Tribune, as to who they might be?"

Lucius looked into the tomb.

"I'm afraid, Philippus," he said, "answering that question is why you are here."

And Where Do You Think You're Going?

Twenty-Five Days until Bethany

Jonah hated being down here. The smell of garbage and offal reminded him too much of his own past, the past he had worked so hard and taken such risks to escape. The growing darkness didn't help matters. Stepping around the squalor, Jonah couldn't believe how far his Mary had fallen. Why was she living in such a place? Jonah understood that since meeting the Nazarene she had given up her old life, and that was a good thing. *But why live here*, he asked himself, *when all she had to do was accept the life that I have offered her?*

He was hidden in an alcove across the alley from the one-room house. Concealed by the dim starlight, he was nearly asleep on his feet. His senses perked up when the lamp inside the house went out. The door opened and Mary, dressed in a long, hooded tunic, came out. She pulled the hood up over her head and made her way deeper into the slums of Jerusalem. Jonah followed. He had Barnabas and his men watching the disciples, Joseph of Arimathea, and Aaron. Mary was the one job he wanted to take care of himself.

The woman Mary was meeting was wealthy. Even in the dim moonlight, he could see the glint of the gold and silver jewerly decorating her wrists. A scarf was wrapped tightly across the lower half of her face. *Whoever she is,* puzzled Jonah, *she doesn't want to be recognized.* She came with her own entourage, two handmaidens and a burly bodyguard. Jonah recognized the guard. He was a member of the temple guards and worked for Caiaphas.

The two women embraced. Jonah wanted to get close enough to hear what the women were saying but couldn't risk being seen.

"Mary, I hope you have a good reason for bringing me out here."

"I do, my lady. The disciples have returned, and they bring good news."

"Good news?"

"Yes, my lady. Jesus has returned to us."

"You've seen Him?"

"The disciples have seen Him in Galilee. That is why I called you. John, Peter, and Thomas are going to speak to us tonight. I wanted you to hear them."

"Then why are we standing around in the dark? Let us be on our way."

"As you wish, my lady."

The women started off, heading deeper into the lower city. The darkness, made even dimmer by the high-walled alleys, was both a help and a hindrance to Jonah. It made his detection less likely, but it also made his quarry harder to keep in sight. The women were leading him on a tour of the poorer sections of the city. They made their way down lightless passages. Rats scurried in the darkness. Wild dogs could be heard scavenging for food. A cat hissed at them from a window ledge. Crossing a small, empty market square, they climbed a slight hill. A line of stone houses stood on top of the hill. They stopped at the third door, and Mary knocked quietly. The door opened, and they all vanished inside.

Jonah found the door bolted. He saw no windows, just the usual small holes near the roof. He was not easily put off. He used his knife to quietly chip away at the plaster that held the hovel's fieldstone walls together. He removed one of the smaller stones near the floor and lay down on the ground for a bird's eye view inside.

He saw a typical house of the working poor. Seven or eight people were kneeling on mats. Their heads were bowed in silent prayer. A single oil lamp was lit. A small brazier provided some protection from the late-night chill. The man guarding Mary's mystery friend had taken up a position by the door. His eyes were everywhere, and his hand was on the hilt of his sword. Mary, her friend, and the two hand maidens were talking to a man Jonah recognized as the disciple Peter. They were joined by the man Jonah remembered as John. The mystery woman gave John a purse, from which he counted out five silver coins. He showed the coins to Peter. Peter took the mystery woman's hands in his and bowed his head slightly in thanks. She shook her head and shrugged her shoulders as if to say it was nothing. Peter motioned for the woman to join them in prayer. As they kneeled, the mystery woman removed her hood and scarf.

Reisa, the wife of the high priest! Jonah pulled his eye away from his spy hole. He needed a moment to think. He sat up, leaned against the side of the house, and struggled to gather his thoughts. Jesus had obviously been more influential than Caiaphas believed. The words of the dead carpenter had seeped right into his own house, his own bed.

Jonah shook his head and sighed. He hated being the bearer of bad news. It was one of the things he liked about his job. He never brought his clients bad news. They came to him with the bad news. He got rid of it for them. What he had to tell Caiaphas would not be good news.

Returning to his spy hole, he saw Peter step forward to speak. "Friends" said Peter, "I know you are fearful. Even those of us who were closest to Jesus fled Jerusalem in fear. We huddled behind locked doors. But we were delivered from our fear. Our door was locked and yet Jesus appeared before us in flesh and blood. He showed us his hands, and we saw the scars. He said to us: 'May you have peace. Just as the Father has sent me forth, I also am sending you,' and then He blew upon us and said, 'receive the Holy Spirit.' So I want you all to know we have nothing to fear. Not from the Sanhedrin and not from Rome. Jesus lives! We must all have faith in that fact."

Peter stood down. A quiet murmur spread amongst the people gathered in the tiny house. Jonah could see the look of surprise on everyone's faces. Eyes were wide, shoulders were raised, and mouths hung open. As he watched, broad smiles slowly replaced the looks of shock and surprise.

John stood up to speak. "My friends, like Peter, I was also afraid. I was afraid of the Romans, afraid of the Sanhedrin, afraid even of my fellow Judeans. What Peter has told you is true. But our Teacher did not stop there. He told us to stay in Jerusalem. To wait for what the Father has promised. And He said that we would all be witnesses to Him. We need only be patient."

The next disciple to speak called himself Thomas. "I know not how I should begin," he said. "I was not there the first time Jesus came to us. When my brothers told me that they had seen Him, I did not believe them. I said that unless I see in His hands the print of the nails, and unless I stick my hand into the wound on His side, I would never believe. Well, my friends, Jesus came again, and this time I was there. I saw His hands. I touched His wound. And Jesus said unto me, 'Do you now believe because you have seen me?' And when I told Him yes, Jesus said, 'That is good, but blessed are those who do not see and yet believe.'"

Still stretched out on the ground, his attention focused on what was happening inside the house, Jonah almost jumped right out of his skin when something nudged his right foot.

"Jonah," whispered a familiar voice, "it's me, Barnabas."

Jonak covered the hole with his hand and looked back over his shoulder. Barnabas was bent over him, his hands on his knees. "What are you doing here, Barnabas?"

"What you pay me to do, boss. Keeping an eye on the priest and the disciples."

"I don't think I said anything about you scaring me half out of my wits."

"Sorry about that, boss, but I thought you should know I was here. Saul is also here."

"You mean the captain is in the house?"

"That's what Saul told me, but you can talk to him yourself, boss. He's on the other side of the square."

Jonah replaced the stone and got to his feet. He followed Barnabas back across the market square to where Saul, an older man, once a farmer who found working for Jonah easier on his back, was waiting for him. Saul was hiding in an alley between two larger houses across the square from where the followers of Jesus were meeting. "Are you sure the captain is inside, Saul?" asked Jonah, entering the alley.

"He was one of the first to show up."

Jonah looked from one tired face to the other. "You guys look exhausted," he said. "Why don't you go on home?"

"Sure, boss," smiled Barnabas, "but how are you going to follow so many people?"

"Don't worry about it. You guys can pick them up in the morning."

Saul and Barnabas looked at each other and shrugged. "Then I'm off, boss," said Barnabas.

"Me to," agreed Saul.

The two men hadn't gone very far when Barnabas stopped and looked back at Jonah. "What is it?" asked Jonah.

Barnabas walked back to Jonah, Saul a step behind him. "I was just wondering, boss, what do you think this means?"

"What does it mean?" asked Jonah, scratching the back of his neck.

"Yeah, you know, everybody gathering here tonight?"

"I don't know that it means anything, Barnabas."

"Chipping out that stone from the wall was a heck of an idea, boss. I'll have to remember it. But, ah, what were you able to hear?"

Jonah looked at the tired faces of his two operatives. *What should I tell them?* he asked himself. *Do they need to know that the disciples are saying the Nazarene has returned from the dead? Or that they claim we will all soon be witnesses to this miracle?* "Not much," said Jonah affably, having decided that the less they knew the better.

"That's too bad," said Saul.

"Yeah, I'd like to know what they're all talking about. Maybe you'll be able to hear a few things when they come out, boss."

"Maybe I will, Barnabas."

Jonah tried to get comfortable. It was more than a simple matter of finding a clean spot to sit down. His mind was uncomfortable as well. The confluence of the disciples, Joseph of Arimathea, Aaron, Mary, and Reisa all tended to support Caiaphas's fears. The followers of the Nazarene were certainly up to something. Aaron being at the meeting was one more piece of evidence pointing towards the Nazarene's followers as the ones responsible for the theft. It was one more nail in Mary's coffin.

All the pieces fit too perfectly. The body had been taken from a tomb belonging to a believer. The tomb had been guarded by a believer. Most importantly, the believers stood to gain the most from the body's disappearance. Jonah didn't believe the claims of the disciples that they had seen the Nazarene. That story was part of their plan to start a new religion. And as anyone who had ever seen a collection plate knew, there was money in religion—lots of it. Jonah had not forgotten the five silver coins that Peter had pocketed from Reisa.

How do I keep Mary out of trouble? he asked himself. He had no answer. He only knew that whatever happened, he had to do everything he could to keep her safe. *I'm not going to fail her. Not like back in Galilee, when I*—Jonah stopped himself. He didn't like to think about how he had left things in Galilee.

His eyes were closing by the time people started walking out of the house. He waited, hidden in the dark alleyway, until everyone had said their good-byes and gone their separate ways. Then he rushed off to catch up with Mary.

He followed Mary back to her simple house. He was about to make his way home for some badly needed sleep when Mary came back out carrying two small bowls, one of water, the other a bit of dried meat mixed with bread. She placed the food and water at her feet then whistled softly into the quiet, late-night air. A thin-faced dog appeared from inside the small burrow he had dug under a pile of rubble not far from where Mary was standing. He was a tough little terrier with short, stout legs. His ears were up, alert for any danger. From the number of teeth he was showing, he looked the type of cur who liked to fight bears. Jonah noticed that the animal had a bandaged left ear. The dog approached Mary cautiously. It knew people. Mary knelt and held out her hand.

"Come on, it's all right," she said in a soft, gentle voice.

Slowly the dog advanced, his senses keen for any sign of trouble; then he ravenously attacked the food bowl. Mary watched, smiling. "There," she said. "Isn't that good?"

The dog licked the bowl clean then turned his attention to the water, licking rabidly. The animal looked up at Mary—a gesture of thanks. She reached out her hand. Jonah expected the dog to bite. Instead it licked her hand.

"There, there," she whispered as she looked into the eyes of the grateful creature and the truth of His words. *Yes,* she thought, *it is better to show mercy than to burn sacrifices.* "Let's take a look at that ear of yours," she said.

The animal emitted a low warning growl but didn't run away. Mary gently unwound the bandage. "Oh yes," she exclaimed happily. "It's coming along splendidly. Another week and you should be as good as new." She gave the wound a good sniff but detected no hint of infection.

She dipped a clean piece of cloth in what was left of the water. She cleaned the wound before wrapping it in a fresh bandage. "There, doesn't that feel better?" she asked with a loving smile.

The dog allowed itself to be petted. Looking into her kind eyes, the animal gave in to the power of her love and nuzzled her hand.

Jonah watched woman and dog experience a pure, simple moment of trust, so different from his own lack of faith in anything but his sword. The dog, perhaps sensing the tenuousness of the moment, lifted its head and trotted off to its burrow. At the entrance, it looked back at Mary one final time. She returned his look with a silent wave of her hand. The animal barked once playfully and then slipped back into its hole.

Jonah stepped out of the shadows. "Good evening, Mary," he said.

"Jonah!" she exclaimed. "What are you doing here?"

"Realizing how much I love you," he said, the depth of his longing sweeping over him. To Jonah, Mary was everything. The mother he barely remembered. The seductress he'd never experienced. The love he'd only hoped for. When he first met Mary he had been captivated by her beauty, especially her face. Oval in shape, fair in complexion with a perfect nose, warm, full lips, limpid, dark eyes that suggested a worldly experience beyond her meagre years, and lush hair that had once cascaded past her shoulders, but which she now cut much shorter. But as he had gotten to know her, his affection had grown beyond her physical beauty, affecting him unlike any other woman he had known.

"How long have you been there?" she asked, breaking the silence.

"Long enough to know you're far too generous with your bread, giving it away to mongrel dogs. Meat too, by the looks of it. Is there anything left for you?"

"We are all God's creatures, Jonah, even mongrel dogs," she said, turning to leave. Jonah reached out, pulling her back.

"Look at you, Mary. You're wearing rags," he said, giving her thin cloak a shake. "And you're living in a hovel."

"Jesus said, 'Why worry about such things?'" she said, jerking her cloak from Jonah's hand. "It won't add a second to your life."

"I'd give you a good life, Mary," he whispered, trying to sound contrite.

Mary looked up into the eyes of the man whose shadow dwarfed her. Slowly, delicately, she ran her finger along the six-inch scar decorating the right side of his face. Standing on her tiptoes, she kissed it. "At what cost, Jonah?" she asked solemnly.

"Would living with me be that bad?" he asked.

"It's not you, Jonah. It's the life you lead."

"Who are you to point fingers?" he asked caustically.

"I point no fingers. I pray for your soul every day that God may help you to see His truth."

"Truth won't feed you when you're old and alone."

"But I won't be alone. God will be with me."

"Very brave of you."

"Not brave, Jonah. Only safe under God's wing."

"You need to start worrying about your future, Mary."

"Why worry about the future, Jonah?"

"Because it's going to be here sooner than you think."

"Tomorrow is a mystery, Jonah, and yesterday just a memory. But today? Today is a gift from God."

"Very profound, Mary, but what are you going to do for money?"

"Jesus said we must either be loyal to God or mammon. I have chosen God."

"And I've chosen mammon?"

"Don't you already know the answer to that question, Jonah?"

"All right, you don't like what I do for a living. But it's not all bad. Yesterday I saved a farmer and his family from Parthians intent on robbing and killing them. What's wrong with that? And what I do pays the bills. You understand that, don't you? You don't really believe we can live without money, do you?"

"No, Jonah," she said, her smiling face still looking up into his. "Only that God will provide."

He held her with bear-like paws. As he looked down into the heavenly glow of her eyes, he was struck by something, something that was not merely another aspect of her beauty. Something indescribable, impalpable, and ephemeral, something he'd never seen before. "God will provide?" he repeated sarcastically. "As simple as that, is it?"

"We need only live by His word."

"I live by my own word," he replied with a sombre finality, letting go of her.

"I know, Jonah, I know. Now, I really must go. I haven't slept, and I'm very tired."

"I'm tired too. I've been watching you all night. Do you have any idea of the danger you are in?"

"I've done nothing wrong, Jonah."

Jonah kept his suspicions to himself. If the followers of the Nazarene were responsible for the body's disappearance, he wanted to believe that Mary knew nothing about it. "These followers of the Nazarene, they are dangerous people," he said finally.

"To some, the truth is always dangerous."

"And don't think Reisa will help you."

"You saw her?"

"If the Romans move against you, they'll arrest her too. She has no power to save you."

Mary looked up into his eyes defiantly. "I'm already saved," was all she said.

"Enough!" He growled impatiently. "I didn't come here to argue with you."

"Then why did you come?" she asked.

"You know, that's a very good question," he said sharply.

"I wish, Jonah, you could find what I've found," she said honestly.

"I gave up children's stories a long time ago, Mary," he replied with contempt. And on those words, he was off.

His anger grew with every step he took. It could turn him into something instinctual, unthinking, savage, violent, and dangerous. Just ask the two dead thieves who had tried to lighten him of his purse. It was a side of him that Mary had seen too often back in Galilee. It was a side he had sworn never to show her again.

Mary watched him go with tears in her eyes. She loved him. But she knew how he made his living. She wished there was some way to bring him to the light. She wiped the tears from her cheeks, and kneeled down. Silently she prayed for him.

The dog's head popped up from its hole in the ground. Seeing Mary on her knees, sensing her sorrow, the animal ambled over. Gently, the dog licked her hand. Mary opened her eyes and saw the dog and smiled. The dog rubbed its nose against her hand. Mary stood up and returned to her home. The dog watched her go and then followed after her. Mary looked down at her new companion. "And where do you think you're going?" she asked. The dog barked and scratched at the door. "Oh, you want to come inside, do you? Well I guess that would be all right," said Mary, opening her door. The dog, tail straight up in the air, pranced right on in as if he'd been living there all his life.

BUT IF YOU WEREN'T THERE, WHO WAS?

TWENTY-FOUR DAYS UNTIL BETHANY

Philippus was waiting for the four temple guards who had been responsible for guarding the empty tomb. Entrenched behind his expensive, ornately carved circular desk in his newly assigned interrogation room, he kept himself busy by reading one of the scrolls Lucius had given him on the Nazarene. The carpenter's growing popularity had caused the tribune to accumulate a file on Him several scrolls long. Philippus planned to read them all.

The room was bright and sunny with an excellent view of the magnificent arches Roman engineers were busy constructing across the Hinnom valley. The walls were decorated with glazed, pastel-coloured tiles. Several four-legged stools stood in front of Philippus's desk. He was seated on a tall curule chair. The curule was normally reserved for magistrates, but Philippus used them because of their height. He liked to look down on those he was interrogating. Overall, the room was exactly what he had requested. He wanted his "guests" to feel relaxed, not threatened. It had been his experience that frightened people tended to talk too much or not at all.

Philippus rolled up the scroll and placed it on a shelf behind him. Based on what he'd read so far, the Nazarene appeared to be the most non-violent man imaginable. Which left Philippus wondering: How did this seemingly harmless man end up crucified? Why had Pilate and Caiaphas seen the man as such a threat?

He picked up two wax tablets. The first was the letter supposedly sent by Gaius Verus Clemens to the legate in Antioch, and the second was a letter that the senator had sent to Philippus a year ago. Philippus placed the two letters side by side and compared the handwriting. He wasn't surprised by what he discovered.

The letter sent to the legate was a forgery. "A good one," admitted Philippus. "But the signatures are different. The question is, who in Judea would have bothered to forge a letter from Gaius Verus Clemens? I can think of only one man: Lucius Verus Clemens."

But why? he asked himself. *Lucius has an eye for my wife, but is that enough to risk forging his father's signature? If Lucius wants me in Jerusalem, it's for money, not copulation. So how does the tribune plan on making money from my Judicium?* Philippus had to admit he had no idea. *Should I tell the tribune that I've discovered his forgery? What good would it do me? Not much, but depending on what sort of trouble the tribune has in mind for me, it might come in handy down the road.*

Perched in his comfortable curule, Philippus studied the faces of the four men standing in front of him. Aaron, Jacob, Ezra, and Azekah stood at attention, waiting for the questioning to get started. "Gentlemen, at ease," smiled Philippus. "Men, I asked you here so that I could show you something I discovered at the tomb."

"The tomb of the Nazarene?" asked Aaron suspiciously. "Why?"

"Why don't we all go and find out?"

Philippus didn't take them to the empty tomb. He walked them over to the olive tree where they had lit their evening campfire. He had had the area roped off to prevent contamination. When the five of them were standing by the rope, Aaron turned to face Philippus. "I don't understand. Why have you brought us here?" he asked.

"I just wanted to show you and your men something that's been bothering me, Captain," replied Philippus, looking over the roped off area. "See if you could help me out."

"Help you out?" asked Aaron uncomfortably.

"Well, you see, Captain, it's like this," started Philippus conversationally as he turned back to face Aaron. "According to your story, you were attacked by a large number of men."

"That is what happened, sir."

"Yes, I'm sure it is, Captain."

"Then what is bothering you?"

Rubbing his chin in thought, Philippus turned back to look at the ground around the olive tree. The remnants of the clay mouldings could still be seen in some of the deeper footprints. "Captain, this is where you and your men were playing dice at the time of the attack, correct?"

"That's right sir. We were gathered around the fire. It was cold that night and very foggy."

"Yes, I know, Captain. But I've made castings of all the footprints I could find here"—Philippus motioned with his hands towards the roped off area—"and unfortunately, I could only find four."

"Four?" exclaimed Aaron. "But I can see dozens of footprints, sir."

"Yes I know," replied Philippus, "and they were all made by the same four sets of feet."

"How do you know that, sir?' demanded Aaron.

"There were only four different foot sizes. So the question I want you fellows to help me with is, what happened to the other footprints?"

"What other footprints, sir?" asked Azekah.

Philippus smiled at Azekah like a condescending parent. "The footprints left behind by the men who attacked you, soldier. And please don't tell me they wiped them away."

"Well, sir, maybe they did," said Azekah, compulsively scratching the side of his face.

Philippus smiled as he watched Azekah scratch away. "Would all of you please take off one of your sandals and hand them to me?"

"Why do you want our sandals, sir?" asked Aaron.

"Just take them off, Captain. Please, for me?"

Aaron and his men each removed a sandal. Sandals in hand, Philippus walked over to the side of the tomb not far from the guard stone. There he found four clay moldings. "Come over here, gentlmen," he said.

Aaron and his men, not sure what else they could do, limped over suspiciously.

"Thank you, men," began Philippus. "What you see here are clay moldings of the four foot sizes we found under the olive tree. I'm going to see if any of your sandals fit any of the moldings."

Philippus fit each of the four sandals into one of the four clay moldings. "A perfect match," commented Philippus. "You men can retrieve your sandals now.

The four guards didn't move. The rookies turned to Aaron, hoping he had a way out for them. "We all seem to be waiting for you, Captain."

Aaron looked from the worried faces of his men to Philippus's beaming smile. "What do you want, sir?" he asked.

"I don't want to get you and your men into trouble, Captain. As far as I'm concerned, whatever happened here, you and your men are not the ones responsible. I want the ones responsible."

Aaron jerked his head in the direction of his men and said, "Let them go, and we can talk."

"Fine," replied Philippus. "You men can leave."

Jacob, Ezra, and Azekah looked at each other and then at their captain. "Go on," shouted Aaron. "Get going!"

The three young men grabbed their sandals and ran away like children being let out of school early. Taking out a flask, Philippus offered it to Aaron. "A little wine, Captain?" he asked.

"Why not?" shrugged Aaron. He wasn't sure what to expect next, but if the man who holds your life in his hands offers you a drink, you take it.

Watching Aaron drink, Philippus went over what he knew about the man standing across from him. According to a report sent to him from Caiaphas's office, the captain had performed his duties both diligently and intelligently. He had been promoted accordingly. He was married with a five-year-old son. *So I wonder,* Philippus asked himself, *how does a man like the captain manage to afford a home in one of the most expensive parts of Jerusalem? And, looking at his clothes, I can't help but notice that his tunic is made of the best Egyptian cotton, but his cuffs are frayed. The captain likes the best, but he has trouble paying for it.*

"So, Captain," asked Philippus, "how do you like the wine?"

"Syrian, I believe," replied Aaron, doing his best to sound conversational. "A Chalybonium—one of the best I've ever tasted, sir."

"You can drop the *sir*, soldier. You like fine wines, Captain?"

"When I can afford them."

"Money a problem for you?"

"Money's a problem for everybody. Why should I be any different?"

"I read in your service record that you own a very expensive home."

"An inheritance after my wife's father died."

"Still, maintenance, taxes, and expensive Chlybonium must be difficult on a Captain's pay."

"As I said, I have an inheritance."

"So you weren't paid to look the other way and lie about what happened at the tomb?"

"What I said, what I ordered my men to say, had nothing to do with money."

"Then why did you lie, Captain?"

Aaron looked down at the ground and shook his head.

"We lied because we ran away," he mumbled his head still pointed at the ground.

"What did you say, Captain?"

Aaron lifted his head and took a deep breath. He stared directly into Philippus's eyes and said in a loud, clear voice, "We ran away. There was an earthquake. I was almost hit by lightning."

"So when the body was actually stolen, you and your men were not there?"

"No."

"Tell me, Captain, do you usually run from your post?"

"No."

"Then why this time?"

"I'm afraid I haven't been able to answer that question. Something just came over me, and I ran."

"Something just came over you?"

"It was as if something had taken control of my mind."

"You were afraid?"

"No, it wasn't fear. I've been afraid before. I've never run from it."

"Then why this time?"

"I wish I knew, sir. I wish I knew."

Philippus gave Aaron a long hard stare. "You swear before the God of your people, you were not present when the body was stolen?" he asked.

"Before God, I swear we were nowhere near the tomb when the body was taken."

"Then I guess whoever did steal the body must have removed their footprints and left only yours in order to frame you and your men, is that what you're telling me?"

"I'm telling you we weren't there."

"Any idea how the robbers were able to tell their footprints from the footprints of you and your men?"

"I only know we weren't there."

"That's too bad. I was hoping you could tell me about the one-way footprints."

"One-way footprints?"

NOT MY WIFE

TWENTY-FOUR DAYS UNTIL BETHANY

Jonah was ushered into Caiaphas's counting room. Caiaphas looked up from his accounting and smiled.

"So what do you have to report?" he asked, leaning forward, pushing his ledgers to one side, and giving Jonah his complete attention.

"I think you're right about the followers of the Nazarene," replied Jonah as he sat down. "They had a meeting last night. They were all there, including that captain of yours."

"Aaron? So he is in on it?"

"He's a true believer, Joseph."

"You're sure of that, Jonah?"

"Why else would he have helped them?"

"Money?"

"If the captain was bought off, he hasn't spent a shekel of it. I talked to the merchants he does business with. None of them reported any unusual purchases by the captain. He owes the carpenter who repaired the roof on his house fifty shekels. According to his commanding officer, he cancelled a family trip to Caesarea. Does that sound like a man who's just come into money?"

Caiaphas leaned back in his chair. A worried hand pulled at his beard. "Excellent work, Jonah," he said keeping the worry from his face.

"All the pieces are falling into place, Joseph: the motive, the opportunity, and now with the captain, the means."

"But you haven't seen the body?" he asked tentatively.

"Not yet, Joseph, but I've got men watching everybody. The disciples, Joseph of Arimathea, and the captain. It's only a matter of time before one of them goes to it. It's human nature. Something that important, you're going to make sure it's safe. Trust me, they always go back."

Caiaphas felt a wave of panic overcome him. The empty tomb was not just a religious issue for him. It wasn't just politics. It was personal. Nothing was more personal. "Don't you understand how important this is? We have to find that body. The future of our people depends upon us finding that body."

"I'm doing everything I can, Joseph," answered Jonah.

Caiaphas brought himself under control. *Relax*, he warned himself. *Of course we'll find the body. We have to.* "I know you are, Jonah," he said apologetically, "I have absolute confidence in you."

"Thank you, Joseph. Your respect means a great deal to me."

"I'm happy to give it, Jonah. You prove yourself worthy of it every day."

"I only do my job, Joseph."

"I know, Jonah. Now, if that's everything…" The high priest sighed, his eyes returning to his ledgers. "I really should get back to work. I'm afraid I've been neglecting my responsibilities—too caught up in all of this subterfuge."

"Actually, Joseph, there is one more thing."

"Yes?" asked Caiaphas, looking up.

"Perhaps it would be better if I showed you."

They waited across the market square, hiding in the alley that Jonah's men had used. Caiaphas recognized several of the men arriving at the house. They were the so-called disciples like the one he had bribed into revealing where the Nazarene could be found.

"If you brought me here to see these men, Jonah, I already know who the disciples are."

"Not the men, the women."

A carriage stopped in front of the humble abode. A well-dressed woman got out. She spoke briefly to her driver, who nodded and drove away. The woman's head was covered by a scarf, but when she looked around to see if anyone was watching, Caiaphas caught a good look at her face in the moonlight. "Joanna, the wife of Chuzza, Antipas's chief steward?" he whispered to Jonah.

"The very same," replied Jonah.

"Is that the woman you wanted me to see?" asked Caiaphas.

"She's one of them," replied Jonah, "but not the one."

A second carriage arrived. Two men got out. "Joseph of Arimathea and Nicodemos," said the high priest.

"They both come regularly, just like all the others."

Joseph of Arimathea and Nicodemus were about to make their way into the house when yet another large carriage pulled to a stop in front.

"That carriage looks familiar," said Caiaphas.

"It should," said Jonah.

The carriage door opened and three women got out. "Reisa!" exclaimed Caiaphas.

Alone in his study, Caiaphas heard his wife and her two handmaidens sneaking themselves back into their beds. Quickly, he blew out the candle that was the room's only light. He knew he should confront her, but he had neither the heart nor the stomach. *What would I say to her?* he asked himself. *And what would she say to me? Fifteen years—fifteen years we've faced everything good and bad together. But if she's joined with these misbelievers, how can we go on?*

Like a summer storm the tears came suddenly and all at once. The clouds of his soul burst, and he cried in powerful torrents. He was surprised that her betrayal could affect him so completely. He thought she had to hear him, but nothing stirred. For Joseph Caiaphas, it was a blessing.

The More I Know, the Less I Understand

Twenty-Three Days until Bethany

C enturion Amicus Favonius could not believe his luck. He'd been assigned by Tribune Lucius Verus Clemens to what so far had been the slackest assignment he'd ever fallen into. "Just make sure Philippus gets whatever he wants" were the tribune's exact instructions. The investigator had been in Jerusalem for a week, and this was the first time the man had asked him for anything. This was fine with Amicus, it having been his experience that bad things tended to happen the second somebody asked him to do something.

Amicus found Philippus, the sun rising in the window behind him, seated at his desk reading a report on the sermons given by the Nazarene. He came to attention and saluted. "Hail Caesar!" he shouted.

Philippus looked up from his reading and smiled weakly at the officer standing rigidly in front of him.

"Centurion Amicus Flavonius reporting, sir!"

"I'm not your superior officer, soldier, so you don't have to call me sir. My name is Philippus. And please don't salute me. Puts me in an awkward position. I have to salute back."

"Yes, sir. I mean, yes, Philippus."

"There you go. Now, I need to have these documents transcribed," said Philippus, picking up several scrolls and handing them to Amicus. "They're transcripts of the Nazarene's sermons. Can you arrange that for me?"

"There is a library scribe," said Amicus, sliding the scrolls under his arm. "I'll have him start copying the documents right away."

"Excellent. When the scrolls are completed, have them delivered to me immediately."

"Consider it done, ah, Philippus."

Looking up at the centurion's smiling face, Philippus knew that considering the work done was one thing; the reality was something else altogether. It would take weeks for the copies to be delivered. With the growing wealth of the Roman world and the rising popularity of both private and public libraries, an entire industry had grown up around the copying of written works. It was a slow, lugubrious process fraught with the likelihood of human error. Authors dictated to groups of scribes, who painstakingly wrote out every word on scrolls, each the equivalent of a small book. Such manuscript rolls were made from papyrus stitched together end on end. Unfurled, the scrolls could be anywhere from twenty to forty meters long, and even a small private library could house up to seventeen hundred scrolls. The library in Alexandria possessed half a million. But words could be misheard or misread. Scholars were often left arguing over different versions of the same thing. "Tell the scribes to take their time. I want the transcribing done correctly, not quickly."

"I'll make sure they do a proper job."

Amicus turned to leave, but Philippus called him back. "Oh, Centurion, one other thing."

"Yes?"

"I need someone followed."

"Followed?"

"The man is a captain in the temple guards by the name of Aaron."

WHY DO YOU WANT HIS SANDALS?

TWENTY-THREE DAYS UNTIL BETHANY

The condemned man fell as he carried his cross up the difficult slope to the top of Golgotha. The sun was making its first appearance, but sweat was already pouring down his face. He had once been a well-to-do farmer until he was caught buying mutton originally meant to feed the Roman cohort stationed in Jerusalem. He had known that the meat was stolen. What he didn't know was that the thieves had killed two legionaries. That made his purchase of the meat a capital offense. To save his family, he had accepted his cross without demanding a trial.

Struggling back to his feet, the condemned man could see the top of the hill looming ever closer. Two crosses, their emaciated victims hanging as if they were already dead, the flies forming dust like halos around their heads, were up and in place. He knew his time was running out. One of the Roman soldiers shoved him from behind. He fell again with a loud thud. The Romans started laughing. They enjoyed watching their prisoners suffer.

The centurion in command looked back at his men. "What is going on?" he asked.

"He fell, sir," answered one of the legionaries.

"Well keep your minds on your work and let's get 'em nailed down and into place. I don't want to be late for lunch."

The centurion's concern over lunch tortured the condemned man more than any of the physical blows he had endured. Lunch—he was never going to eat lunch again. His mind floated off on thoughts of warm bread, honey fresh from the comb, butter right out of the churn, cheese delivered that morning, grapes grown on the southern hillside of Hebron, and to top it all off, a few sweet raisins.

Thoughts of what he would miss replaced fears of what he would soon have to endure. Never again would he hear the laughter of his children, feel the love of his wife, or enjoy the comradeship of his friends. Never again would he feel the sun on his face, the wind in his hair, the good, rich earth of his farm between his toes. All he had to look forward to was pain, deprivation of a kind he'd never even imagined, and then…blackness? The end for all eternity? God? He didn't know.

At the top of the hill, the executioner was waiting for him, two five-inch nails stuck between his teeth like tooth picks. One of the two wizened bodies he was soon to join lifted its head, scaring away a bird going after its left eye. The condemned man dropped to his knees and wretched violently. The bile burned his throat.

Two legionaries lifted the heavy wooden cross from his shoulders and laid it on the stony ground behind him. Two more grabbed him by the shoulders and stripped him naked except for a loin cloth. The legionaries argued briefly amongst themselves as to the relative value of the garment. The near-naked man could only hang his head, sobbing. The Romans were happy that for once they'd been assigned a man whose garments were worth the bother of selling. They got him to the ground by grasping his arms and pulling him backwards. Once on his back, the cross beam was fitted under his neck, and two legionaries knelt on the inside of his elbows.

Seeing that his victim was ready, the executioner knelt beside the man's right hand. The soldier whose knee was resting on the inside of the man's right elbow held the man's forearm in place. The executioner probed the man's wrist to find the hollow spot where there would be no vital artery or vein. Finding it, he took one of the nails from his mouth and held it in place. He brought down his hammer with all the force he could muster.

He screamed. A loud, passionate cry, it shook his entire body before subsiding into a desperate gulping for air. The fingers in his right hand clawed impotently at the sky. He saw the executioner standing over him. "Help meee," he begged. "It hurts. It hurts *so* much. Please, *help.*"

The executioner ignored him. Eyes like a reptile about to eat, he went about his business. Quickly jumping over to the left arm, he hammered a second nail into the man's flesh. The condemned man opened his mouth to scream, but the centurion shoved a sponge dipped in drugged wine into his mouth. The executioner stepped aside.

The legionaries used the ends of the crossbeam to lift the condemned man until his feet left the ground. He hung from the crossbeam by the nails driven into his wrists and begged the legionaries to put him out of his misery. He was granted a second taste of drugged wine. The crossbeam was fitted onto the main beam already in place. The executioner grabbed the man's feet, placed the right one over the left, and drove a third nail through both, eliciting another pitiful scream. And then, mercifully, he passed out.

Philippus saw the condemned hanging from their crosses and thought about turning back. He could always arrange to interview the centurion when he wasn't so busy, but he didn't like to put things off. Centurion Longinus Macro was arguing with a rag dealer over the value of the condemned man's belongings. He took no notice of Philippus, who waited patiently.

The price agreed upon, the rag man reached into his money pouch and took out a dozen bronze quadrans. Longinus accepted the money with a smile. The rag man dumped his newly acquired possessions into the back of his cart and wandered off down the hill.

Business concluded, Longinus took notice of the man standing just off his right shoulder. "If you were hoping to buy the clothes, you're too late."

"I'm here to interview Centurion Longinus Macro."

"Are you the fellow they've got digging into the disappearance of that body?"

"Brought me all the way from Antioch."

"They told me I was to answer all of your questions, but"— Longinus paused to look up at the sun—"I'm late for lunch, so let's make this quick."

"Quick works for me," said Philippus as he looked the centurion over. He was a short, stocky man who had almost no neck and very few teeth. He was a veteran of twenty years and fifteen major engagements. *He was either good or lucky*, thought Philippus. *Probably both.*

"Then get on with it," snarled Longinus, his eyes looking past Philippus's shoulder. The condemned man was awake and sucking back as much wine as he could. He didn't know, or didn't care, that the effect of the wine was to dull his immediate pain and extend his longer-term suffering. The legionary started to remove the sponge from his mouth. The man held on with his teeth. The legionary relented, laughing at the man as he sucked furiously on the sponge.

Philippus followed Longinus's eyes. "How about some wine?" he asked.

"I suppose I'd be dishonouring the regiment if I turned down a free drink."

"A regimental duty we can all accept," replied Philippus, reaching for the wine-skin hanging at his side. He handed it to Longinus who took a long drink followed by a loud, satisfied sigh. "Good wine," he said. "Not like the slop we get back at the barracks."

"I'm glad you like it. It's from a vineyard near where the carpenter you crucified was born."

"You don't say. Ain't that a coincidence?"

"You were in command of that crucifixion, right?" he asked.

"I was."

"As you know, the body has gone missing, and I've been given the job of finding it."

"What does any of that have to do with me?" asked Longinus, the tension visibly returning to his face. "I just crucified the man. I don't know what happened to His body."

"Relax, Centurion, you're not under investigation."

Longinus looked at Philippus with a fixed stare. "Then why the questions?" he asked.

"Look, Centurion, I do not think you took the body."

"Good!"

"So I can ask my questions?"

Longinus relaxed again, smiling for the first time. "Any wine left in that wine skin?" he asked.

"I think so," answered Philippus, giving the skin a good shake.

"Then why don't you ask your questions while I help myself to another drink?"

"Good idea," agreed Philippus, handing the wineskin back to the centurion.

The poor soul on the cross screamed as a large starling landed on his arm. Philippus observed Longinus's back stiffen and felt his own spine tighten as well. A second scream pierced the air as the bird pecked at some blood just below the man's wrist. Longinus immediately brought the skin to his mouth. When he finished, Philippus took his own long drink.

"So, Centurion," began Philippus, handing the skin back to Longinus. "Was there anything unusual about the crucifixion of the Nazarene?"

"You on the level about not being after me or my men?" Longinus asked.

"We served under the same regimental standard. The last thing I want to do is get you in trouble."

"Well, as to unusual"—Longinus shrugged—"I call it unusual when a man goes up on the cross and refuses the drugged wine we offered Him. I call it unusual when a Man forgives you after you've pounded nails into His hands and feet and hung Him up to die slowly in the hot sun. And I call an earthquake at the moment of a man's death very unusual."

"He forgave you?" Philippus asked, not sure if he'd heard Longinus correctly.

Behind them, they could hear the condemned man cursing at the legionaries. His cursing was soon cut off by the difficulty he was experiencing trying to breath. He had to lift himself up, using what little strength he had left in his arms and legs to prevent being slowly asphyxiated.

"The Nazarene looked down on me and smiled. He asked His Father to forgive me."

"His Father?"

"The Man considered Himself the Son of God."

"Yes, that's right. I understand you finished Him off, is that correct?"

"The locals here have a rule against executing a man on the Sabbath. Me and my men were getting ready to return to barracks when a bunch of priests showed up with permission from Pilate to club the men to death before sunset."

"The bodies were mutilated?"

"Not all three of them, just the two thieves we executed along with the Nazarene."

"What happened to the Nazarene?"

"When the priests got to Him, I…"

"Go on, Centurion," Philippus interjected reassuringly.

"Well, I've been fighting Rome's battles for twenty years. I've seen my share of cruelty and blood. So I'm not what you'd call a soft or forgiving man, but there was something about this Jesus of Nazareth—a nobility, a fearlessness, a…I don't know, an air of 'careingness' about Him. It brought to mind a word I hadn't thought about in a long time." Longinus paused. His eyes swept the sky. Looking down, he kicked at a stone lying next to his right foot.

"What word, Centurion?"

Longinus looked up and squared his shoulders. "*Love*," he said forthrightly.

"Love?"

"That's what I said. Most men, like that farmer we just hung up, they curse at you. They threaten your family, promise to come back from the grave and haunt you. But this fellow? He blessed us. He went to His death so calmly. He was so—the Greeks have a word, *stoic*, I think it is. Well this Nazarene was the most stoic man I've ever seen. I only hope I meet my end as well."

"Sounds like quite a man."

"I thought so. Anyway, I just couldn't stand there and let those priests have at Him. So I rode up, and I thrust my close-action spear right between the Man's fourth and fifth rib. And then," Longinus leaned forward as if he were about to tell Philippus a great confidence, "when my blade struck home, the sky darkened and the earth shook."

"What did you make of that?" asked Philippus.

"At the time, I thought perhaps the gods were angry."

"They usually are. What was done with the bodies?"

"We dumped the thieves into a common grave. We were about to do the same with the Nazarene when another priest showed up with orders from Pilate telling me to turn the body over to him."

"What about the Nazarene's clothes?"

"We sold them. We're entitled."

"I know. I was just hoping to buy the Nazarene's sandals. Could you do that for me?"

"I guess I could go talk to the rag dealer."

"There'd be a nice tip in it for you."

"I can try, but I can't promise anything."

"I understand."

"What do you want with His sandals anyway?"

"I want to measure them against some footprints."

"Whatever makes you happy," said Longinus with a shrug as he started to walk away.

"Oh, Centurion," said Philippus.

"Yeah?"

"How are your eyes?"

"My eyes?"

"Yes, I read over your service record, and I noticed you were supposed to be suffering from cataracts. Yet I see no evidence of any disability."

"You know," he said, "you're the second person this morning asking about my eyes."

"Really, who was the first?"

"Some Jew priest, the same one who took the body. I recognized the face."

"He was interested in your eyes?"

"Wanted to know if the Nazarene's blood had gotten into them."

"And had it?"

Longinus' eyes narrowed, his face darkened. "You give me your word as a soldier in Caesar's army what I say here stays here?"

"Before the gods, Centurion, you have my word."

"Because if you go repeating any of this, I'm just going to deny I said it."

"If you didn't steal my body, Centurion, you have absolutely nothing to fear from me."

Longinus glanced over at the farmer hanging motionless from his cross. The sponge was hanging from his mouth. "It was a moment I'll never forget," he said. "After I struck, His blood and water started gushing, and some of it splattered my face, got into my eyes."

"Did you feel anything?"

"I felt a tingling sensation."

"Tingling?"

"I tried to rub it away, but I couldn't get the blood out of my eyes. And then, I swear to you, believe me or not, I was healed. My cataracts just melted away."

"Could it be possible that your eyes were getting better on their own, Centurion?"

"Yeah, maybe, who knows?"

"Yeah, who knows? Well, Centurion, I believe that will be all for now."

"Good," said Longinus, turning to leave.

"Oh, Centurion, you said the priest who took the body came to see you about your eyes?"

"That's right, he was here just before the rag man showed up. That priest has a real strange interest in the Nazarene's blood."

"What makes you say that?"

"After I struck the body, I saw this same priest gather up His blood in a cup."

"This priest have a name?"

"Joseph, he called himself, Joseph of Arimathea."

Longinus returned to his men, making sure the cross was properly secured; nobody wanted the darn thing to fall down. His men were packing up, getting ready to leave. The farmer was pathetically begging for more wine. He was studiously ignored.

Watching Longinus as he collected unused nails, Philippus marvelled at the ease with which he was able to spot them. Had the Nazarene's blood cured him? He wasn't the sort to believe in miracles, but it was hard to ignore what he was seeing with his own eyes.

Suddenly his arm exploded with pain. He clenched his teeth closed his eyes and waited out the spasm. *I'm going to have to make up my mind*, he decided. *It's me or my arm. Too bad I can't decide if a one-armed man is worth having around.*

MORE DANGEROUS THAN HE LOOKS

TWENTY-THREE DAYS UNTIL BETHANY

Caiaphas was at the home of his father-in-law, Annas, not enjoying a simple supper of bread, cheese, and wine. The two men were comfortably sprawled on thickly cushioned cathedra chairs in the spacious tablinium. The room was pleasantly decorated in contrasting marble tiles. The expensive sound of running water could be heard emanating from the former high priest's courtyard. The door was closed. Annas had sent all his servants away.

The former high priest was well into his seventh decade but had lost none of his vigour. Annas still craved command. The day Gratus had deposed him was the saddest of his life. He was a small, thin man, with ferret-like eyes and a mind to match. He had lost his hair and most of his teeth, but everything else was in good working order. "So, Joseph, how's my little girl?" asked Annas, with a less-than-sincere smile.

"Reisa is fine, but she's not your little girl anymore, Father. She's my wife."

Annas sucked on his teeth. His smile became a thin red line. "Yes, she is," he said, "and you are my high priest."

"I'm God's high priest."

"Yes, of course, Joseph," replied Annas, nodding his head sympathetically. "But don't forget who brought you to God's attention."

"I know why your daughter consented to marry me, Father. But that does not give you the right to treat me like an indentured servant."

Annas's eyes hardened. "I'll treat you any way I want to," he said in a whisper that belied the anger that lay behind his words, "because you are mine, Joseph. When Gratus gave you the job, he was acknowledging my influence. I suggest you do the same."

Caiaphas reached for more wine. He'd been drinking more of it lately. A showdown with Annas was something he wanted to avoid. The old man still had the ear of most of the members of the Chamber of Priests. During the trial of the Nazarene, his one great fear had been that Annas would oppose him. Much to his relief, the old man had played along. The wine working its magic, his nervous tension abating, he said, "Is that why you asked for this meeting, Father? So you could threaten me?"

"I don't threaten, Joseph. I was just reminding you of the facts. I asked for this meeting because of the Nazarene."

"As I told you the night of His arrest, the Nazarene had become too dangerous."

"For whom, Joseph?"

"To Rome, and we both know how Rome deals with threats."

"The Nazarene was just a prophet, like John the Baptist. Rome did not take action against him."

"Have you forgotten Pilate's bloody suppression of the Galileans during Passover? That was only one year ago. And where did John the Baptist do his baptising?"

"And yet we are still here, Joseph. Nothing has changed."

"The Nazarene was different."

"In what way?"

"He attacked our money changers. He was against our entire sacrificial system. Like us, He preached about purity of body and spirit, but not through sacrifices and ritual— by repentance and prayer. He talked not of the law but of its redundancy. He called people to God directly. He was the end of religion. He was a revolutionary, and Rome has a low tolerance for revolutionaries."

"But to execute an innocent man, how do you justify that?"

"He was not innocent, Father. He was condemned by His own words. That's why I sent temple guards to break His limbs. To prove He was no Messiah since Isaiah prophesied that 'a bone of the Messiah shall not be broken.'"

"Unfortunately, that centurion ruined your plan. The Nazarene died just as Isaiah said He would."

"That still doesn't make the Nazarene our true Messiah, Father."

"If we had banished Him, the Nazarene would have been just one more wandering prophet."

"Wandering prophets do not have adherents within our own priesthood."

"You mean Nicodemus and Joseph of Arimathea?"

"They are both sympathetic."

"You don't know that."

"Nicodemus spoke up for the Nazarene during His trial. Joseph of Arimathea has been seen meeting with the man's disciples."

"Stop with the excuses, Joseph," scoffed Annas. "You only fool yourself. You didn't convict the Nazarene because two priests were sympathetic. And you didn't do it to save the Sanhedrin. You did this for Rome."

"For Rome?" exclaimed Caiaphas, feeling that little twinge of guilt one gets when forced to face a truth best kept hidden. "Pilate wanted nothing to do with the Nazarene."

"So you took care of it for him. Pilate didn't have to arrest anyone. You did. Pilate didn't have to put anyone on trial. You did. He had to sign the death warrant, but that's Roman law, or you would've done that for him too."

"You can criticize my decision in hindsight, Father, but as I recall, you voted to convict."

"I went along with His conviction, but I was never happy about it."

"Well it's too late to complain now."

"Finally we agree, Joseph. It is too late, and now we've got all this talk about a resurrection."

"More evidence of just how dangerous the Nazarene was."

"Or how dangerous we've made Him. Messiahs can be awfully difficult to fight."

"For the last time, Father, the Nazarene was no Messiah."

"He is if people believe He walked out of His own tomb."

"That's why we have to find the body, put an end to those rumours."

"I assume you're already looking?"

"Of course I'm looking. All of the disciples are being watched and—"

"You think they took the body?"

"They had the most to gain."

Did they? Annas asked himself, his eyes darting from left to right. *Who else might have something to gain from that empty tomb? If the situation worsens, it could create problems for Pilate, which would benefit that old fox in Galilee. And if Antipas is involved, so is his Roman lap dog, Lucius. I'll have to tell my informants in Galilee to keep a sharp eye out for that greedy tribune.* "Well, Joseph, I hope you're right about the disciples."

"Who else stands to gain?"

"Who else indeed," Annas smiled.

Caiaphas stood up to leave. "If that's all we have to discuss, Father, I really should be going."

Annas rose to walk his son-in-law to the door. "I'm sorry things got so late."

"It's all right, Father. I'll try to sleep after the morning sacrifices."

They had reached the door. A servant opened it for them. Annas put his hand on Caiaphas's shoulder. "Ah, one moment, Joseph," he said.

"Yes, Father?"

Annas looked at the servant holding the door and waved him away. "I know you managed to get me and the Chamber of Priests to support you, but—"

"This isn't about the aqueduct, is it?" asked Caiaphas.

"I just wanted to make sure that you had not forgotten your promise. That if the people find out who is paying for their aqueduct, you would take responsibility for using the Corban."

"I will do what I promised, Father."

"Regardless of the consequences?"

"Regardless of the consequences."

It's Time to Retire

Twenty-Two Days until Bethany

Sunrise found Lucius and his body guards coming out of the Antonia without bothering to see if they were being followed. Jonah fell in behind them. To his surprise, they turned south at the temple Mount, making their way into the lower city. They stopped at a wine shop that was no longer in business. One of the guards went to the front door of the boarded up building and banged loudly until the door opened. All three men went inside.

Jonah took a walk around the building. Every window was shuttered. He returned to try the front door. As he suspected, it was locked. He was about to give up when he spotted an open second-floor window.

It wasn't easy. He had to make his way up the side of the building like a rock climber, using small cracks between the bricks as foot and hand holds. Almost falling more than once, he made it to the open window. It opened onto a small storage room that stank of spilled wine. Careful not to make too much noise, he walked over to the door that led from the storage room to a hallway overlooking the main floor. He heard Lucius's voice and inched out into the hallway.

Hidden at the top of the stairs, Jonah took a look at what was going on below him. Ten men were gathered around the tribune, who stood in the middle of the empty room, his body guards on either side of him. "You will all be rewarded," shouted the tribune.

"When?" asked one of the men in the crowd.

"Patience," replied Lucius. "Money takes time to arrange, but as a show of good faith, my body guards will give each of you a tenth of our agreed-upon amount."

"Only a tenth?" shouted a second man.

"Anyone want to walk away from ten percent?" asked Lucius. The room fell silent. "Good," continued Lucius. With a nod, he signalled his body guards to begin paying out the money. "I want to congratulate all of you. You've been doing great work spreading the word that Caiaphas is using the Corban to fund the Aqueduct. But now I want all of you to start telling people that the Nazarene was falsely accused and that the Judicium is merely an attempt to cover up the fact that Caiaphas had an innocent man crucified."

Jonah's eyes widened. Antipas and the tribune were trying to foment revolution by destroying Caiaphas. It was a perfect plan. Use the empty tomb to create religious chaos. That could only be bad for business, and that would be bad for Rome. The instant Tiberius Caesar saw his revenues dropping off Pilate would find himself on his way back to Rome in disgrace. It would also put Antipas on the throne in Caesarea. What was happening downstairs was all part of the tribune's deal with the fox in Galilee. *What won't Romans do to each other for money?* Jonah asked himself. As he turned to leave, his mind still preoccupied with the brilliance of the tribune's simple plan, he tripped over a broken floor board.

Jonah heard the sound of heavy footsteps pounding up the stairs. He made a mad dash for the storage room. From the open window, Jonah paused for one quick look behind him. The bodyguards reached the top of the stairs and spotted Jonah one leg already out the window. He could see the anger in their eyes. There was no time to climb back down. He would have to jump and hope he didn't break a leg. He spotted a farmer with an open cart loaded to the brim with freshly sheared wool. A knife missed his head by inches, embedding itself in the window frame.

In midflight, not sure if he'd land on wool or cobblestone, Jonah thought again about changing occupations—the sooner the better.

It was a matter of inches, but his feet landed at the back end of the cart. He felt himself falling backwards onto the cobblestones and swung his arms furiously in a desperate effort to maintain his balance. The farmer looked over his shoulder in stunned amazement at the sight of a huge man standing in the back of his wagon, swinging his arms uncontrollably. Jonah smiled at him. What else was he going to do? The driver smiled back. A knife, thrown by one of Lucius's bodyguards, landed point first between them, and they both looked up at the angry faces glaring down at them. "Friends of yours?" asked the farmer.

"They're sorry I'm leaving."

"You'd better sit down or you're going to fall."

"I'm trying,"

"Try harder."

Jonah almost laughed. It was touch and go, but he regained his balance. He looked back at Lucius and waved. The tribune smiled at him with all the charm of a venomous snake.

Can Two Wrongs Ever Make a Right?

Twenty-Two Days until Bethany

The sun was setting as the high priest met Jonah in one of the inner cloisters just outside of the court of Israel. "Jonah," said Caiaphas, going to an archway that overlooked the north gates. "What news do you bring me? Have you found the body?"

"Not yet, Joseph, but I know what Antipas and the tribune are plotting."

The bluntness of Jonah's words took Caiaphas by surprise "Am I going to like it?" he asked.

"I don't think so. The tribune is trying to put Antipas on his father's throne by destroying you. To that end, he's hired agents to spread lies about you."

The high priest turned from the archway, his legs feeling weak. He sought out a wooden chair and sat down. "What kind of lies?" he asked, forcing the terror from his voice.

"That you're using money from the Corban to finance the new aqueduct. I know such a thing is ridiculous, Joseph, but there are plenty of people willing to believe it."

The gall of the tribune astounded him. He didn't think for one grain of sand to tell Jonah that the tribune was right. "Is that the only lie he's spreading?" he asked.

"He's also saying that you executed the Nazarene because He was a threat to your power."

The colour left the high priest's face as the truth struck home. Lucius Verus Clemens was actively seeking his destruction. "Jonah," he said, "we must find that body. It is the only hope we have of saving Judea from the horrors of civil war."

For a moment, both men were silent. Caiaphas was the first to break it. A thought had occurred to him. "You don't think Lucius could be behind our missing body, do you, Jonah?"

"I never considered it," replied Jonah, his right hand worrying his chin. "It makes sense if the tribune is out to destroy you, but do you really think the tribune robbed the tomb?"

"I don't know, Joseph. I don't know anything for certain. That's what is so damnably frustrating about all of this."

"Well I think I should be on my way. And don't worry, Joseph. I won't let you down."

"Find the body, Jonah. My very life depends upon it."

Alone, Caiaphas pondered his situation. Was the tribune responsible for the empty tomb? *Regardless, he's using the missing body to tell lies about me. What can I do to stop him? Find the body, of course, but what if Jonah fails me?*

For a moment, the high priest's mind was a blank slate. Then it came to him. It was not something he wanted to do. *But what choice do I have? Surely God will forgive me, won't He? If I spread a few lies to save the future of His people?*

Could Bethany Be the Key?

Twenty-Two Days until Bethany

Candles lit the room as Philippus waited impatiently in his office for his meeting with Amicus. He looked up sternly from his reading when the centurion finally showed up. *Better late than never*, thought Philippus to himself as he watched Amicus nervously close the office door behind him.

Amicus knew he was late and wondered if perhaps he shouldn't have taken the time to eat that last slice of bread and cheese before leaving the dinner table. He certainly didn't want to upset Philippus.

"Well don't just stand there, centurion. What have you got to report?"

"Well, sir—ah, Philippus," began Amicus, cursing himself for his mistake, "I've been watching the captain as you ordered, and, ah, he mostly just goes about his job then goes home to the wife and children."

"That's it?" asked Philippus. "He hasn't visited any abandoned buildings or secluded backyards?"

"Not unless he gave me the slip. Wait a minute."

"What?"

"It was last night. It must've slipped my mind."

"Yes, yes, what slipped your mind?"

"The captain didn't go straight home. He went to some sort of religious gathering."

"What kind of religious gathering? Were any of the disciples there?"

"You mean the men in the drawings you showed me?"

"Yes, did you see any of them?"

"They were all there, except that Judas fellow."

"Did the captain talk to any of them?"

"He talked to a woman called Mary Magdalene."

Mary Magdalene, Philippus said to himself. That name had come up in one of the scrolls Lucius had given him. She was one of the Nazarene's followers. She'd even been seen at His execution. "What did they talk about?" he asked.

"I didn't get close enough to hear very much. But the woman mentioned the Nazarene."

"Did you hear anything else?"

"I was outside on the street, and I had to stay pretty well hidden."

"I understand, Amicus, but try to think. Did you hear anything—a name, a place, anything?"

"Oh! There is one other thing. This Mary Magdalene mentioned Bethany to the captain, if that means anything."

Bethany, considered Philippus. Bethany was the home of Lazarus, the man the Nazarene was supposed to have brought back from the dead. *Could Bethany be where they've hidden the body? It would be the perfect place. Close to the city yet far enough out of the way to avoid easy detection. And most importantly, this Lazarus fellow, being a farmer, would have plenty of safe places to hide a body. I'll have to pay Bethany a visit. Should be interesting. I've never talked to a dead man.* "You did good work, Amicus— very good work."

"Thank you, sir—ah, Philippus."

"And rest assured, I'll mention it to Tribune Clemens," said Philippus.

"Thank you, Philippus. Should I continue to follow the captain?"

"I want you to make the captain your number-one priority. If he goes anywhere out of the ordinary, I want to know about it, especially if he goes to any more of these meetings. Understand?" asked Philippus, looking up at Amicus and raising both eyebrows.

"I understand completely, sir—ah, I mean, Philippus."

"Good."

DECISIONS, DECISIONS

TWENTY DAYS UNTIL BETHANY

Helena was up early. She had agreed to go shopping with Lucius Verus Clemens. She slid out of bed, tiptoed across the marble bedroom floor and into her dressing room, where her slaves had laid out her tunic and walking sandals. As she waited for her personal slave to finish combing her hair and applying her makeup, she debated whether or not she was doing the right thing. She had not completely given up on Philippus, she told herself, but she was not as enthusiastic as she had once been.

It was now becoming clearer than ever that the same old problem would forever stand between them. Philippus would not join her in the Bacchanal. *So the final decision is mine,* she told herself. *Can I live with a husband who does not share my faith? And if I can't, can I walk away?*

She remembered the jewels he'd thrown at her in Antioch. She was wearing one of the bracelets. Just a series of thin gold bands intricately spun into what looked like a piece of golden rope wrapped around her wrist. Of all the jewellery thrown at her that morning, it was her favourite. She remembered trying to throw it away. She still couldn't.

Hair combed and make-up applied, Helena told her slave to tell Philippus that she would be home before dinner and that she had gone shopping—alone. A worried frown on her lips, she slipped out of the apartment hoping to play both ends towards the middle without getting burned.

They were strolling through the markets not far from the Antonia. Lucius had ordered his two body guards to stay well back and out of sight. He wanted to be alone with Helena. The upper city markets were the commercial centre of the city. They walked along the seemingly endless array of market stalls and shops, and stopped to admire the work of coppersmiths, carpenters, weavers, crafts men, painters, and sculptors.

Lucius paid the goods on display scant attention; he had other forms of beauty on his mind. He hadn't fully decided how much he wanted her. Her beauty was undeniable, and the tribune prided himself on his appreciation of beauty. *But this religious obsession of hers is distinctly not my style. Attending one of their Bacchanals for some risqué fun and games is one thing. But to actually take all that eat-the-flesh, drink-the-blood, live-forever nonsense seriously is just, well, beyond my ability to keep a straight face. I could never tolerate any wife of mine carrying on that way in public. On that point, Philippus and I are in complete agreement.*

If not for her religion, though, she'd make an excellent consort for me back in Rome. She lacks the correct bloodlines, but she doesn't lack for sophistication, and she'd look fabulous on my arm. And in bed? Well, I've had the pleasure of her charms, and I must admit they're unrivalled.

So where does that leave her? Rome is out of the question, obviously. I won't be seen in public with a wife anyone can see naked by attending a bacchanal. He let his eyes slide over the flesh that was so clearly on display beneath her nearly shear silk tunic. It was cinched tightly at the waist by a belt that set off her figure to excellent effect. *She is beautiful. More than worth the effort to rekindle what we once had.* He smiled to himself.

By the gods, those were heady days. We went at it so hard I thought we'd kill ourselves, but what a way to go, eh? And she certainly seems interested, if I'm any judge of women. Why not? What would be the harm? Philippus? He does have quite a reputation with the sword. That young tribune back in Rome could testify to that—if Philippus had left the poor fellow in one piece. Ah, a little danger only sweetens the reward.

He took advantage of a slight slip on Helena's part. He got his hands around her waist. Smiling, he pulled her close.

"Please, Lucius," she remonstrated, trying to pry his arms from her waist. "What are you doing?"

"Keeping you from a nasty fall," he said, turning her so that they faced each other.

"Well, you can let go now."

"But you feel so good," he said, not hiding his amusement. He could smell her perfume. Admiring the delicate beauty of her skin, the lustrous sheen of her eyes, he almost kissed her. *Hold on*, he told himself, *this is one filly that needs to be handled with extreme care. I don't want to scare her off. On the other hand, I hate wasting time.*

"What if one of our guards sees us and tells Philippus?" she asked

"They wouldn't dare," he said, pulling her closer, their faces now only inches apart. "I pay them far too well."

"But why take the risk?" she asked demurely, her eyes glancing back at Lucius's two guards walking several feet behind them.

"Forget the guards," he said, taking her chin in his right hand and turning her face back towards his.

"And Phillipus?"

"Surely after our time together in Rome, you know me well enough to know that Philippus is not someone I fear."

"If I didn't, that forged letter you sent to the legate in Antioch was more than enough to convince me. If Philippus finds out, he's not going to be very happy," she said, pushing him back and walking away.

"What do I care?" scoffed Lucius, walking after her.

"He could tell the legate or even Caesar once we're back in Rome," she reminded him sternly.

"Tell them what? That I forged a letter from my father in order to obtain the services of Rome's best investigator so that a rebellion might be nipped in the bud? Caesar would give me a reward for service beyond the call of duty. Besides, it was the only way I could get you to come here," he lied, moving closer, his arm returning to her waist.

"Do I get a say in the matter?" she asked, lifting his arm from her waist and picking up her pace.

He watched her move away and smiled. *Games,* he said to himself. *Why do they always want to play games?* "Only if you agree with me," he said, running up behind her and getting both his arms around her waist.

"You go too far, Lucius," she said, looking down at his hands locked across her waist.

"You're worth it." He grinned.

"Are you sure?" asked Helena, grabbing his index fingers and using them to leverage his arms from around her waist.

"I was," he said, brusquely releasing her. "But suddenly I'm not so sure."

At the stall of a Greek sculptor who worked exclusively in limestone, Helena was particularly taken by a small statue of the goddess Daphne. "Lucius," she asked, picking up the statuette and holding it out for his inspection. "What do you think of this?"

Lucius gave the limestone figure a quick once over from head to toe. "An excellent example of the Corinthian school," he remarked after due consideration.

"You don't think it's perhaps a little too provocative, do you?"

"You mean because she's naked?"

"I certainly don't mind, but you never know how others will react."

"You don't mean Philippus, do you?"

"He could care less. No, I was thinking more of our hosts."

"Pilate and Procula?"

"As a guest, I wouldn't want to upset anyone."

"Trust me. No Roman will raise so much as an eyebrow."

"You're sure?'

"Positive."

"Then I'll take it," she said, addressing the artist who jumped up from his chair.

"A very wise choice, madam," commented the sculptor. "I remember when I finished her, thinking that I might not be able to part with her, so struck was I with her beauty."

"Would fifty sesterce ease your pain?" interjected Lucius.

"Immensely, noble Roman."

Lucius pulled out a small purse and handed it to the artist. "Then we have a deal," he said.

"No, Lucius, I can't let you pay," protested Helena, reluctant to be in the tribune's debt in even this small way.

"Nonsense, Helena, you can't deny me this small indulgence."

"But I can pay. I have my own money," she insisted.

"Helena, you don't understand. I want to pay. I want to offer this as a gift from me to you."

"Well, I suppose if it's a gift," said Helena reluctantly.

"It is." Lucius smiled.

Her purchase completed, they continued their walk. They stopped for a brief lunch of eggs, cheese, olives, and unleavened bread accompanied by a half flask of wine. Coming finally to the end of the market, they entered the store of a rug merchant the quality of whose merchandise Lucius had made note of from a previous visit.

The inside of the store was like the inside of an Arab sheik's tent. Everywhere they looked, their eyes were greeted by brilliantly fashioned examples of the weaver's craft, each one more beautiful than the last. The owner was a solemn, conservative man who valued obeisance before God above all things, even business.

"Sir, madam," he said, coming out from the back of his store, "how may I help you?"

"The lady has need of a rug," replied Lucius.

"Does the lady have anything specific in mind, a colour perhaps, a pattern, a size?"

"I'm not sure really," answered Helena.

"I have rugs from all over the civilized world, but my personal preference is for the Persians. They're more expensive, but well worth the extra cost, as I'm sure a woman of your obvious high rank and taste already knows. Perhaps I could show you some of my better ones?"

"Why don't I just look around, and if I see anything I want to purchase, I'll let you know."

"As you wish, madam. Please look around to your heart's content."

They'd been in the store longer than Lucius could tolerate. The tribune's mind was looking for some means of entertainment. He nudged Helena gently with his elbow and whispered into her ear. "Watch this," he said. "Oh, sir?"

The merchant came right over, face eager with anticipation of a big sale. "Yes, sir, how may I help you?"

"Well," began Lucius, unveiling the sculpture, "I was wondering, as a man of artistic taste and discernment, if you could give me your opinion of this statuette."

At the sight of the naked Lady Daphne, the old man threw his hands up before his face. "Please, sir, I'm sorry, but I must demand that you get that offensive Greek art out of my shop immediately."

"You mean you don't like it?" asked Lucius, a playful smirk spread across his face as he shoved the limestone Daphne into the merchant's red face.

"Please, sir, you must take it outside."

Helena couldn't hold back a giggle. "Oh, for heaven's sake," she said contemptuously. "It's just a sculpture. It won't bite you."

"It is forbidden by God."

"Oh, come on, stop behaving like a child, and tell us what you really think of it," insisted Lucius.

"No, I'm sorry. You must leave my shop."

"You can't be serious," demanded Helena. "I haven't made my purchase yet."

"I don't care. You and that…thing must go now, immediately!" exclaimed the pious merchant before storming off to his private quarters at the back of his shop.

Alone in the now-empty sales room, Helena took her statuette from Lucius, giving him a playful slap on the arm as she did. "That was terrible," she said, "upsetting the poor man like that."

"Didn't keep you from enjoying a laugh."

"I couldn't help myself. The man's reaction was so utterly uncalled for."

"He's one of these orthodox types I was telling you about. I spotted him right away. These religious fanatics, their noses up in the air, are always looking down on the rest of us. They'll be the ruination of this country one day, mark my words."

"Oh I don't know, Lucius. He seemed harmless enough, a little extreme, but harmless."

"Don't you believe it. There are thousands more just like him hiding out in the desert, itching for the chance to rise up against us."

"I'm sure you exaggerate, Lucius."

"I wish I was," replied Lucius, his face hardening. "But I've been in charge of security in this part of the empire for three years. And if I've learned only one thing, it's that these religious zealots are going to drag Judea into war. And then, we will destroy this place."

I Think We Should Tell Mary

Twenty-One Days until Bethany

Philippus enjoyed his walk to Bethany. He had been worried about his wife when he woke up that morning and found her gone. "It's not like Helena to get up so early," he had remarked at the time. "Not like her at all. She usually relishes her beauty sleep too much to ever rise before the end of the first hour." But the feel of the warm afternoon sun had washed his mind clean of worry. It was blazing in the clear blue Levantine sky as he skirted the village, going first to the site of Lazarus's tomb. Standing in front of the small hole dug into the side of the Mount of Olives, he thought about what it must have been like to walk out of his own grave. *I'll have to ask Lazarus when I see him,* he reminded himself.

He saw other sealed tombs, any of which might contain his missing body. He thought about asking Pilate to order the tombs opened, but why bother? The Sanhedrin and the Jewish people would never stand for it, and the prefect would never take the chance. With a shrug of his shoulders, he headed for the village.

He walked down the single main street the few houses that comprised the village scattered along either side of him and took a deep breath of air. It smelt clean and fresh. *If a body is hidden here, it must be buried.* He took a careful tour. A few of the women, outside looking after their children and livestock, gave him a curious look or two. He checked every barn and shed but could smell and see nothing. He checked the ground, looking for any sign of recent digging. His search came up empty except for some garden patches. Finally satisfied that the village was clean, he asked an old woman who was busy washing clothes where he might find Lazarus and his sisters.

It wasn't much of a place, two rooms and a loft for sleeping. A shed with a fence around it served as home for a few sheep and half a dozen chickens. The place was clean and well looked after.

He found the sisters feeding the chickens and cleaning out the stalls. They weren't happy to see him. "What do you want?" asked Martha after scattering the last of the chicken feed. The hungry birds swarmed around her, desperate to find every crumb.

"I'd like to speak to Lazarus. I was told he lives here."

"Why do you want to speak to my brother?"

"My name is Philippus."

"I didn't ask you your name."

"I'd like to ask him a few questions, that's all."

"Questions about what?"

"About his resurrection."

"My brother doesn't know anything about it. He was dead at the time. You'd be better off talking to me and my sister, Mary."

"Then I'd like to ask you and Mary a few questions."

Martha looked at Philippus as if she were buying a piece of fish and couldn't make up her mind as to its freshness. "You're that investigator they brought in, aren't you?"

"I only want some information. I'm not here to arrest anyone."

"What does my brother's resurrection have to do with finding the body of Jesus?"

Philippus had to think about that one. Why did he want to talk to Lazarus? Did it really have a bearing on his missing body? Certainly not in any direct sense. Aaron and the Magdalene woman had mentioned Bethany, but not Lazarus. He did like to learn as much as he could about his suspects, but he couldn't justify interviewing the sisters of a man supposedly resurrected by the Nazarene months ago. If he was going to be honest with himself, he had to admit that it wasn't the job that had dragged him out to this woman's doorstep. It was curiosity—his own. "I'm not sure," he said. "That's why I ask the questions."

Martha stroked her chin thoughtfully and shooed away a chicken that was pecking a little too close to her foot. "Mary!" she called out.

"Yeah?" came a muffled reply from inside the small barn.

"Man here wants to ask us a few questions."

"Questions?" asked Mary, walking out of the barn, dusting dirt off the front of her tunic.

"About Lazarus and his resurrection."

The three of them were seated at the kitchen table. Philippus was at the head of the table, Mary and Martha on either side of him. The women were sipping water and looking at him with calm, curious eyes. Martha broke the silence. "So ask your questions," she said.

Philippus smiled, "I suppose we should start with the obvious," he said. "Are you both absolutely sure that your brother was dead at the time of his burial?"

"Of course we're sure," said Mary a tad indignantly.

"You had a doctor look at him?"

"A doctor," scoffed Martha. "Who has money for a doctor?"

"Our Rabbi pronounced him dead."

"The Rabbi, all right. And how long was your brother in his tomb before the Nazarene arrived?"

"Four days," said Mary quietly.

"We called for Him as soon as Lazarus got sick, but He waited in Galilee. We didn't see Jesus until five days after we sent for him," continued Martha.

"When the Nazarene did finally arrive, did He do anything peculiar?"

"Why would Jesus do anything peculiar?" asked Martha suspiciously.

"Well, actually, now that you mention it, I did find His behaviour a little peculiar," interjected Mary. "I remember telling Jesus that Lazarus had already been buried, and He started to cry."

"I don't see anything peculiar about Him crying," said Philippus.

"It wasn't the crying. It was after, after Jesus stopped crying. He looked at us, and He smiled. And I don't mean the kind of half-hearted smile you give someone when you're trying to cheer them up. This was a big, bright, light-up-your-face kind of smile. Do you remember it, Martha?"

"I do. And now that you bring it up, I also remember thinking it was a little unusual to be smiling like that."

"And do you remember, Martha, what the Nazarene said?"

Martha had to think about it. Scratching her head, she said, "Jesus said we were not to worry. That He was the resurrection and the life—"

"But that isn't all Jesus said," interrupted Mary. "He also said, 'He who believes in me shall live even if he dies. Anyone who believes in Me shall never die in all eternity.'"

"When did the Nazarene go to your brother's tomb?"

"He asked to see it right after His little speech," said Martha.

"Was anyone else present?"

"If I remember right, there was me and Mary, and three or four of our neighbours."

"I assume they'll all verify what happened?"

"Of course they will!" asserted Martha. "It happened. And I'm telling you that, even though I was against it."

"You were against bringing your brother back to life?"

"I didn't think Jesus could bring Lazarus back to life. And remember, our brother had been dead for four days. When Jesus asked that we move the stone out of the way, I told Him no. I told Him the body was putrefying. But He insisted. So Mary and I, we got one of the village children to fetch some of the men, and they rolled the stone out of the way."

"And then what happened?" asked Philippus, his eyes watching both sisters zealously. He was surprised to find that they were both looking directly at him.

"Jesus said a silent prayer," replied Mary. "Then He went to the opening of the tomb and called, 'Lazarus, come out.'"

"I had the sleeve of my tunic up against my nose, expecting the worst," said Martha, coming back in. "But there was nothing to smell. And a few moments later, out hopped our brother."

"Hopped?" asked Philippus.

"Of course he hopped. He was still wrapped in his grave shroud."

"Yes, of course," said Philippus, remembering the shroud left behind in the Nazarene's empty tomb. "And he was unharmed? He felt fine?"

"He was hungry," said Mary.

"Like a lion," added Martha. "We were cooking all day."

Philippus smiled at what must have been an interesting day spent slaving in the kitchen. "I suppose your brother ate as if there was no tomorrow?" joked Philippus.

"He certainly did," chuckled Martha.

"He said he wanted to make up for lost time," added Mary.

"And you're both sure that your brother Lazarus was dead for four days?"

The two sisters looked at each other and then nodded their heads in agreement. Philippus nodded back even though he was sure they were mistaken. He'd seen men given up for dead on the battle field make sudden, seemingly miraculous recoveries. He once witnessed a soldier buried along with several dozen of his comrades in a shallow, mass grave climb up out of the ground like some sort of spectre freshly returned from a voyage down the river Styx.

There were also drugs and poisons that, if taken in small amounts, could induce a condition that closely resembled death. But that would mean Lazarus was either drugged or poisoned. And if he was, the next question for Philippus to answer was by whom? Did his sisters try to do away with him only to be thwarted by the unexpected arrival of the Nazarene?

But they claim they asked for the Nazarene to come and save their brother. *Which brings another issue to mind. Could this entire event be nothing more than a clever publicity stunt? I can't answer any of these questions for sure,* he told himself, *but one thing I do know is that nobody comes back from the dead.* "Well, ladies," he said, getting out of his chair, "I guess I should be going."

"You still want to talk to Lazarus?" asked Martha, as she showed Philippus to the door.

Philippus paused for a moment. "Perhaps a question or two," he said.

"He's tending to some sheep over on the northwest slope."

"Thanks. Well good-bye," said Philippus, making his way out the door. "Oh, one last question," he said with a clever smile. "You and your sister wouldn't know about anything special that might be happening here in Bethany in the next few weeks would you?"

"Special?" asked Martha. "What do you mean by special?"

I don't think she's even aware of it. Philippus smiled. *The way her whole face went red the moment she started lying.* "You know, special," he said. "Like a wedding or some sort of festival or religious gathering?"

"No, Bethany is a pretty dull place. Nothing much ever happens here."

"Except for when people return from the dead," said Philippus.

"Except for that."

"Well thanks again for answering my questions. I suppose I should go and see your brother. Northwest slope you said, right?"

"That's right, you can't miss him."

Philippus walked away, but he didn't go to see Lazarus. He had intended to ask the neighbours a few questions. Did Lazarus and his sisters get along? Would they have any reason for wanting to harm their brother? How close was the Nazarene to Lazarus and his sisters? But the fact he was sure that Martha had lied to him forced him to change his plans.

He circled around to the back of the house. The kitchen had a small, shuttered window. The sisters kept the window open to catch the spring breeze. He sat underneath it, and waited and listened.

Mary was alone in the kitchen. She looked up and smiled weakly as Martha walked in. "He's gone?" she asked.

"He is. He asked me if anything special was going to be happening in Bethany soon."

"Special? Martha, did he say what he meant by special?"

"Like a wedding," he said, "or a religious gathering."

"You didn't tell him anything?"

"Of course not, Mary. What kind of a fool do you take me for?"

"You don't think he knows, do you?"

"How could he know, Mary?"

"The Romans have spies everywhere."

"Not amongst the disciples."

"What about Iscariot?"

"Do you think we should go to Jerusalem and tell Mary Magdelene?" asked Martha tentatively.

"I think we have to, Martha."

Philippus carefully backed away from the window. He'd heard enough. He knew Martha had lied to him, and once again, the name Mary Magdalene had come up. *Why is she so important?* he asked himself. *And what's happening in Bethany? And why did Martha and Mary lie about it?*

Giving up Is Just too Easy

Twenty-One Days until Bethany

Helena was at her dressing table being made even more beautiful. Buzzing around her like honey bees in a cherry orchard were two ornatrices. Their job was to "ornament" the body and face of their mistress. The elderly but professional women had been working on Helena for hours. The ordeal had begun with an extremely hot bath, a vigorous scrub-down, a second bath in purified asses' milk, and finally, a generous application of moisturizers.

Once they had her skin incandescently clean, soft, moist to the touch and smelling ever-so-faintly of rose pedals, the ornatrices moved on to dressing her. They narrowed her waist and controlled her hips with a cestus, which they wrapped tightly around her waist and lower torso. A mamillere was used to help support her breasts. Over her lingerie, they had slipped Helena into a shimmering silk tunic. The tunic left her shoulders enticingly bare and was cut short enough to reveal most of her legs.

Her body accentuated in just the right way, the ornatrices had moved on to Helena's face. A foundation made of chalk, orris root mixed with fat, and tin oxide was lathered over her face. All imperfections, lines, blemishes, and scars were smoothed, covered over, or filled. Over the foundation, rouge was applied, highlighting Helena's prominent cheek bones and giving her face a youthful, ruby-red complexion. Her lips were moistened with a salve then tinted with red ochre. Special attention was paid to her eyes. The eyebrows were painted. Eyeliner was used to further accentuate the beauty of her almond, slightly oriental eyes.

Lastly, they went to work on her hair, already dyed a golden red, "Egyptian russet," it was called, the colour was all the rage in Rome and never failed to arouse her husband's ardour. The golden-red locks were piled high on her head and arranged in layers with golden ringlets falling lustrously down either side of her face.

The ornatrices hurriedly sprayed the room with Helena's favourite perfume, an expensive combination of myrrh, frankincense, and cinnamon, as Philippus dragged himself into their apartment.

Her back was to him. He could see the perfect colour of her hair, the artful way it had been arranged just to please him.

The ornatrices made a hasty and silent retreat. The moment of truth was at hand. She had finally decided that their marriage deserved one final chance. That's why she had subjected herself to an entire day of beautifying torture. Philippus, she had discovered on the road to Jerusalem, meant that much to her. She felt his hands begin to caress her bare shoulders. She smiled and slid on the golden rope bracelet from Antioch.

"You look beautiful," he said, his hands massaging her shoulder muscles.

"I wanted to look my best tonight."

"Well, you succeeded." He smiled, his fingers feeling out the pressure points of pleasure pain.

"Thank you, sweetheart." Helena sighed, relaxing into the rhythmic movements of his hands.

"It must have taken you hours to get ready."

"I've been at it all day."

"Why go to all the trouble?"

"I need a reason to look my best for my husband?"

"This isn't still about Lord Bacchus, is it?" he asked suspiciously.

"Why would I waste my time when you've made yourself very clear on that subject?" she asked slyly.

Watching her relaxed face, he couldn't see any sign that she was lying, but a lifetime of practice had made her a very good liar.

He bent lower to lift her bodily to the bed. A lightning strike of pain shot up his wounded arm, briefly paralyzing it. He yelped in agony.

Her eyes opened as if her body had been convulsed by an electric shock. "Are you all right?" she asked, turning to see him holding his arm gingerly as he examined the festering gash.

"I'm fine," he said between gritted teeth.

"You don't look fine," she said, getting up for a closer look. "Oh my! It's infected! Have you been to the surgeon?" Seeing the raw, puffy, red soreness of the wound, all thought of seduction, of convincing Philippus to drink the wine, was washed from her thoughts. "You're going to lose this arm," she exclaimed, feeling for a second time like a real wife. It struck her as odd. *Women were supposed to love men for their strength, and yet it's his vulnerabilities that rush me to his side.*

"You think I don't know that?" he snapped. "And, no, I haven't been to see the surgeon."

She looked at him like a mother dealing with a frightened child. "So when are you going to see him?" she demanded.

"I don't know if I want to see him."

"What are you talking about? If you don't, you'll die."

"I guess that's my problem isn't it?" he snarled, pulling his arm from her and walking away.

She went to him quietly, softly. He tried to keep his back to her, but she slid around him. With a loving hand she traced the contours of his face. "What's wrong, Philippus?"

"Nothing's wrong, I just haven't felt like seeing a doctor, that's all."

"I haven't forgotten what you tried to do back in Antioch."

"What happened in Antioch? That was nothing. I told you I was drunk."

"Then why haven't you faced this?" she asked, looking down at his wounded limb. "You know you're going to have to sooner or later."

Looking into her imploring eyes, he was surprised to see they were moist. With his good arm, he hugged her to his chest. "Maybe I don't want to face it," he said, "sooner or later."

The tears began to flow, surprising her as much as they did him. "But you can't!" she shouted, pounding tiny fists against his broad chest. "You don't! You—" The pounding fists came to a sudden halt. Looking up at him, she wiped a tear from her cheek. "You don't really mean that."

Philippus didn't answer her question. He couldn't. How do you tell your wife, even in a marriage as troubled as theirs, that you'd rather be a dead man than a one-armed man? That fate had done for him what he had been unable to do for himself? He kissed her forehead. On tiptoes, she gently kissed him back. Careful not to hurt his arm, she turned her back to him. She wrapped his strong arms around her. With a languorous sigh, she released into their comforting warmth. "You're not afraid of losing the arm, are you?" she asked, her voice gentle and soothing.

"No, I'm not afraid," he said, pulling her closer, ignoring the pain it caused.

"Then what is it? You're not ashamed, are you?"

"Ashamed?" he asked. "You think the thought of living the rest of my life as a cripple is too much for my ego to bear?"

"Is it?"

"No, I'm not ashamed," he lied.

"Then you'll go to the surgeon?"

"Yes, all right, I'll go to the surgeon."

"Tomorrow?"

"Sure, tomorrow."

"Good." She sighed. Feeling him so close, the night's original objective came back to her. "Philippus?" she asked turning to look up into his eyes.

"Yes?"

"Is there anything I can get you to help with the pain?"

"No, I don't think so."

"Well," she said with an insouciant smile, "is there anything I can do?" she asked as she pulled off her tunic to stand before him in just her undergarments. "Does this take your mind off of the pain?" she asked.

"I...ah...I'm suddenly painless," he stammered with a smile.

She was so lovely, and like a man lost in the desert, he thirsted for her. Without a second thought about the pain, he took her into his arms. She kissed him and led him to the bed. Mindful of his arm, he laid down first. She looked down at him, a smile splashed across her face. "Do you trust me?" she asked.

"I want to trust you," he answered.

She rushed over to her nightstand. She picked up a ceramic jug and a simple clay cup. She filled the cup and offered it to him. "Drink," she said.

"I thought you weren't going to waste your time?" he asked, placing the cup on the night stand.

"Do you remember right after we were married?" she asked, sitting down on the bed beside him. "You took me to Egypt to see the pyramids? Do you remember hearing the jackals at night? I was so frightened, I couldn't sleep. You put your arms around me and said you'd protect me. Tonight, let me put my arms around you," she said.

"But why must I drink?" he asked, sitting up.

"Because I want you to experience what I have discovered."

"Bacchus?" he asked.

"You won't be able to fully receive him. For that, you have to be properly purified."

"Purified?"

"Purity is at the very centre. Before the divine can take over our bodies, we must be made as clean as possible. We must fast and cleanse ourselves in the baths, but tonight we'll start with the wine. Bacchus has taught us that the growth of the grapevine—their death every autumn and rebirth every spring—is a sign from god, proof of our immortality."

"Immortality?" he asked, the word taking him by surprise. "Is that what your Bacchanal is really all about? Living forever?"

"It is a promise from Bacchus. The grape is its proof."

"There is no such thing as an afterlife," he said, getting out of bed, forcing himself to ignore the pain in his arm.

She watched him walk over to the wine cabinet and hung her head in frustration. "What are you talking about?" she asked plaintively. "Even the gods of Rome talk of an afterlife."

"You don't actually believe all that foolishness about the nine circles of the underworld and the River Styx, do you?" he asked with a sceptical snort as he poured himself a goblet of unadulterated wine.

She gave up, retrieved her tunic and dressed. "Then why go to temple every morning?" she countered accusingly.

"I don't."

"Then why not give Bacchus a chance?"

"I could get arrested."

"Eternity is worth it, don't you think?"

"If I believed in eternity."

"So life for you just ends with death?"

"I have no idea what death ends."

Helena shook her head, pulling on her tunic. "How can you live like that?" she asked.

"Like what?"

"With the thought that any day, any moment, any breath, could be your last for all eternity?"

The question stung like a blow only partially blocked. "I'm prepared to do what life demands of me," he said resignedly.

"Like dying instead of losing an arm?"

Philippus looked down at his infected left arm. The pain had receded for now, but there was no mistaking the green colouration. "If it comes to that," he said stoically.

"But life doesn't demand it of you," she said beseechingly. "Bacchus has promised all his followers salvation and a blessed afterlife."

"And all we have to do is get drunk?" he asked sceptically.

"By drinking the wine, we commune with god. Just let down your defences," she implored him. Picking up the cup from the night table, she held it out to him one last time.

"No. I'm sorry," he replied shaking his head. "I think—"

"Think! Think! Think!" she screamed, pushing the goblet into his face. "You've turned into one of those Greek philosophers you admire so much."

"I think of that as a compliment," he said, pushing the cup away and walking off.

CAN YOU LIE FOR GOD?

TWENTY-ONE DAYS UNTIL BETHANY

B ecause of the late hour, Caiaphas had the three young guards brought to his counting room at his home rather than risk having them come to the temple. He had not invited Aaron. The captain was almost certainly a sympathizer, if not a true believer, and for what he had planned, the high priest needed men who had no allegiance or sympathy for the followers of the Nazarene.

After being marched into the room by one of his guards, Azekah, Jacob, and Ezra stood nervously at attention, waiting for the high priest to tell them why they had been summoned. All three of them were expecting the worst. "Gentlemen, be at ease. I have a small proposition for you."

"What kind of propostion, Excellency?" asked Jacob.

"There's something I'd like you to do for me."

"Do for you, Excellency?" asked Azeka.

"Yes," he said easily. "According to your captain's report, you were attacked while playing dice."

"Yes, Excellency," said Jacob, "and we've already been punished for that."

"We had extra duty for the past week, Excellency," added Ezra.

"I know, and all three of you can relax, because it is not my intention to punish you further. In fact, what I'm offering you is a chance to earn some extra money."

"Did you say extra money, Excellency?" inquired Ezra.

"I did," smiled Caiaphas.

"How much extra money, Excellency?" asked Jacob.

"Oh, well, let's say ten pieces of silver each—to start."

"What would we have to do, Excellency?" asked Ezra.

"I want you to change your story about what happened at the tomb. I want you to say that you know who attacked you."

"But, with all due respect, Excellency, we don't," insisted Jacob.

"For ten pieces of silver, don't you think you could find a way to say that the followers of the Nazarene attacked you and that they are the ones responsible for stealing the body?"

They shuffled their feet. Ezeka scratched his head. Not one of them could find his tongue.

"Come, come, gentlemen. It is a simple request for a very nice fee. But if you are having trouble making up your minds, I'll make it twenty pieces of silver."

Ezra stopped scratching. "Excellency," he said, "for twenty pieces of silver, I'll say anything."

"Excellent. How about the rest of you?"

Jacob and Ezeka looked at each other. They wavered for a moment and then nodded their heads.

"Good! You men have no idea how important this is. For the future of all our people, we must put a stop to these rumours about the Nazarene being alive."

"We'll do our best, Excellency," said Jacob.

"I'm sure you will. I'm sure you will."

WHO CAN WE TRUST?

TWENTY-ONE DAYS UNTIL BETHANY

Arms around her waist, Aaron bent forward to kiss his wife good-bye under the portico that led into their large, Mediterranean-style house. He'd already said his good-bye to his boy before tucking him into bed. Releasing her, Aaron couldn't help but notice that the small crack running across the top of the portico had gotten larger. *I'll need to call a stone mason about that crack,* he reminded himself. *More money I don't have.*

The captain made his way across the northern edge of the upper city, heading east towards the temple mount. The home Aaron had inherited from his father-in-law was located not far from Herod's palace at the northwest edge of the upper city. The priest's house was due east, not far from the temple steps.

Aaron had no reason to think he was being followed. He didn't bother to look behind him or take any evasive action in order to cut off any tail that he might have grown. At one point he thought about ducking into a crowded wine bar, quickly making his way to the back door that led to the latrines and then doubling back to the front of the bar, thus confusing anyone who might be following him. But he couldn't convince himself that it was necessary. Nobody was following him. Besides, he was in a hurry.

Consequently, he never saw Amicus doing a rather poor job of trying to remain unobtrusive as he followed the captain.

Peter and John were the only disciples present at the meeting that night, the others having determined that it was best that they not all congregate in one place at one time. The others at the meeting included the priests Nicodemus and Joseph of Arimathea; Joanna, the tax collector's wife, who had come all the

186 | Gerald Hess

way from Antipas's household in Tiberia; Aaron, who had been invited by Joseph of Arimathea; and Reisa and Mary Magdalene.

They had gathered to hear the news from Peter and John that Jesus was to be near the village of Bethany forty days after His resurrection. A chosen few, the disciples, Mary, and Lazarus's sisters, had known for days, but this was the first more-public announcement. They were all assured that they would be able to see Jesus before He returned to His Father. The announcement had generated great joy amongst those who had gathered to hear it, but also a great anxiousness.

They were all worried about their current and future safety. The sight of Jesus in agony hanging from His cross was still fresh in their memories. They all understood that their legal position was fragile and vague. As followers of a convicted blasphemer, were they subject to the same harsh penalties? No one knew for sure. What they did know was that Rome was the ultimate temporal power in Judea and would do as she pleased. For the moment, Rome appeared to be willing to tolerate them. But was that merely because of their small numbers? What if those numbers grew? Would Rome remain tolerant?

As to the Sanhedrin, no one in the room was under any delusions as to how the Jewish priestly class felt about Jesus—or them.

They were all seated in Joseph of Arimathea's spacious dining room. The servants had been given the night off. Joseph's wife and children were visiting the in-laws. They could all speak freely. Bread, cheese, olives, figs, and tea had been laid out in advance. But no one was interested in eating. Peter, sitting at the head of the table, stood up. "I know we are all excited about Bethany," he said. "Seeing Jesus one more time will be a great blessing for all of us, but let us not deceive ourselves. Bethany could also be a great danger. If Rome or the Sanhedrin find out, they could send troops to try and arrest Jesus and all who show up to see Him."

"Then we have to make sure Rome and the Sanhedrin do not find out," said Nicodemus. He was an older man with grey hair, a long, lined face, and heavily hooded, sad, brown eyes that looked as if they had seen more of the world than they really wanted to.

"I disagree," said Mary Magdalene. "What is to happen in Bethany must not be kept secret."

"I agree with Mary," said John. "If we keep it a secret, would we not be throwing away our best chance to demonstrate His divinity? Should we not do everything we can to tell all who will listen what is about to happen?"

Joanna spoke next. Because of her position in Herod's court, she was the most political. "Perhaps I have a workable solution," she said. "We could refrain from promoting Bethany publicly and, instead, tell only those people we believe we can trust."

"That's good in theory, Joanna," replied Peter, "but we know how people like to talk. If we tell anyone beyond our inner circle, Rome and the Sanhedrin will ultimately find out."

"Peter," asked Mary Magdalene, "couldn't we deal with that problem if and when it arises?"

"And how would we know if our enemies have learned of Bethany? Do you expect them to send us a written message?"

"I don't, but I think we will be able to tell if too many people are talking about Bethany."

"Exactly," chimed in Joanna. "Those who know and love Jesus will not tell Rome or the Sanhedrin, and if word of Bethany does get out amongst the public, we will hear of it as surely as Rome, and we can decide what to do at that time."

"'At that time,'" scoffed Peter. "At that time, it will be too late. Why don't we ask the military man what he thinks?"

All eyes turned to Aaron, who shifted in his chair uncomfortably. "Honestly," he said, "I don't feel qualified to speak here tonight."

"Nonsense," said Nicodermus, who was seated next to Aaron. "Who is better qualified to speak about matters of security than a captain in the temple guards?"

Aaron cleared his throat. "I would say that telling the general public would be a huge mistake. But even if you told no one beyond those who already know, Bethany would still be dangerous. Caiaphas sees all of us as a danger, not just to the Sanhedrin, but to all of Judea."

"Reisa," asked Peter, "do you agree with what Aaron has said?"

Reisa looked around the table before speaking. "Aaron is right," she began in a voice barely above a whisper. "If my husband finds out about Bethany, he will do everything he can to stop us. He will use force—deadly force if necessary. Not because he is a cruel man. He is just sure that he is doing what is right for Judea and for God." She paused to let her words sink in.

A tremour of fear rumbled across the cedar table. Nervous looks were exchanged. This was something they had all talked about. To get through the day they did their best not think about it. And when they did think about it, they found comfort in the thought that God was with them. But the bottom line was that none of them could afford to deny that spreading the words of Jesus might cost them their lives.

Peter broke the silence. "What about Rome? Will Pilate send Roman soldiers to stop us?"

"Rome, I'm not so sure about," continued Reisa, happy to move on. "Pilate is nervous, and nervous people are unpredictable. But I know my husband will advise Pilate that he must act against us."

John, seated at the other end of the table opposite Peter, rose to speak. "I think before we make a final decision, we should all remember what Jesus said to us back in Galilee. He told us that he was sending us forth, and by hiding Bethany from the people, by seeking our own safety more than we seek to spread His truth means we are not going forth, we are not following His wishes."

"So what do you think we should do, John?" asked Joseph of Arimathea.

"I think we should tell everyone we can of the miracle that is soon to take place in Bethany."

"And if we're arrested," asked Nicodemus, "how do we go forth from a jail cell?"

"I don't believe following the wishes of Jesus will put us in jail. I understand that you do not feel the same way. So I recommend that we agree to Joanna's compromise. Let us tell only those we can trust. That way, most, if not all, who want to see Jesus will be in Bethany."

Peter saw the heads nodding in agreement. "Well," he said, "it would appear that we have reached a decision. We will make no public announcement but will quietly tell those we trust. I only pray that those we trust do not let us down."

"Fear not, Peter." John smiled. "Jesus will be there to protect us in any case."

"Yes, John," replied Peter. "It is in Jesus we must put our trust."

They all left together. It took Amicus a few tense seconds to spot Aaron as he hugged Joseph of Arimathea good-bye. He was hiding behind a small bench placed right across the street from Arimathea's home so that it overlooked the Tyropoeon valley.

As he came out from behind the bench, Amicus didn't see Barnabas hiding in the shadow of the indented front door of a small bakery just off to the right of the bench. The weasel-faced spy watched Amicus fall into line behind the captain. Even in the modest moonlight, he could make out Amicus's military sandals and cloak.

Later that night, after a few hours sleep, Aaron was on his way to work when he found Jacob standing around in the Court of the Gentiles, not far from the site of Solomon's Portico. The place was almost empty, but a few pilgrims were starting to drift in before the dawn sacrifices. Jacob was calling them over individually. As Aaron got closer, he could just make out what was being said. He couldn't believe his ears. Jacob was spinning a tale about how it was the disciples of the Nazarene who had attacked him and taken away the body.

So it is true, marvelled Aaron. He had heard stories about what the three rookies were doing, but he had refused to believe them. Moving in on Jacob from behind, he shoved him so hard the lad almost fell over. "What do you think you're doing?" he asked grimly.

"Aaron!" replied Jacob, once he'd regained his balance. "Why are you here so early?"

"I'll ask the questions, soldier," snapped Aaron, eyes grinding into Jacob.

"Well, sir, I'm…ah…just…ah waiting for the dawn sacrifices."

Aaron looked at him sceptically. "You can stop lying, soldier. I heard what you were saying."

"Don't worry, sir, everything fits with our original story. It's just that, now I'm remembering a detail I'd forgotten."

"Some detail. Who's paying you to do this?"

Jacob looked around nervously before speaking. "Just between you and me, sir, it's the high priest. He wants us to tell people that the body was stolen by the Nazarene's disciples."

"And you went along with it?"

"He is the high priest, sir."

"But it's a lie, soldier."

"It's twenty pieces of silver, sir."

"Are the other two in on this—this fiction?"

Jacob nodded his head sheepishly, looking down at his feet.

Aaron stormed off. He wasn't sure what he should do next, but he knew someone who would.

WHAT'S IN A NAME?

TWENTY DAYS UNTIL BETHANY

Aaron had to wait until after work before meeting with Joseph of Arimathea. He had wanted to have this meeting earlier, but he'd been forced to do double duty because of all the pilgrims still camped around the city. Their numbers had shrunk appreciably, but they were still creating overflow crowds at the temple. This evening was the first opportunity he'd had to get away, and he was desperate to let the disciples know about the lies being told about them and who was behind them.

Joseph of Arimathea was alone in his study. On his desk sat the chalice. He had gone to his study immediately after dinner, locking the door behind him, guaranteeing that he would be alone and undisturbed. He looked deeply into the dark red ichor trying to decide what he should do. Unlike any blood he had ever seen before, the blood in the chalice was not evaporating or coagulating. Three weeks had passed since the Nazarene's death, but his blood looked as fresh as when he had first collected it. Joseph contemplated whether the few inches of red fluid were actually capable of miracles. Even more importantly, was there any way he could prove it? Looking into the opaque liquid, Joseph thought it was a perfect metaphor for what had been happening to his life. *Like this blood*, he told himself, *nothing is clear anymore*.

He was jolted from his reverie by a throbbing arthritic pain in his right hand. He'd had the problem for years. He worried that it would soon force him to give up his work charting the stars. Since his days as a boy, Joseph had looked at the stars and wondered about their true meaning. As he grew older, he came to understand that the impulse that drove him to study the stars also lay behind his desire to become a priest: That the lucumbration of mystery was an essential religious impulse.

The idea came to him as he was softly rubbing away the ache in his hand. He dipped a cloth into the blood and rubbed it on his sore hand. He had just put away the chalice when his manservant Isaac knocked at the locked door. Joseph unlocked the door and asked, "Is something wrong, Isaac?"

"You have a visitor, sir."

"Does this visitor have a name?"

"Aaron, sir. Said he was a captain in the temple guards."

"Tell the captain I'll see him in the courtyard."

"Yes, sir."

Aaron was waiting when Joseph walked into the courtyard. Torches had been lit to provide a little light and a jug of wine had been placed on a wooden table surrounded by four wicker chairs. "Captain, I hope I haven't kept you waiting too long?"

"No, sir, I'm so glad you could see me on such short notice."

"Please, Captain, sit down. Can I get you anything? Something to eat? I see wine has been brought."

"No, sir, I'm fine," replied Aaron as he sat down in of the wicker chairs.

"Your message, Captain," said Joseph sitting down in the chair across from Aaron, "said you had something to tell me of the gravest urgency."

"Yes, sir. I didn't know who else I could tell."

"So what is it you want to say?"

"Well, sir, when I was guarding the tomb, I had three men under my command, and it has come to my attention that those men have been paid to spread the lie that the disciples attacked us and stole the body."

"Paid? By whom?"

"The high priest, sir."

Joseph looked up at the night sky. "I must thank you for bringing this to my attention, Captain."

"Sir, you must go to the disciples. They must do what they can to combat these lies."

"I agree, Captain, but everyone is worried about Bethany. The disciples are not going to be seen in public until then."

"So you think we should just let Caiaphas's lies stand unopposed?"

"Until after Bethany."

"That's almost three weeks. The lies can be heard by a lot of people in that time."

"Yes, and Bethany will prove to everyone that they are lies."

"Not if we are the only ones there. You must convince the disciples to reconsider their decision to stay hidden. They must come forward and deny these lies."

"I'll do what I can, Captain, but I don't think I'll be able to change their minds."

After the captain left, Joseph had his servants take urgent messages to Mary, Peter, and John that they meet at his home immediately. Two hours later, the four of them were sitting in a circle on straight-backed wooden chairs, sipping Chinese tea as Joseph told them the bad news.

"Oh, no." Peter moaned. "That can't be true."

"I'm afraid it is, Peter," replied Joseph of Arimathea.

"And Caiaphas is paying them to do it?" asked John.

"That is what Aaron told me."

"But why?" pleaded John.

"I think the reason is obvious," replied Peter ominously. "Caiaphas fears us and intends to destroy us."

"So what are we going to do, Peter?"

"Aaron thinks you should go out amongst the people and tell them the truth."

"Out of the question, Joseph," snapped Peter. "We would only succeed in getting ourselves arrested."

"What about Bethany?" asked John uneasily.

"These lies only make Bethany more dangerous, John," answered Peter.

Mary looked at all the nervous faces. "I have more bad news about Bethany," she said. "Lazarus's sisters came to see me. The Roman investigator has been to Bethany. He asked them if anything special was happening in the next few weeks."

"But how, Mary? How could he have found out?" asked John.

"Mary and Martha didn't think Philippus knew anything for sure, but he is suspicious."

"So what are we going to do?" asked Peter.

"We must put our trust in God," said John. "He will protect us."

Joseph of Arimathea stood up to speak. "What if we arranged a distraction for the Romans?" he asked, his eyes looking furtively around the room.

"What kind of a distraction?" asked Peter.

"Here's what I'm thinking," said Joseph leaning in, getting excited about what he was about to say. "I have met with Aaron, the captain in the temple guards. He spoke at our last meeting. I could go to him and ask him to go to Lucius and tell the tribune that our Lord will be in, oh, say Galilee, on the fortieth morning."

"Yes, I see what you mean," nodded John, "The Romans would go to Galilee, not Bethany."

"But we would have lied," said Mary.

"It's a good idea, Joseph," said Peter, "but we can never agree to it."

"And that is your unanimous opinion?" asked Joseph.

"Yes, Joseph," said Peter. "So is that all we needed to discuss?"

"Wait a minute," pleaded Joseph, "how can we move on when we still haven't decided what to do about Bethany?"

"I thought, Joseph," replied Peter "that we would leave Bethany in the capable hands of God?"

"Yes, yes, of course, but does that mean we do nothing?" asked Joseph, a touch of desperation in his voice as his eyes went from face to face.

"Joseph," said John, "trusting in God is not nothing."

"No, I suppose it isn't." Joseph sighed, reluctantly sitting down.

"So, if that's all, I think we can go home," continued Peter.

"There is one more thing we need to settle," said Mary quietly.

"And what is that, Mary?" asked Peter.

"Followers of the way are asking me what they should call our teacher."

"Why not call Him Jesus?" asked Joseph.

"Yes, Joseph, of course, Jesus. But is Jesus the Messiah or the Christos?" asked Mary.

"Jesus is the Messiah, we all agree on that, don't we?" asked John.

"That is the Jewish name, but it is a Greek world that we must reach out to," replied Mary.

"So you think we should call Jesus the Christos?" asked Joseph.

"It will be more pleasant for Roman ears," said Mary.

"Is that so important—pleasing Roman ears?" questioned John.

"Mary is right," said Peter, entering the debate. "For us, He will always be the Messiah, but for the rest of the world, He must be the Christos."

"Then it's settled." Joseph smiled. "Jesus is now Jesus Christos."

She Doesn't Seem So Bad

Nineteen Days until Bethany

First-hour meetings with Amicus were hardly the norm, so Philippus was more than a little surprised when he was informed by the guard outside his office door that the centurion was already inside waiting for him. "Amicus?" He frowned, walking into the room and closing the door behind him. "What brings you here at such an early hour?"

Amicus, who had fallen asleep while he waited, jumped to attention, knocking over his chair and bringing a smile to Philippus's lips. "Sorry, sir...I mean...ah...Philippus, but I thought you'd want to know this as soon as possible."

"Know what, Centurion?" asked Philippus, sitting down behind his desk.

"Well...ah...Philippus," began Amicus hestitantly, bending down to right his fallen chair, "I've been following Aaron, making him my top priority like you said, and he's started seeing this priest, and—"

"Which priest?" interrupted Philippus, the centurion having caught his attention.

"Joseph of Arimathea, at least, that's who pays the taxes on the house where they meet."

"You checked up on that, Centurion?"

"I did, sir—Philippus," replied Amicus proudly.

"Good for you. Shows initiative! I like that."

Amicus's smile broadened. "Anyway, the captain is not alone when he visits the priest."

"He isn't?"

"No, two of those disciples you told me about are also there—Peter and John, I think—plus some women I don't know and a few others I didn't recognize."

"Good work, Centurion."

"Thank you, sir, I mean, Philippus. Do you want me to switch from the captain to the priest?"

"Stay with the captain. I'll deal with Joseph of Arimathea."

"Anything you say...ah...Philippus."

"Good, I think that will be all for now. I've an appointment to see some legionaries."

Philippus met the eight legionaries he had seconded from the cohort stationed at the Antonia near the entrance to the empty tomb. At the sight of their temporary commander, the slovenly group got slowly to its feet. They were a motley bunch of conscripts, dragged in from every corner of the empire. "Not a single Roman amongst the lot of them," grumbled Philippus as the eight men failed to come to attention.

Their job this morning was to help him determine if Aaron and his men could have rolled the stone without help. "All right, men, we're going to see how many of you it takes to move this stone," shouted Philippus, walking over and, using his good arm, giving the bear-sized rock a hearty slap. "We'll start with you two," commanded Philippus, pointing at the two legionaries standing closest to the tomb entrance. "Pick up a couple of these poles, lever them underneath the stone, and let's see if you can move it. And, you there, at the other end, go stand guard by the path leading to the tomb. Don't let anyone approach the tomb without talking to me first."

It was just after the third legionary had picked up a pole that Philippus heard the commotion coming from where the legionary assigned the guard detail had taken up his position. He caught sight of the guard shoving a woman to the ground.

"What seems to be the problem?" asked Philippus, arriving on the scene.

"Woman won't take no for an answer," came the gruff reply from the legionary.

"I only want to pray," complained the woman, sitting up.

"No one is allowed near the tomb," said Philippus, using his good hand to help her up.

"How close can I get?" she asked, taking his offered hand.

Philippus considered the woman standing defiantly in front of him. *Not altogether unpleasant to look at,* he thought. *But that's not what has me captivated. It's her eyes; I can't look away. What is it about those eyes? They're not as beautiful as Helena's, but they possess something.*

"Can I at least kneel in front of the tomb and pray?" she asked.

Sorrow, Philippus finally told himself. *This woman has confronted more than her fair share of pain. I've seen this look before. Right after a battle when the blood is still fresh on our uniforms and the cries of the wounded and dying are all we can hear. And we lucky few, the survivors, go about the awful job of dispatching enemy wounded and burying our dead. We have in our eyes that very same look.*

Tearing himself away from her sad eyes, he checked the tomb entrance, where his three legionaries were struggling unsuccessfully to budge the large stone. "I don't think we need to chase her away," he said, returning his attention to the guard.

"You mean you're going to let me pray?" she asked.

"As long as you stay outside the tomb," replied Philippus. "Entering is strictly forbidden."

"I don't need to go inside, only to be close to where He lay."

The woman started off when Philippus called her back. "Hold on a moment."

"Yes?" she asked, her mouth forming a worried frown.

"Why?" he asked. "Why pray at this man's tomb?"

"He saved my soul," she said, the pain in her eyes fading.

"Does this soul come with a name?'

"Mary Magdalene."

So this is the woman Aaron was seen talking to. The woman Lazarus's sisters decided they had to tell about my visit to Bethany. "Well, Mary," he said pleasantly, "go and pray, but be careful in case that rock starts rolling."

Mary looked over at the legionaries and smiled. "I don't think I have much to worry about."

"I'd be careful anyway."

Phillipus had seven men at work for the better part of half an hour. *Well, I guess that clears the guards,* he said to himself, *unless they had help. But if they had help, why are there only four sets of footprints? Why did the men who helped them wipe away only their own prints? And how were they able to separate their footprints from those of the captain and his men? I know I couldn't have done it. I'll have to ask them after I catch them.*

He watched the big stone start to roll and could only shake his head in amazment as the stone picked up steam. It left the legionaries and their poles behind and rolled across the front of the tomb. The hill sloped gently down from the entrance of the tomb to where Mary was praying. The stone, following the slope, was headed right for her.

Mary opened her eyes. Doom was coming straight for her. Philippus saw the frozen look of fear in her eyes and knew she wasn't going to get out of the way in time. *Just like men in battle right before somebody runs them through,* he thought.

He didn't understand why. He didn't know this woman except as a suspect. He didn't owe her anything, certainly not his life, but he risked it anyway. With a burst of speed he didn't think he still had in him, he reached her a split second before the stone. Too late to lift her to safety, but maybe, just maybe, in time to knock her out of the way. With every ounce of strength his legs could muster, he left his feet, thrusting his shoulder into her chest, knocking her clear.

He was unable to do the same for himself. He looked up from the dirt and gravel. He saw the stone bearing down on him. *Oh well.* He smiled. *At least I won't have to worry about my arm anymore.*

He closed his eyes. He heard Mary scream and shouts of panic from the men. He was expecting to feel the pain of rock ripping flesh and crushing bone. Instead, he heard a crunching sound followed by a gust of wind, followed by a loud crash and a shower of dust. He opened his eyes and was more than surprised. The stone had been shattered into small pieces a foot away from where he had fallen.

The legionaries helped him to his feet. They explained to him that just as the stone seemed poised to crush him, it hit a second rock buried in the ground in front of him. The collision knocked the stone off its course and sent it crashing to the ground.

Mary was the first to notice the blood. "You're bleeding!" she exclaimed.

"I've seen worse."

"But it must hurt," she said, looking at the blood as it dripped profusely onto the ground.

"Means I'm still alive," he joked.

"What do you want us to do now?" asked the legionary who had been on guard duty.

"You can stay on guard duty," said Philippus. "The rest of you can report back to the Antonia."

The guards left. Mary tore off the left sleeve of her threadbare cloak. "Please," she remonstrated, "you must let me bandage your wound."

"That won't be necessary."

"But you could bleed to death, or the wound could become infected."

"It's already infected."

"And I've already torn my cloak," she pleaded, holding up the torn sleeve.

"You didn't have to do that," he said.

"We must all be good Samaritans, for in the eyes of God we are all equal," she replied, carefully wrapping the torn sleeve around his wounded upper arm.

"Didn't the man in that tomb speak of a good Samaritan?"

"He did. You heard Him speak?" she asked.

"I was denied that opportunity, but I've read some of His sermons."

"You have them written down?"

"Scrolls of His sermons are kept in the palace library."

"That's wonderful! I didn't know. I had no idea. How is that possible?"

"Rome had men following the Nazarene with orders to write down what He said."

"I wish I could read them."

"Perhaps I could arrange for a copy to be transcribed for you."

"That would be truly a blessing—to have a record of His sermons—even to have a few of the sermons."

Philippus smiled contentedly, seeing the pain drain from her eyes. "I'll do what I can," he said.

Mary looked deeply into his eyes and nodded her head. "Yes," she said, "I believe you will, and I thank you for it."

"I've read most of the sermons, but not all. The Nazarene had quite a lot to say."

"Yes, He did," smiled Mary.

"What about His message had the greatest impact on you?"

Her eyes changed again. A far-away, thoughtful look came over them. Bringing her left hand up to her face, she rubbed her cheek as if she had a toothache. "That's an interesting question," she said. "Everything Jesus said was important and true. Treat others as you would like to be treated, meet hate with love—but for me, I suppose my life has been changed the most by His call to charity. Like the Samaritan, we must all do what we can to help the less fortunate."

"I don't know what good it does, helping the poor. What do you hope to accomplish?"

"It's not about results. It's about love for our fellow man."

"So we help no matter what?" he asked.

"And if we do, we discover that giving rewards those who give as much as those who receive."

"Rewards the giver? What do you mean? Does God reward the giver?"

"Let me explain it to you this way. When I go amongst the poorest of the poor with food or a little kindness, afterwards, I feel so, so blessed. It's as if I should be the one saying thank you."

"For the privilege of giving?"

"We are all God's children. And so charity nourishes something fundamental to our nature."

Philippus thought about what he had just heard. "What about forgiveness?" he asked. "Are you saying we should just forgive people their weaknesses, their shortcomings?"

"Jesus said hate the sin but love the sinner."

"Yes, I remember reading that." Philippus smiled. "And I remember not understanding it. But I think you've just made it clear to me. Maybe I'll give charity a try sometime," he said.

"It would be a blessing—for those who receive and for you as well. Never forget that we serve God by serving our fellow man. There, that should stop the bleeding. Is it too tight?"

"It feels fine," he said, forcing himself not to bring his hand up to scratch his face, a clear sign that he was lying. The wound didn't feel fine. It hurt terribly, throbbing away underneath Mary's improvised bandage.

"Good," she said, "but please, I think you should have a doctor look at it."

Philippus looked at his wounded limb and sighed. "Seems to be the majority opinion," he said.

"You don't agree?"

"This wound isn't going to heal. Here, give it a good smell." He held the arm up under her nose. It was unmistakable. A sickly sweet aroma that was the first sign of rot as the bacteria went about their deadly business. Philippus could see the sadness return to her eyes.

"You are going to lose your arm," she said calmly.

"Not necessarily."

"But surely if you don't, you will—"

"Die?" he asked, finishing her question for her. "That's the diagnosis. But who wants to live with only one arm?"

"You can't possibly believe that life without an arm has no value?"

"It is only my left arm, but if its not there, what's going to hold up my shield?"

"But life—your life—is a precious gift from God. You must not willfully destroy it."

"Then God better figure out a way for me to keep both of my arms," he said, raising them above his head. As he lowered them, a thought occurred to him. "Oh, I was visiting Bethany," he said as conversationally as he could. "Not a bad little town. Do you know the place?"

Mary looked down at her hands. "Bethany? Why would you want to go there? It's a small place and very poor. There are much better places."

Philippus didn't miss the way she talked to her hands instead of him. *She can't look me in the eye and talk about Bethany at the same time. Maybe I should poke her a little bit more.* "I spoke to the sisters of that farmer—Lazarus. The man whose body I'm looking for is said to have raised Lazarus from the dead. I thought his sisters might have something to say about who took the body."

"Lazarus is a good, simple, and righteous man. He didn't steal your body, and neither did his sisters."

"That's what they told me."

"Well, I must be going," she said, quickly getting to her feet.

"Can we talk again?" he asked.

"If you'd like," she answered, walking away hurriedly.

"Yes," he said, "I think I would." *And sooner than you suppose*, Philippus thought to himself. *I'll probably be carrying an arrest warrant.*

WE MUST DO SOMETHING

NINETEEN DAYS UNTIL BETHANY

The sun had set, and Joseph of Arimathea was thankful that Aaron had agreed to meet with him in his observatory. Aaron let his eyes take in the cluttered room. He was amazed at all the glass windows, each one looking out at a different part of the sky. Once again, Aaron was impressed by how well the Sanhedrin lived.

They were seated in wooden chairs that looked out onto the western horizon. The late-night sky was clear and filled with stars. Joseph poured two cups of wine to sip as they enjoyed the view. "I've been thinking about Bethany," he said.

"What about it, sir?"

"The Romans are suspicious. The investigator has been asking questions."

"You think he knows about what is to happen on the fortieth day?"

"If he doesn't, I believe he soon will. The question is how do we prevent the Romans from arresting everyone?"

"I thought we were only going to tell people we could trust about Bethany?"

"That was the plan, but somehow word must have leaked out, and now we must do something."

"What are you proposing? We certainly can't stop them by the force of arms."

"No, of course not, Captain. I believe you are familiar with the tribune Lucius Versus Clemons?"

Aaron swallowed. "I know the man," he said cautiously.

"You were seen running to the tribune the morning of the resurrection."

"Your witness must be mistaken."

"You have nothing to fear from me, Captain. I asked you here not to accuse you of anything but to ask you for your help."

"My help? What can I do?"

Joseph smiled kindly at Aaron. "What I want to do is set up a decoy. Trick the Romans into believing that Jesus will be appearing not in Bethany but Galilee."

"How do you plan to do that?"

"By feeding the Romans false information, which is where you fit in."

"What do you want me to do?"

After the captain left, Joseph was sitting under one of his new windows. Out of habit, he rubbed his arthritic hand, when it suddenly occurred to him that it wasn't sore anymore.

Must It Be So Hard?

Eighteen Days until Bethany

On his way to Mary's, Jonah tried not to worry about Barnabas's latest bit of information: that the Roman investigator had a man watching the captain when he attended meetings at the home of Joseph of Arimathea, meetings where Mary had also been present. It was no longer a matter of conjecture. Mary and the rest of the followers of the Nazarene were the investigator's prime suspects. The only good news was that there continued to be no hard evidence that they had actually taken the body or were planning a revolt of any kind.

Perhaps the Roman investigator will realize that and leave them alone. But if he doesn't, I don't know how I'm going to protect Mary. If only I could convince her to leave Judea, but she refuses to listen to me.

Mary and her four-legged friend greeted Jonah at the front door. She gave him a big hug. The dog kept his distance. "Don't worry about him," said Mary, seeing that Jonah and the dog were staying a respectful distance from each other. "He just doesn't know you yet."

"As long as he doesn't bite," replied Jonah.

"Please, Jonah, sit," she said, pointing at the two mats she had spread out on the dirt floor. He selected the mat that kept his back to the far wall, giving him a good view of the door. Mary sat down across from him. "I brought you a few things, Mary," he said, handing her a cloth sack.

"Thank you, Jonah," she said, accepting the sack and looking inside.

"Just some food, a little wine," he mumbled.

"Oh, Jonah, it's wonderful," she exclaimed, taking out the fresh bread, olives, dried meat, and cheese. "Look boy," she said, showing the food to the dog. Without waiting, she tore off a piece of meat and gave it to him.

"Mary, what are you doing?"

"Sharing your kind gift."

"But not with the dog."

"Why not, Jonah? He is hungry too. I only wish I could offer you something."

"Don't worry about me, Mary. I'm fine."

Mary looked at Jonah. She kissed him on the cheek. "Thank you," she said.

"Knowing you've got something to eat is thanks enough," he said. "If you don't give it all away."

"Well, why don't I make us some lunch?" she asked.

"No I don't want anything. I didn't bring you this food so you could give it back to me."

"And why is that?" she asked. "Is the blessing of charity only for you?"

"I can afford it," he grumbled, suddenly unable to look directly into her trusting eyes.

"Let me tell you a story, Jonah."

"No! No stories," he snapped. "I've heard enough of your stories. I know you want to give everything away. But we all have to eat."

"We cannot live by bread alone."

"And we can't live without it."

"The greater the sacrifice, the greater the gift."

Jonah gave Mary a stern, steely-eyed stare that had frozen the blood of more than one strong man. She was clutching his care package in her arms. "I want you to promise me, Mary," he said sharply, "that you won't give any of this food away."

Mary lowered her head but said nothing.

Jonah reached out to take her firmly by the shoulders. "Mary," he said. "Give me your word."

"Let me finish my story," she said, removing his hands, putting down the package then gently taking his hands in hers. "Jesus was teaching in Judea near the border with Galilee when a rich, important man ran up to Him and knelt. And this man asked Jesus, 'What must I do to inherit eternal life?' And Jesus said to him, 'Obey the commandments, keep them.' And the man replied, 'Good teacher, I've done all these things. What else can I do?' And do you know how Jesus answered him?"

"You mean all of that wasn't enough?" asked Jonah, surprised at the cost of salvation.

"Jesus said to that man, 'If you want to be perfect, sell everything you own and give the money to the poor. That will gain you great riches in heaven.'"

"So did he do it?" asked Jonah.

"He turned and walked away."

"Of course he did," siad Jonah, pulling his hands away.

Mary smiled at him. "I know it's hard for you," she said. "And Jesus knows it's hard. Believe me, He does. He knows we will fail. But it is still something we must strive for."

"It's not hard, Mary. It is impossible!"

"That's right, Jonah. It is impossible, but only if you do it in obeisance to law rather than out of love for God."

"You mean love God rather than fear Him?"

"Yes, Jonah. Love God and, because you do, try to act in ways that would make Him happy."

"Like giving away my money to the poor?"

"But not out of fear of being punished—because you want to, because you love God."

"That's asking a lot, even if the motive is love."

"The sacrifice is great, but so is the reward—eternal life."

"If you do as you're told."

"No, Jonah, you still don't understand. It isn't about 'doing as you're told.'"

"No, of course not. But if we don't, we get punished, right?"

"Not anymore, Jonah. Because of Jesus, we don't have to worry about our failures, for forgivness has come to us from beyond the grave."

Jonah looked at her with a quizzical grin. He didn't believe that anything or anyone had "come to us from beyond the grave." But he had learned a long time ago that you didn't argue with people about their religion. "You said something about going up to the roof?" he asked, deciding he'd let her share the food. *I'll just bring her more.* He smiled to himself.

A rickety ladder took them to a trap door built into the roof. It wasn't much, but there was a breeze, and the setting sun lowered the temperature even more. She put down her plate with the olives, bread, meat, and cheese. She and Jonah sat down around it. He opened the wine and poured a little for both of them.

"I was surprised to see you again, Jonah, especially so soon. The last time we spoke, I got the feeling that I was seeing you for the last time."

"Mary, you know that is never going to happen. If we can't be man and wife, we can be friends."

"Then let's drink to our friendship," she said, lifting her cup.

Their rooftop picnic passed pleasantly. Jonah was pouring more wine as they watched the sunset. "Mary," he said, "it's late, and there is something I have to ask you before I leave."

"You may ask me anything, Jonah."

"When we parted back in Galilee, you were..." Jonah hesitated, unsure of the right word.

"I was possessed, Jonah."

Jonah remembered those black days in Galilee. Mary had been an animal, frothing at the mouth and shouting the most hideous things at anyone foolish enough to go near her. By the time he left her, she had eaten nothing for days. The last thing he recalled was Mary tied to a bed, emaciated, delirious, and near death. He'd thought her mad and was sure he was leaving her for the last time. "What happened?" he asked. "How were you cured?"

"Not cured, Jonah, saved. It was shortly after you left—"

"I'm sorry about that," interrupted Jonah, "but I couldn't be there to watch you die. I only hope you can forgive me."

"There is nothing to forgive. Just as there was nothing you could do." Mary closed her eyes. When she opened them, Jonah could see the tears she was struggling to hold back. "I had broken free of the ropes that held me to my bed and was wandering the wilderness, barely alive, my soul in constant torment. I must have wandered into a ditch, because I remember I was rolling in the mud like some wild pig, screaming profanities at the sky. Suddenly, Jesus was standing over me, looking down at me with the most beatific smile I have ever seen. And He pointed at me, and then He cried, 'Come out of that woman, you filthy devil.' And the devil, speaking through my mouth, shouted back at Him, 'What have I to do with you, Jesus, Son of the Most High?' And then Jesus asked the demon its name, and the demon responded that he had seven names, for there were seven of them inside me."

"Seven?" Jonah asked. "And you think Jesus cast them out?"

"I know it," she said with a look of such certainty that it forced him to turn away, unable to see it as anything but smugness. "And He did more than cast out demons. He saved me, Jonah. And Jesus can save you."

"Not if it's going to cost me everything I own," he scoffed, getting up and walking to the roof's edge. "I don't need saving that badly."

"Not everything, Jonah. As I told you before, we follow the word of God, but not as if it were the word of Rome. Ceasar gives us orders; God gives us love. We follow Rome because we must, and we try to get away with as much as we can. But for the ones we love, we *do* as much as we can. We bend laws, but love, true love, never bends. Would you not gladly give your life out of love for your wife or children?"

"You know I would, Mary."

"But there is no law commanding you to give up your life. Yet you would do it anyway. Can you not see the difference between the law and love?"

She waited patiently for an answer to her question, but none was forth coming.

She watched him standing there with his back to her. "Oh, Jonah," she cried out after him. "How am I ever going to open that heart of yours?"

"An open heart is a weak heart," he said, turning back to face her. "I like mine the way it is—closed."

"No you don't."

"What makes you so sure?"

"A closed heart would not have brought me this wonderful picnic."

"What about a foolish one?" he asked, unable to keep a smile from his lips.

On his way home, Mary's words were still with him. Was he the man of stone he claimed to be? Did he still want to be? *If I'm honest with myself, I have to admit that I don't.* He thought again of Mary. Despite her poverty, he was more than a little envious. *To have so little, but to want even less. What must that be like?* he asked himself. He could come up with no clear answer.

Later that night, he followed her again. She went to a market place deep in the poorest part of Jerusalem. She found the poorest of the poor, lepers and the crippled, the blind, the helpless, and the hopeless, and as he had expected, she gave away all the food. "Probably saved a bit for that mongrel dog," he muttered to himself.

Mary took the last of her food to a dying man. He lay on a moth-eaten blanket in a filthy alleyway. She helped him to sit up, resting his back against the alley wall. His flesh was pock-marked with bites and sores where the rats and insects had attacked him. Patiently, she gave the man a little water and a mouthful of food.

Hidden by the darkness, Jonah slid closer. The dying man was on his third mouthful when he suddenly choked and started throwing up. Mary wiped his mouth with the piece of cloth the food had been wrapped in. He took some more water. "Are you all right?' she asked.

"I'm feeling a little better. I guess I shouldn't take such large mouthfuls."

"Would you like a little more? Perhaps some water?"

"No, not right now."

"Is there anything I can get you?"

"You've already brought me the one thing I thought I'd never see—kindness."

"I wish I could do more."

"No, you don't understand. For so long—as long as I can remember—all I have known is cruelty. Now, as I face death, I have known a little kindness. Thank you."

Jonah was unable to put his finger on what it was that caused him to suddenly reveal himself. Perhaps he was finally starting to understand the Nazarene's message of love over law. Perhaps he could finally see the difference between acting because the law commands it and acting solely for love. Silently walking over to Mary, he took off his warm, wool cloak and handed it to Mary, who took the cloak but said not a word.

She was surprised to see Jonah, but she was even more surprised by the donation of his cloak. "It'll help keep the poor man warm," he said before walking away.

"Thank you, Jonah," she called out to him.

He turned as if to say something, but too confused by the conflicting emotions and thoughts colliding inside of him, he just waved good-bye then continued on his way.

Mary wrapped the old man in Jonah's cloak. She stayed with him until, just before dawn he closed his eyes for the last time.

EVIL PAYS A VISIT

SEVENTEEN DAYS UNTIL BETHANY

Mary was sharing the last of Jonah's gift, providing her four-legged friend with a late-night snack. They were standing by her front door. The dog had his head buried in his food bowl. Mary, her back turned to the alley that connected her house with the main street, waited patiently for him to finish. Suddenly, the dog's ears snapped to attention. The dog lifted his head and, turning in the direction of the approaching intruder, growled quietly. "What's wrong boy?" she asked, still unaware of the approaching threat.

He came at them from out of the shadows of the alley. The dog moved to the attack, getting between Mary and the intruder, forcing him to keep his distance. "Uzziah!" shrieked Mary. She had not seen the man for years, not since the demons had taken possession of her.

He was a tall, thin man with a long, pointed face, ferociously bad breath, and a smile that never quite looked sincere. He gave Mary a quick once over and grunted. He was not happy about what he saw. "What have you done to yourself, Mary?" he asked dismissively. "The Mary I know knew how to make the most of what she had. But now?" he said, looking her over a second time. "Woman, you look like a damn peasant."

"I am a peasant, Uzziah."

"When you ran away back in Galilee, I thought the demons had gotten you for sure."

"Well, you were wrong. I was saved."

"So I see. So I see. You know a little work on your hair, your face." Uzziah paused to reach out and run his hand along her right cheek. "You might still be worth something."

The dog snapped at the man's offending hand, forcing Uzziah to jump back. He looked down at the creature snarling at his feet. He shoved the dog away with the heel of his boot. A petty thief and a pimp, he made his living by hurting things.

Seeing the blow coming, the dog dodged the kick and bit into Uzziah's ankle. Uzziah angrily tried to shake his leg free of the dog. The dog was having none of it. The pimp reached for the knife tucked into his belt.

Mary knelt down and got her hands around the dog. "There, fellow," she said soothingly. "It's all right. Let go of his ankle now."

In deference to Mary's insistence, the dog relinquished the ankle. Her arm around the dog's neck, she whispered into his ear. "Don't you worry, boy. He'll be gone soon."

Uzziah reached down to check his ankle. "You'd better do something about that cur, Mary."

"He does as he pleases," she said, the dog continuing to growl menacingly from her arms.

"Looks thin as well as mean. I'll bet he's hungry." Uzziah reached inside his cloak. "Well let's see what we've got here," he said, pulling out a piece of chicken. "My lunch," he said, waving the flesh in the dog's face. The growling abated. "Hey, you like that? You want it? Go get it!" He threw the meat as far as he could. The animal jumped out of Mary's arms and made a beeline for the chicken. "That solves that problem," Uzziah said with a smirk. "So, Mary," he said, moving closer. "I've got a little proposition for you."

"I can't help you, Uzziah. I've changed."

"So I've heard," said Uzziah caustically. Mary moved for her door. He cut her off with a surprising, cat-like quickness. "Going somewhere, Mary?"

"I'd like to go inside," she said.

He stepped closer. His foul breath forced Mary's back to the wall. "What?" he asked. "You haven't got a moment to spare for an old friend?"

"What is it you want?" she asked, not wanting to hear the answer.

"I want you," he said, deftly placing a powerful forearm on either side of her head.

The meaning of his words caused her knees to wobble. *I have only my faith to protect me,* she thought, *but it is enough?* "I'm not the woman you remember," she said calmly.

"You look the same," he said, smiling. "A little worse for wear, but still worth a shekel or two."

"Please, Uzziah, I have to go back inside. There is much I have to do." Ducking under Uzziah's left arm, she tried again to reach the door. She didn't get very far.

He caught her by the shoulder and pulled her into his chest. He smiled at her. "You know, Mary, if I didn't know better, I'd say you weren't happy to see me."

Mary looked up at him defiantly. "I'm finished with people like you, Uzziah."

Uzziah shoved her into the wall. Her breath left her in a whoosh. "That's too bad," he said, "because I'm holding a party for some centurions."

"I can no…longer…work for you."

The smile disappeared. A dark cloud passed over his face. In a deliberately savage motion, he grabbed Mary by the throat and banged her head against the wall. Loose bits of mortar fell to the ground. "This is what you're going to do, Mary," he said in an angry whisper. "You are going to get yourself prettied up." He shoved a few coins into her hand. "Buy some new clothes. In a week, I'm going to come back, and you are going to give some fine Roman gentlemen a lesson in love."

Fear she could taste it at the back of her throat and feel it in her legs. "Take back your money," she said, pushing the coins back into his hand. "I want nothing to do with you."

Uzziah looked at the coins and thrust them into his cloak pocket. "We'll see about that," he said, lifting her off her feet and forcibly carrying her into her tiny house.

The dog looked up from his food just in time to see Uzziah carry her into the house. The front door was still open. He could hear Mary fighting inside. He made for it.

Mary was on the ground on her back, facing the door. Uzziah was standing over her. Grinning, he threw off his cloak. He undid his belt, and it slid off his hips. Mary noticed the glint of the knife bouncing off the floor.

He heard the dog at the last second but was too slow to fend him off. The dog's fangs dug in where neck meets shoulder. Uzziah reached for his knife. It wasn't there. He searched the room for an alternative. Mary stuck out her leg, trying to trip him, missing by inches. No weapon at hand, Uzziah backed up against a wall, sandwiching the dog between him and the wall. Then he thrust his back into the wall. The animal squealed then slid lifelessly to the floor.

What followed was too vicious to be remembered clearly. A kick to her solar plexus knocked the wind out of her, and she was gasping painfully for breath as Uzziah threw off his blood-stained tunic to stand above her naked.

He finished quickly.

Mary drifted in and out of consciousness. He took the coins she had returned to him and put them back into her hand. Putting on his blood-soaked tunic, cloak, and belt, he walked away.

Mary watched him leave, the coins falling slowly, one by one, from her hand.

I WON'T LET HER DOWN

SEVENTEEN DAYS UNTIL BETHANY

Jonah found Mary on the floor, conscious, but unable to get up. The dog was at her side licking her face, its right hind leg broken, blood dripping from the wound at the back of its head. Going to Mary, Jonah incurred the animal's growl. Mary, summoning all the strength she could, scratched the top of its head. The decibel level of the growl faded. He got as close as he dared then he squatted down for a better look. "Are you hurt badly, Mary?" he asked.

"I don't think so."

"Can you get up?"

"I tried a little while ago, but lifting my head causes the room to spin horribly."

"Then stay still."

"How is the dog, Jonah?"

"The back of his head is bloody, and I think he's broken a leg."

"Oh my goodness," she exclaimed. "Here, let me take a look," she said, trying to sit up.

He reached out to stop her, and the dog grabbed for the sleeve of his tunic. Moving with only three legs wasn't easy, but he did his best. Jonah pulled back his hand. "Please, Mary," he remonstrated, "don't try to move."

Mary lifted her head a foot or so off the floor, her weight supported by her elbows. A wave of nausea swept over her. "Oh my," she said.

"Mary what is it?"

"I don't know? I just...oh, I better lay down," she replied, setting her head back on the floor.

"That's good, Mary. Stay down." Jonah took off his cloak, thinking to use it as a pillow, but when he went to slide the cloak under Mary's head, the dog would have none of it. He had to circle around Mary's prostrate body and slide his rolled-up cloak under her head from the other side. "How does that feel, Mary?" he asked, standing up.

"Better, Jonah, better. I thought I was going to be sick, but it's passed now."

"It's because you tried to get up. Just stay still. I'll get some help."

"What about the dog, Jonah?" she asked, her hand scratching the dog's chin.

"I'll get help for him too," he said. "Don't worry, Mary," he said gravely. "I won't let you down. Not like last time—not like Galilee."

Mary smiled weakly at him. "I know you won't, Jonah."

He ran to the end of the alley and stopped. He knew of a good Greek doctor. He had used the man several times in the past. The doctor's office was near the top of the upper city. He could try to run it, but it was a long way, most of it up hill. Off in the distance, he heard the tingle of a dairy man's bell; he was making his early morning deliveries. It was coming from the east and getting closer.

He had to buy the farmer's entire stock before the man agreed to take Jonah to his Greek doctor. The doctor was busy. Jonah's money convinced him that he wasn't as busy as he thought.

Mary was unconscious, the dog at her side. The animal managed to stand on his three good legs and growl defiantly as Jonah and the doctor entered the house. "I'm sorry," exclaimed the doctor, stopping beside Jonah just inside the doorway, "but you didn't say anything about a wild dog."

"Shut up, doctor. The animal's half dead."

"That's when they're the most dangerous." The doctor tried to leave.

Jonah took hold of his arm and pulled him back inside. "You're not going anywhere, doctor."

"I will do as I please," declared the doctor defiantly, trying unsuccessfully to disengage his arm from Jonah's iron grip. Jonah tightened his hold. He used the arm to hoist the doctor up on his toes. "Hey, let go, Jonah, that hurts!"

Jonah looked deeply into the doctor's eyes. "The dog is hurt, not rabid," he said coldly. "And that woman's life is worth more to me than ten of yours. So you're going to stay, and you're going to help her, or so help me God, this hut will be the last thing you ever see."

The doctor looked from Jonah's determined face to the growling sneer of the dog. "Look, Jonah, be reasonable," he said, "there's not much I can do with that dog trying to bite my face off, now is there?"

Jonah looked back at the dog, its teeth bared. Reluctantly, he granted the doctor his point. "I'll take care of the dog," he said.

"Fine, now let go of my arm, please?"

Jonah tired to determine if the doctor was likely to make another run for it. In the end he couldn't see what choice he had. "All right," he said, releasing his grip, "but if you try to run away, I'll—"

"You'll kill me. Yes, I know," interrupted the doctor. "I've heard it somewhere before, but you said something about taking care of our canine friend?"

Jonah looked at the dog and felt a sudden burst of admiration. The pain from the broken leg had to be excruciating. His head was leaking blood. Yet there he was, decisive, defiant, determined to defend his friend.

Jonah nodded his head out of respect for the animal's loyalty. He saw Mary's eyes open, and a smile spread across his face. "Mary," he whispered, "you're awake."

"Jonah?" she called out weakly. "Is that you?"

"Yes, Mary. I'm right here. I've brought a doctor."

At the sound of her voice, the dog limped closer and licked her face.

Jonah, taking advantage of the dog's preoccupation with Mary, crept closer. The dog leapt over Mary. Jumping on three legs wasn't easy, and landing was impossible. As the weight of his body hit the floor, the pain from his broken leg was too much. With a heart-wrenching yelp, the animal fell flat on its face. Jonah took another step closer. The dog lifted its head, baring its teeth.

Jonah stopped dead in his tracks. "Don't worry, fella," he said in a comforting tone. "We're not here to hurt Mary. I love her too."

The dog tried to charge and fell again. "Get it now!" shouted the doctor excitedly.

"Keep quiet, you fool. You're only making things worse," said Jonah, glaring angrily at the doctor. He circled slowly to his left, trying to get around the dog, who had somehow managed to get back on its feet. This time, the animal looked to be more comfortable on only three legs. He wobbled across the floor just fast enough to stay between Jonah and his Mary.

The dog wasn't going to let him get near Mary, so Jonah stopped trying. He called out to her. "Mary," he whispered, "can you hear me? It's about the dog."

"What do you want me to do?" she asked hoarsely.

"We need to get the dog away from you, Mary, for the doctor."

"He's not going to like that," replied Mary.

"I know, but if you keep talking to him, keep him calm, then he might let me take him outside."

"He could bite you."

"Wouldn't be the first time. Now start talking, Mary. Get him to relax."

Mary talked to the dog about moments they had shared together. She talked to him about the rat he brought to her as a present. She reminded him of the big bone she had given him. The growling stopped.

Slowly, Jonah inched forward. From his relative safety by the door the doctor watched intently, anxious to see what was going to happen next.

Mary scratching his head, the sound of her voice soothing his fears, the dog took no notice of Jonah's slow encroachment. When he got close enough to touch the dog, he added his own voice to Mary's. "That's a good dog," he said. "Nobody is going to hurt you." Slowly he reached out his hand to join Mary's in scratching its head. The dog growled but did not bite.

Jonah, crouching low so as to appear less threatening, took out a piece of meat that was supposed to be his lunch and offered it to the dog. The dog sniffed at it then wolfed it down.

"Good boy," said Jonah. "You like that?" he asked.

The dog barked hungrily in response. A smile came over Jonah's face. "Of course you do. Here, have some more," he said, pulling out another piece. The dog accepted it gleefully.

"I think he likes you," said Mary.

"He likes my lunch." Jonah smiled before trying to pick him up.

The growling returned. As his paws left the floor, the growl became a snarl. Jonah stopped lifting.

She almost passed out, but somehow, Mary hoisted herself up on one elbow. She reached around with her other arm and hugged the dog. Suspended in Jonah's strong arms, Mary hugging him, her face pressed up against his flank, the dog relented. The snarling stopped.

Jonah continued lifting. The dog looked to Mary. Her comforting eyes assured him that it was all right.

Jonah carried the dog towards the door. The doctor slid nervously out of his way. Jonah paused, letting the dog get a good look outside. Mary was still offering words of encouragement. Jonah gave the dog the last of his meat. Then he stepped outside.

Jonah held his breath, waiting for the animal to rip out his throat. To his great relief, it didn't.

He got the farmer to keep his mouth shut by promising him a few more coins. He then placed the dog on a blanket in the back of the cart. "There you go," he said. "You rest here. Mary will be with you in no time." Jonah gave him a playful scratch on the top of the head and turned back to Mary.

The dog, seeing that he was being left behind, struggled to its feet and barked at Jonah's departing form. Jonah saw the dog standing shakily on three legs. It had lost a lot of blood. His broken leg was shooting fresh waves of pain through his nervous system, but he wasn't going to leave Mary. He wasn't going to desert her. "Just relax," said Jonah, walking back to the cart and trying to get the dog to lie down, "Mary is going to be all right. You just take it easy, and the doctor will tend to your wounds in a little while."

The dog seemed to reluctantly give in to Jonah's gentle but persistent efforts. "There, that's a good dog," Jonah said, giving the animal a pat on the head. He was about to step back inside the house when he heard something hit the ground behind him, followed by a painful howl.

It moved him more than he would have thought possible. The wounded dog, its broken leg thrust out from its body at a cruel and unnatural angle, was crawling towards him. He watched the dog, and he remembered Galilee. He remembered how running from Mary had been so easy. He remembered how much she had needed him and how difficult it had been to be near her. Watching as the demons slowly destroyed her. And he realized that the dog was teaching him a lesson, the same lesson Mary had been trying to teach him. The dog was not obeying any orders. He was acting out of love. Only love. It was a lesson Jonah was never going to forget. "All right, boy," he said. "You win." He picked up the animal and carried him into the house.

"I've changed my mind," he said. "This fella has earned the right to be here." The doctor opened his mouth to protest, but seeing the dark look in Jonah's eyes, kept his complaints to himself.

In between looks over his shoulder at Jonah and the dog, the doctor took her pulse, listened to her breathing, and felt her forehead to check her temperature. "Her pulse is good," he said. "She has no temperature, and her breathing is unobstructed."

"So she's going to be all right?"

"I think so." The doctor mixed a white powder in some water and had Mary drink it.

"What is it, doctor?" asked Jonah.

"It's an opiate. It will ease her pain."

"What about the dizziness?" asked Mary.

"That should leave you over time."

"But when will I be able to get up?"

"Who can say? You've suffered a blow to the brain. There's nothing we can do but wait for your brain to heal."

"But surely, doctor," inquired Jonah, "you have some idea of how long that will be?"

"A few hours, a few days, a few months, who can say? Now, Jonah, she'll need someone to look after her and a proper bed to sleep on."

"Don't worry, doctor, I'll take care of both of them," said Jonah, scratching under the dog's chin."

Placing a cool damp cloth upon Mary's head, the doctor turned his attention to the dog. He used more of the opiate to put the animal to sleep and then set the leg. Jonah carried both patients out to the farmer's cart, neither of them feeling any pain. The farmer, after Jonah dropped even more coins into his hand, agreed to take everyone back to Jonah's home.

They were about to leave when the doctor pulled Jonah aside and spoke to him privately. "She's been raped, Jonah," said the doctor.

Jonah's eyes widened. The relief he had felt over getting both patients safely into the farmer's cart left him. An ominous anger passed over him. "Are you sure?" he asked.

"Of course I'm sure. I offered her a mixture of Silphium and wine, but she refused."

"Did you tell her the silphium would prevent any pregnancy?"

"I did, but she said she would not kill a life to make her own easier. I assumed she was still suffering from the effects of the attack, so I saved some of the mixture. Here," said the doctor, handing Jonah a small vial, "this should be enough to help her, but she must take it soon."

"Thank you, doctor," said Jonah, taking the vial but knowing Mary would never use it. "Why don't you get in the cart, doctor? I'll be along. I just want a final look around."

Back in the hut, he took a careful inventory of the room. He saw the dog's blood on the wall. He saw the coins. He picked them up then nodded his head knowingly. "Uzziah," he muttered angrily under his breath.

FORGIVENESS

SIXTEEN DAYS UNTIL BETHANY

It was located near the top of the eastern slope of the upper city, overlooking the Zion Bridge that spanned the Tyropeon valley. It was a fine house once owned by a caravan merchant who had fallen on hard times. The merchant owed one of Jonah's clients a substantial amount of money. He sold Jonah the Mediterranean style home, with its open courtyard and beautiful mosaic floors, in return for Jonah taking care of his debt. Jonah settled the debt for half of the outstanding amount. It was the only way he could have afforded such a luxurious home.

Jonah had been doing something he had never done before: He had willingly placed the needs of others above his own. Even the dog had only to cry out, and he was immediately at its side. He had given the mutt a name—Odysseus, because of his loyalty.

Jonah had discovered something he would not have believed possible. It had been late last night. He had just returned from taking Odysseus for his evening stroll. Tired, he lay down upon his bed. Before falling off to sleep, he thought about how happy he was. *I've been serving Mary and Odysseus like a slave, and I've never been happier. Could it be?* he asked himself. *That true joy can only be found in the service of others?*

He never showed her the silphium. When he asked about the possibility of her being with child, she had smiled at him, saying only that if it was God's will that she bring a new life into this world she would not do anything to oppose it. He had thought about the idea of having Uzziah's child walking around beside her, and he had been unable to accept it. *I don't know what I'll do*, he told himself. *But if it's what Mary wants, I'll do my best to respect it.*

He didn't press her about what happened. He waited until he was sure she was feeling better. The woman he had coming in to help with the cooking and cleaning had left for the night. Mary was seated by the fire, Odysseus at her feet. He walked over and stood beside her. "So tell me," he said casually, "and the truth now. Who did this to you?"

"What does it matter?" she asked, looking up at his worried face. "I'm well now."

Jonah's eyes narrowed; his jaw stiffened. He was determined to control his temper. But the rage that swept over him whenever he contemplated the horror of what had been done to her could not be held in check. "Whoever did this to you must pay."

"Vengeance," she said quietly, "will not change what has been done."

"The man who did this to you must be punished."

"Punishment—an eye for an eye—right, Jonah?"

"Is that not what the Bible says, Mary?"

"Jesus said we should bless them that curse us, do good to them that hate us, and pray for them who despitefully use us and persecute us."

"Surely Jesus was not referring to the sort of man who attacked you?"

"You tell me, Jonah. Who was Jesus referring to when He said, 'God sends rain on the just and on the unjust'?"

"God can be forgiving, Mary, but I'm just a man."

Mary rested her cheek upon Jonah's hand. The feel of her cheek forced a smile to his lips, but it did not take the anger from his heart. "Give me his name," he said gravely.

Letting go of his hands, she sat back. "And if I do, what will you do?"

"I will see to it that he does not go unpunished."

"Leave his punishment to God," she implored him.

"God will have His chance. I just want to make it sooner rather than later."

"And that is why I cannot give you his name."

Jonah reached into his pocket and took out Uzziah's coins. "Who gave you these?" he asked, his voice thick with accusation.

At the sight of the coins, she looked away.

"It was Uzziah, wasn't it?"

Mary couldn't lie, and she couldn't tell him the truth. She knew the tears were coming. She jumped up, pushed her way past him and ran to her room. Odysseus, jostled out of his sleep, started to follow her then stopped to look at Jonah, not understanding what had happened. "Go on, boy," Jonah encouraged. "Go to Mary." The dog barked and then scampered off to her room.

Jonah looked at the coins, wishing he'd never asked the question and that there was some way he could get beyond his anger and instinctive need for revenge. But he knew what his darker side demanded of him. There was only one way to quench the demon that lived inside him. That was with the sword. He tossed the coins into the fire. He knew what he had to do.

He left Mary with Odysseus and went in search of Uzziah. The owner of a tavern where Uzziah trolled for customers informed him that Uzziah, apparently having eaten something that did not agree with him, had gone home early to rest.

Jonah headed straight for the address given to him by the owner of the bar. Overhead, storm clouds were gathering. Lightning illuminated the sky, followed by the ominous rumbling of distant thunder. Jonah's anger grew with every step. The hate he felt for Uzziah knew no bounds. Like a virus, it started somewhere deep in the most ancient, reptilian part of his brain then worked its way down his spinal cord until it reached his stomach, where it twisted in his bowels. Pausing to catch his breath, Jonah could feel his heart pounding, the blood raging through his veins. Just around the corner from Uzziah's house, Jonah stopped to check the condition of his blade. The pimp was a man well practised in the art of killing. He would not die easily. He was holding up his sword, trying to examine the blade in the light of his torch, when the sky exploded.

The lightning shattered his sword. Only the fact that he had been holding the ivory handle saved his life. Even so, the strike left him unconscious. He awoke minutes later to the sound of soldiers nearby. He got to his feet and stumbled along in the direction of the soldiers.

They were attacking Uzziah's home. From inside the house, Jonah could hear cursing, the sound of blades clashing, and furniture being overturned. A man cried out in pain, then another. Then Uzziah's voice, squealing, was followed by a final, anguished scream. Then silence. A moment later, they carried out Uzziah's body, dumping the pimp onto a cart. Jonah watched the cart move off and contemplated his luck. If not for the lightning, he would have ended up beside the pimp, the two of them headed for a common grave.

Jonah walked past the shredded remnants of his sword and shook his head. He looked up at a sky that was now unexpectedly clear and winked knowingly. He had no idea why, but God had saved him. He only hoped he would prove worthy.

Later that night, before a roaring fire, Odysseus sleeping between them, the dog's leg still heavily wrapped, Jonah told Mary what had happened. "I was dead set on killing him after what he did to you. I know I promised no more violence, but I couldn't let him live."

"So why did you not kill him? What stopped you?"

"A storm rolled in from the desert. The last thing I remember, I was examining my sword before waking up on my back, on the pavement, my sword shattered into a dozen pieces."

"You were struck by lightning?"

"I think so."

"Are you hurt?"

"A sore back, but I'm fine."

"And what of Uzziah?" she asked.

"He's dead."

"But I thought you said—"

"I didn't kill him, Mary. Roman soldiers did. They were after Uzziah for killing a Roman officer over a bad debt. They showed up to arrest Uzziah just after I was struck. He put up a fight. He lost. The lightning saved my life. I would have been with Uzziah when the Romans arrived. God saved me, Mary. Despite all my sins, He saved me."

"All life is precious, even the life of sinners. God loves us all, Jonah."

"I know that, Mary. I thought I knew it before, but now I truly understand. It's helped me to understand why you did not take the silphium."

Long after Mary had gone to bed, Odysseus at her side, Jonah went to say thank you. He left the city by the gate of Gennath and went straight to Golgotha. There, he climbed up to His place of execution and asked the Son of God to forgive him. Eyes closed, head raised towards the heavens, he kept repeating the same words over and over again.

"Lord, make me worthy of your forgiveness. Lord, make me worthy of your forgiveness."

And as he prayed, the hate he felt for his father, for a world that had always shown him the back of its hand, the hate he had carried with him like a favourite childhood toy, too precious, too full of memories to ever part with, slowly receded from his soul.

Love in His Heart

Fifteen Days until Bethany

H e sent the cook away. When Mary and Odysseus entered the kitchen, they found him preparing breakfast. "Jonah, what are you doing?" she asked.

"Breakfast," he replied, deftly moving about the kitchen like a man who knew what he was doing.

"I didn't know you could cook?" she marvelled, walking over to where he was taking fresh bread out of a small clay oven.

"As a boy, my master assigned me to help in the kitchen. I picked up a few things. Now sit down have a little wine. Breakfast will be served in just a moment."

And a fine breakfast it was. Fresh bread with lots of butter and honey, fresh grapes and figs, a heaping plate of eggs scrambled with a delicious local cheese, a delicately seasoned, slightly cold roast chicken, and to wash it all down, his last bottle of Chalybonium.

They ate heartily, and afterwards, Jonah helped Mary take the leftovers to those who lived in the squalor of the lower city. The sun was high in the sky by the time they returned home. Seated together on a stone bench in the courtyard, Jonah could not keep from smiling. It was then that Mary mentioned going home.

"Why can't you stay?" he pleaded. "There's lots of room."

"Jonah, I am grateful for your help, but I can't continue to live here as if I were your wife."

Jonah leaned forward. He'd been planning to plead his case to her one more time, waiting for the right moment. "Mary," he began "I'm glad you mentioned *wife* because—"

"Oh, Jonah, I thought we had settled this?"

"I want to change, Mary. I've saved enough money to buy a farm, a good farm."

"You'd give up your way of life?"

"I want to, Mary, but I need your help. With you, I can be reborn."

"What you ask of me—you don't understand. I promised God. I promised myself."

"Do you love me, Mary?'

"I love the man you could be."

"Help me be that man."

Mary looked at him, her eyes brimming with tears. "I can't give you an answer this morning. If you must have it now, it will be no. I need time to pray for guidance."

"Take all the time you need. Only stay."

"But I've already been here too long."

"So a few more days won't matter."

Alone in her room, Mary tried to sort out her feelings. She would not lie to herself. She would not deny that something true and real had passed between her and Jonah. The man who had deserted her in Galilee had saved her life and that of Odysseus. He had given of himself willingly. And this morning, as they had handed out food to the hungry, she had not seen the old Jonah with anger in his heart, vengeance on his mind, and a sword in his hand. This morning, Jonah had love in his heart, charity on his mind, and a basket of food in his hand.

YES!

FIFTEEN DAYS UNTIL BETHANY

That night, Mary found Jonah in the courtyard, praying. She hesitated before going to him, not wanting to interrupt, but also because she was still not sure what she wanted to tell him. Since the death of Uzziah, only one question had been on her mind. *What does God want me to do?*

Before Jonah had returned to her a new man, her future had been set in stone. She would serve God. Any consideration of marriage, children, or what most would call a normal life was out of the question. From the moment Jesus had delivered her from the demons, there had never been any doubt. Whatever the personal sacrifice, her life had a higher calling.

So how had this man shaken her resolve? She'd always had a soft spot in her heart for him. She had been a whore, and Jonah had been a violent man who made his living by the sword. Yet they had seen something human in each other. It drew them together. In Galilee they had reached out to each other amidst the dehumanized and dehumanizing creatures that came in and out of their lives like so much flotsam, never staying very long and leaving a slimy film in their wake.

They had lived together, although neither of them had ever considered marriage. They had not been the marrying kind. He had given her a taste of what a normal life could be like. He had protected her from Uzziah and had seen to both their needs.

But something deep within her could not abide the life Jonah had offered. The days were too long, the nights too short. As sordid as it had been, her old life possessed a certain excitement that sitting in front of a fire before turning in for the night just didn't replace.

And so, she had left him and returned to Uzziah. Throwing away her last chance, she had embraced her sinfulness with complete and utter abandon. Uzziah no longer had to scare her into doing as she was told. She was a willing employee. No client was too disgusting, no act too degrading. She was Uzziah's favourite girl. And then the demons had come.

Jesus of Nazareth had saved her. She would never forget His peaceful and serene eyes looking down at her as she had glared at him from her road-side ditch, her body covered in offal and mud, deliriously shouting obscenities at no one and everyone.

To those eyes she had dedicated herself until...now?

His prayers completed, Jonah looked up. "What are you doing?" he asked.

Mary smiled. "Realizing how much I love you," she said, wiping away an unexpected tear.

"You mean you're staying?" he asked, getting off his knees.

"I'm staying."

"Oh, Mary," he said, rapturously sweeping her up in his arms. "You've made me happy, truly happy for the first time in my life. Thank you. Thank you. Thank you," he repeated over and over again as he kissed her right cheek then her left cheek then the tip of her nose and the bottom of her chin. He looked into her eyes and saw that she was crying. Gently, he kissed them away. "God has answered my prayers, Mary," he said, smiling.

"We both have reason to thank Him," she said, taking hold of his face with her two hands and kissing him passionately.

Jonah broke off the kiss. For a moment blessed by God, he looked into the brown eyes that for too long had reflected only sorrow and saw only joy. "I love you, Mary, and out of love, I want to protect you. I want to keep you safe. Look after you when times are hard and make sure that mine is the one you reach out for when you need a helping hand."

He carried her to her bedroom and set her gently upon the bed. He hovered above her, their lips mere inches apart. An unspoken urgency passed between them.

"I should go," he said finally.

"After we're married," she whispered back to him.

He stood up. She smiled. "There's a farm I'm thinking of buying," he said. "A modest place, a few vineyards, some olive trees, a little livestock, a few cedar trees, a living, I think."

"It sounds wonderful."

"There's not much of a house."

"We don't need much."

"I'm going to build you a new house with plenty of room for children, Mary, if they come."

"When can I see this farm?"

"I was thinking perhaps in a few days."

"I can't wait."

Somehow, his smile managed to widen. "I'll make the arrangements," he said.

NOT A WASTE, A NEW BEGINNING

FOURTEEN DAYS UNTIL BETHANY

B efore going to Caiaphas, Jonah had one other stop to make. He had to visit a blacksmith who specialized in iron farm tools. After quibbling over the price, the man agreed to provide Jonah with the latest in farming technology: a plow with an iron blade. Jonah was about to leave when he looked down at the sword strapped at his side. It was no ordinary blade, but the first sword he had bought after leaving the Roman army. Jonah unsheathed the blade. "Is there something else, Jonah?" asked the blacksmith.

"Yes," said Jonah. "I was thinking maybe you could use my sword to make the blade."

"For the plow, you mean?"

"Could you do it?"

"I don't know, Jonah. Let me see the sword."

Jonah handed the sword to his friend. "Quite a blade, Jonah. Must have cost you a small fortune."

"Can you use it?"

"Sure, but such fine metal, it would be a waste to use it for a plow."

Jonah took back the blade. It had been his for eighteen years. It was more like an old friend than a mere possession. He ran his hand along the flat of the blade. He thought about how many times this long, thin piece of metal had saved his life and how many lives it had ended. He kissed it gently and then handed it over to the blacksmith. "Not a waste," he said solemnly, "a new beginning."

Jonah had worked for the high priest since his appointment by Gratus fifteen years ago. Over that time, he had come to respect and like the man. It wasn't going to be easy to tell him that he was quitting.

He really didn't want to bother Caiaphas at such a late hour, but Jonah felt as if he couldn't wait another day to get it over with. He had his employer's servants get the high priest from his bed.

"What is this about, Jonah?" asked Caiaphas, wrapping a robe around himself as he walked into the courtyard where Jonah was waiting for him. "You haven't found our body, have you?"

"That's what I wanted to talk about, Joseph."

"You mean you have found it?" asked Caiaphas exultantly.

"No, Joseph, I haven't found your missing body."

"Is there something you're not telling me, Jonah?"

"Yes, Joseph, there is." Taking out the last purse his friend had given him, Jonah handed it back to the high priest.

"What's this?" asked Caiaphas.

"Don't worry, it's all there."

"What's all there?"

"The money you paid me."

"But I don't want the money, Jonah. I want you watching Lucius and Aaron and the disciples and all the other followers of the Nazarene. I need you helping me."

"You will have to find someone else to help you."

"Jonah, whatever are you talking about?"

"I've bought a farm, Joseph."

"You're going to be a farmer?" asked a surprised Caiaphas.

"I'm going to try."

"Farming is a noble profession, Jonah, but what do you know about working the land?"

"I can learn."

"Then I pray that you succeed and that somehow I get along without you."

"You'll be fine. You're too smart to be destroyed by a man like Lucius and his decadent paymaster in Tiberias."

"I hope you're right, Jonah. Can you answer me one question?"

"I can try."

"Why?"

Jonah was never able to explain it. He had been determined not to reveal the whole truth to Caiaphas. The smart play was to tell the high priest he was going to be a farmer and leave it at that. But God had come into his life, and something inside of him wasn't going to let him walk away without acknowledging that fact. "I have found God," he said.

Caiaphas smiled. "That's wonderful, Jonah, but what does it have to do with working for me?"

"I can't work for you because I don't believe the body of Jesus was stolen. There is no body, Joseph."

"There has to be a body, Jonah."

"Jesus lives, Joseph."

"Jonah, you don't believe that?"

"I believe it with every fibre of my being, Joseph," said Jonah as he turned and walked away.

BREAD AND A LITTLE LOVE

THIRTEEN DAYS UNTIL BETHANY

Philippus experienced another sleepless night thanks to the constant throbbing of his infected arm. He had spent the night reading about how the Nazarene had fed thousands of people from just a loaf of bread and a fish. *The more I read about this Jesus of Nazareth*, marvelled Philippus, *the more incredible He becomes.*

He needed a break from his reading and walked over to the shuttered window. Opening the shutters, he looked out into the dark night sky. The window opened to the east, and he was hoping for a glimpse of the sun. All he saw was blackness. He was closing the shutters when, far off on the eastern horizon, the morning sun winked at him. He watched the soft white light spread over the horizon like warm butter, an inspiration overcame him.

He sought out a baker near the lower city. He bought as much fresh bread as he could carry. A farmer on his way to market gave him directions to a public square known as a place where beggars spent the night.

Not sure what he might face alone amongst the poorest of the poor, he found the square awash in hopeless souls. Most were still asleep. They came awake at the smell of so much bread. Like a pack of wild animals desperate to get theirs before the bread ran out, they came at him. He didn't want to frighten anyone but saw no alternative, he drew his sword.

The glint of the sharp metal in the early morning sunshine stopped the hungry in their tracks. In a panic, they backed away. Sheathing his sword, he held up his hands, palms out. "Don't run," he told them. "I've brought plenty for everyone." The hungry mass looked at him, unsure what to make of him. They wanted the bread, but not the sword.

Philippus broke off a piece of bread and offered it to the man closest to him. The man hesitated for a second then grabbed the bread from his hand. The others surged forward. Philippus fed as many as he could.

The bread vanished in the blink of an eye. He bought more. That vanished too. A third load finally sated the hungry mob. He was on his way to the tomb, when something tugged at the hem of his tunic. He saw a dirt-encrusted child, her eyes filled with tears, staring up at him. "Please, sir," she said. "Might I have a little bread too?"

"Where are your parents?" he asked her.

"They're gone," she said.

"Gone?"

"I haven't seen them since…since I don't remember."

"Then who looks after you?"

The child shrugged. "I do," she said.

He looked her over closely for the first time. Her skin was sallow, her eyes watery. On her arms and legs were sores that looked as if they would never heal. Her hair was scraggly and dirty. Her tunic, or what was left of it, had a hard time qualifying as a rag. She stank and was constantly scratching at the flea bites that covered her body. Smiling at her, offering her his hand, he said, "Let's get you something to eat."

He took her to a small cafe on the edge of the lower city. They shared a good breakfast of fresh bread, boiled eggs, and sweet raisins. She really liked the raisins. She told him her name was Ruth. Her father had been a farmer who had lost his farm. Her family had come to the city, her father hoping to find work. They ended up beggars. They slept where they could in alleys, doorways, or sidewalks. One morning, she wasn't sure how long ago, she woke up and her parents were gone. She'd fended for herself ever since.

After breakfast, they were standing on the street in front of the café. Philippus couldn't decide what he was going to do with her. *I can't just return her to the street, but what choice do I have?* He looked at her and did his best to smile. She smiled back. For a long moment, they stood there looking at one another. Then she took his hand. Her tiny fingers clung to his. Philippus knew his decision had been made. She wasn't going to let go, and neither was he.

He took her back to the palace, where he got her cleaned up and gave her a new tunic. Then he took her to the tomb. He hadn't decided on the long term. He only knew he wasn't sending her back out to live on the street. Ruth was impressed when the guards at the tomb saluted Philippus then moved respectfully out of his way. "You must be very important," she said.

"Not really," he answered.

"But those soldiers, they saluted you."

"They don't know any better."

"So why are we here?"

The question brought him up short. *Why am I here?* he asked himself. "The body that was buried here has been stolen," he said. "It's my job to find out who did it."

"So you're looking for clues?" she asked.

He told Ruth she was right, even though he knew she wasn't. He'd been over every square inch of this tomb. There was nothing new for him to find, and yet here he was. One of the guards approached. "Yes? What is it?" he asked.

"Sorry to bother you, sir, but there's a woman asking to see you."

"A woman?"

"She says she knows you, sir."

"Did she say what she wanted?"

"She wants to pray at the tomb—said you'd authorized it in the past."

Philippus didn't need to ask for her name. "Let her pass," he said. The guard turned and, with a wave of his hand, ordered his compatriots to step aside. Mary made her way to the tomb. Turning to Ruth, he said, "You're going to like this woman."

"I am?"

"Yes, Ruth, you are." He didn't mention that Mary was one of his prime suspects. "Mary." He smiled. "You've come to pray?"

"I have. And who is this cute little thing?" she asked, smiling at Ruth.

"My name is Ruth. I'm with Philippus."

"You didn't tell me you had a child."

"I didn't. We met today."

"He was feeding people bread, only he ran out before I could get any, so he bought me breakfast. And now we're best friends, right?" she asked, looking up at Philippus.

"Right," exclaimed Philippus, nodding good naturedly.

"Really?" asked Mary, turning to look at Philippus.

"Don't ask me why," said Philippus with a shrug.

"Of course you know why," said Mary. "You did it because you knew it was right."

"He did it because he likes me," Ruth said, clutching Philippus's hand to her cheek.

"I do like you, Ruth," he said. Smiling at the scruffy creature clinging to his hand, Philippus felt himself imbued with an unexpected sense of well-being. He might even have called it happiness. He wasn't sure. He hadn't been happy for a long time. He remembered the jewellery he'd extorted from the follower of Bacchus back in Antioch. He remembered throwing the jewellery at Helena's feet and how much unhappiness it had brought. "Yes, acquiring those jewels really did both of us a world of good," he muttered sarcastically to himself.

Ruth started playing with his fingers. She was so unlike the little girl who had first pulled on his tunic. She was happy. He had made her happy, and yes—now he was sure—that made him happy. *Do unto others*, he thought to himself.

"Are you and Ruth going to spend the day together?" asked Mary.

"I'd like that!" said Ruth.

He smiled at Ruth. The smile vanished as he looked at Mary. "She has no parents, no home."

"So what are you going to do?"

Philippus paused before answering. "I don't know, Mary."

"Can't I stay with you?" asked Ruth, the happiness gone from her voice.

Philippus crouched down to speak to her face-to-face. "Ruth, you don't want to stay with me."

"Yes I do."

"But I live in Rome."

"I don't care."

Philippus stood up and shrugged halfheartedly at Mary. "I think," said Mary good naturedly, "that I know of two good people who would love to adopt Ruth."

"I don't want to be adopted," cried Ruth, hiding behind Philippus. "I want to stay with Philippus."

With the frightened child hiding behind him, Philippus felt as if a knife had pierced his heart. "Are you sure, Mary?" he asked. "They'd give Ruth a good home?"

"They have a small farm. God has not blessed them with a child, and no one would be happier to give Ruth a loving home than they would."

Crouching again, he asked, "Ruth wouldn't you like to have a real home of your own?"

"Why can't I have a real home with you?"

Philippus didn't know how to answer. *How*, he asked himself, *do you tell a child about divorce? How do I tell her that unless I change my mind and allow the surgeon to remove my arm, I'll soon be dead?* "I'm sorry, Ruth, but that just isn't possible," was all he could think of.

Her eyes watered. She was about to start crying when Mary bent down and whispered into her ear. Slowly Ruth dried her tears. "What did you say?" asked Philippus.

"I told her that her new family had lots of baby animals that she could play with and that you'd come by to visit her as often as you could."

Philippus smiled. He took Ruth's hand into his. "I'm glad I met you," he said.

"And I'm ever so glad I met you."

He watched them go. Ruth turned and waved good-bye. Philippus waved back. He thought of Mary's possible arrest and crucifixion. His sense of well-being vanished. He fervently wished that he was wrong. He didn't think he was.

A Final Parting

Thirteen Days until Bethany

Helena was waiting for him when he made his way back to their apartment. She had opened the windows, flooding the apartment in sunlight. She was dressed in her ceremonial toga. The incense had been lit, the wine prepared. A miniature clay phallus was sitting in the centre of the living room. The slaves had been sent away. This would be Philippus's last chance.

She ran to him, throwing her arms around him. "Where have you been?" she asked.

"I couldn't sleep, so I went to the tomb."

"The Nazarene's tomb?" she asked, releasing him and stepping away.

"I suddenly felt an urge to see it."

"Well, I'm glad you're finally back. I've been waiting all day."

"So I see. What is this all for, Helena?"

"Prayers—to Bacchus."

Philippus tried to force a smile. He failed miserably. "I thought we had settled this. You and I are not looking for the same thing," he said, walking away from her.

"And what are you looking for, Philippus?" she asked, walking after him.

"I'm not sure," he said, turning to face her, "but I'm not going to find it in drugged wine, incense, and phallic idols."

"You mean you don't think you can find it with me. Isn't that what you're really saying?"

"No, Helena, that's not what I'm saying," he replied, an unexpected sadness in his voice.

"Then what are you saying?" she pleaded.

He gripped her by the shoulders and brought her face close to his. "I'm saying," he said slowly, "that whatever future we still have, it can't be held together by Bacchus."

"But I don't understand," she replied, tears moistening her eyes.

"Neither do I, not completely," he said, releasing his grip on her shoulders.

"It's this dead Jew, isn't it?" she asked disgustedly.

"This isn't about the Nazarene or Bacchus," he replied. "This is about us. We need to find our own reason to be together."

She turned away from him. Putting his hand on her shoulder, he spun her back towards him. "I thought you said you didn't want to lose me?" he asked.

"I want to lose Lord Bacchus even less."

"Can't we agree to disagree?"

"Don't you want to believe?" she asked.

Philippus looked at his wife as if he'd just stepped into a bear trap. *Do I want to believe?* he asked himself. Unable to answer her question, even to himself, he just shrugged.

"Don't you understand?" she asked beseechingly. "We need to believe as much as we need to eat, drink, or breath. It's the way we're built. It's what makes us human."

"Then I guess I'm not human."

The fury came over her like a sudden rash, turning her cheeks a bright blood red. All thought of bringing Philippus to the bacchanal left her. "If you won't pray to Bacchus, why don't you at least go and pray to your dead Jew?"

"What makes you think I pray at all?"

"We all pray, Philippus, even if it's just to ourselves."

He walked out to the balcony. It was a clear day, the sky brightly lit by the sun. Staring up into its majesty, he wondered if maybe she had a point. Since the day, too long ago to remember, when the gods of Rome had slipped through his fingers for the last time, he had felt a need—a longing difficult to define but real nonetheless. He had kept it hidden behind his carefully constructed wall of cynicism and sarcasm, but since coming to Jerusalem, holes had appeared in that wall. Holes that grew larger everyday and that seemed beyond his ability to repair.

She came to him, a goblet of wine in each hand. "Peace offering," she suggested, handing him one of the goblets.

"It's just wine?" he asked, taking a goblet from her.

"Just wine." She smiled. "I swear before Bacchus."

"To peace then," he said, lifting his goblet in a toast.

"To peace," she replied, and together they drank deeply.

"It's a beautiful day," he said, looking up at the blue sunlit sky.

"Makes you think we can't be all there is, doesn't it?"

"The truth?"

"Not for me, Philippus, for yourself."

"The truth is, you're right."

"So why not open yourself to Bacchus?"

"So he can grant me the powers I seek?"

"What good are the gods if they're not going to grant us our wishes? What does this dead Jew promise you?"

That one made him pause. Why was he drawn to the Nazarene? He had to admit that he wasn't sure. Then, in a flash of inspiration, he said, "That's the difference between Bacchus and the Nazarene. Bacchus teaches that happiness comes from power, from personal satisfaction. Jesus teaches that happiness comes not from serving ourselves, but from serving others."

"You don't actually believe that?" she asked.

"You should read some of His sermons. He explains it better than I ever could."

"You want me to read the words of a dead Jew?"

"Do unto others as you would have them do unto you. My dead Jew said that."

"Good advice...for a slave."

"You know what I did this morning? I bought a dozen loaves of bread, and I gave them away. I don't think anything I have ever done brought me greater joy."

"You're telling me the truth. You gave away some bread to a bunch of strangers, and it made you happy?"

"Not happy, Helena, ecstatic! Seeing their happy faces, especially the children," he said, remembering Ruth's look of excitement and anticipation as their waitress had brought them their food. "You should have been there."

"And what if you had been attacked by some of these poor people? How much happiness would you feel then?"

He looked into her defiant eyes. He thought of the joy Ruth had brought him. He remembered how willing Mary had been to help. The juxtaposition with Helena was too much for him. "You know, Helena, you once said there was an emptiness in me, and you didn't know how you had tolerated it for so long. Well there's a cruelty in you. And I don't know how I've tolerated it for so long."

"You won't have to tolerate it for very much longer," she said dryly, walking away for good.

She threw herself across her bed. The tears started slowly rolling one by one down her cheeks. Then the flood gates opened wide.

Philippus watched her cry from the open doorway. His first instinct had been to take her in his arms. Let her cry herself out on his shoulder. But those days were over. The final parting had arrived. He had to admit it was ironic that two people who had once viewed religion as nothing more than a bad habit were now saying good-bye because they couldn't worship the same god.

The curtains were drawn shut against the morning light, which still managed to penetrate the room in flickering glimpses highlighting her beauty by rationing it. Looking at her stretched out across the bed, she not only excited his senses; she tore at his heart. He wanted to give her what she asked for, but he knew he couldn't. He'd seen the bacchanal. It had disgusted rather than inspired. He saw no wisdom there, no rightness in Lord Bacchus. As long as Helena remained a believer, it would stand between them. With a sigh, he walked away in search of more wine.

Some sixth sense told her he'd left. Looking up from her pillow, she called out for him. "Philippus," she cried. He didn't answer.

She looked into the darkness for a husband who was no longer there; then she came to a decision. She took off her betrothal ring and threw it across the floor. She remembered the gold bracelet and slid it off her wrist. She walked out onto the balcony adjoining their bedroom, and threw it as far as she could.

THE DEVIL HAS HIS WAY WITH HER

THIRTEEN DAYS UNTIL BETHANY

She was waiting for him dressed in one of her finest and most revealing togas, a goblet of wine in one hand and a plate of oysters in the other. "You can relax," she said as she walked towards him. "Philippus isn't here. You're too late for dinner. I thought you might enjoy a small snack."

I'm late, but not too late, Lucius told himself. A greedy smile came to his lips. *Philippus must have disappointed her, as I predicted he would.* He couldn't decide which of his appetites he wanted to slake first. He ended up reaching for the oysters. She led him over to a sitting room with a good view of the city where they could eat in comfort on two large reclining chairs. He noticed they were completely alone.

"How do you find the wine?" she asked, scratching a thigh, pulling up her toga, giving him a clear and deliberate view.

"It's good. Local?" he asked, eyes fixated on the well-toned leg, sensually revealed to him.

"Yes, I find I quite like the local vintages."

"Did Philippus say how long he'd be away?"

"My former husband has his own apartment now," she said, holding up her hand to reveal the absence of a betrothal ring.

Lucius smiled at the sight of her bare finger. "These oysters are delicious," he said. "They'll taste even better afterwards."

"After what?" she asked, eyes wide with seeming innocence.

"Come now," he said, putting down the oysters, coming towards her. "We're not going to continue with this game of *will she or won't she*, are we?"

"No more games, Lucius," she replied, pushing him back, "but I haven't forgotten how we ended back in Rome."

"Neither have I," he said, the smile leaving his face as he pushed her arms out of his way. He pinned her against the end of the couch. Outside, the Judean sky darkened. A storm was rolling in.

Holding her wrists above her head, he kissed her. She kissed back. He held the kiss longer than she had expected, forcing her mouth open, taking her with his tongue. She couldn't fight him.

Afterwards, Lucius was pouring more wine. Helena was still in bed. "Are you sure you want to do this?" she asked.

He came to her, handing her a silver goblet. "I think I've already answered that question," he said.

"You'd embrace Lord Bacchus?" she asked, taking the wine.

"Drink the wine, eat the flesh, everything," he said. Helena took no notice of the way his eyes flicked away from hers as he finished saying those simple words.

The Happiest Man Alive

Twelve Days until Bethany

The farm was a long day's ride west of Jerusalem, not far from the Jordan River. It was fifty acres of good land, most of it in grapes with a few acres of olive trees and a nice stand of cedars. If smartly harvested, the cedars would be a significant source of income on an ongoing basis.

The current owner met Jonah and Mary at the front door of the main house, which was really little more than a shack. He was unsure about letting Odysseus into his home until Jonah assured him that the dog wouldn't bite. It was a modest place, just a large single room with a hard-packed dirt floor and a stone fireplace for cooking. A simple, wooden ladder led to a loft bedroom. A back door led to an outhouse. Water could be taken from a well by the side of the house.

Jonah had already looked over the stables and storage buildings, so after viewing the house, the owner saddled up two horses, and, Odysseus at their side, they went for a ride to survey the fifty acres. It was a beautiful place anchored by a hill at the northwest corner of the property that afforded the owner a magnificent view of the River Jordan.

When they reached the top of the hill, Mary was surprised by what looked like the frame for a new house. "What's this?" she asked.

"It will be our new home, Mary. The farm house is too small and old. I'm going to build you a grand, cedar house with a view of the river and plenty of bedrooms."

"You don't need to, Jonah."

"I know I don't need to, Mary. I want to. You wouldn't deny me this act of charity, would you?"

"Of course not, Jonah. It will be a fine house."

Jonah had built a wooden bench not far from the site of what would one day be their new home. They took advantage of the bench's excellent view of the farm to rest and enjoy a light repast. As they sat enjoying the sunshine and eating their lunch, Odysseus chased birds and generally took full advantage of what was probably his first taste of anything but city squalor.

Jonah didn't have to ask; the look of contentment on Mary's face told him everything he needed to know. "I hope you like the bench," he said.

"Oh, I do, Jonah. It's such a wonderful view."

"I made it for us, Mary. This will be our bench. We'll watch our children grow up from here, and our grandchildren. We'll grow old together on this bench. There is only one thing I ask."

"And what is that, Jonah?"

"That you outlive me, Mary."

"Heavens, Jonah, what a thing to ask."

"I know, but now that you are a part of my life, I don't ever want to be alone again."

Mary's eyes watered, defying her best efforts to control them. She rested her head against Jonah's powerful shoulder. "Do not worry, my love. In death, as in life, we shall always be together."

Jonah had to suck back his own tears. *I'm the happiest man alive,* he told himself.

My Best Link

Ten Days until Bethany

Philippus had been watching Mary's one-room house for several days but had seen no sign of her. He was no longer certain that the Nazarene's followers had the body, but they were the best lead he had. As well, he couldn't deny the fact that he was curious. *Something happened at that tomb,* he told himself. *And whatever it was, these followers seem to be in on it. They're keeping a secret. I have to find out what that secret is.*

The sun was rising on yet another day when Mary dropped by to pick up her clothes. Philippus followed her back to the luxurious mansion she was now apparently calling home.

He didn't have to wait long outside of Mary's new home before she came back out. He followed her to the Jaffa gate. There she met up with two disciples, John and Peter.

The three of them continued west, deeper into the upper city. The streets got wider and cleaner, the houses larger and more luxurious. The air smelt fresher. In front of a home just a few hundred yards below that of the high priest's, Mary and her two friends met another familiar face—Aaron. The captain greeted all three of them warmly, handing Peter a small purse and giving Mary a few coins as well. The four them then entered the house. The face of the man who opened the door for them was well-lit by the morning sunlight. It was Joseph of Arimathea.

Philippus was using a side alley to circle around to the back of the house, looking for an unlocked door or an open window, when everything went black.

Jonah hadn't wanted to hit him. He had been worried for quite a while that Mary might become a person of interest to the Roman Judicium. The appearance of this Roman confirmed his worst fears.

Mary had warned him that situations would arise where his instincts would push him one way and God another. He had felt certain that when those times came, he would have no trouble resisting the pull of his old ways. That's what he had told himself, but in the real world, living according to the words of Jesus was not so easy.

He stared down at Philippus and came to a decision. He had sinned, given in to his anger, but that single sin need not lead to a second. Though every fibre of his being told him to slit the Roman's throat, he would do as he had promised. No further harm would come to the Roman. He would reason with the man. Prove to him that Rome had nothing to fear from his Mary or from the words of Jesus. Lowering his head, he silently prayed for guidance.

When Philippus came to, he was lying on a mat on the floor of what looked like a mud shack. There was a fire blazing away in a nearby stove, which Philippus couldn't see because a large man was standing between him and the stove. "Where have you taken me?" he demanded, trying to lift his head, causing it to throb so painfully he put it back on its pillow immediately.

The man moved closer. "I'm sorry about your head," he said.

"So am I."

"I only hit you because I wanted to know why a Roman investigator was following Mary."

"Why didn't you just ask me?"

"Because that's how I used to deal with people."

"You hit them?"

"Old habits die hard."

"Too hard," moaned Philippus, using his hand to touch a large bump at the back of his head.

"Are you going to answer my question?"

"About Mary?"

"Have I asked any others?"

"Why don't we start with a name?"

"You want to know my name?"

"You know who I am. It seems only fair."

"You can call me Jonah."

"And you can call me Philippus, but you already know that."

"Are you ever going to answer my question?"

"I was hoping she'd lead me to the body of the Nazarene."

"Mary has no idea where the body is."

"I think she does, or at least, she knows people who do."

"How do I know you won't torture Mary?" he asked.

"That's not my way."

"I know how Rome operates. People who don't tell you what you want to know get hurt."

"I guess you're going to have to trust me."

"Why should I?" asked Jonah, his eyes narrowing.

"Because you have no choice?"

Jonah began pacing. Feeling a headache coming on, he stopped pacing and began massaging his forehead.

"Listen," said Philippus, "if I wanted to torture Mary for information, why would I bother following her? Couldn't I just torture her instead?"

Jonah stopped rubbing his forehead. The Roman had a point. Why was he following her? *One thing you could say on behalf of my old ways—they were simple. Jesus is more complicated.*

"I know what you're thinking," said Philippus, breaking into Jonah's thoughts. "You're thinking why not kill me? But you don't want to do that. Rome would get very angry—kill a lot of innocent people. It would all get very messy."

"How can I convince you to leave Mary alone?"

"My only interest is in finding out what happened to the Nazarene's body. Mary has nothing to fear from me, so long as she tells me the truth."

"Let me talk to him, Jonah—alone," spoke a voice from the other side of the room.

"All right, Mary," consented Jonah, "but I think I should stay."

"That's all right, Jonah. Let me talk to Philippus by myself."

"Who will protect you, Mary?"

"The Roman means me no harm, Jonah."

Jonah hesitated and then left, pausing to give Philippus one last whithering look of warning. "Don't hurt her," he said. "Or God or no God, I will kill you."

"Go on, Jonah," insisted Mary, watching until Jonah had left. "Why are you following me, Philippus?"

He ignored the question. "As I told your large friend, I'm only interested in finding my missing body."

"There is no body."

Philippus shrugged. "Sooner or later," he said, "you're going to have to tell me the truth."

"That is the truth."

"Listen, Mary, I know you and the rest of the followers of the Nazarene took the body."

"How could we take something that does not exist'

"It's time to stop lying, Mary."

"But I'm not lying. I would never lie. To lie is to sin."

Philipus sighed dejectedly. "Look, you, the disciples, and all the other followers have the best motive for stealing my body. I know that whoever took the body, they did it with the help of Aaron and his men. I also know that Aaron has been attending your meetings. Is that when you paid him off?"

"Paid him off? Philippus, I have no money. In fact, Aaron was kind enough to donate a few shekels to me so that I could do more to feed the hungry."

"That doesn't prove anything. Others who do have money, like Joseph of Arimathea, probably paid Aaron."

"We did not pay anyone to help steal His body."

"You and Aaron were overheard talking about Bethany. Is that where you hid the body?"

"For the last time, Philippus, you must try to understand that Jesus is alive."

"Then when can I see Him?"

She almost told him about Bethany. "Soon," she said. "I can't tell you more than that."

"Then let me tell you something, Mary. I could have you arrested right now, you and everybody else associated with the Nazarene. I could order you tortured until one of you told me the truth."

"I have told you the truth. You are investigating a crime that never happened."

"Is that your final word?" he asked her.

"It is the truth."

"Fine." He shrugged. "But rest assured, I'm going to get to the bottom of this, Mary. I'm going to find out what happened to my body." He turned and walked away.

She shouted after him, "But you must believe me!"

Philippus stopped and turned to face her. "Why?"

"Because it is the truth."

"I'll give you one last chance. What is going to happen in Bethany?"

"Forget about Bethany. Rome has nothing to fear from Bethany."

Philippus shook his head. "I hope you know what you're doing," he said, storming out the door.

Philippus thought it must be an hour or two before sunset. His arm hurt, and he felt like nothing more than a hot bath, dinner, and a warm bed. As he made his way southwest to the palace, he thought again about arresting Mary, but for what? He had plenty of circumstantial evidence but no physical evidence, like a body, linking Mary or any of the Nazarene's followers to the theft. He could arrest Aaron, but he couldn't charge the captain with anything more serious than deserting his post. That wasn't a crime against Rome.

And what if she really is telling me the truth? He wanted to dismiss the thought as too farfetched, but after visiting Bethany, after seeing the one-way footprints and all the other unanswered questions at the tomb, he just couldn't. Waiting for the guards to open the palace gate, he knew he wouldn't arrest Mary, not when she was his best link to the Son of God.

Fate Finally Steps In

Ten Days until Bethany

Lucius had asked the priest to come to the palace, but Annas preferred meeting at his home in the upper city. Caiaphas had spies all over the palace, according to the former high priest. *That's something I'll have to look into,* Lucius reminded himself.

The late hour was another aggravation. *Why couldn't we meet while the sun was still up?* he asked himself. Of course, the tribune knew exactly why. *Annas is afraid his son-in-law might see me and ask why his father-in-law is meeting with Pilate's second in command. Annas can't tell Caiaphas the truth, that he's using me to payoff Antipas in the hope that the tetrarch will give him his son-in-law's job. Conspiring against your daughter's husband might not go over all that well at the next family dinner.*

Lucius had first learned that the former high priest wanted his old job back when a member of Annas's staff approached him about meeting with his boss. At that first meeting, Annas had surprised Lucius by informing the tribune that he had contacts close to the tetrarch of Galilee. He put it to Lucius that the tribune had been meeting with Antipas and that he knew why. When Lucius claimed not to know what Annas was talking about, the former high priest had looked Lucius straight in the eye and told him to stop lying. "Just admit that you're conspiring with Antipas to replace Pilate," he had admonished Lucius. Annas had gone on to say that he didn't care who sat on the throne in Caesarea, Antipas or Pilate. As far as he was concerned, the one who ran the temple was more important than the one who ran the government. Annas had assured Lucius that he would not reveal what the tetrarch and the tribune were up to, but only if Antipas promised to once again make him high priest.

Lucius had seen only opportunity in Annas's threat. *I have to get the old man to understand that he's more likely to get what he wants with honey as opposed to vinegar,* he remembered telling himself. With a smile that actually unnerved Annas, Lucius had informed the old priest that threatening Antipas was a good way to meet up with an untimely accident. The tetrarch, he promised Annas, responded better to bribes than threats.

At the mention of the word *bribe*, Annas had immediately asked, "How much?" Lucius had kicked a number of figures around in his head, trying to decide how much he should go for. Then he told himself to ask for twice what he wanted.

Annas had almost fainted when he first heard the number. One hundred thousand shekels was not a sum the former high priest was used to paying for anything. Lucius had made no mention of the fact that half the money was staying in his pocket.

After he had recovered his breath, Annas had decided that the souls of his people were worth it, that since he was the only one capable of running the Sanhedrin properly, of balancing the interests of Judea against the demands of Rome, he would have to pay whatever was necessary. He owed it to God. He owed it to his people. The fact that he owed it to his own ambition was something he tried not to think about. He had told Lucius he would raise the money but that it would take some time.

That had been six months ago. Lucius had given up hope of ever seeing Annas's money when a messenger had brought word that the former high priest wanted to meet right away.

Annas's home, like that of his son-in-law's, was spacious with every comfort. The floors were polished marble, the ceilings high and coffered, the walls beautifully painted in soft, comforting pastels. They met in a small, secluded courtyard at the back of the house. A servant brought fresh pastries and tea from China then left discreetly. "These pastries are wonderful," said Lucius, sitting in a wicker chair across a small wooden table from Annas. An oil lamp provided them with a little light and warmth.

Annas, who wasn't much for small talk with decadent Romans, got right to the point. "I have the money," he said.

Lucius looked up from the pastry plate, an almond cookie on its way to his mouth, and smiled. "Want to get right down to business, do you?"

"I don't want anyone to see you here, Tribune."

"Fine," said Lucius, biting off half of the cookie and chewing loudly. "You have the entire one hundred thousand?"

"Every shekel," said Annas, untying a purse from the leather belt that circled his rotund waist and waving it at Lucius. "But before you get your hands on it, Tribune, I want a guarantee that Antipas is going to replace Pilate."

At the sight of the bulging purse, Lucius knew he had to get his hands on all that money. *But I can't give the old man a guarantee, not until Antipas is safely ensconced in Caesarea. On the other hand, why not give the old man his gurantee? I do believe that Pilate will soon be history, but if he's not, so what? What can this old man do to me? If I fail, and he comes looking for his money, I'll threaten to go public about how he bribed a Roman official. That would shut him up.* Lucius looked at Annas with as much sincerity as he could muster. "Sir," he began, "I guarantee you that Antipas will be the tetrarch of Judea. The seeds of Pilate's destruction have been planted, and if you wait until Antipas is in Caesarea, you'll be one of many voices importuning the new tetrarch of Judea. In that case, even one hundred thousand would be no guarantee of satisfaction."

Annas considered what the tribune had said. As much as he hated to admit it, Lucius had a point. His money would be more effective sooner rather than later. "I'll tell you what I'll do," he said. "I'll give you half, and you can tell Antipas he'll get the rest when he makes me high priest."

Lucius sighed. Half a loaf was better than none. "A wise decision, sir," he said.

"So," asked Annas as he counted out fifty thousand, "what's holding things up? Why isn't Antipas in Caesarea yet?"

Lucius wasn't sure how to answer such a direct question. *What does this old man need to know? No more than he already does. Then again, he knows Judean politics as well as anyone. He might have a useful suggestion to offer.* "We need a way to link Caiaphas to the body of the Nazarene."

Annas thought about the problem and then said, "I'm privy to some information that might be of use to you, Tribune. There's a temple guard by the name of Abner, and it has come to my attention—and my attention alone—that the man has hung himself."

"How is it, sir that you are the only one to know?"

"I own the building. And my man came to me before the authorities."

"And he has yet to report the incident?"

"Isn't that what I just said, Tribune?"

"Sorry, sir, I only want to get the facts straight. Why did this Abner hang himself?"

"How should I know, Tribune? Perhaps he was upset over the execution of the Nazarene. He was a follower of that renegade priest."

"With all due respect, sir, this is all very interesting, but how does this temple guard help me tie your son-in-law to the missing body?"

"Think of it this way, Tribune. Caiaphas is linked to Abner because as a temple guard, Abner worked for him. He is linked to the Nazarene because I have witnesses who will testify that Abner was seen attending several of the Nazarene's sermons."

"I understand, but Abner is not linked to the theft of the body."

"No, but if you could plant some evidence that linked Abner to the theft, you'd be able to go after Caiaphas as a co-conspirator."

"Evidence? What kind of evidence?"

"Do I have to do all of your thinking for you? Something from the tomb would do the trick. The Nazarene's body would be best."

THE HAPPIEST MAN
IN JERUSALEM

NINE DAYS UNTIL BETHANY

Dawn found Philippus, his arm throbbing, back behind his desk. He was taking advantage of the quiet time to return to his study of the Nazarene's words. "Do onto others what you would have them do onto you," he said to himself. *Such a simple, straight-forward idea*, he thought, *but, like so much of what the Nazarene had to say, it runs contrary to basic human nature. We all want to be well treated, but the human condition boils down to them or us. As a Roman, had Hannibal won, I would have wanted the Carthaginians to be merciful. But after our victory, we did what we had to do.*

It's not always possible to treat your enemies as you want to be treated, he decided, once again struggling to understand the Nazarene's logic. *He spoke beautiful words and had grand ideas, but He expected too much from His fellow man.* Philippus's thoughts were interrupted by the arrival of Amicus. "Yes," snapped Philippus, irritated at being disturbed.

"Sorry to bother you, sir, I mean, Philippus, but I have the arrest record you wanted on that woman, Magdalene. And that Jewish contractor…ah…"

"Elijah?" asked Philippus helpfully.

"Yes, that's the name. He still wants to see you. Says it's—"

"Important, yes, I know," interrupted Philippus with a sigh. "It always is. Tell him I'm too busy to see him. He'll have to come back another time." Standing up, he took Mary's criminal record from Amicus. "Thank you," he said.

"And I'll take care of that contractor," replied Amicus, turning and leaving.

Philippus skimmed through the arrest report. Mary Magdalene had been arrested more than once. He looked over the list of her known associates. None of the names were associated with Jesus. So whatever criminal associations she once had, they were not connected with this case. He was rolling up the scroll when Lucius walked in. "Tribune, you're up early."

"I have excellent news," smiled Lucius.

"Really? And what might that be?"

"I think we may soon be able to send you back to Rome."

Philippus looked up from his writing, "Nothing would make me happier."

Philippus and Lucius reached the rundown apartment building located not far from Herod's hippodrome just as the morning sun was beginning its slow climb. Lucius led the way down a dark, shabby hallway until they came to an open apartment door. They walked right in. A near-toothless fellow in desperate need of a drink jumped to his feet at the sight of them. "Tribune," he shouted a little too enthusiastically.

"Well," said Lucius sternly, "what have you to show me?"

"This way, Tribune."

The agent motioned them into a smaller room that served as a bedroom. Hanging by his neck from a rafter was a man the agent identified as Abner, a member of the temple guards."

"Very interesting," speculated Philippus, "but what does it have to do with my missing body?"

"This way," said the man. He led them out a back door that opened to a small courtyard with a communal well in the centre of it. Several men were hoisting something out of the well.

As Lucius and Philippus stood by watching, the body of a naked man was pulled out of the well and deposited at their feet.

Philippus leaned in for a closer look. He took note of the wounds on the man's hands and feet, the scars on his forehead, and the wound under his ribs.

"Looks like we've found our missing body," smiled Lucius.

"So it would seem," said Philippus. He grabbed a torch and crouched down for a better look. The man was the right age, and his state of decomposition suggested that he'd been dead the right amount of time. Philippus shook his head in amazement. After all the doubt and confusion, the Nazarene had turned out to be just a man thrown down a well. All his unanswered questions about the miracles, the one-way footprints, he pushed to the back of his mind. He stood up and patted Lucius on the shoulder. "Lucius, you've just made me the happiest man in Jerusalem," he said. "This Judicium is over."

It's Not Easy to Change

Nine Days until Bethany

Caiaphas was not used to waking up alone. Since the fateful night of Jonah's revelation, he had quietly slipped out of the master bedroom that he had shared with his wife for the past fifteen years and into a guest bedroom at the opposite end of the house. The room was comfortable enough, with a pair of small easterly facing windows that allowed the sun to greet him every morning. And, although no one knew better than Joseph Caiaphas that his marriage had been more political than romantic, he'd grown used to Reisa. Despite her betrayal, he missed her. He feared he always would.

He was up early this morning. It was going to be a big day at the temple. Tiberius Caesar had made the grand gesture of offering two hundred beasts for ritual sacrifice. Pilgrims had been gathering since last night, anxiously awaiting the appearance of the beasts. Their moment had arrived.

Caiaphas had arranged for seven hundred priests to be gathered on the great platform. As his servants dressed him, he thought about the long day ahead of him. Not only would the high priest have to oversee the ritual butchery of Caesar's two hundred animals, but hundreds of pilgrims had offered up individual sacrifices as well. The slaughter would be enormous. Caiaphas and his priests would have to work fast. The sheer size of the slaughter demanded that the carving of the carcasses be done as efficiently as possible. The platform where the slaughter was to be carried out was not solid but hollow, functioning as a gigantic flushing system. The necessary water was stored inside thirty-four cisterns. The largest was capable of holding over two million gallons. Pipes carried the water up to the platform surface where a multitude of drains carried off the flood of blood and water.

Caiaphas ate a full breakfast of fresh bread, boiled eggs, honey, and cheese. He washed it all down with several cups of tea. It was such a fine morning that he waved away his carriage in favour of walking to the temple mount. Four temple guards were waiting for him at the gate to his home—his escort.

He had spent his entire life around it, but he still felt a tremendous sense of awe whenever he approached Herod's Grand Temple. As he made his way across the bridge to the temple mount he ordered his escort to wait while he took a moment to gaze upon Herod's masterpiece.

It really is magnificent, he said to himself, his eyes taking in Herod's vision. He had had to double the size of the temple mount from Solomon's sixty cubits to one hundred. *But it was worth every shekel,* considered the high priest. He even increased the size of the sanctuary from Solomon's sixty cubits to one hundred. And Herod wasn't a member of a priestly family. He couldn't even enter the inner court.

Not that he spared any expense on the outer court, marvelled Caiaphas, forced to shield his eyes from the glare of the sunlight bouncing off the gold and silver decorations covering the gates and walls. So much gold and silver, visitors could see it glittering in the bright Levantine sunlight from miles away.

Such splendour had always brought a smile to the high priest's face. Today, his eyes squinting in the sunlight, he wasn't so sure. *What if the Nazarene was right?* he asked himself. *What if it truly is more important to God that we be pure in thought and action and not so busy burning incense and slaughtering animals? What if God wants more mercy and love and less sacrifice and blood? What if trappings like Herod's great temple, meant to honour and bring us closer to God, actually dishonour and take us away from Him? What if our great temple enslaves us?* These difficult questions were new to him, and he wasn't sure how to answer them. He only knew that since the Nazarene had first come into his life they had been bothering him more and more.

Before entering the holy of holies, the high priest had to be properly dressed. He had to stand on his right leg first and then his left as his servants pulled up his michnasyim or linen pants. A Ketonet, or simple tunic, was slipped over the pants. Next, the Avnet or sash was draped over one shoulder. Only the high priest's was embroidered. A mitznetfet, or turban, was placed on his head, his being larger than anyone elses.

All of these garments were worn in common with the other priests. But on top of these, the high priest had four pieces of clothing exclusive to his rank. First, there was the *me'il*, or robe, of the Ephod, a sleeveless, blue robe, the hem of which was fringed with golden bells and coloured tassels. Over this, he also wore a richly embroidered vest. Over the vest, his servants fitted a breastplate with twelve gem stones, one for each of the tribes. Lastly, a gold crown was placed around the turban inscribed with the words "Holy unto God."

Once inside the holy of holies, the high priest immersed himself in the mikvah and washed his hands and feet, then barefoot, like the other seven hundred priests he walked onto the platform. Behind him, he could hear the ululating cries of the animals being led in for the morning sacrifice. The doors to the inner sanctuary were open so that ordinary male Jews could see inside, although none were allowed to enter. Caiaphas closed his eyes and listened to the unearthly symphony, the high notes played by the terrified cattle while the ritual chanting of the priests carried the baseline. Opening his eyes, he watched the first animal brought up onto the altar. The killing had begun.

Caiaphas and the other priests handled the carcases with the skill of well-trained, professional butchers. As the unlucky animals were being dispatched, the flow of blood soon threatened to overwhelm the multitude of drains designed to carry off the red torrents.

Caiaphas heard the reaction to what happened next before he saw it. One of the drains was backing up. A piece of flesh, large enough to block the drain, had fallen from the altar. It had been carried away by the huge volume of fluid and had lodged itself at a point where the drain fed into the gutter that carried the blood and water into the vats below the platform. Fresh blood was backing up. It was flooding the sacrificial platform.

Caiaphas watched the blood wash over the bare feet of the agitated priests. The sight of all that blood affected him profoundly. Had God just spoken to him? Was the failure of the drains God's way to answer his difficult questions for him?

THE EVIDENCE MOUNTS

NINE DAYS UNTIL BETHANY

The high priest wasn't smiling as he made his way up the Mount of Olives that early spring afternoon. The day's killing was still fresh in his mind, and the questions it raised were still unanswered, but he had no time to dwell on them. He had more pressing worries. At first, the news that Rome had found the body was a source of great relief for him. Then he received word that the body had been found in a well used by a temple guard and that the guard was believed to be the thief.

So the doubt that had vanished briefly when he heard the body had been found returned with a vengeance. Confronting the possibility that he had made a huge and tragic mistake was becoming more and more difficult. *There's only one way out of this*, he finally admitted to himself. *I have to resolve this mystery for myself.*

He had already travelled to Nazareth to speak with the Rabbi there. The Rabbi had only deepened his misgivings by proving to the high priest that the carpenter had not been born in Nazareth. That meant, as Caiaphas feared, He could have been born in Bethlehem. That He could have been the "new king" that the wise men from Babylon had spoken to Herod about. But how sure were the Babylonians that they were indeed seeking out a new-born king? The high priest knew of only one man still alive who could answer that question.

It was a small, stone house just below the village overlooking the Kidron valley. Walking up to the front door, Caiaphas knocked. A spy hole in the door opened up, and an eyeball gave him a careful once over. "What do you want?" shouted a voice from behind the door.

"I'm here to speak with Judah," replied Caiaphas.

"Is Judah expecting you?"

"He knows I'm coming."

"I need a name."

Joseph hesitated. His name was something he did not want to reveal. He did not want news of his visit to become common gossip. He did not want to have to explain to anyone what he was doing here. "Just tell Judah that the friend he is expecting is here to see him."

"Wait here," said the voice. The spy hole closed. A moment later, the door opened and a very large, well-armed man motioned for Caiaphas to enter.

He was led down a short hallway that emptied into a cozy little room that was being warmed by a roaring fire in a stone fireplace. Seated across from the fire was an old man who looked as if he'd been around since the beginning of time. As Caiaphas entered, the old man looked up and smiled warmly. "Sorry about the locked door," he said, "but these are dangerous times."

"No need to apologise, Judah. May I sit down?"

"Of course, please, make yourself comfortable," replied Judah, waving a bony hand at an old but comfortable chair next to him facing the fire.

"Thank you." Caiaphas smiled as he sat down and warmed his hands before the fire.

"So, Pontiff, how can I help you?"

Caiaphas was not sure how he wanted to answer that question. He didn't want Judah to suspect what was really on his mind, the doubt that was tormenting his soul. "You were Herod's astrologer when the three Babylonians came to see him, were you not?" he asked.

"I was. Does this have anything to do with that carpenter you had Pilate crucify?"

The old man's question struck Caiaphas like a knife. *The old man already suspects the truth,* he warned himself. "If you don't mind, Judah," he said, "I'll ask the questions."

"So ask."

"What brought those three men to Judea?" asked Caiaphas, getting right to the point. *So what if the old man suspects the truth? What does it matter really?*

"They said they were following Jupiter," answered Judah.

"The star of kings?" Caiaphas asked breathlessly.

"That is correct. Jupiter was rising in the east in the sign of Aries."

"And Aries is the sign of Judea."

"Which is why they came here. They were also interested because the Sun and Moon were flanking Jupiter as it rose in Aries."

"Are not the Sun and Moon the rulers of Aries?"

"Correct again. You know your astrology, Joseph."

"Did the Babylonians say what they thought the rising of Jupiter in Aries might mean?"

"They believed it meant a new king was being born in Judea, a king who would be of great importance to all of mankind."

"Did they know of the prophecy?"

"Herod told them that it had been prophesied that a king would be born in Bethlehem, that the prophet Micah had predicted that Bethlehem would be the home of the Messiah. So they went to Bethlehem. Of course, as you know, when they didn't report back, Herod had every child under the age of two put to the sword."

"Do you think they found their king?"

"I don't know, Joseph, but I believe whatever they found, they believed it was important. That's why they didn't tell Herod. They didn't trust him."

"Thank you, Judah, you've been most helpful."

"You know, Joseph, I've often wondered if the Babylonians did find a new-born king, did they warn the child's parents? And if they did, were the parents able to get out of Bethlehem in time?"

"So you think the child might have escaped Herod's wrath?" asked Caiaphas fearfully.

"If he did, the child would now be the same age as the Nazarene you had crucified."

"A coincidence, Judah, nothing more," said Caiaphas a little too confidently.

"But did the carpenter not claim to be the King of the Jews?" asked the old man.

"He claimed many things, but I'm afraid I must be leaving you now," said Caiaphas, getting up from his chair.

"But that's why you're here, isn't it? You think you might have executed the wrong man."

"I think nothing of the sort," replied Caiaphas curtly, turning for the door.

"Have you spoken to Lazarus?" asked Judah, chasing after Caiaphas.

"I spoke to his neighbors," replied Caiaphas, picking up his pace as he headed for the door.

"Then you know he's alive. If Jesus could save Lazarus, why not himself?"

"I don't believe Lazarus was ever dead," exclaimed Caiaphas with more confidence than he actually felt.

"Then how did he survive for four days in his tomb?"

"He wouldn't be the first man to go four days without food or water."

"You are fooling only yourself, Joseph."

"We'll know who the fool is soon enough," replied the high priest, fearing that he would soon be forced to realize that he was far worse than a fool. He was almost out the door when Judah finally caught up with him, grabbing him by the sleeve.

"Don't blame yourself, Joseph." he admonished. "You had no way of knowing. You did only what you thought was best."

"I have no idea what you are talking about, Judah," lied Caiaphas, shaking his arm free of the old man's grip and walking out the door.

A Moment of Reconciliation and Faith

Eight Days until Bethany

Reisa suspected that her husband had somehow discovered her involvement with Jesus. *It's that big man, Jonah, I think he calls himself, the one Joseph hires to do his spying for him. He probably followed me.*

She knew she was going to have to talk to her husband. Hiding from each other solved nothing. *What if he leaves me?* she worried. *What would I do? How would I live? Would father take me back? Not now. Not now that I've taken Jesus as my saviour.* She remembered Mary telling her that she did not fear for the future because she had put all her trust in Jesus. *That's what I must do*, she told herself. *I must trust in the Lord, and I must speak to my husband.*

She had planned to wait until he returned from the temple and was more than a little surprised when Caiaphas's personal guards informed her that the high priest had not gone to temple and had instead gone to the empty tomb—alone. *Now why would Joseph go to the tomb of Jesus?* she asked herself. *Especially by himself?*

"Joseph," she called out as she approached the sepulchre.

Caiaphas was on his knees, his back to Reisa. Looking up from his prayers, he had to look twice before believing what his eyes were telling him. "Reisa?" he asked.

"Yes, it's me," she said, surprised to see the tears on his cheeks.

"What are you doing here?" he asked.

"The same thing you are," she answered.

"I'm glad you found me," he said, wiping away his tears. "There are things I need to tell you."

"I was about to say the same thing," she replied, stopping beside his left shoulder.

"I guess we have avoided each other for too long."

"Much too long, Joseph."

"Kneel beside me, dear." Resia joined her husband, kneeling beside him. "I've come to a very difficult conclusion," he said, hanging his head in shame.

Seeing her husband on his knees, unable to look her in the eye, cheeks wet with tears, she took him into her arms. Although she had nothing to go on, she knew in her soul what he was trying to say. "You only did what you thought was best."

Joseph looked clear-eyed at his wife. Taking a deep breath, he let it out slowly. In a voice barely above a whisper and almost choked off by tears, he said, "I crucified the Son of God."

Reisa smiled serenely at her husband. She knew the first step in overcoming sin was to admit that you had sinned. "You only have to ask for His forgiveness, Joseph. If you are sincere, God will forgive you. He has to. You were part of His plan."

Caiaphas pulled away. He looked hard into her eyes. "What plan?"

"Jesus did not die uselessly, Joseph. He died for our sins. He died so that all who worship Him may live. But none of that would be possible had you not done what you believed to be right."

Caiaphas's eyebrows went up. His pupils dilated. His heart rate rose. *Is she saying that I had God's blessing?* he asked himself. "Do you really believe that?" he asked incredulously. "Do you really believe God wanted me to condemn His only Son?"

"My dearest," began Reisa, holding her husband's hands in her own, "no other explanation is possible."

"I don't know what to say."

"There is nothing to say, Joseph. Just be thankful that God had a purpose for what you did."

For a moment, he just looked at her. An uneasy stillness settled in between them. But the more he considered her words, the more truth he found in them. "Yes." He finally nodded thoughtfully. "I am thankful, truly."

Reisa's smile broadened. Keeling beside her husband, she knew she wouldn't have to argue with it anymore. Her heart had changed its mind—something hearts do very rarely. She squeezed his hands just a little too hard. "I am so happy for you," she said.

"Are you going to Bethany?" he asked.

"You know about Bethany?" she asked nervously.

"The rumour is all over the city."

"Then the Romans know?"

"I should think so."

"Romans or no Romans, I will be there."

"Let us go together."

She placed his hand over her heart. "Together," she said softly.

The air changed suddenly. They felt another presence come over them. Like a wave, it washed away all their doubts and all their fears, cleansing them.

Caiaphas took Resia in his arms. Kneeling before the empty tomb, he found the strength to accept his error, and, in accepting, he came to understand that God forgave him and still loved him—that God loves us all.

He looked up at the magnificently blue, Judean sky, and breathed deeply the cool, clear air. He felt like a yoke had been lifted from his shoulders. The sound of birds springing to life could be heard all around him. "God is truly all around us," he said.

"Yes, dear, He is," replied Resia, her heart singing with a joy she had long despaired of ever feeling.

Hand in hand they closed their eyes and they prayed.

CONFIDENTIAL SORCES

EIGHT DAYS UNTIL BETHANY

Philippus found his wife sharing a cup with Lucius. The two of them were stretched out on lounging couches, cups in hand, slaves standing at their elbows, wine jugs filled to brimming. They were laughing and giggling about something. *Probably some cleverly vacuous insight from the tribune's painted lips,* thought Philippus as he interrupted their fun. "Philippus," slurred Helena, "where have you been all night?"

Looking from one smirking face to the other, Philippus grasped with the finality of death that his marriage was lost. "Do you really care?" he asked dully.

"He's right," she said to Lucius, laughing contemptuously. "I don't."

A heavy, elegiac silence filled the room. Lucius looked to Helena. She looked back at him. "Well, I hope one of you has the courage to say the obvious," demanded Philippus, breaking the silence.

"I want a divorce," she said, her voice as flat as the Dead Sea.

"Found someone else to keep you out of prison and pay the bills?" he asked, directing a caustic smile at Lucius. The tribune smiled back drunkenly. Raising his glass to Philippus, listing a little too far to starboard, he almost fell off his couch.

Helena stumbled to her feet, spilling wine. A nearby slave rushed to clean it up. "This has nothing to do with what anyone can do," she slurred. "This has to do with what we've found." She looked at Lucius. He was having a hard time keeping his eyes open. "Me and Lucius."

"And what might that be?" asked Philippus.

Helena turned her gaze back to Philippus. She emptied her goblet and threw it into the fireplace. A slave ran to offer her a new one. She waved him away, stumbling drunkenly as she did. "Lucius and I have found a common faith, haven't we?" she asked, looking back over her shoulder at her barely conscious tribune.

"In Lucius?" asked Philippus with a contemptuous snort.

"Poor Philippus, such a sceptic—such a cynic," said Helena contemptuously to her newfound lover. Lucius didn't answer. He was too busy having a slave feed oysters into his open mouth.

"You forgot stoic," added Philippus, smiling thinly, his arm starting to ache intensely.

"He also thinks he's clever," said Helena.

She's hiding it well, Philippus said to himself. The wine helps, but I can see the sadness. The way the corners of her mouth droop, the way her eyes never quite look into mine when she's talking to me. She wants to run from my arms but not necessarily into his. "Listen, Helena," he said, "leaving me is one thing. We both know it's been over between us for a long time, maybe since the day we first met. But whatever you think you've found in Lucius, well, that will prove false."

Philippus paused, and Lucius punctuated his sentence by bolting upright and vomiting into a nearby urn. "He'll hurt you, Helena," he continued, pointing an accusing finger at the disgorging Tribune. "He'll hurt you, just as surely as I have," said Philippus, starting for the door. A slave entered and bowed. "Yes?" asked Philippus, his eyes grinding into the slave.

"Excuse me, sir," started the slave, his head remaining bowed, "but this message just arrived for you." The slave reached out a hand, which was holding a small wax tablet.

Philippus took the proffered tablet. "You may go now," he said. Looking down, he saw a brief message. It read: "Philippus, please come and see me at once on a matter most urgent." It was signed Procula Pilate. The postscript read: "Under no circumstances should you tell Lucius of our meeting."

"What is it?" asked Helena.

"Somebody wants to see me."

"Who?" inquired Lucius looking up from his urn.

"None of your business, Tribune."

He met her in a small waiting room just off the master bedroom. Philippus inquired as to the whereabouts of the prefect and was told that her husband was sleeping soundly and wouldn't be bothering them.

"I'm so glad you could see me on such short notice," said Procula once they had been seated and her servants had left.

"What is this all about, my lady?" asked Philippus.

"I've been told that you've found our missing body," she said, fanning herself.

"That's correct. A body has been found. Although, I'm not the one who found it."

"I understand Lucius is the one responsible," she said discursively.

"Correct again. Um, is there any reason why we're meeting so late at night?" Philippus watched her fan go from languid to frantic and smiled. "The reason I ask is, well, I thought it might be because you didn't want your husband to find out."

"Find out what?" she asked, her fan putting a bumble bee to shame.

"That the two of us were talking."

Procula closed her fan abruptly. "Do you tell your wife about everyone you talk to?" she asked.

"Of course not, but my business is all about finding and keeping secrets."

"And so is the business of a prefect's wife."

Philippus nodded his head as if to say he understood. "So what secrets do you want to discuss?"

"What if I told you I have reason to believe that the body Lucius found is a fake?"

Philippus'eyes widened in surprise."I'd say that was information you should be sharing with your husband."

"I don't think my husband would believe me."

"Why not?" he asked.

Procula looked pensively at Philippus. "Can I trust you?" she asked. "Trust you to keep a secret?"

"Depends on the secret."

"I have a source of information that cannot be made public."

"Protecting confidential sources is something I do every day," replied Philippus with a smile.

"My information comes to me from one of the tribune's slaves. The slave told me that his master paid two grave robbers to provide him with that body. Since my information comes from a slave, Pontius would see it as unpersuasive."

"That can be a problem," he said.

"That's why I want to hire you to come up with persuasive evidence. You have a week before you've been ordered to leave. I want you to spend that week proving the body is a fake."

Philippus considered the offer. Normally he would have said no. He didn't need the money, and a week to relax and get ready for his trip home was a pleasant enough idea. But these were not normal times. First of all, unless he changed his mind, his arm meant that this case would be his last, and the question of what really happened to Jesus of Nazareth still intrigued him greatly. His reaction to what Procula had just told him proved that. "How much?" he asked.

Procula took a furtive look around then reached into a secret sleeve pocket of her cloak. She took out a small purse and handed it to Philippus. "I presume this will be enough for one week. If you need more, tell me, and I'll arrange it for you."

It was difficult with only one hand, but he managed to open the purse. "This will be fine," he said, sliding the purse into a pocket. "But a week doesn't give me much time."

"Then I suggest you get to work immediately. And you'd better do something about that arm."

"Right," said Philippus, turning to leave.

"Oh, wait, one more thing."

"Yes?" asked Philippus, looking over his shoulder at her.

Procula waved him closer. "I don't care to shout," she said. "I just wanted to make it clear to you that this is very important."

"I understand."

"I'm not sure you do. The tribune is plotting something. I don't know what, but this fake body must have something to do with it."

"Couldn't it be that Lucius wants to put an end to all this nonsense about a resurrection before things get out of control and we end up with a full-scale revolt?"

Anger hardened Procula's face. "I have no idea what Lucius wants to put an end to. But let me assure you of this, he means no one any good but himself."

I Always Do

Seven Days until Bethany

Amicus couldn't believe how much the tribune was willing to pay. He was standing at attention in the tribune's office just before the start of the third hour. The office was spacious but sparsely furnished. Just two ladder-backed, wooden chairs sat opposite the tribune on the other side of his elaborately carved cedar desk. From a drawer, the tribune retrieved a heavy purse and handed it to Amicus. "This is very generous of you, sir," smiled Amicus, taking a quick look inside the purse.

"I only hope you are as generous with your information," smiled Lucius, chugging a cup of wine to help him swallow the headache powder he had just taken. He was still hungover after the previous night's excesses with Helena.

Amicus tied the purse to his belt; he could feel it resting against his leg. "It seems, sir," he began, "that Philippus has taken a keen interest in that body you found."

At the mention of the body, Lucius's eyes widened. "Really?" he asked. "What makes you say that?"

"Well, sir, Philippus has asked me to order the centurion Longinus to identify the body personally. He also wants this Mary Magdalene woman to do the same."

Identify the body? wondered Lucius, doing his best to remain calm while his brain churned over the possibilities. *What game is Philippus playing? Does he suspect the body's authenticity? And even if he does, what difference does it make to him? He's been paid. Pilate is happy. Real or fake, the body has served its purpose. Philippus should be packing, not calling in eye witnesses. Unless,* Lucius suddenly realized, *he has a new client, a client for whom the body's authenticity has real importance.* In a flash, he remembered Philippus's late-night message. "Has Philippus seen anyone unusual?" he asked.

"Well, sir, just before he got interested in the body, he met with Pilate's wife."

Lucius raised a sceptical eyebrow. "How do you know that?" he asked.

"A member of her ladyship's entourage paid the investigator a visit first thing this morning, sir."

"That doesn't prove anything."

"No, sir, but I got the guard to let me into the office to clean up, and, once I was inside, I went straight to the investigator's desk."

"And?" asked Lucius impatiently.

"I noticed a wax tablet. The words *Procula, second hour, tomorrow,* and *temple mount* were written across the top."

The churning inside the tribune's brain doubled in intensity. Could Procula be his new client? Why would Procula be interested in the body? *She can't suspect what I have planned for her husband? I just have to stay calm, stick to my plan.* "You've done good work, Amicus," he said.

"Thank you, sir."

"Do you know where the body is right now?"

"A room below the Antonia near the cells. Philippus had it moved there yesterday."

"Good. I think that will be all, Amicus. Continue to keep your eyes and ears open, and there will be more gold for you. You have my word on it."

"Thank you, sir." Amicus smiled, his right hand gently tapping the purse hanging from his belt.

Lucius stood before one of his many full-length mirrors, trying not to notice how the worry lines around his eyes were deepening. His fake body was the key to everything. His plan to unseat Pilate depended on linking Caiaphas to that body. He had several clues and witnesses that he was about to reveal that would seal the high priest's fate. But if Philippus proved that the body wasn't real, his evidence would be worthless. *I have to prevent Philippus from finding out the truth,* he told himself. *I just don't know how. But I will,* he promised himself, his smile returning. *I always do.*

IT'S ALL ABOUT THE ANGLES

SEVEN DAYS UNTIL BETHANY

Philippus had had the body moved to an examination room not far from the prison cells under the Antonia. The room was cold and damp and, of course, lacked any windows. It was not an ideal location for a month-old corpse. The body was layed out on a wooden table in the centre of the large room. He held a perfumed cloth to his face and looked down at the decayed face.

After a month of decomposition, the entire body was shrouded, head to toe, in a cloak of adipocere, an oily, gooey substance with the consistency of very thick cream, and an unmistakable, rancid odor. Thick layers of it were slathered over the remains of the face like cake icing left too long in the sun. Maggots were still hard at work, devouring what was left of the dead man's flesh. The journey from the temple guard's well to the Antonia hadn't bothered them at all. The legs were black, bloated tubes. The belly was enormous, swollen by the gasses that were seeping out of the man's anus.

The feet and hands were sweetbreads gone very, very bad. Randomly along the body, greyish, green bones poked through the discoloured flesh. At the joints, the cartilage was a sickly yellow. The teeth still looked human. Two rows of yellowed, poorly cared for ivories grinned at Philippus from the severely desiccated face.

Mary had already looked at the body. She had claimed that it was a fake. Being a follower of the Nazarene, she had a good reason for lying. But Philippus had watched her closely and was convinced she had told him the truth as she understood it.

He measured the feet of the dead man and then compared them to the measurements he'd taken from the one-way footprints from inside the tomb. He wasn't surprised when they didn't match.

He meticulously examined the scaring around the forehead. It was consistent with the crown of thorns the Nazarene had worn. He fitted nails, exactly like the ones used during the crucifixion, into the wounds on the hands and feet. They fit perfectly.

He had tried everything he could think of, but he had found nothing that he could take to Pilate. He'd even had a body, entombed around the time of the Nazarene's internment, exhumed so that he could compare the rates of decomposition. See if they were similar. They were.

But Mary had insisted that the body was a fake. If he didn't come up with some solid evidence that proved otherwise, Pilate was never going to reopen the Judicium. Lucius would be free to go ahead with whatever he was planning. *Oh well.* Philippus sighed. *Perhaps Longinus will be able to help me.*

He was putting away the nails when Longinus was escorted into the examination room. "Longinus," he said after the escort had left, "thanks for taking the time to see me again."

"I've got those sandals you wanted," replied Longinus. "Why isn't this poor fellow under ground?" he asked, bringing his hand up to cover his nose and mouth.

"He will be soon enough. Here, use this," said Philippus, handing Longinus a perfumed cloth.

The centurion took the cloth and handed Philippus the sandals. "The ragman was more than happy to sell them back to me, especially after he found out what you were offering."

"You're sure these belonged to the Nazarene?" asked Philippus.

"Of course I'm sure. What's so important about these sandals anyway?"

"I think they're going to solve a mystery."

"How?"

"By proving a miracle."

"Like my eyes?"

"Like your eyes."

"So how can I help you?" asked Longinus.

Philippus pointed at the body. "I want you to tell me if you think it's the man you crucified."

"I'll do my best," said Longinus. He took his time, despite the smell. Starting at the head, he slowly made his way down the length of the body. "It certainly looks like the Nazarene," he said.

"Is there anything you can see that shouldn't be there? Like a mark, a wound that's out of place?"

"All the wounds look to be in all the right places." Longinus looked at Philippus. His eyes narrowed. "You don't think it's the right body, do you?"

"Let's say I have my doubts and leave it at that."

Longinus shrugged. He cast his eyes back over the body. "I'm sorry, Philippus. I wish I could help you, but this looks like the right body to me."

"Well don't give up. Keep looking."

With another shrug, Longinus continued looking. "I wonder if the wound between his fourth and fifth rib here, the one I finished Him off with, is the right size?"

"The right size?"

"If you're right and this body is a fake, then somebody besides me must have cut'em right here between the fourth and fifth rib," said Longinus, pointing at the wound.

"And you want to see if they used the right spear?"

"Exactly," answered Longinus, as he rested the tip of his spear against the wound. It was the right width and length. "Sorry, Philippus, but it's a perfect match."

"And you're sure that's the spear you used?"

"Absolutely. I remember looking up at the Nazarene as I—"

"What?" asked Philippus, looking at Longinus as if he didn't quite recognize him. "Did you just say you looked up at Him?"

"Of course I looked up," replied Longinus. "He was hanging from His cross."

"Yes, yes, of course He was! So you had to strike upwards!"

"I did, but I don't see what you're trying to get at."

"Here," said Philippus, "give me a hand with this body."

The smell and the feel of the body almost knocked them out, but using an old blanket, they lifted the body off the examination table. Longinus tied it to a hook hanging from the ceiling while Philippus held the body upright. Taking the centurion's spear, Philippus placed the tip against the wound as if he were striking from below. "See?" he asked Longinus.

"See what?"

"How the tip of your spear doesn't fit into this wound if I thrust from below."

Longinus looked closely at the tip of his sword as Philippus fitted it into the wound at a forty-five degree angle to the body. The tip fit perfectly. "If we assume that you were standing parallel with the Nazarene, your spear is a perfect match with the wound. But"—Phillipus paused long enough to adjust the angle of entry so that the blade was now meeting the wound at a ninety degree angle—"if you assume the Nazarene was suspended above you on a cross, and you adjust the angle of entry accordingly, your spear tip no longer fits into the wound."

"The angle of entry is wrong," marvelled Longinus, smiling.

"The wound on this corpse was made with a level thrust instead of an upward one, and that means that this is not the body of the Nazarene."

LET HIM HAVE HIS WEEK

SEVEN DAYS UNTIL BETHANY

Philippus had already told Procula the good news, and she had offered him a bonus for producing such satisfactory results so quickly. Much to his surprise, he had turned it down. It would have been greedy to accept it. It wasn't how he would have wanted to be treated if he were the one paying the bills. That sort of thing seemed to matter more to him now.

After seeing his new client, Philippus paid a visit to his old one.

Pilate was uncomfortably seated in the palace throne room. The prefect had not counted on anything as fortunate as finding the body at the bottom of a dry well, and now Philippus, who had told him just days ago that the case was closed, was refusing to accept victory? Well, he was going to see about that! Turning a baleful glare on Philippus, he asked, "Wasn't it you who told me to declare victory?"

"The body we found in the well is a fake, sir," Philippus said perfunctorily.

"The hell it is!" Pilate said, slamming his fist onto the throne's armrest.

Philippus couldn't miss the flaring nostrils, the narrowing of Pilate's eyes. The way the two worry lines, beginning where his eyebrows met and ending at his forehead, deepened. "Sir, despite the fact that this is not our body, I do believe that we've made significant progress."

"We've found our missing body! What makes you so certain that we've got the wrong body? Why are you right and everybody else wrong?"

"It's the angle of entry, sir."

"Angle of entry?"

"On the wound between the fourth and fifth rib, sir."

"What about it?"

"Well, sir, I've interviewed the centurion, and he has assured me that he struck the blow while the Nazarene was still hanging from His cross."

"So what?"

"The wound on our body was not inflicted from below, sir."

"How do you know that?" asked Pilate.

"It's perpendicular, sir."

"It's preposterous."

"Sir, if you'd look at the corpse for yourself, I could demonstrate exactly what I mean."

"I don't need to look at any corpse. We have our body. This Judicium is over."

"With all due respect, Prefect, this Judicium ends when I say it does."

Pilate wheeled on Philippus. He pointed a stern, well-chewed finger in his face and said in a cold, flat voice, "Now you listen to me. I ordered you here, and I can order you to leave any time I want to, now get out!"

"Again, sir, with all due respect, I work for Rome, not you. My contract is with Caesar, not the prefect of Judea."

Pilate's face hardened. "In Judea," he said, "I speak for Caesar."

"But, sir, I've taken some important steps forward. I should stay until I find the real body."

At this point, Lucius had heard enough. "Are you saying," he interjected, "that someone either found an appropriate body or murdered an innocent man to get one then dumped it down that well for us to find?"

"I'm not saying it, Tribune. I can prove it."

"Because of this ridiculous, angle-of-entry theory of yours," scoffed Pilate.

"It's not a theory, sir."

"I want you on the next galley back to Rome," barked Pilate, his patience at an end.

"Sir, let me delay my departure for Rome by a week. Give me a chance to prove to you I'm right."

"You can't, because you're wrong."

"Then what harm can one more week do, sir?"

There was nothing the prefect wanted more than to be rid of his pesky investigator. Oh how he regretted condemning that carpenter. Oh how he wished Antipas had taken the case off of his hands. If only the crowd hadn't asked for Barabus. *If only, if only*, he moaned to himself. *So why give this trouble maker another seven days to torment my mind and ruin my sleep? As if my sleep isn't restless enough as it is. But what if the real body turns up? People would think I was responsible for the deceit. Caesar would— well, it's best not to think about what Caesar would do.* "All right, Philippus," he sighed, "one more week, but then I want you gone, understood?"

"You have my word, sir."

Pilate could barely wait long enough for Philippus to leave the room. "What if he's right?" he plaintively asked his second in command, chewing on his left thumb.

Lucius plucked a fig from a nearby tray. "The figs are delicious, sir. You should try one. I guarantee they taste better than your thumb."

There's that damn smile again. I swear before Jupiter, one day, I'm going to wipe that smile off of his face once and for all. Holding onto his temper he asked, "Will you just answer the question?"

Lucius turned to check out his reflection in a nearby mirror. He had on a new tunic just arrived by caravan from Rome. It had a particularly wide laticlava. He liked what he saw, and a broad smile came to his lips. He turned back to address Pilate. "Sir, there's no need to answer your question. Philippus is not right."

Pilate pulled his thumb from his mouth. "I certainly hope so, because the last thing we need is for the real body to turn up."

"Sir, we have the real body."

"I'll look like a fool, and Caesar does not like fools."

"Sir, the only thing we need to worry about is who hid our body down that well."

"We already know—it was this temple guard."

"Surely, sir, you don't think a mere temple guard is behind the theft?"

"Who else?"

"Sir," began Lucius, wandering back to the fruit tray, "The temple guard must have been working for somebody. That's the man we want."

"That could be anybody."

"It could be, sir, but I think we both know who it really is."

"Caiaphas?" asked Pilate, getting up from his throne and starting to pace.

"It has to be, sir. Caiaphas is the only man who—"

"Even if you're right, Tribune," interjected Pilate, keeping his hands locked together behind his back as far away from his mouth as possible, "there's no way I'm ordering the high priest's arrest, not without a lot more evidence."

"What more do you need, sir? We know this entire affair, beginning with the Nazarene's arrest, conviction, and crucifixion, all started with the high priest."

"That doesn't prove anything."

"What about opportunity, sir? Caiaphas, through Joseph of Arimathea, had control of the tomb, and his guards were watching over it."

"Only because I refused Roman guards. Are you suggesting I'm part of this conspiracy?"

"Caiaphas knew you'd turn him down, and, when you did, you gave him a perfect alibi, sir."

"This is all very interesting, Tribune, but it doesn't prove anything."

"Aren't you forgetting about motive, sir?"

"Motive?"

"Sir, remember when I told you our real threat lies in Galilee?"

Pilate stopped pacing. His right thumb went unthinkingly to his mouth. "Antipas?" he asked.

"Caiaphas wants one of his own in Caesarea."

Pilate very deliberately crossed his arms in front of his chest. "So you keep telling me, Tribune," he said. "But I can't order the arrest of the high priest of the Sanhedrin without sparking the very rebellion Caiaphas has been trying to create. I could only do it with overwhelming and irrefutable evidence—so much evidence even Antipas would be forced to support the arrest."

"Don't worry, sir, the evidence is out there, and I promise you I'll find it. In fact, I believe I will have something to show you later tonight."

"You can't tell me now?"

That Popping Sound

Seven Days until Bethany

Joseph of Arimathea couldn't believe what had happened to him. He was a man of wealth and power, a member of the Sanhedrin, and yet he had been crudely dragged from his bed in the dead of night. His wife and children had cried piteously, watching in terror as their home was ransacked and their servants arrested as material witnesses.

The screams started after Joseph was thrown into his cell in the bowels of the Antonia—at times, sharp and piercing, at others, soft and moaning, falling off into lamentable groans, they stretched his nerves to the point where the simple clatter of a knife falling to the floor caused him to jump right out of his skin. His cell was hot and clammy. He was covered in a cold sweat. The bucket that served as his only toilet hadn't been emptied. A handful of industrious flies buzzed around it like real-estate salesmen assessing the value of a home newly placed on the market. The smell was overpowering, pushing him to the brink of nausea. He'd been given nothing to sleep on except a moth-eaten blanket alive with fleas. He was already scratching obsessively. He hadn't been fed, and, although he was dying for a drink, the water they had given him smelled worse than his night bucket. His gut felt as if it were twisted into a Gordian knot so tight even Alexander could not have cut it.

The tribune entered the cell along with two large, violent-looking quaestiones. Professional torturers, they were both highly trained and well-experienced in the practice of inflicting pain without killing. Lucius couldn't wait for them to begin their work. His heart was pounding, his mouth dry in anticipation. He felt within him a rising sensuality that he couldn't and didn't want to control.

Joseph backed away as they entered. Cowering in a corner of his cell, he asked, "Why are you doing this to me, Tribune?"

"I only want to ask you a few questions, Joseph," smiled Lucius.

There was something in the smile that made Joseph's blood run cold. "Then why have you arrested my servants?"

"I wanted to ask them a few questions as well."

"You tortured them. I could hear them screaming."

"That was their fault. They didn't want to answer my questions. Now it's your turn." With a nod of his head, Lucius signalled the quaestiones.

They grabbed Joseph roughly by the arms and dragged him out of his cell. They hustled him down a long, dark hallway until they came to a large circular room. Once inside, Joseph could see the hideous purpose of the room. Everywhere, men were in pain.

A half-naked man was hanging from a hook while a foul smelling creature subjected him to a metal-tipped whip that ripped open his flesh. In the centre of the room was a large fireplace. Next to it, a naked man had been chained to the floor. As Joseph watched, a hot iron was applied to the man's back. Further on, a man was having a small incision sliced into his abdomen. The man screamed, his body writhing horribly, as his flesh was cruelly parted. Joseph did not know the men being tortured, but, when they dragged him over to a rack, his horror was greatly amplified. Isaac, his personal servant, a man who had been with him for twenty years, was tied to the foul device.

It was a simple, rectangular instrument made of wood and slightly raised from the floor. At the top was a wooden roller, at the bottom, a fixed bar. The feet of Joseph's loyal servant were securely tied to the bar, his hands to the top roller. One of the quaetiones stood beside a ratchet attached to the roller at the top

298 | Gerald Hess

of the rack. Very gradually, the quaestiones increased the tension. Isaac let out a soft moan, feeling his body tighten.

"So, Joseph," began Lucius, forcibly turning the priest's face away from the rack and towards him. He wanted to watch Joseph's eyes. He knew it would excite him. "I brought you here to show you what will happen to you if you don't confess to your crimes,"

"Please, I beg you, release Isaac and let him go home. He's done nothing wrong."

"I will, Joseph, the moment you confess to your crimes."

"What crimes? I've committed no crimes," pleaded a terror-stricken Joseph.

"Come, come, Joseph, you know that's not true. I have testimony from your servants that they have seen you conspiring with the high priest Caiaphas."

Joseph's eyes widened, not with fear but anger. "Those are lies!" he shouted. "I had nothing to do with what happened to the body. And far from conspiring with Caiaphas, I opposed his decision to put Jesus on trial in the first place."

"Oh, I do wish people would just admit things. Otherwise, it gets so messy," commented Lucius casually to one of the quaestiones, who shrugged his shoulders. With a nod of his head, Lucius signalled for the torture to continue.

"Let him go," shouted Joseph, as he watched his loyal servant's body slowly stretched to the breaking point.

"I do hope you decide to do the right thing before we start to hear those awful popping noises when the ligaments snap," Lucius lied. He was looking forward to it, especially the high-pitched screams that usually preceded the actual popping.

He whispered in Joseph's ear. "Your servant's muscle fibres will soon be stretched past the point of no return. They'll lose their ability to contract. The poor man will be a cripple for the rest of his life."

Isaac's screams reached a much higher pitch. A loud popping sound, like a branch being violently snapped in two, echoed back and forth across the room. Isaac's head dropped like a stone, his chin resting languidly upon his chest. His loyal servant fell silent. The innocent man hung lifelessly from his leather restraints.

Just before Isaac's' final scream, Lucius had closed his eyes, waiting anxiously for the *pop*. Opening his eyes, the tribune took a moment to wipe the sweat from his brow. He took a deep breath and let it out slowly. An uncontrollable shudder overcame him. For a moment he thought he might fall down.

Lucius smiled at Joseph. *He's white as a ghost,* Lucius told himself. *If I don't break this old priest soon, he's going to pass out on me.* Leaning forward, getting into Joseph's face, the tribune offered the priest a way out. "It's not you I want, Joseph," he said. "I'm interested in Caiaphas. All you have to do is admit the truth—"

"But it's a lie!" shouted Joseph, interrupting the tribune. "It's a lie."

Lucius shook his head. "The truth, a lie, what's the difference as long as the suffering ends?"

Isaac was jolted back to life by a bucket of cold water. The torturer returned to his wheel, ratcheting up the pain. Joseph heard another loud *pop*. Isaac, beyond screaming, gurgled in despair, his pain-fevered mind floating somewhere between consciousness and darkness. Above it all, Joseph could hear Lucius telling him that time was running short. Isaac had only seconds before he would never walk again.

Joseph turned to look into the cruelly smiling face of the tribune. "Make it stop," was all he said.

Later that night, Isaac, in unspeakable pain, unable to walk, or even stand, was laid gently into his bed by Joseph's servants. His arms and legs, the ball joints having been pulled from their sockets, dangled from his torso like overcooked noodles. His entire body, right down to his bones, ached intensely.

Joseph held the hand of his servant as the doctor made Isaac's suffering worse when he, with the help of a large, burly assistant, forced the joints back into their sockets. Even the opiate the doctor had given him before proceeding could not quell the pain.

The doctor informed Joseph that he held out little hope of his servant ever walking again. Later, after the doctor had left, and he and Isaac were alone, Joseph, not knowing what else he could do, went to his locked cabinet. He removed the chalice and brought it to Isaac. "Drink," he said.

"Is this—?" asked Isaac in a painful whisper.

"Yes, Isaac, the blood of God."

Unable to lift his head, Isaac took a deep drink just before passing out.

The scroll containing Joseph's signed confession tightly in hand, Lucius thought about going immediately to Pilate. But the sun was still several hours away. His blood was flush from the sense that victory would soon be his. He wanted to savour the fact that his complicated, daring, and dangerous plan had worked out so perfectly. Well, not quite perfectly. Philippus had certainly not been worth the trouble, although his wife had made up for it.

At the door to the apartment of his favourite female slave, he parted the curtains and looked inside. The room was silent and dark. Closing the curtains behind him, he made directly for her bed.

BETHANY WILL SHOW EVERYONE THE TRUTH

SEVEN DAYS UNTIL BETHANY

Despite the hour, the high priest could not sleep. Alone with his fears, he had spent the night in his study, silently rereading the words of the ancients. *We must never forget the wisdom of the dead,* he reminded himself as he unrolled the scroll he had taken from the shelf behind his desk. He tried to draw strength from the story of Moses and his perilous fight against Pharaoh. His spies inside the palace had told him of Joseph of Arimathea's forced confession. The only good news was that an arrest warrant had not yet been signed. He knew it was only a matter of time.

He had considered running. He had friends in Bactria, where Rome had no jurisdiction. He and Reisa could make a home there.

He had been on the edge of packing his bags when another part of him entered the discussion. *What of my people?* he asked himself. It was not an idle question. With all his heart and soul, Caiaphas believed his people were on the cusp of making a tragic mistake, one that would prove to be genocidal. Moses could have looked after himself. But he risked everything on behalf of his people. *I'm not Moses,* he admitted, *but like him, I must not run. My arrest and trial will bring all of Judea to a boil. But if, from my jail cell, I call on my people not to revolt, to look to God and not their swords, perhaps I can prevent the worst from happening.*

Having decided to meet his fate head on, Caiaphas's thoughts turned to his wife. *She'll have to seek safety in her father's home,* he decided. Surely Lucius would not dare to come after her there?

Caiaphas emptied his wine cup and got up from his desk. He returned the scrolls he'd been reading to their proper place in his library. He bent over and blew out the candles, pitching the room into darkness. He was about to leave when an unexpected candle lit the room. "Reisa, what are you doing up?"

"What's wrong, Joseph?"

Caiaphas looked at her, wishing that he could say nothing. "I think I will soon be arrested."

"For what?"

"For stealing the body," he said.

"I thought the Romans were blaming that on some temple guard?"

"Joseph of Arimathea has confessed that I paid the guard to steal the Nazarene's body."

"I don't believe it. He would not do that."

"They tortured his servants, threatened his family. A man will say anything."

"So what are you going to do?"

"I was going to suggest we go to Bactria, but I've changed my mind."

"You're going to stay and fight?"

"I am. And I'm going to try and keep Judea from exploding."

"But this is all so foolish. We both know Jesus is not dead."

"I haven't been arrested yet. If I stay free long enough, then Bethany will show everyone the truth."

So You Keep Telling Me

Seven Days until Bethany

Afraid to wait until dawn, Procula went straight to Philippus's new apartment after hearing about Joseph of Arimathea's confession. Luckily, she didn't have to have him pulled from his bed. He was still up, packing for his return to Rome. "What are you doing?" she asked in shock.

Philippus looked up from his packing, doing his best not to move his left arm, "I am returning to Rome."

"I thought my husband gave you one more week?"

"Haven't you heard? Lucius has proven that Caiaphas is responsible for everything—the Nazarene's arrest, His crucifixion, stealing the body, dumping it down that well, everything."

"You don't—you can't believe that confession Lucius coerced from Joseph of Arimathea?"

"I believe there are too many unanswered questions. But your husband believes it. He's ordered Caiaphas arrested," he replied, wrapping one of his short swords in goatskin before placing it inside one of his traveling trunks. They were standing in the apartment's tiny bedroom, tiptoeing around piles of clothes, weapons, and armour that Philippus had yet to stow away.

"What?"

"Lucius is going to arrest the high priest tomorrow morning as he makes his way to the temple."

Swept up in a wave of intense panick, the prefect's wife started to pace uncontrollably. Philippus watched her ambulate back and forth, haphazardly negotiating her way around several traveling trunks. He wished there was something he could do to alleviate her distress. Nothing came to mind. "I don't believe you!" she shouted, her pacing coming to a sudden halt. "My Pontius is too cautious," she continued less emphatically.

"He's already signed the arrest order," replied Philippus, picking up another sword. He layed the sword on the bed and wrapped it in a second goatskin.

Procula stood across the bed from Philippus with her hands on her hips. "Then you've got to change his mind," she said. The second sword wrapped, Philippus placed it inside an open trunk. "What do you expect me to do?" he asked plaintively.

"I don't know. Tell Pontius that he's making a mistake, that you've discovered new evidence. Tell him anything. But get him to rescind that arrest warrant."

"New evidence?" asked Philippus, laying a breastplate and a pair of greaves on top of the carefully wrapped swords. "I don't have any new evidence."

"Tell him you do!" snapped Procula, reaching out with her right hand and taking hold of Philippus.

"You want me to lie?" asked Philippus, looking down at the woman's hand clutching his cloak as if it were her only life line.

"I want you to help me save a good man's life, as well as my own."

"So you want me to tell Pilate I have new evidence when I don't?"

"Yes."

"Then what?"

"Pontius postpones the arrest while you uncover your new evidence."

"Mind my asking what this new evidence might be?" he asked, slowly removing her hand.

"How should I know?" she asked, returning to her pacing. "All I know for sure is that Caiaphas did not dump a body down any well."

"Too bad we don't know who did."

"It's the tribune," said Procula. Her pacing stopped. She looked Philippus in the eye. "I can't prove it, but in my bones I know it."

"Too bad we can't use your bones as evidence."

"But if you can get Pontius to give you more time, you could find some real evidence."

"I'm glad you have so much confidence in me."

"I have confidence in the tribune's guilt."

Pilate was not amused. "What new evidence?" He moaned like a sick child.

Philippus looked from Procula's smiling face back to the glowering face of the prefect. His arm was killing him, and the last place he wanted to be was in between Pilate and his wife. But he did want to get to the truth. "Well, sir," he said, "I'd rather not say."

"Rather not say?" asked Pilate. Turning to his wife he asked, "Why am I talking to this man?"

"Because, dear, Philippus needs you to give him back his extra week."

"Why?"

"So that he can determine the validity of his new evidence."

Pilate threw his hands in the air dejectedly. "But I don't need new evidence," he quailed. "The body has been found. The man responsible for stealing it is dead. The man behind him will soon be under arrest. The matter is closed. I should think under the circumstances that Philippus here would want to be on his way back to Rome as soon as possible. Isn't that right, Philippus?"

Philippus looked to Procula for support. All he got was a wan smile. "Well, sir," he said, "under normal circumstances, I would be the first one in line to leave, but this new evidence—"

"What new evidence?" asked Pilate again.

"Well, sir, as I said, I can't say until I can determine whether or not the evidence is true or false."

"You hear that?" he asked his wife. "He can't even determine if the evidence is true or false."

"That's why he needs his week back, Pontius."

"But I don't need—I don't even want—new evidence."

"Pontius, what you want is not important right now."

"Oh really, and what is important right now?"

"That you not make the greatest mistake of your life."

"And what would that be?"

"If you arrest Caiaphas, you'll ignite a revolt that will certainly cost both of us our heads."

"Not if Caiaphas is guilty, and I can prove it."

"That is why we must give Philippus the necessary time to follow every bit of evidence. You have to be absolutely certain that you're arresting the right man. What do a few more days matter when we're putting our very heads at risk?"

"Well," said Pilate, "when you put it like that, I suppose you have a point. "All right," he said with a loud sigh of relief. "I won't arrest Caiaphas. You've got your week."

"Thank you, sir."

"You're doing the right thing, dear."

"So you keep telling me."

OUT FLANKED

SIX DAYS UNTIL BETHANY

Philippus made his way directly to Abner's home. Meticulously, he searched the two small rooms. *The tribune's men have really made a mess of this place,* he said to himself. *I can't imagine they've missed anything.* As Philippus suspected, a search of the two rooms revealed nothing of value. Outside was to prove more valuable.

Philippus was examining the outside of the well. He was about to give up when a break in the clouds provided him with a burst of light. Something sparkled. It was hidden underneath a clump of tall weeds that had taken hold around the edge of the well. He bent down for a closer look, and was able to ascertain that it was a Roman military belt buckle. Attached to the buckle was a regulation military belt. *The man who wore this took it off because he was lifting something heavy, like a body, and then forgot it or couldn't find it in the weeds. Well, I'd better go to the Antonia and see who recently applied for a new belt.* He smiled.

The office of the quarter master assigned the task of keeping the Jerusalem cohorts properly supplied was tucked away in the northwest corner of the Antonia. It would have had a nice view of the temple if it had had any windows. Unfortunately, the room was a barn piled to the rafters with all the material and equipment necessary for the proper functioning of a Roman army. Windows were not a priority.

Philippus went straight to the chief centurion, hoping the man would assist a former legionary. He wasn't too optimistic.

The centurion looked up from his chair as Philippus approached. "How can I help you?" he asked suspiciously.

"You could answer a simple question."

The chief centurion gave Philippus the once over. "Depends on the question," he said.

"I was wondering if you've had any legionaries come by and request a new belt."

"I don't see how that is any of your business," he said dismissively. "Now if you don't mind, I've got work to do." The chief centurion went back to unloading a new shipment of swords just arrived from a foundry in Rome.

Philippus wasn't sure it would work, but a bluff seemed better than nothing. "You do understand that I'm an investigator under contract to Tiberius Caesar and that the information I'm requesting is pertinent to the Judicium I'm currently conducting?"

That caught the chief centurion's interest. "What Judicium?" he asked suspiciously.

"I'm looking for the missing body of the Nazarene."

"I thought that investigation had been concluded?"

"Then you thought wrong. Pilate has decided to extend it."

"But I heard they'd found the body?"

"A body has been found. I'm trying to make sure it's the right one. Now, are you going to answer my question, or do I go back to Pilate and inform him of your lack of cooperation?"

The chief looked up from his swords. "No need to bother the prefect," he said, smiling.

"That's what I was hoping to hear."

"Because, now that you mention it, I did have a legionary come by for a belt recently."

"I'll need a name."

"It'll take me a few minutes. I'll have to check my records."

"Take your time I'm in no hurry."

The chief centurion went to a rack containing numerous scrolls, pulled one out, unfurled it, and started reading. "Ah, here it is. Man's name is Marcellus Macro."

The barracks were not far from the Quarter Master's office, just a short walk across the parade square. A staff tribune told Philippus where Marcellus was billeted.

Marcellus Macro was currently off duty, trying to catch some sleep after being on guard duty all night. *Lucky break*, thought Philippus. *They're always easier to intimidate right after you wake them.* "Marcellus Macro?" he asked, poking Marcellus in the ribs with a finger.

"Hey!" cried out Marcellus. "Who are you?"

"My name doesn't matter, but yours does. Now are you Marcellus Macro?"

"Yeah, I'm Marcellus Macro," he said, sitting up. Marcellus was a short, squat man with slits for eyes and just enough battle scares to make him look dangerous. His head was shaved. His left ear was missing.

"You received a new belt recently?"

"Yeah? I paid for it too," Marcellus barked, angrily rubbing his eyes, doing his best to wake up.

"You mind telling me what you were doing dumping a body down a well?"

Marcellus's sleepy eyes widened. "I haven't dumped anything anywhere."

"Then what was your belt doing lying by the side of a well with a body at the bottom?"

Marcellus blinked several times. "You can't prove that's my belt," he said.

"Yes I can," he said, smiling broadly. "It's really not that difficult. I just go to the chief centurion. Then I have him check to see how many new belts have been ordered in the past month."

"Go ahead."

"Already have, and guess what? Your name is the only one that comes up."

Marcellus shifted uneasily in his bed. "What is it you want?" he asked haltingly.

Philippus put on the warmest, most reassuring smile he could muster. He didn't want to intimidate Marcellus. He wanted the centurion to look upon him as a way out of what would otherwise be a very difficult situation for him. "You seem like a good man, Marcellus—loyal Roman, decent citizen. I don't want to get you into trouble. I just want to know whose orders you were following."

"You say you don't want to get me in trouble, right?"

"I don't just say it, Marcellus. I mean it."

"If I talk to you, trouble is exactly what I will get."

"Whatever you say will remain between you and me—our little secret."

"I don't have to swear to anything?"

"Who said anything about swearing?"

"You promise to keep my name out of your report?"

"You're just leverage to help me get the big fish. That's who I'm really after."

"Is the senior tribune big enough for you? He paid me to dump that body."

That evening, reporting back to Pilate, Philippus was surprised to see Lucius smiling as he walked into the throne room. Next to Lucius was a second surprise—Marcellus Macro. He was also smiling.

"So, Philippus," said Pilate, "I'm so glad you're here."

"I came as soon as I could, sir. What is this all about?"

"It appears that Lucius has uncovered some very interesting evidence about our body."

"What evidence, sir?"

"Why don't we let Lucius do the explaining?"

"Thank you, sir," said Lucius, striding over from his position just off to Pilate's right to stand directly in front of Philippus.

Clearing his throat, he started lying one more time. "Some time ago, sir, it came to my attention that Marcellus had a Jewish mother and spoke the local language, so I approached him to do some undercover work for me."

"Undercover?" asked Philippus.

"That's right. Marcellus was able to gain the confidence of several temple guards. I like to keep an eye on what the guards are saying to one another. After all, they are the largest non-Roman military force in Judea. In any case, one of the guards by the name of Abner...and...well, sir, why don't we let Marcellus explain the rest?"

"Yes, by all means, let us hear from Marcellus," said a very confused Philippus.

"Not much more to say, sir," said Marcellus, his voice cracking a little from the strain of having to address Pilate directly. "It's pretty much like what the tribune said. At his orders, I went to work for this Abner fellow."

"And what did you do for him, soldier?" asked an impatient Pilate.

"Well, sir, I helped him dump a body down a well."

"I presume," inquired Pilate, "that you were well paid?"

"I was, sir, and Abner told me that the money came from a priest."

"Which priest?" asked Pilate.

"Abner told me his name was Joseph of Arimathea and that he arranged the theft under orders from the high priest."

"So you see, sir," said Lucius, jumping back in, "this witness affirms the validity of Joseph of Arimathea's confession and the guilt of the high priest."

"Anything you care to add to that, Philippus?" asked Pilate, eyes wide with anticipation.

Philippus looked around at the unfriendly faces. There was no point in fighting the inevitable. "No, sir," he said. "Only that when I questioned the legionary, he told me Lucius is the one who paid him. So the man was lying then or is lying now. Either way, I don't think he can be trusted."

"Of course." Pilate chuckled. "What else could you say?"

"Sir, can I assume that, after the legionary's testimony, the arrest order for Caiaphas still stands?"

"Tomorrow morning, Tribune, as soon as the high priest leaves his home but before he reaches the temple mount."

THE LAST TRAIRII

FIVE DAYS UNTIL BETHANY

Procula hustled her way from her residence to Philippus's office, the palace hallway dark and empty at such an early hour. She was amazed at how fate always managed to surprise her. She had done all she could to keep Pilate from ordering a Judicium into the disappearance of the Nazarene's body. Yet here she was, running to the very man she would have prevented from even coming to Jerusalem in the first place.

Philippus was in his office not enjoying the sunrise. The request from Elijah seeking a moment of his time was already waiting for him. His defeat at the hands of Lucius had left him sleepless and without any interest in anything but getting out of Judea, unless his arm killed him first. The pain was worse than ever. Philippus figured he would soon be feverish. He forced himself not to think about the fatal decision his procrastination was making for him. He cursed himself for underestimating the tribune's subtlety and diabolic cunning. He had been tricked brilliantly. There was nothing he could do but accept his defeat gracefully. He was about to finally get around to seeing this Jewish contractor who had been hounding him for an appointment for weeks when Procula walked in unannounced, her face ashen. "Caiaphas's arrest has been ordered for this very morning," she said. "What happened?"

"Lucius happened." Philippus shrugged from behind his desk. "He tricked me. He had one of his agents lie to Pilate. The man incriminated Joseph of Arimathea and the high priest."

"So what are you going to do?" she asked.

"There's nothing I can do."

"What?" she asked, her eyebrows raised in dismay as she placed her hands on the top of his desk and leaned in on him. "You do understand that once Caiaphas is arrested…" she stopped mid-sentence. Her face contorted. Philippus could see her fighting back the tears. "By the gods, Philippus, what am I going to do?"

"I wish I knew. Looks like we've come to the last trairii," he said, solomnly referring to a Roman legion's final line of defense.

"Except there isn't one," answered Procula, taking her hands from the desk and straightening up as Amicus entered the room.

"Yes, what is it Amicus?" asked Philippus.

"It's this contractor, Elijah. He's demanding that he be allowed to see you."

Philippus glanced down at the written request sitting on his desk and shrugged. "Well I suppose I might as well see the man."

Amicus ushered Elijah into the room then slid off to the side innocuously.

"So, Elijah, what is this all about?"

"First, sir, let me express my gratitude that you have finally found the time to see me."

"Don't worry about it. Just get to the point."

"Well, sir, the point is that Rome has been paying for nails that have never been delivered. The point is that the tribune has been putting the money thus embezzled into his own pocket. The point is that I'm not going to be the one who gets arrested for it."

"Can you prove these allegations?"

"I've got all the receipts proving that I am not the one responsible and that I have not benefited."

Procula and Philippus exchanged a look of amazement. Philippus smiled from ear to ear. "I think, Procula," he said, "that we may have found our trairii."

Elijah had wanted no part of testifying before Pilate, but when Philippus mentioned charging the contractor as a co-conspirator, he changed his mind immediately.

As the three of them entered the throne room, Pilate had no idea what to make of it. He had been told by his secretary that his wife was demanding that he see her at once.

"Please don't tell me Lucius has already left?" asked Procula, as the three of them entered the throne room.

It wasn't so much what she said that bothered Pilate, but how she said it. Something was wrong very wrong. "He just left. Why? What is so important?"

"Pontius, you have to reverse Caiaphas's arrest order and issue one for the tribune instead."

"What? Philippus, do you know what she's talking about?"

"Sir, Lucius is guilty of embezzlement."

"That's ridiculous," sputtered Pilate.

"It's not ridiculous, Pontius," added Procula. "Elijah here has the receipts to prove it."

It took a couple of less-than-polite shoves from Procula before Elijah found the courage to approach the prefect and hand him the physical evidence. Pilate had barely begun to look the documents over when Procula grabbed them out of his hands. "Pontius, there isn't time for you to read these. Besides, I've read them, and Lucius is guilty. What you have to do is get an arrest squad on the move to apprehend the tribune and rescind the order against Caiaphas."

"Wait just a moment here," blustered a somewhat overcome Pilate. "Just because Lucius is guilty of embezzlement, that doesn't affect the guilt of the high priest."

"Pontius, the man responsible for the evidence against Caiaphas is a swindler and a thief. You can't possibly risk your neck and mine on the word of a proven liar. I won't let you!"

Pilate looked deeply into his wife's frightened eyes. He knew her to be as tough as any man and not prone to emotional outbursts. Yet the tears were welling up. The sight of those moistening eyes struck him deeply. Who was right, who was wrong, didn't matter anymore. With a wave of his hand, he summoned his secretary. "Send men to arrest Lucius Verus Clemens."

"But, sir, no papers have been prepared. What are the charges?"

"The charge is embezzlement!" shouted Procula. "And you can get your paper work later."

The secretary looked from Procula to Pilate and then back again. "As you wish, my lady," he said, starting for the door.

"And hurry!" shouted Procula. "If the tribune isn't arrested in time, I'll see to it that you lose your head before I lose mine."

The secretary broke into a run, screaming orders at his subordinates as he left the throne room.

"Do you think there's enough time?" asked Elijah.

Philippus sighed. "Depends on how much of a lead Lucius has."

"Lucius may not have even left the palace yet," mumbled Pilate.

"I hope you're right, Pontius, my love. Our lives depend upon it."

Lucius was in the lead as his squad of legionaries made its way to the home of the high priest. They were only a block away from intersecting the high priest when the smell of freshly baked bread caught his attention. They were making their way across a small market square, the farmers and craftsmen busy setting up their stalls in the early morning sunshine. A baker was pulling out a tray of honey rolls from a large wood oven in front of his bakery as Lucius marched by. The earthy, almost smoky smell of the fresh rolls combined with the sweet fragrance of the honey was simply too much for Lucius to pass up.

Raising his hand for the squad to halt, he walked over to the source of the divine aromas and entered the bakery. He was in the middle of his second roll when Amicus walked in. "What are you doing here, Amicus?" asked Lucius in between swallows.

"Sir, there's something I have to tell you."

"So tell me?"

"This should be said in private, sir."

All of Lucius's warning bells sounded. He had been surprised by Amicus's unexpected arrival, but not worried. Now he was worried. "Why in private?" he asked.

Amicus took a quick look around. They were alone except for the baker. "With all due respect, sir, the reason why is also private."

"I have no idea what you're talking about, but I can assure you this baker is not someone we need worry about."

"Whatever you say, sir. I've just come from the palace. Sir a squad of legionaries is on its way to arrest you."

"On what charge?"

"Embezzlement, sir. I believe it has something to do with the new aqueduct."

"Are you sure about this, Amicus?"

"I'm sure, sir. I was in the room when this Jewish contractor—"

"Elijah?" asked Lucius, his face turning ashen as the gravity of the situation became clear to him.

"Yes, sir, that was the Jew's name. He told Philippus that he had receipts that proved you'd been putting money meant for the aqueduct straight into your own purse."

"I should have had that man put to the sword," cursed Lucius under his breath. "You've done good work, Amicus, but I think for both of our sakes it's time for us to say good-bye."

Amicus left immediately. The baker handed Lucius the rest of his purchases. He looked at the baked goods, hot and fresh in his hands and for the first time in his life regretted having stopped for food.

Leaving the bakery behind him, the first thing Lucius saw was a squad of legionaries obviously sent to arrest him. He immediately formulated his escape plan. He tossed aside the baked goods and ran back into the bakery.

A moment later, Lucius, disguised in a baker's hat apron and smock came out the front door of the bakery and quietly, head down, made his way out of the square. He went to a house

318 | Gerald Hess

he owned under an assumed name and rented to one of his bodyguards. The bodyguard left the house as ordered and went to purchase a horse for Lucius. Once he was alone, Lucius went straight to where he had hidden several thousand sesterces along with a handful of precious stones and a small purse filled with gold. It was his emergency money. *And if this is not an emergency,* he told himself, *I don't know what is.*

IT'S BACK ON

FIVE DAYS UNTIL BETHANY

Lucius was on his way to Tiberia at almost the same time that Pilate's secretary was nervously explaining the situation to Pilate, Procula, and Philippus. "Sir, I'm sorry to report that the tribune has managed to escape arrest."

"What about Caiaphas!" exclaimed Procula. "Was he arrested?"

"On that, I have good news to report. The high priest was not bothered and is at this very moment performing his duties at the temple."

The look of relief that came over Procula's face brought joy to Pilate's. He had read over Elijah's evidence, and he now understood that his second in command belonged in prison. "So what's next?" he asked to no one in particular.

"The tribune will be sent back to Rome to face charges," replied Philippus.

"We'll have to catch him first," added Procula, helping herself to a goblet of wine.

"Isn't it a bit early for you, dear?" asked Pilate.

"It's been that kind of a morning." Procula sighed.

"I wouldn't worry about catching Lucius," said Philippus, joining Procula in a goblet of wine. It had been a long morning for him as well. "He can't go far."

"What about the missing body?" asked Pilate.

"Sir, are you saying the Judicium is to resume?" asked Philippus.

"Of course that's what I'm saying. Now, you were saying you'd made some progress?"

The question caught Philippus off guard. He couldn't possibly inform Pilate that the progress he'd mentioned had been a ruse he and Procula had used to get him to change his mind. "Well, sir, it's all still very tentative, but I believe I may be close to determining what happened to the body, and where we might be able to find it."

"You believe you may be? What about an arrest?"

"Time will tell, sir."

"That's the best you can do?"

Philippus considered telling Pilate about the real evidence he had uncovered. *How do I explain the healing of Longinus's eyes? Or the one-way footprints or the mystery of how the stone was moved? How do I explain Lazarus?* "I'm afraid so, sir," was all he could bring himself to say.

"Did you hear that, dear?" he asked Procula.

"I did, Pontius, but you remember I told you not to order a Judicium?"

"How can I forget?"

Walking over to Pilate, she took his hand into hers. "I was wrong, very wrong."

Pilate looked down at Procula's hands clutching his. Lifting her hand to his lips, he kissed it then turned back to Philippus. "Do you think you might soon have a suspect?"

"Sir, the followers of the Nazarene are planning a public gathering on the morning of the fortieth day since the tomb went empty. I think that's when we'll get our answers." Philippus didn't bother to add what he thought those answers would be.

"So you think the Nazarene's people took the body?"

"That's what I'm hoping to find out on the fortieth, sir," obfuscated Philippus.

"So when is the fortieth morning?"

"In five days, dear," said Procula, squeezing Pilate's hand a little harder.

BETTER HIS HEAD THAN MINE

FOUR DAYS UNTIL BETHANY

The tribune was in Tiberias just after sunrise. He had been riding all night, too frightened by the thought of bandits to risk stopping to sleep. He was shown directly into the throne room. Antipas didn't get up to greet him. "Tribune, what brings you here so unexpectedly?" he asked.

Lucius told Antipas the tragedy that had befallen him, leaving out only a few details, like the fact that he was wanted for embezzlement. He told his story as if he had been the victim of a plot designed to make him responsible for the failure of the Judicium.

"What about the body you left in that well?" asked Antipas, his eyes taking on a suspicious slant. His spies at the palace had already informed the tetrarch of the tribune's impending arrest on charges of embezzlement. "The one that was supposed to put me on the throne in Caesarea?"

"Rejected, Excellency," said Lucius, dropping into a reclining couch opposite Antipas.

The tetrarch's eyes followed the tribune's legs as they stretched out on the couch. *I wouldn't get too comfortable, Tribune. You won't be staying all that long*, he commented to himself. "Rejected?" he asked, raising an eyebrow. "Why?"

"They know it's a fake, Excellency," replied Lucius. "Something about the angle of entry. You don't have anything to eat, do you, Excellency. I'm famished."

"Angle of entry?" asked Antipas, signalling a nearby slave.

"Apparently, Excellency, the final blow was struck while the Nazarene was still hanging from His cross. So the blade had to have entered the body on an upward angle."

"So?"

"Well, Excellency, the wound on my body is perpendicular."

"How unpropitious for you, Tribune, but what exactly have you been charged with?"

"Well, Excellency, Philippus has convinced Pilate that I'm the one responsible for the fake body."

"But I thought you paid off that centurion, Marcellus, to point the finger at Joseph of Arimathea who you then tortured until he implicated Caiaphas? You told me that the high priest's arrest was imminent. What happened to all of that?"

"As I just said, Excellency, the angle of entry happened."

"Oh yes, the angle of entry."

The slave returned with a large serving plate filled with bread, assorted cheeses, fresh dates, pomegranates, plums, and figs. "Ah," exclaimed Lucius, his mouth watering at the sight of the brimming plate as it was set down on a small circular table. "This looks excellent." He smiled.

"But on what evidence have they charged you?" asked Antipas.

"My centurion, Marcellus, Excellency, has agreed to testify against me. You wouldn't have any wine, would you?" asked Lucius, holding up a golden goblet that was sitting empty on the table next to the plate. "And perhaps some meat? Some lamb would be divine."

Antipas rolled his eyes and then nodded at a slave who came forward with a jug of wine. A second slave ran off to the kitchen. "That hardly guarantees a conviction, Tribune."

"Excellency, with all due respect, I'd rather not take the chance."

Antipas considered his plaintive Roman. The sight of the man sickened him. *He thinks me a fool,* he told himself. *That I don't know what is going on. That I don't know he's lying to me. That I don't know the charges against him have nothing to do with the Judicium. That he's wanted for embezzling.* "That's up to you, Tribune, but what do you expect me to do?"

"Yes, well, Excellency," mumbled Lucius in between mouthfuls of fresh bread slathered with honey and cheese, "I was thinking of heading east, perhaps as far as India. Ah, the lamb smells delicious, Excellency," commented Lucius, the second slave returning from the kitchen with a plate piled high with sliced lamb.

"Do you need someone to point you in the right direction?" inquired Antipas sarcastically.

"Actually, Excellency, I was hoping…that is…you have many contacts in the East. You could arrange safe conduct for me and letters of introduction."

"And why would I do that, Tribune?"

"Because I'm in trouble for trying to help you, Excellency."

"For which you were paid well."

"Partially paid, Excellency."

"For a job only partially completed."

"Excellency, with all due respect, I have performed every service promised."

"Am I sitting on my Father's throne?"

"No, Excellency, but that is not the consequence of my failure."

"Are you suggesting that it's the consequence of my failure?"

"No, of course not, Excellency."

"So, once again, Tribune, why are you here?"

"But…Excellency," he stammered, "what of our friendship?"

"That has already cost me enough."

"I could pay, Excellency. I have plenty of money."

"Most of it mine."

"Here's your chance to get it back, Excellency."

"Your assets will soon be seized by Pilate, if that hasn't already happened."

Lucius was about to devour a particularly large piece of lamb. His hand was halfway to his already wide open mouth when it stopped in mid-air. "You've heard about the embezzlement charges?" he asked.

Antipas smiled smugly. "Of course I've heard," he said.

"Then there's nothing you can do for me?"

"If I help you, Tribune, Tiberius will want my head as much as he will soon want yours."

"Then there's nothing else I can say?"

"Nothing at all, Tribune."

Lucius had barely been shown the door when Antipas called over the captain of his personal guards for a private chat. "How may I be of assistance, Excellency?" inquired the captain.

"The tribune is headed back to Jerusalem?"

"Yes, Excellency, that's the road he took."

"See to it that he never arrives."

Lucius stopped at the first inn he came to on his way back to Jerusalem. It was an unpretentious place catering to the common traveler with simple fare and cheap rooms. The third hour had just ended, and Lucius could barely keep his eyes open. He hadn't slept in over twenty-four hours. But he had one final task to take care of. He noticed the inn had a wine bar and headed straight for it. He spotted what he was looking for right away.

Sitting at a table near a window was a youngish man of no more than thirty years. *He's the right age, size, and hair colour,* Lucius said to himself as he walked over and sat down in a chair right across from him. The young man was drinking alone. From the look of his worn-out, dust-covered sandals, he'd been on the road for a long time and lacked the price of a new pair of sandals. "Long day?" asked Lucius.

"What's it to you?" replied the young man, his eyes contemplating the well dressed Roman.

"Just making conversation, friend," answered Lucius, flashing the man a greasy smile.

"We're not friends, stranger, and I've no time for conversation, so"—he, paused to empty his cup—"you'll have to excuse me."

"No, stay," said Lucius, grabbing the man by the arm. "Can I buy you a drink?" he asked.

The man's eyes glanced at the hand gripping his sleeve. He couldn't miss the sparkle of the gemstones or the glint of the gold that decorated the tribune's fleshy hand. Glaring suspiciously at Lucius, he asked, "Why would you want to buy me a drink, stranger?"

Lucius put on the most accomadating smile he could manage. "Well," he started, "I've been on the road all day like you, and I wouldn't mind a little company, that's all."

"Company?"

"A friendly voice, and I'm willing to pay for it. So, can I buy you that drink or not?"

The young man removed Lucius's hand and sat down. "Why not?" he said. "My name is Simon."

"Glad to meet you, Simon. My name is, ah, Marcellus Macro. Where are you headed?"

"Tiberias."

Excellent, thought Lucius. *Yes, my friend, you'll do very well indeed.*

The first cup turned into several more before Lucius mentioned what was actually on his mind. "Simon, my friend," he began.

"Yes, Marcellus, my friend," replied Simon, his words slightly slurred.

"I have a favour to ask of you."

"A favour? What kind of favour?"

"Well, Simon, I've gotten myself into a bit of trouble."

"Trouble?"

"I got myself involved with a married woman—you know how it is?"

"No, but I'd like to." Simon smiled.

"Her husband has found out, and he's been chasing me all the way from Tiberias. I'm afraid if he catches me, it'll be with a knife in his hand."

"Sounds pretty bad, but how do I fit in?"

"I was hoping I might buy your clothes, as a disguise, to fool the husband."

"But what will I wear?"

"You can have mine."

"But won't the husband think I'm you?"

"Not once he gets a look at you. What do you say?"

"What's it worth to you?" replied Simon.

Lucius paused. He didn't want to seem too eager, as it might invite suspicion. "What's it worth to me?" he asked, feinting disbelief. "Simon, I thought we were friends?"

"And a friend wouldn't ask a friend to do him a favour that could get him in trouble without offering to pay. Besides, Marcellus, you look like you can afford it."

Lucius smiled. The fish had taken the bait. "How does twenty sesterces sound?" he asked.

A smile came to Simon's drunken face. "Sounds just about right," he said, emptying his cup.

Lucius watched Simon ride off in the direction of Tiberias then decided he could finally allow himself a few hours for sleep. He instructed the owner of the inn to wake him for dinner then retired to his room to sleep away the afternoon.

After a modest dinner, Lucius continued on his way. He hoped he was wrong. He really did. He had grown to like Simon and didn't want to see him murdered by Antipas's thugs. But he had seen the cunning look in Antipas's eyes. *I know what he's thinking. He hopes to gain favour with Caesar by handing him my head. Can't blame Antipas. I'd do the same thing. So better Simon's head than mine.*

Antipas's men were surprised to see Lucius headed back towards Tiberias. But that didn't stop them from putting an arrow through Simon's right eye. He was dead instantly.

HE WAS NO MAN

FOUR DAYS UNTIL BETHANY

The opium the doctor had given him to help him sleep wore off before sunset. Rested after his first good night's sleep in days, Philippus rolled out of bed and went to the window of his new apartment. He looked out at the city. He had to admit that the past few weeks had changed him. *I'm not the man I was*, he assured himself. He decided to make one last trip to the tomb. He knew there was nothing new for him to discover, but the tomb was calling him like the house he grew up in.

He wasn't surprised when the guards told him that Mary Magdalene was already at the tomb. "Mary," he called out as he walked towards her. "Why am I not surprised to find you here?"

"You told me it was all right, Philippus," she said cautiously, looking up at him with quizzical eyes.

"It is all right," he replied, coming to a stop beside her.

"Because, otherwise, I would not be here," she continued.

"No, I want you to come. I've told the guards to let you pass."

"I come here to pray, Philippus. Why are you here?"

"I'm not sure," he said, crouching down. "I haven't been sleeping very well. My arm," he said, holding up the wounded wing. "And I was watching the sunrise when it just came over me."

"Came over you?"

"Don't ask me to explain it. All I can tell you is it has nothing to do with my investigation."

"Something personal then?"

"Yes, I think it is. I think that it has something to do with what's happened to me."

"Happened to you?"

"This investigation, the miracles, the...I don't know...it's just that—"

"Jesus happened to you."

"Maybe. I don't know if I'd go that far."

An anxious silence settled between them. Philippus stood up. Both of them knew that Mary was right. That Jesus had penetrated his defences and entered his soul. Was he ready to believe, believe for the first time in his life? He was. He just wasn't ready to admit it.

The moment lingered until Mary broke it. "I've been to see Ruth," she said. "I spoke with her new father. He told me she was doing well and that she speaks often of you, asks how you are doing and if she will be able to see you soon."

"What do they tell her—her new parents?"

"They tell her you've returned to Rome."

"Good," he said, idly kicking at a piece of the great stone. "How well did you know the Nazarene?" he asked, changing the subject.

"He saved me," she answered forthrightly, her dark eyes staring directly into his. "I was possessed by demons. Jesus drove them out, and then He showed me how to live."

"How to live?" he asked scratching the side of his head.

"What is truly important in life," she continued.

"And what is truly important?"

"Our relationship with God," she said, watching for his reaction.

"Our relationship with God," he repeated, returning to his crouch, drawn in. "God is for the next world, if there is a next world. What about our relationship with things that matter in this world?"

"God is what matters."

"Really? What makes you so sure?'

"Our time in this world is short. Our time with God is forever."

"So this world doesn't matter? Only God matters?"

"You asked me what is truly important. God is truly important."

Philippus looked once again into the empty tomb. There was nothing to see, the morning light having yet to penetrate its darkness. "What was Jesus like?" he asked, staring into the unknown.

"He was gentle and yet strong. He saw the good in everyone, even those who would do Him harm, but he had no tolerance for the bad. He wanted no part of earthly power, instead calling on all of us to see the true power of Heaven that he represented."

"Ever since I arrived in Jerusalem, people have been trying to get me to believe something. My wife wants me to believe in Bacchus. You want me to believe in Jesus."

"I don't want you to believe in anything."

"You don't?"

"I want you to come to God, Philippus, the one true God. But I want you to do it in your own time, in your own way, when you are ready."

"So you don't think I'm ready?"

"Only you can answer that question. Are you ready?"

"I don't know. I was always quite comfortable not believing in anything, but now—"

"Now you're not so sure?"

"Now I'm not so sure. What do you think I should do?"

"Just become who you are."

He smiled at her. "Become who I am. Very clever, Mary—an answer without an answer."

"What I mean, Philippus, is that we are all created in God's image. So to become who you are is to become closer to God."

"All created in God's image?" pondered Philippus. "Does that include the blood-thirsty crowds at the coliseum?"

"Even those who gather to watch men kill each other are priceless in the eyes of God."

"If that's true, I can't say I have a very high opinion of God."

"Philippus, please, since the first time we met, you have obsessed over what you think of God. Why don't you try worrying more about what God thinks of you instead?"

"What God thinks of me? You mean have I given enough in sacrifices and donations?"

"I mean do you strive to rid your life of sin every day?"

Sin, thought Philippus. *The Nazarene had talked a lot about sin.* For Jesus and His followers, to sin was to not live up to God's law, to let God down, and to hurt Him. For Philippus and most Romans, sin was understood as having to do with justice. One paid the consequences for one's actions. Fight others, and others would fight back. The strongest and cleverest would emerge victorious. Sin had nothing to do with breaking the commandments of God. It simply acknowledged that if one was stupid and weak and behaved stupidly and weakly, he would suffer the consequences. The idea that anyone could be successful and sinful was going to take Philippus awhile to get used to. "I'm not sure I even know what sin is," he said.

"Sin is not that complicated. In its simplest form, to sin is to fail to treat others the way you would like to be treated."

"That's all there is to it?"

"There's more, but if you follow that one rule, God will look favourably upon you."

"And what of the sins I've already committed?"

"For those, you must pray for forgiveness."

"God will forgive us?"

"God did not send us His only Son for the benefit of the best and brightest. Jesus came for sinners. Sinners like you and I. He came to save us, Philippus."

"Sounds like Jesus was quite a man."

"He was no man."

"Well, He died like one," said Philippus, standing up and walking away.

If the Shoe Fits

Four Days until Bethany

Lucius used the cover of a large caravan to smuggle himself back into Jerusalem. The men driving the caravan were exhausted, having been up all night in order to reach Jerusalem before the midday rush. They didn't see Lucius untie the flap of the last wagon in the caravan and jump inside. The wagon was loaded with bales of cotton. Careful not to make any noise, he wedged himself behind two of the larger bales so that he was hidden from view.

Everything went smoothly until one of the guards at the west gate noticed the untied flap. Lucius felt himself sweating as he heard the guard ask the driver why the flap wasn't tied down. The driver said he had no idea because he remembered tying it off. The guard pulled back the flap then jumped into the wagon for a look around. The tribune thought he was caught for sure, but the guard didn't bother with a thorough search. He merely satisfied himself that the wagon was filled with cotton before jumping back down.

Philippus returned to his new rooms at the palace poured himself a large goblet of wine and collapsed into a reclining chair. The opium had worn off. He tried to ignore the pain and relax. His mind wouldn't let him. It was too busy trying to understand what was happening to him. He was falling under the spell of the Nazarene. His words had persuaded him, and His miracles had convinced him. *But it's not easy to change*, he told himself. *I'm pretty settled in my ways. I don't know if I even want to change.*

332 | Gerald Hess

He got up, filled his pipe, and lit it. He returned to his chair as the opium soothed the pain but not the questions that were swirling around inside of him. Surrendering his purely logical and materialistic view of the universe filled him with dread. So much of his life depended upon a cold, dispassionate, and logical viewing of the facts. He had always made great efforts when starting a case to avoid having faith in anything—not witnesses, not confessions, not even physical evidence. All of them had to be viewed sceptically, double and triple checked, until proven to be genuine. Faith was for suckers and fools, not investigators.

Then what about hunches? he asked himself. *That feeling I get in the pit of my stomach when the facts don't feel right but I can't say why? Was that not a form of faith? Don't I have to have faith in my gut to follow up on a hunch the facts don't substantiate? Of course I do. So how is faith in God any different?*

Well, for one thing, it's more consequential. Putting your faith in the one true God is significantly more important than trusting your gut to tell you there's something wrong about the cook when all the evidence points to the gardener. But does being different in degree make them any different in kind? In both instances, you have to submit to a higher power.

Submission—is that the true stumbling block? Is my retreat into logic really just covering up for my unwillingness to submit myself to God's will? To turn over the question of how I should live my life to someone, or something, greater than myself? Am I even capable of that?

The opium carrying him off to the very edge of consciousness, Philippus contemplated the loss of so much power. He found himself rolling over in his mind a perfect example of what that loss could mean in the real world. He imagined himself on a battle field, watching the approach of an onrushing horde of blood-thirsty barbarians. He imagined himself not raising his sword but merely turning his cheek. He couldn't help himself. He laughed out loud at the very thought of it.

He emptied his goblet and forced himself to get up to refill it. He had to admit that no matter how ridiculous it would look on the battle field, it certainly would take a prodigious amount of courage. *More courage*, he thought, *than any man could possibly summon. A man could head out to meet his enemies with only non-violence in his heart, but when all that stands between him and certain death is his sword, how many men would not use it?*

And even if I could find an army of men with that kind of courage, wouldn't it, in the end, prove to be a useless and futile gesture? Would not the brave soldiers of God be cut down? Their families and friends murdered or enslaved?

Back in his chair, eyes closed, enjoying the effects of the opium, he imagined thousands and thousands of brave men and women, their faith in God so absolute they did not fear—not even death—greeting with smiles and open hands a great army of barbarians bent on destroying them.

At the moment the two great forces meet, the barbarians are confused. Some, the blood running too high, slice mercilessly into their smiling adversaries, but most stand face to face with those they had intended to kill, unable to decide what to do next. Eventually even the ones doing the killing join their comrades in stupefied amazement. One of God's warriors offers a wine skin to one of the barbarians. The barbarian takes a long drink before handing it off to the man next to him. Suddenly, thousands of wineskins are being passed back and forth. All thought of killing melts away. Hands are shaken, shoulders clasped.

His eyes growing heavy, sleep approaching, Philippus had one final conscious thought—Bethany. On that reassuring thought, unconsciousness overtook him.

Worried about being spotted during the daylight hours, Lucius rented a room and caught up on his sleep. Just after sunset, making his way towards the palace, Lucius could think of only one person who might still be both willing and able to help him.

Getting past the palace guards was tricky, but he knew when the guard was changed. Taking advantage of the time it took for the new guards to take up their positions, he hustled past the guard house.

He used the servants' stairs to avoid being seen. He reached Helena's apartment and stepped into the main hallway. A quick look around assured him that the hall was empty. He made a dash for Helena's door, hoping that she would be alone.

Although not expecting him, Helena was pleased to see Lucius when he unexpectedly appeared in her living room. "Lucius!" She smiled. "What a surprise."

"Is Philippus here?" he whispered, his eyes looking everywhere for danger.

"I have no idea where he is. Lucius, what's wrong?"

"Nothing. Is he expected back soon?"

"Philippus has his own apartment now."

"Of course, I'd forgotten."

"Lucius, something is troubling you. What is it?"

Lucius grabbed Helena by the shoulders and shook her. "Stop questioning me!" he shouted into her startled face. "Now listen to me, Helena. I'm hungry and I'm thirsty. Order your slaves to feed me and bring some wine. After I've eaten, I'll answer all of your questions, all right?"

Unable to speak, she nodded her head and left to order Lucius some dinner. As she left for the kitchen, a slave rushed forward with a goblet of wine. Lucius grabbed it from the slave's hands taking a long deep drink.

His arm woke him. Philippus thought about taking more opium but decided he'd hold out a little longer. Trying to take his mind off of the pain, he went to the window. He wasn't surprised to discover that the sun had set. He'd slept away the entire day. *Drugs will do that to you.* He smiled to himself. His arm had gotten much worse. The infection was spreading throughout his body. The chills would start soon and then turn to fever. He looked at himself in a mirror, his face pale, his eyes deathly, he decided he'd better find out if he could prove a miracle.

Philippus found the tomb exactly as he'd left it. He lit a torch and carefully made his way along the plank that led to the front of the altar. He shoved his torch into the crack created by the mysterious lightning strike. He positioned the torch so that it illuminated the ground directly in front of the altar. He carefully fitted the clay moulding of the one-way footprints into the sandal he'd gotten from Longinus. He wasn't surprised when it fit perfectly.

He was about to leave when something made him stop. Standing in the entrance to the tomb, one foot in, the other out, he turned and looked inside. In the wavering light of his torch, the tomb had a strange, surreal appearance, as if he were looking at it but not really seeing it. A sudden gust of wind came up, bending the flame of his torch towards the bottom of the altar like a spotlight. For what seemed like minutes but was no more than a single breath, the one-way footprints were all he could see.

Philippus looked down at the sandals still clutched in his other hand. He felt a shudder run through him as he finally accepted the truth. His cynicism, his doubt, the materialism that had ruled his life—they were all utterly false. He was conscious of a higher power, a higher purpose, something more than mere existence. *We are not just bags of flesh, bones, and blood*, he told himself. He shed his self-importance, his role as the great sceptic, the man who saw through all the false pieties and who saw the world for what it was and dealt with it on his own terms according to his own morality. He faced his own unimportance. He faced the mystery and the majesty of God.

His legs unable to hold him, he fell to his knees. He hadn't merely shed his old ways. He had shed vital parts of his own identity. On his knees, in front of the empty altar, he came to understand that love was the measure of a man, not intellect or money or power. *We are—we* become *what we cherish, not what we accomplish.*

The torch tumbled from his hand. Holding firm to the sandals, he lifted his face skyward.

He couldn't remember the last time he had prayed. The gods of Rome had long ago lost their appeal. Religion for him was a form of politics and nothing more. The priests, like politicians, played to the sympathies of the crowd, offering false hopes in return for real coin. What he felt now was unlike anything he had ever experienced before. Not on the battle field, not in the bed of a lover, not from the thrill of a case solved, and certainly never in a Roman temple.

Closing his eyes, he did the best he could.

Lucius pushed away his plate, picked up his silver goblet, and emptied it. He ordered a slave to refill it, and then, after a loud belch, he relaxed.

"So are you ready to tell me what is wrong?" she asked.

He tried to size her up. Could she help him? Her father had money, and from what he'd seen back in Rome, he denied his precious daughter nothing. He needed money, that much was obvious, but money for what? Running was easier said than done. He was wanted by Rome, and Rome was everywhere. And then it hit him! The followers of Bacchus knew all about running from Rome. "I need your help," he said cagily.

"And of course you shall have it, darling, but why? What is wrong?"

"Let's just say I tried one trick too many and leave it at that."

"No, Lucius," she said sternly. "I want to know what's going on, or you can leave right now."

"I don't see why you need to know anything, dear. What possible good will it do you or me?"

"You said you needed my help. Talk, or you won't get my help. It's up to you."

The tone of her voice surprised him. He had expected suspicion but not defiance. "All right," he said. "I'm in charge of the accounts for the new aqueduct. It's a lot of money, a huge temptation."

"Lucius, you didn't!"

"I couldn't help myself. Pilate was so busy with the actual construction, and everybody else took their orders from me. I had no one looking over my shoulder."

"Did you embezzle Roman or Jewish money?"

"Money is money. It all spends."

"How do you think I can help you?"

"Your fellow believers, many of them have had to go into hiding. Such friends could hide me."

"I don't know, Lucius. You're not even—I mean, you haven't been baptized."

"I've already told you I'll convert."

"So that we'll hide you?"

"Originally, it was so that we could be together."

"And now?"

"And now it still is," he lied, eyes darting down and to the left.

By the time Philippus made it back to his apartment, his arm was throbbing worse than ever. The bright red colouring had given way to a yellowish green that was now starting to turn black.

He went to his bedroom and took his small vial of opium from the side table. Back in the living room, he filled a pipe and took a long draw. Immediately, the pain started to recede. He sat down and let the opium do its work when he heard a knock at his door. "Come in," he shouted dreamily from his couch. A legionary marched in and saluted.

"Sorry to bother you, sir," he said, sniffing the opium in the air and smirking. "A Mary Magdalene is waiting to see you. She says it's urgent, and she's brought a child with her, sir."

"A child?"

"A little girl, sir."

He had Mary and the girl ushered directly into his apartment. He wasn't surprised to see the girl was Ruth. "What is it, Mary?"

"I have bad news," she said, gripping Ruth's hand firmly. "Ruth's new parents are dead."

"What?"

"They were killed by bandits. They hid Ruth in a root cellar."

Ruth ran to Philippus, wrapping her arms around his legs. "I'm sorry," she cried.

"Ruth, sweetheart," he said, running his hand through her hair. "This isn't your fault. No one blames you, but"—he looked at Mary—"what are we going to do now?" he asked.

"I don't know, but Ruth needs a home."

"Can't I stay with you?" she asked, looking up into Philippus's eyes. Philippus tore himself away from those sad pleading eyes and looked at Mary with an expression of hopelessness.

"She could stay with me, Philippus, but—"

"No! I want to stay with Philippus!" cried Ruth.

"Of course you can stay with me, Ruth," he said, unable to say anything else, "but why don't you step out onto the balcony and look at the stars while Mary and I have a little talk, all right, dear?"

Ruth wiped newly formed tears from her eyes. "Really?" she asked. "I can stay with you?"

Philippus nodded his head and said, "Really."

"Okay." Ruth smiled bravely as she headed for the balcony wiping away the tears as she went.

"That was a lie you told her, wasn't it?" asked Mary as soon as Ruth was out of ear shot.

"No, Mary, it wasn't a lie, but there is another problem. It's my arm."

"Are you going to have it amputated?"

"I'm afraid it's too late for that now."

Mary went to him and, gently lifting his left arm, examined it closely. "You fool," she said. "You've thrown away your life."

"I didn't think, with just one arm, my life had any purpose anymore."

Mary glanced out at Ruth on the balcony. "And now you realize that it does."

"Can't you help her?"

"Yes, I can help her, but it's you she loves. You're all she talks about. When I found her she was still in that root cellar. She hadn't eaten or had anything to drink. If I hadn't come by to visit, who knows? She might have died right there. I only found her hiding place because she heard me calling out her name. You know what she said to me from her hiding place?"

Philippus hung his head, unable to look Mary in the eye. "What did she say?" he asked.

"'Take me to Philippus. I want to see Philippus.' She wouldn't leave her hiding place—not for food, not for water, not for anything. Only after I promised her that I'd take her to you did she come out. I wasn't sure if coming here was the right thing, but you said if anything went wrong…I see I was mistaken."

Philippus lifted his head and looked at Mary. His eyes were moist. "I didn't know," he said. "How could I? I thought the only one who'd miss me was me, and I didn't care anymore."

"Jesus cares about all of us."

"Yes…Jesus. I guess I should tell you. I've proven that you're right. Jesus is alive."

Mary smiled at him. "It's good that you've finally come to the truth."

"It's too bad Jesus isn't here right now. He could fix my arm." Philippus looked out onto the balcony. Ruth was staring up into the night sky. He could see her pointing with her finger; her lips were moving. *She's counting the stars,* he said to himself. He remembered that fateful morning only six weeks ago when he had almost taken his own life. *How easy it is,* he thought to himself, *to end it all when you're the only thing that matters. How meaningless our lives can become unless we're connected to something bigger, even if that something is just a lonely little girl. How right the Nazarene was to make how we treat others so crucial to what He was trying to teach.* Philippus went over to a side table and poured himself a goblet of wine. He looked down into his goblet. The red liquid sparkled, catching the candle light. "Wait!" he exclaimed. "Jesus is here, or, at least, His blood is."

"His blood?" asked Mary.

"Yes, Mary, His blood—on His burial shroud. And the blood of Jesus cured Longinus's eyes. Maybe it can cure my arm."

He went to the lockbox where he had placed the shroud after taking it from the tomb that first day. Using his knife, he scrapped some of the dried blood into a cup. He mixed the dried blood with water then he poured the mixture of dried blood and water into and over his putrefying arm. "Well, that's it," he said. "We'll have to wait and see if it works."

"What about Ruth?"

"You take her for now. If I survive, I'll see you in Bethany, and I'll take her back."

"Forever?"

"Forever."

"You'll have to convert immediately," said Helena. "And you must fully commit yourself to Lord Bacchus," she continued, pointing an accusatory finger at Lucius, who was back at the dinner table enjoying a little honey and fresh bread. "It cannot be merely for your convenience."

"Whatever you say," he said, his attention on the piece of bread he was slathering with honey.

"No!" she shouted, standing directly in front of Lucius and slapping the bread out of his hand. "This is about whatever you say. And unless I believe that your conversion is genuine, I won't risk the safety of my fellow believers."

Lucius's eyes narrowed. "I did not want to say this, dear," he said in a very level and calm voice, "but I'm afraid I can't afford to negotiate. I need your help and the help of your friends. If that help is not willingly offered, I'm ready to coerce it."

"Are you threatening me?" she asked, angrily placing her hands on her hips.

"Only if you refuse me. I'll tell Rome everything I know about you and your fellow believers."

"You are threatening me!"

"More like a promise."

Alone with his arm, Ruth having left with Mary, Philippus couldn't deny that although it had been less than an hour, he was already feeling positive results. *I'm due for some more opium*, he thought, *but I don't need it.*

There was no denying that the black discolouration, the final stage of the bacterial decay, was gone. The swelling had also gone down. He had to admit it. He had been healed.

He walked out onto his balcony and looked up into the dark, star-covered sky. He whispered a small thank you to God then he wiped away a tear.

He was headed for his bedroom when a nervous sentry requested permission to enter his apartment. "Come in," shouted Philippus, hoping that whatever the legionary had to say wasn't going to take too long.

"Sorry to disturb you, sir," began the legionary after saluting, "but one of the kitchen slaves believes he saw Lucius Verus Clemens using the servant's stairs to enter the palace."

Philippus's eyes widened in shock. *Could Lucius really have returned to the palace? Who could he possibly be hoping to see?* It didn't take him long to answer his own question.

"It appears that you have left me no choice," said Helena.

"Then you'll help me?"

Lucius never got an answer to his question. "Philippus!" exclaimed Helena. "What are you doing here?"

"I came by to warn you to be on the look out for—"

"For me, Philippus?"

"Tribune." Philippus smiled, turning to see Lucius for the first time. "People have been looking all over for you."

"And here I am."

"So you are," replied Philippus.

Lucius was on his feet, knocking over his chair and drawing his sword. "Draw your sword," he said, his eyes taking on a malevolent glitter. "It's time we found out how good you really are."

"I'm not going to fight you, Lucius. I'm placing you under arrest."

"Not without drawing your sword."

Philippus slid to his left, avoiding Lucius's first slashing swing. He felt the breeze as Lucius's sword sailed past his head. Taking a step backwards, he drew his sword.

"Now, that's more like it." Lucius smiled, slashing back across his body. Phillipus used his sword to parry the tribune's second swipe then struck his own blow. The tribune was ready for him.

Slicing his blade across his body to the left, he struck Philippus's sword, almost knocking it out of his hand. The two men circled each other, their swords shrieking as blows and counter blows were parried.

With a desperate yell, Lucius swung viciously at Philippus. At the last second, Philippus managed to get his sword in front of the tribune's. The blow, striking his sword, bounced, and glanced off his left arm. "Wounded arm hurt?" asked Lucius. "Not as strong as you hoped?" he joked, rushing at him.

Cutting and thrusting, Lucius came at Philippus with everything he had, forcing Philippus to retreat across the room. Seconds turning into minutes, the tribune began to labour, all those morning pastries catching up with him. Philippus managed to stay tantilizingly close but always out of reach.

The tribune backed Philippus into a corner. Parrying the tribune's assault, Philippus didn't realize he was trapped until it was too late. The tribune faked to his left then nimbly shifted to his right as Philippus moved to slide past his faked blow. His escape blocked, Philippus cursed himself for buying into the fake and retreated into the corner.

With the last of his strength, Lucius hacked at Philippus again and again and again. Philippus, with no room to manuver, did his best to block the tribune's assualt. He could sense his opponent was running out of oxygen. Then, the unexpected happened. Lucius's sword deflected off of his, almost slicing off one of Philippus's fingers before slicing into his right forearm. Philippus's sword fell from his hand.

Helena screamed. Lucius smiled and raised his sword. Desperate for breath, he had to pause for just a second. Philippus saw his chance. Stepping inside what was to be the tribune's final stroke, he thrust his left shoulder into the the exhausted tribune's chest, sending him to the floor. As he landed, Lucius couldn't believe his moment of triumph had so suddenly turned into defeat.

Philippus picked up his sword and placed it against Lucius's exposed throat.

"Philippus, please, don't kill him," cried Helena.

The muscles in his right arm began to stiffen. He was going to kill him. At the last second, something held him back. He remembered Mary telling him to treat others the way he would like to be treated. Slowly, his mind cleared. The anger, the emotional fire, the hate of battle left him. "I have no intention of killing you, Tribune."

"What are you going to do?" Lucius asked.

"I'm letting you go. But if I were you, I'd go home and do the honourable thing. It's time to open your wrists, Tribune." Philippus watched Lucius struggle to his feet. He went for his sword, but Philippus warned him off. He looked at Helena, shrugged silently then scurried away. After he left, Philippus asked Helena, "Were you seriously thinking of helping him?"

It took a moment for her to compose herself. "I don't know. I think so," she said hesitantly.

"Because he'll only hurt you."

"What do you care?"

"I know it's over between us, Helena, but I will always care about you."

"I don't need your pity."

"Come with me to Bethany. The Nazarene is going to be there."

"You don't really believe that, do you?"

"I don't believe it, Helena. I know it."

"Then you truly are mad. I'm going home, Philippus. My father is begging me to return to Rome."

"What about Bacchus?"

"I've eaten of his flesh, drank of his blood. He'll always be with me."

"Remember you said you felt sorry for me?"

"I still do."

"Well you can stop, because I've found my reason why."

"Then I'm happy for you."

"Does that mean you might change your mind?"

"I'm not going to Bethany."

Philippus nodded his head, accepting her refusal as final. "Good-bye, Helena," he said, walking out the door. He was going to tell her about Ruth, but what would be the point? Their life together was over.

"Good-bye, Philippus," she said to his back.

NOT TO BE UNDERESTIMATED

FOUR DAYS UTNIL BETHANY

Lucius had no intention of opening his wrists. In his mind there was nothing worse than death. The end of the only thing that had ever mattered to him was more than he could bear. He was determined to put personal extinction off for as long as possible and to suck as much juice out of the time fate afforded him as he could. Giving up was not his style. He had a better idea.

It was a gamble, but there were no safe avenues of escape open to him anymore. This particular gamble appealed to the tribune because it was a gamble on the only man he trusted—himself.

The plan was simple enough. He would present himself to Pilate, but before he could be taken away, he would attempt one final gambit. He would take advantage of Pilate's single greatest weakness: His sense of inferiority. He would underscore for Pilate the tenuousness of his own hold on power. Explain how the problems of his second in command could, in the eyes of an already suspicious and paranoid Tiberius, become Pilate's problems as well.

He was arrested as he made his way to the throne room. He offered no resistance, asking only that he be taken to Pilate. The guards informed him that they had orders to do exactly that.

Pilate watched Lucius as he marched ahead of his escort, forcing them to hurry to keep up. He stopped ten feet in front of the prefect and saluted.

"Tribune," said Pilate sternly, "you have been charged with embezzling imperial funds placed under your authority. You are to be sent back to Rome at the earliest convenience to face trial on these charges. Do you have anything to say for yourself?"

Lucius smiled broadly. "Yes, sir," he said forthrightly, "I do have something to say."

"Then get on with it."

"First, let me say, sir, that I think we should have this conversation privately."

The request caught Pilate by surprise. "Why should we be alone?"

"Because, sir, I have things to say that you would not want to be made public."

Pilate looked around the throne room. Turning to the commander of the guards, he asked, "Has the tribune been properly searched?"

"Yes, sir, I searched the tribune personally."

With a signal to the captain, the room was emptied. Pilate turned a baleful eye upon his former second in command. "So what is it you have to say, Tribune?"

Lucius swallowed hard. His moment of truth was at hand. Whether he would live or die would be determined by what he said over the next few minutes. "Sir, I find my throat more than a little dry. Might I have a cup of wine?"

Pilate gestured in the direction of a wine jug on a table next to him. "Help yourself," he said.

Lucius poured a cup, drank it, and poured a second. Then he walked back to stand in front of the prefect. He spoke slowly and deliberately. "Sir," he began, "I understand that if you decide to go forward with this prosecution, I will be the first to lose my head, but you can't believe that I will be the last."

"Are you threatening me?" asked Pilate, his hand sliding to the knife hidden under the armrest of his chair.

"Of course not, sir," said Lucius, his eyes taking note of the prefect's not-so-subtle move for his knife. "I have nothing to threaten you with. I want only to advise you of the facts. Like the fact that Tiberius's revenge can be impossible to predict or contain once it gets started."

Pilate tried to swallow but found his throat suddenly dry. "What do you want, Tribune?"

Lucius took a step forward. Pilate's hand tightened around the haft on his knife. Lucius stopped in midstep and smiled boldly at Pilate. "You won't need the knife, sir," he said disarmingly. "I'm unarmed, and besides, I'm not here to threaten your life. I'm here to protect it."

"Protect me how?"

"By reminding you sir–that we are in this together."

Pilate's eyes widened. "That's preposterous!" he shouted.

"What's preposterous, sir is the idea that Tiberius will believe you had no knowledge of my crimes and did not benefit from them."

"B-but...I...I didn't benefit!" sputtered Pilate, the potential danger becoming clear to him.

"Try and see this from Caesar's point of view, sir. Tiberius knows how involved you are in the construction of his aqueduct. Is he likely to believe that I was able to keep you completely in the dark?"

"But you did keep me completely in the dark!"

"Yes, sir, but is Caesar likely to believe that? And if he doesn't, what do you think he'll do?"

Pilate's mind was reeling, his heart racing, his blood pressure reaching dangerous levels. He started to chew on a knuckle then forced himself to stop. What the tribune had just said could not be denied. One had only to look at the ruthless, unending revenge Tiberius had inflicted on Sejanus's relatives, friends, and even acquaintances.

His mind turned to Procula. It would be one thing for his lifeless body to be tossed down the steps of mourning because of his failure to keep a better eye on Lucius, but Procula? It was too much to contemplate. Whatever the cost, he had to protect her. He had to make sure that she did not suffer. "There will be plenty of witnesses to testify to my innocence," he said, sounding vastly more confident than he felt.

"Of course, sir, but what if I testified?"

"You'd testify against me?" asked Pilate, his mouth agape.

"Not willingly, sir, but under torture…" Lucius didn't finish his sentence. He didn't have to.

Emptying his wine goblet, Pilate forced himself to calm down. "So what are you proposing we do, Tribune?" he asked.

Hearing the plural pronoun, Lucius allowed himself to relax for the first time in a long time. Pilate was his. "Forget my arrest order, sir," he said confidently. "Reinstate me as second in command, and let me go to Bethany."

"Bethany?"

"Yes, sir. According to my informants, this Jesus impostor is supposed to be making an appearance in Bethany. I'll go there with a centura and arrest the impostor along with all of his so-called disciples. I'll end this entire affair once and for all."

"What about Philippus?"

"Order him back to Rome."

"What? He'll report everything to Caesar."

"No he won't, sir. I'll assign two of my most trustworthy men to escort Philippus to Caesarea for his return trip to Rome. They'll make sure he never arrives."

Pilate was taken aback by the tribune's unruffled ruthlessness. But he was right. It was the only way out. Make the arrest, nip any revolt in the bud, and silence the only witness they had to worry about. He hated to say yes, but he knew he would. He told himself it was for Procula. His conscience knew better.

The first thing Lucius did after securing Pilate's reluctant support was break into Philippus's interrogation room. He searched the room until he found the forged letter. Smiling like a cat with a feather sticking out of its mouth, he destroyed the letter by crushing the wax tablet under the heel of his boot. *One more problem solved,* he said to himself. *Now it's onto the biggest problem of them all.*

His arm healed, Philippus was in a sleep so deep even dreams could not penetrate it. Suddenly, rough hands were shaking him back to consciousness. "Get up! Get dressed!" shouted the larger of Lucius's two bodyguards.

"What is going on?" demanded Philippus, straining to clear the cobwebs. He was still in that half-awake state where one is never sure where dreams end and reality begins. Surrounding the bed and glaring down on him were Lucius's bodyguards. "You're taking a trip," said the one who had shaken him awake.

"You're going home."

The two men watched Philippus get dressed and then marched him out to the living room, where Lucius was waiting for him. "What are you doing out of jail, Tribune?"

A self-important smile slowly worked its way across Lucius's face. "There's something you should know about me, Philippus. It is never wise to count me out."

"So I'm discovering."

"Don't look so glum, Philippus. I have good news for you."

"Why do I find that hard to believe?"

"You're not still holding that little disagreement we had against me, are you?"

"I thought I might."

"Well don't, and don't worry about that letter from my father."

"You mean the one you forged?"

"Unfortunately, the letter has been destroyed."

"How convient for you," replied Philippus, controlling his anger with a mighty effort.

"Oh, come on, Philippus, smile. I bring you good news. Don't I, men?" Lucius asked the loitering guards. They chuckled as if privy to some inside joke. "I've been ordered to see to it that you're on a galley bound for Rome as soon as possible."

"You're sending me home?"

"It wasn't my idea. I suggested to Pontius that you'd be much less trouble dead, but he insisted, and orders are orders."

Philippus shrugged. He had already figured out that the tribune had no intention of sending him back to Rome alive. *I've got too much on him.* "So tell me, Lucius, how did you convince Pilate not to throw you into prison?"

"It wasn't nearly as difficult as you might imagine. I just informed our beloved prefect that once I was on trial in Rome, his name was bound to come up, and not in the most flattering of terms. Now, I've a busy day ahead of me, so I'm afraid you don't have any time to pack."

"Why the hurry?"

"I suppose I can tell you. What harm can come of it? The Nazarene is rumoured to be making an appearance in three days at a small village called Bethany. All of his disciples and close followers will be there. I'm going to arrest them."

"Can't you just leave them alone? They're no threat to Rome."

"Sorry, that's out of the question, but first we have to get you on your way back to Rome."

Philippus looked into Lucius's smiling eyes and could see the man was serious. He knew there was nothing he could say that was going to change things, but there was something he could do. He could get to Mary before the tribune did. The question was *how.*

He had an idea, and with a bit of luck or divine intervention, it might work. The first move was his. He had to convince Lucius to grant him a favour. "All right, I'll go without packing," he said.

"I wasn't offering you a choice."

"But I would like one small favour."

"What small favour?"

"While you were renewing your acquaintance with my wife, I've…ah…met someone here in Jerusalem, and I'd like to—"

"You want to say good-bye?" asked Lucius with a knowing smile.

"And give her a little money. You understand."

"One of those, is she?"

"Let's just say I owe her."

"Your galley leaves at dawn tomorrow, so I can't give you much time."

"That's all right, Tribune. I won't need much."

Lucius's carriage pulled up to the alley that led to Mary's tiny abode. Philippus knew she wouldn't be home, that she and Ruth would be on their way back to Jonah's farm. "Is this where she lives?" asked Lucius, his nose curling from the stench in the air. He was seated across from Philippus, who was trapped between the two burly guards.

"She lives at the end of the alley."

"My, you really like them low rent, don't you?"

"You take love where you can find it."

"Is that what you call it, Philippus? Love?"

"Companionship sounds so false, and sex, so crass."

"Well, whatever it was, you're going to have to walk the rest of the way. I don't think the carriage will fit down this alley."

"It's a short walk."

"These two will go with you," said Lucius, nodding at Philippus's two seat mates.

"Fine by me." Philippus shrugged.

At Mary's front door, Philippus stopped and turned to the men who had escorted him from the carriage. "Now, men," he said, "I'm not asking for a lot here, but this woman was…ah…good to me, if you know what I mean." The two guards grinned foolishly at each other. "I knew you would," continued Philippus. "All I'm asking is that you wait outside, and if you hear anything—you know, pots breaking, a scream or two, rest assured, everything is under control, all right?"

The guards nodded knowingly. "Sure," said the larger one, "we know how it is."

"Thank you," said Philippus, patting the two men on the back and opening the front door.

The house was empty, as Philippus had known it would be. Unable to find a back door, he was about to try his luck at kicking a hole in the back wall when he saw the ladder leading up to the roof. Quickly making his way up the ladder, he opened the trap door and climbed onto the roof. As quickly as he could, he crawled to the back of the house and jumped down into the alley.

Landing on a pile of garbage and twisting his ankle, Philippus couldn't help but let out a cry of pain.

At the sound of the scream, the guards grinned and winked at each other. "Sounds like he's saying good-bye in a big way," joked the larger of the two.

"How big can it be?" cracked his smaller friend. "He said he only needed a couple of minutes."

Back inside the carriage, Lucius was wondering what was taking so long. He got out of the carriage and reluctantly tiptoed his way down the alley to Mary's front door.

The ankle ached more with every step, but Philippus knew he had to keep going. The guards would not wait forever. Unfortunately, the alley offered no good hiding places.

At the front door, Lucius's bodyguards jumped to attention at the appearance of the tribune. Lucius didn't waste any time in idle chatter. He barrelled his way past the two men and kicked in the front door. Entering the house, he couldn't miss the open trap door. He sent his larger bodyguard up the alley, the other down. Then he returned to the carriage.

The alley was bordered on all sides by the back walls of ramshackle, one-story homes. There was no place to hide. He could hear the footsteps of the pursuing guard getting closer and closer. "What am I going to do?" Philippus asked himself. "Punch a hole in the back wall of one of these homes?" The question was barely articulated when Philippus went crashing through the wall of the next house he came to. The elderly couple asleep on the floor stopped screaming when Philippus dropped several silver coins on their only table as he ran out the front door.

Out on the street, Philippus spotted a farmer delivering milk in a small cart pulled by a tired, solitary donkey. A few more coins and he was on his way, uncomfortably ensconced in the back of the cart next to the cheese.

At first Philippus thought it would be too dangerous, but then he reconsidered. *After all*, he told himself, *the palace library is the last place Lucius would look for me.*

The scribes in the copying room had the scrolls ready and waiting for Philippus. After making sure all the sermons had been transcribed, he gave the ink-stained wretches in their windowless dungeon of a room a nice bonus. Then he got out while the getting was good. He had a long ride ahead of him, and the second hour was already about to begin.

A Treasure beyond Words

Three Days until Bethany

Since cutting his ties with Caiaphas, Jonah had spent his time trying to master the skills of his new profession. He had never picked up a shovel or guided a plow, but with his future livelihood and that of Mary and their soon-to-be family depending on it, Jonah knew he was going to have to learn, and fast.

To that end, he had hired Daniel, a man who had spent his entire thirty years on a farm. A man who, for twelve years, had provided for himself, his wife, and their five children until a gang of robbers showed up while he was out in the fields. They took his family as slaves before setting fire to everything else. Since that sorrowful day, he had rented himself out as an experienced farmhand.

The sun was setting when Daniel first saw the approaching rider. Jonah was too busy stacking baskets of olives. Nudging Jonah with his elbow, he pointed. "Someone's coming, Jonah, you'd better have a look."

Jonah used his hand to shield his eyes from the sun. He gave the approaching rider a good long look. "I don't believe it," he said. "What is he doing here?"

"He?" asked Daniel.

"Philippus Publius Marcus, a Roman investigator."

"What does he want with us?"

"I have no idea, Daniel," he lied.

They watched as Philippus rode up, waved hello, and then dismounted. "Jonah," he shouted, walking briskly towards them. "I'm so glad I found you."

"What do you want?" demanded Jonah.

"I've got something for Mary," said Philippus, showing Jonah the scrolls. "All of the Nazarene's sermons, every word."

"What?" asked Jonah sceptically.

"Lucius had agents writing down every word ever spoken by Jesus, in case He said something contrary to the interests of Rome. I had a copy made, that's all."

Jonah took one of the scrolls and opened it. He read the first few words, and smiled. "This is wonderful," he said. "Mary will be very pleased."

"I thought it was something that needed to be done. Now we have a record of what He said."

"We'll have to make copies," Jonah said.

"We'll make more copies as soon as we can, Jonah," said Philippus, anxious to talk to Mary. "But first, I have to warn Mary not to go to Bethany. Pilate is sending Lucius Verus Clemens to arrest Jesus and everyone close to Him."

"You'll never convince Mary not to go."

"Maybe with your help, Jonah."

"Saying good-bye to Jesus is all she talks about."

"She'll be in great danger."

"I'll be with her."

"You'll be arrested too."

Jonah considered what Philippus had just told him. He knew that if Roman soldiers showed up in force, there would be nothing he could do to protect Mary. "You're sure they intend to arrest her?" he asked.

"Lucius is taking along a whole centura just to make sure no one escapes."

"Mary is back at the house with Ruth," he said.

Mary and Ruth were in the kitchen, preparing a dinner of lamb stew and flat bread. Odysseus was at their side, begging for scraps as usual. Mary had her head over a large pot, taking in the aroma of the stew as she stirred. Ruth was busy cutting up vegetables when she saw them. "It's Jonah—and Philippus!" she shouted, watching the two men approach through the kitchen window.

"Philippus?" asked a surprised Mary, looking up from her stew.

"Out there," replied Ruth. Putting down her knife, she was out the door, Odysseus right behind her. Mary went to the window. She watched Ruth run to him. Seeing how excited the child was to see Philippus brought a smile to her lips.

Philippus saw the child's smile and couldn't help but smile himself.

Jonah looked from one smiling face to another, but didn't join in.

From the saddle, Philippus scooped Ruth up in his arms and set her down on the saddle in front of him. Odysseus tried to join her, but there was no room. Slipping off the side of the saddle, he fell back to the ground, yelping. Jonah called him, and he ran to him.

"Philippus," Ruth said excitedly. "I'm so glad to see you."

"And I'm glad to see you."

"But what are you doing here?" she asked, turning her head to look back at him.

"I've come to visit you."

"Are you staying long? Please say you're staying," she said.

"Only until the morning."

Ruth looked away. "Philippus," she said, "will I be leaving with you?"

Philippus smiled at the back of her head. Gripping the reins with his pain-free left hand, he used his right to turn her face towards him. "I was hoping we could all leave together," he said.

Ruth threw her arms around Philiipus. "You mean it?" she asked, struggling to keep her voice level.

"Of course I mean it. I want you to know one thing, Ruth. I will never lie to you."

"I know," she said, hugging him closer. "I know, I know, I know." She loosened her grip around his waist, and asked, "Where will we be going?"

"Egypt, and from there, to Rome."

"Rome," she said, not quite believing what she had just been told.

Mary greeted them just outside the front door of the old farm house. "Mary, Mary," exclaimed Ruth, running to her after Philippus had set her back on the ground, Odysseus barking at her feet. "We're going to Egypt and Rome—all of us together."

"Are we?" asked Mary, taking hold of Ruth's hand, waiting for Philippus and Jonah to join them before going back inside.

"I hope so," said Philippus, dismounting.

"We can talk about it inside," replied Mary tensely.

Jonah was going to say something, but the words didn't come to him. "I'll tie your horse up in the barn," he said to Phillipus, dismounting.

"Thank you, Jonah," replied Philippus, handing Jonah the reins to his horse. With a nod of his head, Jonah walked both animals into the barn.

"I've brought you a present," said Philippus, walking over to Mary and handing her the scrolls.

"What are they?" asked Mary, unrolling one of the scrolls.

"The words of Jesus," said Jonah, returning from the barn.

Once they were all back in the kitchen, Mary started reading one of the scrolls. It took her breath away. "It's a treasure beyond words," she said.

"I just thought someone besides the tribune should have a copy," said Philippus.

"I can't thank you enough," said Mary.

By mutual consent they waited until after they'd enjoyed a meal of chicken, olives, and bread, before confronting the real reason for Philippus's visit. The three adults were alone at the kitchen table, Ruth having taken Odysseus for a walk, when Philippus finally broached the subject of Bethany. "I'm not running anywhere, Philippus," asserted Mary. "I'm going to Bethany."

"You can't, Mary. Pilate is sending soldiers under the tribune's command to arrest you."

"Let them come. Let them see for themselves."

"Please, Mary, I have a friend who runs caravans between Egypt and Jerusalem. He owes me a favour. He could take us all to Egypt."

"No, Philippus. I can't leave until after Bethany."

"There's nothing I can say?"

"Nothing, Philippus, for I am not afraid."

"Not even of Rome's torturers?"

"What is one instant of pain, Philippus, if afterwards we pass into the very heart of God?"

"And when you get arrested, what happens to spreading His teachings?"

"Philippus is right, Mary," said Jonah, deciding to join the argument. "How many times have you told me about the need to do His work?"

"I want only to say good-bye, Jonah."

Jonah stared into Mary's unchanging eyes. He could see her mind was made up. Then he realized the flaw in her argument. "You don't have to be in Bethany to say good-bye. Jesus is always with us. 'Wherever we are, He will hear our prayers.' You told me that, Mary."

Mary looked at Jonah and smiled. Looking to Philippus, she said, "I know you both have the best of intentions, but I simply must see Him."

Philippus looked at Jonah. "And what about you?" he asked.

"You heard Mary. She's going, so I'll be there with her."

"And what about Ruth?" asked Philippus pointedly. "Are you going to risk her safety and freedom as well?"

"I thought you were taking Ruth to Egypt," replied Mary.

"I don't believe this!" Philippus shouted. "Have you lost your mind, Mary? You'll be walking right into a trap. How can you do such a stupid, pointless thing?"

"Seeing Jesus one last time is not stupid," Mary said, returning to her scroll, signalling an end to the conversation.

Phillipus looked once again to Jonah for help. All he got was a shrug. "You know, Mary, I went to a lot of trouble and personal risk to get you those scrolls."

"You've done a wonderful thing, Philippus, preserving His words."

"I did it for you—for you to have them and read them, but also because I thought you'd want to take those words to the world. I guess I was wrong about that."

Mary looked up from her reading. Sternly, she said to Philippus, "You know that is not true."

"It's exactly true. After you're arrested, soldiers will be sent here and to your home in Jerusalem. They will confiscate everything they find. The tribune will end up with these scrolls. I don't know what he'll do with them, but I don't think he'll be spreading the good news, do you?"

"I understand, but Jesus gave me back my life, a life I had thrown away. If I lose it now because I need to see Him, I will die contented. Grateful for the time He gave back to me."

Jonah got up from his chair and went to the window. "Looks like rain," he said.

Philippus stood up. "So that's it?" he asked. Mary and Jonah exchanged a look but said nothing. Philippus headed for the front door. His hand on the door, he looked back at Jonah. "Maybe you can talk some sense to her," he said and walked out.

Jonah gathered his thoughts.

God was testing him, and this time with a choice more difficult than any he could have imagined. Leaving the window, he walked over to where Mary was reading her scroll. Standing behind her chair, he said, "Mary, you know how much I love you."

"As I love you, Jonah," she answered, turning her head to look up at him.

Her brown eyes only made what he had to say more difficult. "Mary," he managed to choke out, "I'm not an educated man. Look at these scrolls. I could never even conceive of such a thing."

"What are you trying to say, Jonah?"

"You must leave Judea, Mary, and…you must…leave with him."

"Jonah—you can't be serious?"

"Mary, what you have to do doesn't involve this farm, doesn't involve"—for a swallow he couldn't find his voice—"doesn't involve me."

"No, Jonah that's not—"

"Yes it is, Mary. You know it's true. God wants you. He needs you to help Philippus. Help him fulfill his destiny."

"But you can come with us."

"Philippus needs you, Mary."

She started to interrupt but he cut her off. "Yes—Yes he does, Mary. You've said it yourself. If the words of Jesus are to go forward, they must be heard in Rome. Isn't that why you decided to call Jesus the Christos? Truth needs someone to shout His name. Shout it so loud the whole world will hear it. Philippus can be that someone, but not without you. And you can't be at his side with me standing in the middle."

"And what of your—our happiness?"

"We'll be happy, Mary, and if we're not, we'll at least know that for a short time, we were. We'll know our love prevailed. We'll always have that memory. But right now, happiness is not what matters. What matters—the only thing that matters—is the truth. The truth we were chosen to witness.

"Being alive at the time of Jesus was a blessing, Mary, but it was also a responsibility. Having been shown the road to salvation, we must put up sign posts to show others the way. You'll put up more signs with him. My love cannot be the reason why you don't."

"So you're leaving me, Jonah?"

"You're leaving me, Mary. Philippus is the man you need to be with. He can help you, and you can help him. Together, you can help God."

"What will you do?"

"I won't go back to my old life, if that's what you're worried about. You showed me a truer path. I won't stray from it. I'm going to be a farmer, Mary. I'm going to try and make my living growing things instead of killing them."

"I could help you."

"Go and tell the world, Mary. Tell them there is a God, that He loves us, and that He died for our sins."

She looked at him almost in disbelief. "I'm so proud of you, Jonah. My heart is so big," she said, spreading her arms as wide as they would reach.

Philippus was waiting for her. He was sitting on a fence post, his back to the tiny farm house. Slowly, almost regretfully, she walked over to where he was sitting. She had the scrolls in her hands, and before she spoke, she paused to look at them once more. She couldn't wait to show them to the disciples. "Philippus," she said.

He turned to face her. "Have you changed your mind?' he asked, not expecting to get the answer he wanted to hear.

"These scrolls…I…I don't know how to thank you."

"You could tell me you're going to Egypt with them."

"Why is that so important to you?"

It was a fair question, one that forced him to answer a question of his own. *Do I want her to come with me for God or for myself? Is this about what she can do for Him or for me?* "Mary," he said seriously, "something miraculous happened here thirty-seven days ago. I want you to come to Egypt with me so that we can tell the world. But that's not my only reason. I barely know you, Mary, but...I'm sorry. I've never been very good at saying these kinds of things." Embarrassed, Philippus looked off into the distance.

"It's all right," she said.

Philippus gave his head a shake. *What am I doing?* he asked himself. *This is hard enough for her without me throwing myself at her feet.* He brought his eyes back to hers. "No, it's not all right, Mary. Forget about what I was trying to say. What matters is getting you out of Judea."

"I agree."

"What?"

"I said I agree with you."

"Then you'll come with me to Egypt?"

"Yes," she said, her voice gentle and soft.

Chapter Seventy:
The Way Only a Dog
Can Know

Two Days until Bethany

It was easy to see that Odysseus did not understand. The sun was just peeking above the eastern horizon. The four of them were gathered in front of the old farm house. Philippus and Ruth were already mounted; Philippus on his horse, Ruth a donkey. Mary was delaying their departure as long as she could. Crouching down, her arms wrapped around Odysseus's neck, she was doing her best not to cry, hoping not to give the game away. In all likelihood, she would never see Odysseus again. Jonah stood nearby.

Mary hugged the dog tightly, too tightly; then she started to cry. Seeing her tears, Odysseus tried his best to lick them away. He turned questioning eyes to Jonah, he barked impatiently. When Jonah shrugged in response, Odysseus whimpered like a puppy and tried to snuggle closer to the woman responsible for saving his life.

Mary reached into a cloak pocket. She took out a piece of dried meat—chicken, Odysseus' favourite—and fed it to him. For a few brief seconds, his anxiety vanished as he wolfed down the tasty morsel. She covered her eyes with her sleeve, struggling to suppress a sob. She felt as if her heart might burst.

"What's wrong, Mary?' asked Ruth from on top of her donkey.

"Nothing's wrong, dear," she said, removing her sleeve from her eyes.

"Then let's go! Egypt's a long way away."

"Yes, dear, I know. You're right. I'm coming." She stood up and gave the dog's head a scratch. "Good-bye, old friend," she said. She took one last look to imprint his image in her memory, she smiled weakly at Jonah. She held his eyes longingly, and then, fearing that if she waited a moment longer she might not leave at all, she walked away. She paused, standing beside her donkey as if she'd forgotten what she was doing. She ran to Jonah and wrapped her arms around his neck, hugging him close. Jonah did his best not to cry. He almost succeeded. She looked up at him. Her lips quivered. Her eyes watered. She smiled weakly. She kissed him on the cheek. "Good-bye, my love," she whispered into his ear.

"Good-bye, Mary," he whispered, biting his lower lip. A pensive silence settled over the four of them. Mary held Jonah close as if she would never let go. Jonah looked to Philippus and made a helpless gesture. Philippus shrugged hesitantly in response. Ruth opened her mouth to encourage Mary to hurry up then changed her mind.

Odysseus barked angrily. Jonah and Mary gave the top of his head a good scratch. The dog squirmed closer, pushing his nose into the small space between their legs.

Mary let go of Jonah and mounted up. Odysseus tried to run after her, but Jonah held him back. The dog looked at Jonah and barked softly. Jonah had to hold onto Odysseus's collar as they watched them ride away. But Odysseus broke free. He ran after them, barking loudly. When they didn't slow down or wave for him to hurry up, he stopped and looked back at Jonah. He heard Jonah calling for him to come home. He barked at him impatiently. Jonah called for him to come back. Mary was fading further and further away. Tail between his legs, he reluctantly returned to Jonah's side.

Jonah looked down at Odysseus and did his best to look happy. "Don't worry, boy," he said. "I'll take good care of you. And who knows? She might come back to visit us."

They lingered there, man and dog, the sun strong in their faces, until they could see them no more. Then they walked back inside, closing the door on the woman who had meant so much to both of them.

He waited until night fall; he wanted to make sure Mary and Philippus didn't see any smoke. He grabbed two wine jugs a torch and left the old farm house, Odysseus a constant companion. He headed for the site of his half-finished home. *A fitting symbol for a life half ruined*, he thought as he started his way up the hill.

The climb to the top gave him plenty of time to empty the first jug. His mind drifted back to Mary. *How ironic.* He smiled. *I'm only here, starting a new life because of her, but she won't be here to share it with me.* As he crested the hill, the house that, as far as he was concerned, would always be Mary's, came eerily into view, the wooden joists and beams looking strangely skeletal, giving the structure a forlorn, emaciated appearance.

He looked at it in the shadowy moonlight. For the first time, he saw it not as the start to a happy future but the finish to an unhappy past. *I was building it for Mary anyway*, he told himself, opening the second jug and helping himself to a long, languorous swallow. "She's gone, boy. Mary's gone, but she'll always be with us in our hearts," he said, pounding his chest. "In our hearts, in our memories, and in our prayers."

He walked into the house, the house that would never be home to the love of a man and a woman or the laughter of children, and he drunkenly stacked wood in the centre of the unfinished living room. He looked around at what he had almost built and laughed. When the laughter ended, he discovered he was finally okay with it. She was gone, and it was right that she was gone. His old life was over, and it was right that it was over. This house would never be built, and it was right that it never be built. He poured what was left of the wine over the bonfire he had constructed.

He lit the fire, and then he and Odysseus went back outside. He watched the flames build and wiped away a stray tear. He could already feel the heat on his face. It felt cleansing somehow. In the flickering silver flames, he could picture her, feel her touch, taste her lips; he could hear her voice, see her sleeping in their bed, and he longed for her embrace, her smile. He looked up into the night sky, fell to his knees and bowed his head, more than timber going up in smoke.

The next morning found Jonah wrapped in a blanket. He had spent the night right where he had kneeled to pray. The warm rays of the rising sun woke him from his sleep. Getting to his feet, his body stiff from the damp, morning cold, he ambled over to what was left of his house. The ruins were still smouldering. He looked out over the verdant fields illuminated by the morning sunlight. Colours seemed more vibrant than ever to him, the wild flowers more beautiful, their perfume more exquisite. The warmth of the sun on his face, Jonah felt very close to God. He decided he would go to Bethany. He would say good-bye to the Son of God regardless of the risk. Reaching out to scratch Odysseus's head, he noticed for the first time that the dog was missing. "Odysseus!" he shouted. "Now where has that dog gotten to?"

CHAPTER SEVENTY-ONE:
THEY EAT EVERY BITE

TWO DAYS UNTIL BETHANY

Philippus's friend Omar had his caravan camped a few miles south of Jerusalem before setting out for Egypt. It was a large camp—several large tents, dozens of animals and carts, plus twenty well-armed men. Mary and Philippus arrived just after the sun went down. They were stopped by two men guarding the north entrance to the camp site. Philippus showed them a tablet signed by Omar. The guards waved them through.

Once inside the camp, they were met by a beehive of activity, everyone rushing to get ready to head out with the sun's first morning rays. Tents were being pulled down and loaded onto carts. Mules were harnessed. Elaborate saddles for camels, consisting of two perfectly balanced boxes almost four feet in length which hung on either side of the animal were being repaired and cleaned for the long journey ahead.

They found Omar overseeing the loading of massive barrels of olive oil onto large, flat bed carts. The barrels had to be properly secured in order to keep them from rolling around and breaking. Looking up from his work to see Philippus, Mary, and Ruth approaching, he rushed over to welcome them with open arms. "My friend, what brings you to my humble camp at such an hour?"

"I'm glad I found you, Omar," began Philippus, climbing off his horse and then helping Ruth and Mary down from their donkeys. "I have a favour to ask."

"What is it you need, my friend? Silk, jewels, perhaps a fine horse? I can get you the best prices."

"We need a ride Omar, all the way to Alexandria."

"How can I turn you down?" asked Omar rhetorically, looking from Mary to Ruth. "And who are these two lovely ladies?"

"Omar," said Philippus, "I'd like to introduce you to Mary Magdalene and her…niece, Ruth."

"Ladies, you honour my caravan with your presence."

"It is a pleasure to meet you, Omar," Mary said.

"Me too," Ruth chimed in.

"Well," said Omar, looking at his three new passengers, "I have much to do if we are to leave with tomorrow's first light. So I will leave you now." And with another slight bow, he was off.

"Where will we be staying?" asked Mary.

"I'm sure Omar will find a comfortable tent for the two of you until it is time to leave."

"And where will you be?" asked Ruth.

"On my way to Bethany."

"You're not coming with us?" cried Ruth in a panicked tone.

"Not right away, sweetheart. I'm going to Bethany first."

"Bethany? But you said it would be dangerous!" asked Mary.

"Dangerous?" repeated Ruth.

"Not for me. I'm a Roman citizen. The worst they can do to me is put me on a slow boat to Rome," he lied, covering it with a huge grin.

"So you'll be coming back for sure?" asked Ruth tentatively.

"I'll catch up with you in a day or two."

"Please, let us leave together," said Mary.

"Yeah," agreed Ruth, "together!"

"I'll flip you for it," said Philippus.

"You're going to let a coin make such an important decision?" asked Mary.

"Heads, we all leave together, and tails, you two go on alone," said Philippus, tossing a coin into the air, catching it, and slapping it down on his wrist. Lifting his hand, he peaked underneath. "I better get going." He smiled, mounting up.

"No! Don't go! You can't go! I won't let you!" shrieked Ruth, grabbing at Philippus's leg, refusing to let him go.

"Ruth, please, let go."

"No! I won't! I won't! I won't!"

"Now, Ruth, you have to let him go," pleaded Mary.

"I don't! I don't! I don't!"

Philuppus looked down at the child clutching his leg. Feeling her love, her need, he almost picked her up and took her with him. "I'll be back before you even know I'm gone," he said, forcing himself to remain firm. "I promise you."

Ruth didn't look at him. His words only made her cling to him even more. "No," she cried. "I'll never see you again."

"Ruth, dear," said Mary, crouching down and looking into the child's eyes. "You have to let go."

"But what if he doesn't come back?" asked Ruth, her eyes pleading with Mary.

"He'll come back, dear. He promised us," replied Mary, trying to look as confident as possible.

"For sure?" Ruth asked, letting go of his leg and looking up at Philippus, tears in her eyes.

"For sure." Philippus smiled. He bent over and picked Ruth up. He sat her in front of him, and hugged her tightly. "Don't you worry," he whispered in her ear. "I'm never going to leave you. I'll be back—for you and for Mary."

Ruth dried a tear. Slowly, a smile came to her lips. She kissed Phillipus on the cheek, and he carefully sat her down. He turned his horse to leave.

"God be with you," said Mary.

"That's what I'm hoping to find out," he said.

Alone in the tent Omar had provided for their convenience, Ruth found herself falling asleep. She had promised Mary that she wasn't going to sleep until Philippus returned. Mary had complied with a knowing smile. They had sat up most of the night. Mary reading to Ruth from the scrolls Philippus had given her. Ruth resisted as best she could, but, eyes half closed, she reluctantly allowed Mary to tuck her in under the covers. She was asleep by the time Mary kissed ker on the forehead and whispered good night.

Alone with her thoughts for the first time since leaving the farm, Mary started to have second thoughts about her decision. Did she really want to leave Judea? Everyone and everything she knew was in Judea. Jonah was in Judea.

Philippus is a fine man, she thought. He will do important work in Rome. But he doesn't need me to do it. He thinks he does, but his strength does not come from me. It comes from God. In time, he'll realize that.

And then there was Jonah. She missed him. From the very beginning, she had been dragged along by him. His enthusiasm, his confidence, his love had brought them together, not hers. She had resisted. She had told him it wasn't possible. He had changed her mind. But the last few days, watching him work on their new home, something unexpected had happened to her. *I fell in love,* she suddenly realized. *I fell in love with my Jonah!*

It was Jonah who told me I must go to Rome. He said we had to make choices, difficult choices. Not for ourselves but for a greater purpose. Was he wrong about that? Would it be right to let Philippus go to Rome by himself because I'm in love? Jesus told the disciples, "Just as the Father sent me forth, I also am sending you." Wasn't Jesus speaking to all of us so blessed to have known Him? Have I not said as much myself?

Torn between her love of a man and her love of God, Mary went to her knees to pray. Eyes firmly closed, she asked for a sign, for guidance.

Mary opened her eyes. She heard it first. A dog was barking. The barking was getting closer. Going to the door of the tent, she pulled back the flap, and there was a sight that brought a smile to her face and tears of joy to her eyes.

It was Odysseus, looking a little ragged from his long run, being chased by several of Omar's men. They weren't too happy about a stray dog wandering into their camp site.

At the sight of Mary, the dog began to run faster. "Odysseus!" she shouted, her arms spread wide to greet him. The tears were flowing freely now down both cheeks. He jumped up into her arms. She hugged him close. Omar's men left them alone, returning to their work. "What are you doing here, boy?" she asked after setting him down on a rug inside her tent. Odysseus barked his hello, tail wagging furiously. Mary wiped away tears on the sleeve of her cloak.

"Odysseus!" shouted Ruth, the dog's barking having woken her. The dog jumped into her arms.

"I'll bet you're hungry," said Mary, going to a table where one of Omar's men had brought her a plate of eggs, cheese, bread, dried meats, and olives. At the time, she had been too upset to eat anything, but now with Odysseus's unexpected arrival, she was suddenly hungry, and so was her visitor. Together they eat every bite.

I'll See You There

One Day until Bethany

With Bethany only a day away, Joseph and Aaron decided the time was now to spring their hoped-for deception on the tribune. As he had thirty-nine short days ago, Aaron arranged to meet Lucius in the guard house at the main gate to the Antonia. Lucius was not in uniform this time. He greeted Aaron in a fine cotton toga that combined elegance with comfort. "So, Captain." Lucius smiled. "What useful morsels do you have for me today?"

"I came as soon as I heard."

"Heard what, Captain?"

"A man claiming to be the Nazarene is going to be in Galilee tomorrow morning."

At the mention of Galilee, Lucius raised an eyebrow. *Galilee?* he asked himself. *My information was that the impostor was going to be in Bethany. Could the followers of the Nazarene have changed their minds? Or was Bethany a feint?* "Are you sure it's to be Galilee, Captain?"

"I smuggled myself into one of their meetings. Everyone was excited about seeing the Nazarene in Galilee tomorrow morning."

Now Lucius was certain that Aaron was lying. *Smuggled himself into a meeting?* he asked himself. *Who does he think he's fooling? The captain has been seen regularly attending their meetings.* "Isn't Galilee rather a long way from Jerusalem?" he asked.

"They wanted to be outside of Pilate's jurisdiction."

"They feel safer with the tetrarch?"

"Well, it was Pilate who ordered the crucifixion."

Lucius considered everything he had just heard, balanced against what he already knew. He felt certain the captain was lying. *But what if I'm wrong?* he wondered. *I can't be in two places at once. I'm going to have to make a choice.* Then an idea came to him. It was an old trick, but it had always worked for him in the past. "Well, Captain, I guess I'll be going to Galilee," he said.

"Will you be making any arrests?"

"Why else would I be going, Captain?"

"Yes, of course."

"Will you be there, Captain?"

"Oh, I'll be there, Tribune, and if I hear anything useful, I'll be sure to pass along every word."

"Excellent, Captain. Will ten gold coins be enough?" asked Lucius.

"More than enough," replied Aaron.

"Ten gold coins it is," replied Lucis, smiling broadly as he counted out the coins. He wanted the captain to lower his guard.

Aaron accepted the coins and was turning to leave when Lucius sprang his trap. "See you in Bethany," he said, as casually as possible.

Before Aaron could catch himself, the words were out of his mouth. "I'll see you there," he said confidently.

Lucius didn't say a word. He just kept on smiling as he watched Aaron walk away. *Bethany it is,* he said to himself.

BETHANY, THE FORTIETH DAY

Dressed in an old tunic, his head hidden beneath the hood of his travelling cloak, Philippus made his way through the crowded village of Bethany. Every alleyway, barn, shed, and shade tree had its full complement of huddled pilgrims. He listened to their hushed conversations and heard Greek, Latin, Aramaic, Egyptian, Parthian, Bactrian, Iberian, and even barbarian tongues from Gaul and Germany. Every corner of the Empire was represented. Finding the stables open, he saw to his horse. He stepped out of the stables and looked up at the eastern sky. He could barely see the sun behind the gathering storm clouds.

Procula was stepping into her silk-lined palanquin when Pilate caught up with her. She had tried to slip away without her husband finding out, but the guards felt they had an obligation to inform their commander that his wife was leaving the palace before the first hour with only a six-man escort. Still half asleep, Pilate had pulled on a tunic and a pair of walking sandals and stormed off to see first hand what was going on. "Procula!" he bellowed, walking up to where she was seated in her palanquin. "What do you think you're doing?"

"I'm going on a short trip," she said, averting her eyes.

"Would you mind telling me where?"

"I don't see how that's any of your business, Pontius."

"Not my business?" he erupted angrily. "Do you at least have a proper escort?"

"I've asked for a six-man escort."

"Six? In whose command?" sputtered Pilate.

"That would be me, sir," said a stocky, battle-scarred centurion, stepping forward for the first time.

376 | Gerald Hess

"And you are?" asked Pilate impatiently.

"Centurion Gaius Longinus, sir."

Pilate looked Longinus over. The centurion seemed to know his business. He had the hard, cautious look of a man who had fought and survived more than his fair share of battles. "Weren't you the centurion assigned the crucifixion of the Nazarene?" he asked.

"That I was, sir."

"I thought your eyes were bad? How can a half-blind centurion protect my wife?"

"My eyes have been cured, sir."

"Cured?" asked Pilate suspiciously.

"Yes, sir."

"How?" scoffed Pilate, a mocking challenging tone to his question.

"I'm not sure, sir, but my eyes got better after the blood of the Nazarene was splashed on them."

What madness is this? Pilate thought to himself. "Centurion," he began, "are you suggesting that the blood of this...heretic cured you?"

"I'm only telling you what happened, sir."

"I suppose how you were cured isn't important. What's important is whether or not you can see."

"I can see, sir. Or I wouldn't have been removed from the crucifixion detail."

The answer seemed to satisfy Pilate. "Well, Centurion, do you think a six-man escort is adequate protection for my wife?"

"Sir, I recommended a dozen, but her ladyship insisted on no more than six and assured me we would never be out of site of the city walls, sir."

Pontius turned a questioning eye on his wife. "Is what he said the truth?"

"The truth, Pontius, is that I didn't want an escort at all."

Hanging onto his temper, but just barely, Pilate said dully, "Unless you tell me where you are going and take a proper escort with you, you aren't leaving the palace gates."

Procula turned a pair of penetrating eyes on her husband. "If you don't let me go, I will never speak to you again."

"Can't you at least tell me where you are going?" he pleaded.

"Bethany," she said, signalling for the palanquin to be lifted.

"Bethany!" he exclaimed. "But Lucius is going to—"

"What about Lucius?" she interrupted.

He almost told her the truth. "Nothing," he said, looking at his feet as he chewed his left thumb nail. "I just wanted to tell you that I arrested Lucius last night, that's all."

Thinking the thumb-nail chewing was concern for her safety, Procula softened. "Don't worry," she said. "I'll be careful, and Longinus is a good man. And please stop chewing on your thumb."

He watched her go. He still couldn't believe that his wife was going to see a fake who was supposed to have walked out of His own tomb. *What has happened to her?* He frowned.

Joseph and Reisa made their way up the southeastern slope of the Mount of Olives. The morning was grey and overcast, the sky filled with dark, ominous, and opaque clouds. They were just starting their mile-and-a-half climb up the gently sloping hill when Reisa paused by one of the many olive trees that gave the mount its name. As she looked around, she was wonderstruck by the beauty and grandeur of God's creation bursting into bloom all around her. The growth on the olives trees was young, fresh, and vibrantly green—a delicate, almost yellowy spring green that seemed to glow in the sparse morning light. In the bare patches between the trees, honeysuckle, its purple spring foliage highlighting clusters of fragrant white flowers, was creeping over every bush. "What a glorious world God has made for us," she said enthusiastically.

"He truly means for us to be happy."

"That is why He has sent His only Son to save us."

"We are so blessed."

"Yes we are," she said, her voice soft and gentle. Taking her husband's hand in hers, she kissed it tenderly and then looked up into his eyes.

He beamed at her. Unable to say a word, truly in love, he kissed her.

On the other side of the mountain, Jonah was amongst a small group of pilgrims making their way to Bethany from the north. He had searched frantically for Odysseus before leaving the farm but had been unable to find any trace of him.

Having climbed the mile and a half, Jonah and the other pilgrims made their way around the mountain to the south east. "Looks like rain," he said to himself, checking the dark sky. He wished Mary was with him. *She's safer where she is*, he assured himself.

It hadn't been easy, but Mary managed to convince Omar to give her a cart and horse, a little water, and permission to leave. Omar's camp was a few miles south east of Jerusalem, about an hour's journey by cart from the Mount of Olives. The three of them were bouncing along comfortably, Odysseus resting in Ruth's arms while Mary held the reins. "I'll bet you anything Philippus will be happy to see us," shouted Ruth.

"I'm sure he will be, Ruth—very happy," she said, unsure if he really would be.

"Do you think we'll see Jesus?"

"Of that, I have no doubt, Ruth."

Mary looked over at Ruth and Odysseus, who was doing his best to lick Ruth's face, and smiled. They were in sight of Jerusalem. She sighed, certain now that they would reach Bethany in time.

Her decision to take Bethany over Omar's caravan was not only about seeing Jesus. A mistake had been made, and she needed to correct it. Jonah was wrong. Philippus was wrong. She was wrong. Her future did not lie in Rome with Philippus, but in Judea with Jonah and Odysseus and Ruth. She looked again at the child and smiled maternally.

Joseph of Arimathea was having a hard time keeping up with Aaron. *It's a good thing Issac decided not to come along,* he thought. In his current condition, he would never have been able to make it. Issaac had made a remarkable recovery but was still too weak for anything but a short walk. Seeing the older man's troubles, Aaron slackened his pace.

Lucius's centura was forming up in a business-like manner on the Antonia's parade square. Eighty men in full armour and light summer cloaks were gathered up in ten disciplined, eight-man lines in the faint, dawn sunlight. The tribune, not wanting to waste any time, gave them a cursory inspection and then marched them out of the parade square.

As more and more people arrived, they were forced to spread out farther and farther down the mountain's eastern slope. Some of them sat on blankets, others on the dew-covered ground. No one seemed to know what to do. They had all heard that the risen Christ was to appear near Bethany this morning, and so they had come. More than that, they did not know.

Procula's entourage had just finished crossing Kidron creek and was beginning the long trek up the eastern slope. Feeling the harshness of the incline and hearing the exhausted grunts of the men carrying her, she ordered everyone to stop. Climbing out of her palanquin, she asked Longinus if she might have a word.

"Of course, your ladyship."

"In private, Centurion."

"Whatever you wish."

"Good, then come with me." She walked the two of them off to a nearby olive tree. She smiled at Longinus. "Was it true?" she asked. "Were your eyes really cured by the blood of Jesus?"

Longinus looked down into the imploring eyes that were staring up at him and knew he could tell her the truth. "I believe that they were, your ladyship."

"I believe you do," she said. "Well here's what I want to say to you. I don't want to go on with all these...people. I want you all to go back."

"But, your ladyship, I can't let you go on alone."

"I'm perfectly safe, Longinus. And please stop calling me your ladyship. My name is Procula."

Longinus looked around at the people making their way up the hill. All he could see were unarmed pilgrims, a look of hope and peace etched onto their faces.

"See, Longinus," explained Procula. "These people mean me no harm."

"All right, your...Procula," he said, "I suppose I have no choice but to let you go."

"Alone?"

"If you insist."

He watched her make her way up the hill, talking to other pilgrims, helping an old man who had stumbled. He ordered everyone back to the palace and then hurried to catch up with her.

Lucius's men had been waved through the eastern gate. The tribune, perhaps remembering what happened the last time he had bothered to stop for baked goods, resisted the urge to pick up fresh pastries from a roadside merchant. They were making their way across Kidron creek when one of the legionaries shouted. "Up a head, Tribune, I can see campfires."

They left the horse and cart with a famer and made the climb up the Mount of Olives on foot. There were too many people for them to attempt riding all the way to Bethany. "Look at all the people," exclaimed Ruth. "Did you think there'd be this many, Mary?"

"No, Ruth, I had no idea."

"How will we find Philippus?"

"Just keep your eyes open."

"Maybe he'll find us."

"Maybe," said Mary. She needed to talk to Philippus, but she was looking for Jonah.

Odysseus saw him first. Jonah was waiting at the bottom edge of the crowd. Barking enthusiastically, he was off. "Odysseus," shouted Ruth.

"It's all right, Ruth. He knows where he's going," Mary said, spotting the top of Jonah's head.

He heard the barking. "Odysseus!" he exclaimed exultantly. "What are you doing here?" The only answer he got was the dog jumping up into his arms tail wagging.

Looking beyond the dog, he thought his eyes must have been playing tricks on him. *Is that Mary?* he asked himself. *No, it's just someone who looks like her. Hold on. Is that Ruth? Oh God, it is!*

He started towards them. The crowd jostled him this way and that. A month ago, he would have shoved these people out of his way. Today, he let himself be jostled. He tiptoed his way through the crowd, one arm carrying Odysseus, the other waving at Mary, he wished Jesus had come into his life years earlier.

Mary waved at him over the heads of the people packed between them. "I can see him now," shouted Ruth. "It's Jonah. He sees us!"

Tired of getting his face licked, Jonah put Odysseus on the ground. The dog made straight for Mary. The barking caught the attention of the people standing between Mary and Jonah. One by one, they squeezed out of the way, clearing a path.

After he reached Mary, Odysseus turned and led the way back to Jonah. Following Odysseus, Mary ran to him. He lifted her off of her feet, hugging her close. Odysseus was barking, trying to jump up into their arms. Ruth pulled him out of the way. All around them, people were watching and smiling. Their happiness was contagious.

"Mary, what are you doing here?" asked Jonah, after he had put her down.

"I couldn't stay away. I had to be here."

"Where's Philippus? Didn't he come with you?"

"He left before me on his own."

"Then he must already be here."

"Do you know where he is?" asked Ruth.

The evidence may have told Phillipus what to expect, but the sight of Jesus in the flesh took his breath away. He took out the sandals that had matched the one-way footprints and ran to Jesus. Peter moved to stop him. Jesus waved Peter away. Smiling at Philippus, Jesus nodded at the sandals. "Thank you for returning my sandals," He said.

"My pleasure," replied Philippus. "Would it be all right if I put them on your feet?"

"If you'd like to."

Jesus lifted His right foot. Philippus slid on the sandal. It fit perfectly. Looking up at Jesus, he nodded. Jesus nodded back. "Now do you know the truth?" He asked.

"I do," answered Philippus.

Caught at the back of the crowd, Procula had been unable to see anything. With Longinus's help, the two of them managed to climb up on the roof of a house that afforded them a view of the entire crowd. There were over five hundred of them. They were no longer spread out along the mountain side but had gathered together in front of where Jesus was standing, waiting for Him to speak. "Can you see Him?" asked Procula.

"I can see someone, but it can't be the Nazarene."

"Trust me, Centurion, it is."

"You don't really believe the Nazarene has returned from the dead, do you, Procula?"

"Isn't that why we are here?"

"My children," shouted Jesus, "listen unto me. Go into the world and preach the good news to all of creation. He that believes shall be saved! Make disciples in every land. Baptise them in the name of the Father, the Son, and the Holy Spirit. Teach them to be obedient to every command I have given you, right unto the end of all time." The Son of God paused and looked skyward.

An uncertain stillness fell over the crowd.

From her rooftop perch, Procula saw them first. "Centurion!"

"Yes, Procula?"

"Is that who I think it is?" she asked, pointing at the Roman soldiers entering the main street and making their way towards them.

"I thought the tribune was under arrest," he said.

"I was there when my husband signed the arrest warrant."

"What do you think he's doing?"

"He's here to arrest the Son of God," she said.

The legionaries completed their encirclement of the crowd. Then they began to close in.

"Jonah, what's going on?" asked Mary, trying to keep the fear from her voice. Her hand firmly gripped around Ruth's.

"It's Lucius!" answered Jonah. "He must be here to arrest Jesus."

"Don't worry about those soldiers," cried Ruth. "Philippus will order them to go away."

"If only he could," said Jonah.

"But he can," insisted Ruth. "He took me to the tomb, and he just told the Roman guards to get out of our way, and they did. Roman soldiers listen to Philippus."

"I'm sure they do, dear," explained Mary, "but these soldiers are different. Jonah! Where are you going?" Mary shouted, as Jonah moved to confront the legionaries.

"Just stay where you are, Mary. Don't worry about me."

"Jonah! Please!" cried Mary. "You don't know what you're doing!"

"No, Mary, for the first time in my life, I know exactly what I'm doing."

"Are you here to help us arrest this imposter, Philippus?" Lucius asked, his droll tone masking the tension he felt when Philippus stepped between his soldiers and Jesus. *This is it*, he told himself. *My last chance.* Despite the fact that he had masterminded every devious detail of his own demise, he felt remarkably confident of his ability to salvage not just his life but his fortune as well. And it didn't appear as if it was going to be all that difficult. *The crowd might prove a problem,* he worried, wishing he'd brought more men, but this imposter didn't look as if He or His disciples were going to put up much of a fight. As to Philippus, well, his actions were a gift from the gods. *What better excuse could I have for killing*

him than the fact that he was interfering with the execution of a legal arrest warrant?

"I'm ordering your men to disperse, Tribune," Philippus shouted, pushing two legionaries out of his way.

"These men don't take orders from you, Philippus. They're operating under direct orders from Pontius Pilate. Now move out of the way and let me execute my arrest order," shouted the tribune.

"Not another step, Tribune!" Philippus punctuated his words by drawing his sword.

This is just getting better and better, thought Lucius. "Am I going to have to arrest you as well, Philippus?"

"I wouldn't if I were you," said Philippus, widening his stance.

Lucius yawned pointedly. "I must say, you certainly do look frightening, Philippus, but I have eighty men, and there is only one of you."

"Count again," said Jonah, taking up a position beside Philippus.

Philippus looked at the large, formidable man standing next to him, "Jonah?" he asked.

"At your service."

Lucius shrugged. "So now it's two, so what?"

"So make it three," cried Aaron, joining Philippus and Jonah.

"Make it four," added Longinus, standing beside Aaron.

Lucius shrugged. "If they get in your way, kill them!" he shouted.

Surrounded and outnumbered, Philippus and his three brave friends stood side by side, while all around them, the legionaries tightened their noose. Philippus shouted to the other three, "Watch their eyes. If the pupils widen, get ready for an attack."

"I don't think they have the stomach for it," Jonah shouted back.

Out of the corner of his eye, Philippus caught site of Jesus standing just off to his right. He was looking at Philippus and smiling. Jesus spread his arms wide as if He were about to embrace a long lost friend. "Look to your right, men," shouted Philippus.

Not sure why, Aaron, Longinus, and Jonah looked anyway. They saw Jesus smiling, His arms held wide. Not a word was spoken, but the message was clear. Together they looked at their swords and then at each other. Together, they looked one more time at Jesus, who nodded his assent. Together they dropped their swords. "Why don't we all drop our weapons?" Philippus asked the centurion standing closest to him. "We have no reason to fight. We have no reason to kill each other. Let us drink together and put away all thoughts of violence."

The centurion couldn't believe what he was seeing when Philippus offered him his wine skin. A puzzled look came over the man's face, but having never turned down a free drink in his entire life, he shrugged and accepted the skin.

Following Philippus's lead, Jonah, Aaron, and Longinus offered their wineskins as well. Throughout the crowd, people saw what Philippus had done and began offering the soldiers what they could. All around him, Philippus saw his dream come true as pilgrim and legionary shared drinks, food, and laughter.

Infuriated, Lucius raised his sword.

Then, any thought of arresting anyone left everyone's consciousness.

The earth shook violently beneath their feet. Lucius fell from his horse and covered his head in fear. Above them, the sky erupted with a flash of lightning and a roar of thunder such as no one had ever heard before! The clouds rolled back. Suddenly, the sky was afire, the light intolerably bright. People covered their eyes. Many fell to their knees. All were fearful. A beam of light seemingly stretching back into the farthest reaches of the universe illuminated Jesus in a brilliant, white, sublime light.

Something emerged from the centre of the great, heavenly beam. Shapes appeared, ghost like. Slowly, the apparitions became clearer. It was an escort of angels. Clad in robes intensely white, they were almost impossible to see. Over them, like a celestial guardian, hovered a star glowing with a steady, white light of its own. Even the legionaries fell to their knees.

Mary watched Jesus ascending to the clouds. At this wonderful moment of triumph, of fulfilment, her thoughts strayed back to that horrible day at Golgotha. She remembered the faces—the hard, cruel faces of the Romans, the sanctimonious and self-righteous faces of the priests, the angry, vengeful faces of the mob, and the faces of those whose hearts, like her own, were broken. And she remembered His anguish, His pain, His blood, and how at the moment of His death, she had felt both glad for the end of His suffering and yet wanted nothing more but for Him to live.

And now, as He vanished into the heavens, His last words rang in her ears:

"I shall always be with you!"

On the other side of the mountain, an old man wearing a long, dark robe, a cloak pulled up over his head, watched the miracle before limping his way towards Jerusalem. Stopping to mop his brow, the old man looked up at the sky and nodded knowingly. "Always be with you," he muttered to himself, "Well, so shall I."

Resuming his journey, a gust of wind blew back his hood revealing a face more beast than man.